Praise for *Any Other Name* and the Longmire series

"Like the greatest crime novelists, Johnson is a student of human nature. Walt Longmire is strong but fallible, a man whose devil-may-care stoicism masks a heightened sensitivity to the horrors he's witnessed. Unlike traditional genre novelists who obsess mainly over every hairpin plot turn, Johnson's books are also preoccupied with the mystery of his characters' psyches."   —*Los Angeles Times*

"It's the scenery—and the big guy standing in front of the scenery—that keeps us coming back to Craig Johnson's lean and leathery mysteries."
     —Marilyn Stasio, *The New York Times Book Review*

"[*Any Other Name* is] well-crafted . . . filled with endearing characters and nonstop action."   —*Library Journal* (starred review)

"Johnson's pacing is tight and his dialogue snaps."
     —*Entertainment Weekly*

"Wyoming sheriff Walt Longmire's eleventh case takes him out of his jurisdiction. . . . Those who have followed the series all along will find no reason to stop now."   —*Booklist*

"There's a convincing feel to the whole package: a sense that you're viewing this territory through the eyes of someone who knows it as adoring lover and skeptical onlooker at the same time."
     —*The Washington Post*

"Great characters, witty banter, serious sleuthing, and a love of Wyoming bigger than a stack of derelict cars."   —*The Boston Globe*

"Stepping into Walt's world is like slipping on a favorite pair of slippers, and it's where those slippers lead that provides a thrill. Johnson pens a series that should become a 'must' read, so curl up, get comfortable, and enjoy the ride." —*The Denver Post*

"Reading Craig Johnson is a treat. . . . [He] tells great stories, casts wonderful characters, and writes in a style that compels the reader forward." —*Wyoming Tribune Eagle*

"Suspenseful and always entertaining. . . . The eleventh Walt Longmire mystery is one of the best yet." —*The Oklahoman Review*

"Experience the West in all its grandeur while Walt battles the evils trying to encroach upon his beloved county. Blending the literary novel with the western and the mystery Craig Johnson continues to deliver exceptional reads." —*Shelf Awareness*

"*Any Other Name* is yet another fast-paced novel filled with Johnson's brand of Wild West humor and quick wit." —*Deseret News*

A PENGUIN MYSTERY

ANY OTHER NAME

Craig Johnson is the *New York Times* bestselling author of the Longmire mysteries, the basis for the hit Netflix original series *Longmire*. He is the recipient of the Western Writers of America Spur Award for fiction, and his novella, *Spirit of Steamboat*, was the first One Book Wyoming selection. He lives in Ucross, Wyoming, population twenty-five.

By Craig Johnson

THE LONGMIRE SERIES

The Cold Dish
Death Without Company
Kindness Goes Unpunished
Another Man's Moccasins
The Dark Horse
Junkyard Dogs
Hell Is Empty
As the Crow Flies
A Serpent's Tooth
Any Other Name
Dry Bones
An Obvious Fact
The Western Star
Depth of Winter

ALSO BY CRAIG JOHNSON

Spirit of Steamboat (a novella)
Wait for Signs (short stories)
The Highwayman (a novella)

STAND-ALONE E-STORIES

Christmas in Absaroka County
(includes four stories, also in *Wait for Signs*)
Divorce Horse (also in *Wait for Signs*)
Messenger (also in *Wait for Signs*)

CRAIG JOHNSON

ANY OTHER NAME

PENGUIN BOOKS

PENGUIN BOOKS
An imprint of Penguin Random House LLC
375 Hudson Street
New York, New York 10014
penguin.com

First published in the United States of America by Viking Penguin,
a member of Penguin Group (USA) LLC, 2014
Published in Penguin Books 2015

THE LIBRARY OF CONGRESS HAS CATALOGED THE HARDCOVER EDITION AS FOLLOWS:
Johnson, Craig, 1961–
author.
Any other name : a Longmire mystery / Craig Johnson.
pages cm
ISBN 978-0-670-02646-3 (hc.)
ISBN 978-0-14-312697-3 (pbk.)
1. Longmire, Walt (Fictitious character)—Fiction.
2. Sheriffs—Wyoming—Fiction. 3. Mystery fiction. I. Title.
PS3610.O325A74 2014
813'.6—dc23 2013047845

Printed in the United States of America
10

Set in Dante MT Std
Designed by Alissa Rose Theodor

For Lola, Act I

That which we call a rose by any other name would smell as sweet.

—William Shakespeare,
Romeo and Juliet, Act 2, Scene 2

We sleep safely at night because rough men stand ready to visit violence on those that would harm us.

—Winston Churchill

ACKNOWLEDGMENTS

First off I owe an apology to Campbell County, Wyoming, for getting all noir whenever Walt heads over there; it seems as though it's always the dead of winter when I cross the Powder River country, but I promise that someday I'll do a bright and cheery book that takes place in the spring or summer. Honest. Speaking of summer, thanks to the fine folks at the State Game Lodge in Custer National Park for the ghostly tour.

Finally, this novel sprang up with the fertile assistance of Dr. David "Nasturtium" Nickerson as well as the numerous train experts who helped me in spreading the fertilizer and Auda "Snap Dragon" DeLeon and Marlen "Larkspur" Larson for the Spanish language lessons.

Not much grows in the high plains winter, but I had more than a few hothouse beauties helping me up on this one like Gail "Hydrangea" Hochman and Marianne "Magnolia" Merola. The pruning and cutting was ably handled by Kathryn "Columbine" Court, Lindsay "Star of Bethlehem" Schwoeri, copyeditor Barbara "Chrysanthemum" Campo, and Scott "Cactus" Cohen. The bouquet that makes the road smell sweet is Carolyn "Calendula" Coleburn, Ben "Plumeria" Petrone, Maureen "Dahlia" Donnelly, and Angie "Indian Paintbrush" Messina.

And, most of all, my rose by any name, Judy "Sweet-Pea" Johnson.

ANY OTHER NAME

Any Other Name

1

Joseph Conrad said that if you wanted to know the age of the earth, look upon the sea in a storm; if you want to know the age of the Powder River country, just be on the wrong side of a coal train. A guy who worked for the Burlington Northern Santa Fe once told me that the trains in northern Wyoming are about a hundred and forty cars and a mile and a half long, but it sure seems longer than that when you're waiting on one.

Lucian Connally, my old boss and the retired sheriff of Absaroka County, reached into his pocket and pulled out his beaded tobacco pouch the Cheyenne elders had given him along with the name *Nedon Nes Stigo*—He Who Sheds His Leg. "Damn, this is a long one." He also pulled his briarwood pipe from the inside pocket of his light jacket, much too light for the weather, and fingered a small packet of wooden matches along with it. "We used to get calls from the railroad detectives, what a useless bunch, wanting us to come down and identify the hobos that climbed in the hoppers back in Chicago and Milwaukee, and with the slick sides on the railcar walls, they couldn't get out . . ." He stuffed a small amount of the tobacco into the bowl of his pipe. "They'd pull those cars into the mines and dump tons of coal onto 'em—imagine their surprise."

"Homeless."

He turned to look at me. "What?"

"Homeless; they don't call them hobos anymore."

He nodded his head and looked back at the train. "Flat as a damn pancake is what I called 'em."

I watched the cars roll and felt the ground shake. The single most plentiful source of coal in the United States, the Powder River Basin contains one of the largest deposits in the world and has made Wyoming the top coal-producing state since the late eighties.

He pulled a match from the pack and made ready to strike. "Pulverized pepper steak; wasn't a lot to identify, I can tell ya that much."

The major cities of the Wyoming portion of the basin are Gillette and Sheridan; in Montana, Miles City. The rest of the twenty-four thousand square miles is what they call sparsely populated and I call Durant and home.

It was a Saturday.

"Flat as a flitter."

I was tired.

"Identify my ass."

And I was about to lose my patience.

"Looked like hamburger."

I scrubbed a hand across my face. "Old man, you're not going to light that pipe in my truck."

He looked over at me for a moment, the silence between us carrying the electric charge of decades, grunted, and then pulled the door handle and climbed out of the Bullet. The clanging of the warning bells amplified through the open door before he slammed it behind him and hobbled on his one real and one fake leg to the corner of my grille guard, at which point he recommenced lighting his pipe with a great deal of dramatic flourish.

It was December on the high plains, but you'd never know it to look at him, cupping his knotted hands together without a shiver or gloves for that matter and ducking his Stetson Open Road model hat down against the wind. Amplified by the flashing red lights of the railroad-crossing barrier, the brief flicker of orange glowed, reinforcing the impression that he was the devil and that the deal I had struck with him was venal and binding.

He raised his head, the consistent wind that battled the onward rushing of the train pulling at the brim of his hat like a miniature tornado, his eyes almost squeezed shut with nothing showing but the stained, walnut-colored irises glinting black in the half-light.

I looked down at the letter lying on the center console; the postmark was from a week ago, and the return address was Gillette, in the Iron Horse Subdivision, which was located on the other side of the rumbling coal cars. Gillette was in Campbell County, technically out of my jurisdiction as the Absaroka County sheriff.

My daughter was having a baby in a matter of days, and I was supposed to be visiting her in Philadelphia; instead, I was here, helping Lucian resolve his debt to a dead man.

A barely audible whine keened from the backseat, and I reached around and ruffled the fur behind Dog's ears. The combination St. Bernard/German shepherd/dire wolf glanced at Lucian. The brim of my mentor's hat was pressed against the crown of his forehead, making it seem as if he was galloping at high speed like some soul-damned ghost rider in the sky.

I thought about how easy it would be to just throw the big

three-quarter-ton into reverse and back out, turn around, and take Route 14/16 back up to the Gillette airport to jump on a plane, but they likely wouldn't allow Dog, so that was out.

Wondering what it was I was doing here, other than playing the role of chauffeur, I leaned back into my leather seat and felt the pressure of my Colt 1911. "Maybe they'll have this talk, and then we'll turn around and go home."

I looked at Dog again, but he didn't seem convinced.

Turning back and watching the old sheriff stare at the train, I sighed. "Yep, me neither."

Pulling the collar of my sheepskin coat a little tighter and cranking my hat down so that it didn't follow the train to Oregon, I pulled the handle on my door and slid my boots to the gravel surface. I crunched around to the front of the Bullet to lean on the grille guard with him. I spoke loudly, in the field voice my father had never let me use in the house, just to be heard above the endless procession of open cars and the bells that hammered their warning. "They still do."

He studied me with a clinched eyeball and said nothing, puffing on his pipe like he was pulling the mile of coal himself.

"Find bodies in the hopper cars."

The ass end of the train went by, another disappointment in that it was not a caboose but rather a set of locomotives helping to push from the rear, and I got that familiar feeling I always did whenever a train passed; that I should be on it, but it was going the wrong way.

Suddenly the bony arms of the crossing gates rose, and the incessant clanging stopped. We listened to the wind for a while, and then the old man beat his pipe empty on the hard surface of the grille guard, unintentionally repeating the coda of the claxons. "Hard times."

With this singular pronouncement he turned and climbed back in, leaving me watching the skies peeled back in folds of gray, darker and darker to the horizon.

He honked the horn behind me.

Flakes were streaking in the wind like bad reception as we pulled up to the house, an unassuming one, one that you'd drive right by, thinking that there must be happy people inside—at least that's the way I liked to think.

We both sat there, dreading what was coming.

He cleared his throat and started to say something.

"What?"

Gazing out the side window at a deflated Santa Claus that looked as if it might've overimbibed in holiday festivities, he grumbled, "Boom or bust."

"What?"

"Oil, natural gas, and coal; they used to have bumper stickers over here that read CAMPBELL COUNTY—GIVE US ONE MORE BOOM AND WE WON'T SCREW IT UP." He continued to study the Santa, looking even more like it might've arrived in the bottom of a train car. "Used to see a woman here back in the day; used to drive over here on Sundays. She lived alone in this big old house and had money— used to like spending it on me. Never saw her out on the town, never mentioned other men, never bothered me calling or anything like that and was always glad to see me. Whenever we got together we'd end up in motels over in Rapid or up in Billings—we'd mix drinks in this big champagne-gold '62 Cadillac she had . . ."

"What ever happened to her?"

He stayed like that for a moment, not moving, and then nodded once. "Hell if I know."

Lucian got out of the truck, and I trudged along after him through the snow that had just started blowing to South Dakota, made a detour into the yard, and reattached the small air compressor to the hose that led to Santa's boot heel. The jolly old elf rippled on the ground as if trying to crawl away but then slowly grew and stood with an arm raised, a fine patina of coal dust covering his jaunty red suit.

I walked onto the porch where Lucian had rung the bell.

"That your civic duty for the day?"

"Evidently not. Here I am with you when I should be in Philadelphia with Cady."

Nothing happened so he turned the knob and walked in.

"What are you doing?"

He looked at me still standing on the front porch in the wind and scattered snow. He didn't say anything but limped off into the house; I had the choice of following him or standing out there freezing my butt off.

I entered, careful to wipe my feet before stepping onto the unusually wide plastic runners that lay on the white carpeting, and, leaning to the side, saw Lucian round a corner past a room divider to go into the kitchen.

I unbuttoned my coat and stuffed my gloves in my pockets and followed, hoping that if somebody got shot it would be him and not me—he was gristly and could take it.

When I got to the kitchen no one was there, only an electric wheelchair parked beside a door open at the far end of the room that led to a basement with one of those fancy stairway elevators that you see in the octogenarian catalogs I've been receiving far too often lately.

I reached over and touched the joystick on the spacey-looking wheelchair and it jumped forward, crashing into my leg. "Ouch."

I gently pushed the stick back so that the contraption parked itself in the exact same spot.

Glancing around the kitchen, I was struck by how clean and orderly and white it was—like a museum or somebody's heaven.

There was a humming sound from the basement and what sounded like typing and, peering down the steps, I could see that lights were on down there, flickering blue ones as if from a couple of televisions.

Easing myself around the track for the chair elevator, I started down the steps—Lucian was sitting on an overstuffed leather sofa and was leafing through a magazine. At the bottom of the stairs, I got a better view of the dimly lit room, which was dominated by three huge flat-screen televisions surrounding a counter with two computer monitors; an older, platinum-haired woman, seated in another wheelchair, raised her hand and waved at me. I took off my hat and waved back.

She smiled and shrugged, her head encased in a massive set of headphones, her eyes redirected to one of the screens and what I could now see was an end-of-the-season football game—Oakland and San Diego.

Stepping around the counter in front of Lucian, I watched as she casually tapped the elongated keys of the stenotype-like machines at her fingertips, belying the speed at which the words were magically appearing up on the closed-captioned portions of the screen.

After a while, with no other recourse, I sat on the sofa with Lucian and waited. There was another door, which must've led to another room, but little else. "She does closed captioning for the NFL?"

He flipped another page in the *Wyoming Wildlife* magazine and glanced up at Phyllis Holman, still tapping away like Morse code. "Football, baseball, hockey . . . you name it, she does it." His head dropped back to the tips on wild turkey hunting. "Knows more about sports than any man I know."

"Hi." She had pulled one of the ear cups back and was looking at me. "Commercial break."

"Nice to meet you, Mrs. Holman." I glanced around at all the technology. "Quite a setup you've got here."

She shrugged. "It keeps me occupied."

I looked at one of the TVs, my mind playing pinball in an attempt to find something to say as the talking heads came back on the screen. "Who's your favorite announcer?"

She quickly pulled the headphone back over her ear, her attention returning to the keyboards. "Anyone who talks slowly and distinctly."

I watched her work for a while and then, with my interest not being piqued by either of the teams or by any of the *Wyoming Wildlife* turkey tips, I sidled into the corner of the sofa and pulled my hat over my face.

It was not a new dream, the one that overtook me; rather a continuation of an experience that I'd had back in the spring. There was snow, there was always snow in my dreams or visions, as my good buddy Henry Standing Bear called them.

In this one I was postholing my way in thigh-deep snow, old and laden—both me and the snow. The collar was up on my coat, and my hat was hard on my head, defending against the wind. The visibility was horrible, and I could see only about ten feet in front of me. I was following something, something that didn't want to be followed. There were other shapes, darker ones that hurtled around me, but the creature continued on.

The shapes continued to dodge their way around me, and I could hear their breathing, heavy and dangerous. The tracks were difficult to see in the whiteout, and I reached down to clutch the side of my hip where my sidearm should have been resting under my coat, but there was nothing there—and that was when I saw that the thing had turned and what I was following had horns.

". . . You know Gerald, Lucian. He never would've done something like this; it just wasn't like him."

I didn't move, just stayed as I was—a stakeout under a hat.

Lucian's voice sounded tired, and I started to weaken, thinking of all the conversations like this that he'd had to endure. "He was a good man, Phyllis, but I'm not so sure there's anything anybody can do about this. I spoke with Sandy Sandburg and he said—"

"Don't mention that man's name in this house."

There was a silence. "Nonetheless, he said that—"

"They wrapped it up too quickly, Lucian."

He made a guttural noise in his throat. "Goddamn it, Phyllis, it was the investigators down in Cheyenne that did the autopsy at DCI. You know as well as I do that when a man like Gerald Holman dies they have to do a complete—"

"They didn't like him; they didn't like him, and they're trying to cover something up, I can tell by the way they look at me. I was a court reporter, remember, and I developed an ability to read people; I can tell when people are lying, believe me, I've heard enough of it." Another long pause. "You know as well as I do that these things happen for two reasons: either it's trouble at home or trouble on the job. Now I know there wasn't any trouble at home, so—"

"How's your daughter, how's Izzy?"

There was a pause, and then she answered. "Connie's fine." I could feel the two of them staring at each other. "We haven't had to use the room, if that's what you're asking."

"Do you know what it was he was working on?"

"They won't tell me. What did they tell you?"

"They said he was carrying a full caseload, including a missing persons—"

"The stripper—that whore, doesn't it figure that that's the case they would focus on."

The old sheriff adjusted himself on the sofa in order to sit forward. "Were there other things you know about?"

"Things that would make a lot of very important people in this town more than a little nervous. Yes."

Lucian sighed. "Things like what?"

"I'm not sure I want to tell you about them if you're not going to help me." Another longer pause. "He was a good man, Lucian. He helped you when nobody else would, and now he's dead; I think you owe him something more than a phone call."

I could feel him nodding. "Not as young as I used to be, Phyllis."

"I'm assuming that's why you brought him."

Even with my hat over my face, I could feel their eyes shift to me.

"It is."

"He as good as they say?"

I waited and listened.

"When I hired him I told him two things: no man has any sense till age thirty-five and damn few afterwards . . ."

"Amen to that, and the other?"

"Never go after a man to arrest him unless you are certain you are legally right, but then arrest him or die." I felt him shift and was sure he was looking straight at me now. "In all the time I've known him, I've never seen him quit, which is where most of 'em ain't up to snuff—they give out. If he's got any give in him, ain't nobody found it yet."

"He's big."

"That he is, but that ain't the half of it." He got up from the sofa, and I could hear him limp over to her. "Is that the room over there, the one where you kept Connie?" She didn't say anything, so he continued. "I want to warn you that if you put Walter on this you're going to find out what it's all about, one way or the other." Another pause, and I could imagine the face that was peering down at her, a visage to which I was accustomed. "You're sure you want that? Because he's like a gun; once you point him and pull the trigger, it's too late to change your mind."

"Oh jeez, if it isn't dangerous and dangerouser." Sandy Sandburg, the sheriff of Campbell County, pulled out a chair, sat at our table, and propped up a large manila folder on the windowsill beside him, careful to pick a spot where the condensation wouldn't do any damage.

It was cold in the little Mexican restaurant in Gillette's industrial section beside the interstate highway; late on a Sunday night the patrons were few and far between—as a matter of fact, we were the only ones around. A skinny waitress came from behind the counter and sat a cup of coffee in front of Sandy. "¿Cómo estás?"

"Hola, guapa. ¿Qué tal?"

"Cansada."

Sandburg reached out and gripped one of her thin arms and slid the sleeve of her sweater up to reveal a speckling of old scabs. *"¿Te mantienes limpia?"*

She shrugged, pulled her arm away, and yanked a pad and pencil from her apron. *"Me bañe en la mañana."*

His eyes diverted to us as he let the girl go. "As you might expect, the burritos are pretty damn good." He glanced back at the waitress and held up three fingers. *"Tres, por favor.* Beef with the green stuff." He watched her go and then turned back to the two of us. "Gentlemen, there's no mystery."

Lucian cocked his hat back on his head, looking like Will Rogers ready to make a run on a casino. "Phyllis Holman, by God, seems to think otherwise."

"The bereaved widow . . . Well, she would."

I volunteered. "She doesn't seem to like you."

Lucian glanced at me, now sure I had been awake on the sofa.

"Yeah, I get that, too." Sandy shrugged. "Hell, I don't know what I did to her but offer her retired husband a job on the Cold Case Task Force."

"Maybe that was it." I eased back in my chair as far as I could without fear of breaking it. "How many on the Cold Case Task Force anyway?"

"One." Sandy grinned with his matinee idol smile, the one that got other people in trouble, his teeth white against the tan he acquired at Coco View Resort in Honduras every Christmas. "Started it up just so Gerald would have something to do." The smile faded. "Then this happens; I gotta tell you, of all the fellas I would've thought would go out this way, Gerry would've been the last."

I sipped my already cold coffee. "Why?"

Sandy clicked his eyes to mine. "Ever meet him?"

"No."

"He was so by-the-book that he might as well have published the damn thing." He looked at Lucian. "Am I right, or am I right?"

"Gerald Holman never broke a rule by force of bending one, that's for damn sure." He glanced at the folder next to Sandy's elbow. "That the report?"

"It is. We've got a DCI field office up here with two cashiers and a bag boy." The colorful euphemisms the sheriff used were a result of the Division of Criminal Investigation's headquarters in Cheyenne being an old grocery store. "But they drove the Death Mobile up here anyway and did a full autopsy."

I sat my mug down with more of a *thunk* than I'd really wanted; they both looked at me.

Sandy reached over and opened the folder and read: "On December 13th, one Gerald Holman placed the barrel of his issued sidearm, a .357 revolver, in his mouth and pulled the trigger. It was established by agents of the Division of Criminal Investigation that the individual, locked in the room from the inside, had opportunity and the condition for the decedent to have self-inflicted his injury. Further investigation revealed that no one else had been in the room, verified by eyewitnesses, position of the decedent's body in relation to the unlikely position the assailant would have to have assumed, blood spatter, and the gunpowder residue on the decedent's hand. A gun-cleaning kit was found on the bed beside the decedent, but it was determined that the firing of the weapon was not accidental."

"'Less he was licking the damn thing clean."

I ignored Lucian's remark. "Demonstrations of intent?"

Sandy continued reading. "He used a pillow to muffle the noise."

I looked out the window at the reflection of three men attempting to understand why one of their own had done what he had done. "Personal effects?"

"Untouched."

"Note?"

"Nope." He studied me. "There's nothing here, Walt."

"Can I have the report?"

He folded it up and started to hand it to me but then stopped as my fingers touched it. "Promise to bring it back?"

I didn't move. "Make copies if you want."

He shoved it at me. "I trust you."

I began looking at the photos and reading the summary report from the DCI investigators. "Who is Rankaj Patel?"

"Oh, the Pakistani guy that owns the Wrangler Motel where the incident took place, about a mile east of here . . ."

"Indian."

Sandy studied me. "What?"

"Indian; the man's Indian."

I watched him think about it. "No, he ain't Indian—"

Lucian interrupted. "Dot, not feather."

"Huh?"

I continued leafing through the folder—the photos were, as usual, gruesome. "About a third of all motel owners in the U.S. are called Patel—it's a surname that indicates that they're members of a Gujarati Hindu subcaste." I looked up at his confused face and figured I might as well educate him on the subject. "The Indian caste structure has four principal divisions and a myriad of subcastes, of which Patel is one; Vaishyas, or traders, were at one time employed to calculate the tithes that were owed to medieval kings by farmers in Gujarat, an Indian province on the Arabian Sea."

Sandy shook his head and looked at Lucian. "Was he like this when you hired him?"

He nodded. "Better than a bookmobile."

I put the folder behind me, uninterested in looking at it any more before I ate. "What was he working on?"

"Lots of things—nothing earthshaking."

"Can I see those files?"

"Richard Harvey says he'd be glad to meet with you tomorrow morning."

I nodded. "That his replacement?"

Sandy smiled again, and I knew the real trouble had begun. "Of sorts."

The Wrangler Motel sat on the eastern side of Gillette like it was run out of town. With a lone strip of eight ground-floor and nine second-floor units, it was anchored to the high plains by a decrepit café/bar, the Aces & Eights, on one end and an equally run-down office on the other.

I was standing in said office arguing with Rankaj Patel about a twenty-dollar pet fee for Dog; he was a tiny man and, as I'd suspected, of Indian descent. I looked down at the worn, stained carpet and collapsed chairs and up at the moth-stained art on the walls. "You're kidding."

He responded in a singsong lilt. "It is corporate policy, sir."

"What corporation?"

He spread his hands in a gesture of largesse. "The Wrangler Motel Corporation, sir."

"Of which you are the chairman of the board and CEO?" I

pulled out my wallet and adjusted my thinking to the fact that I was paying half as much for Dog as I was for Lucian and me. "I'll also need the key to room twelve."

He half turned with the key to room 5, the one he had selected for us, and froze. "I'm afraid that room is not available, sir."

I pulled my new badge wallet from the back pocket of my jeans.

"There was an accident."

"I know . . ." The stiffness of the leather caused the thing to fall from my fingers and land on the counter between us like a shot quail, ruining what I had hoped to be a dramatic effect. I reached down and spread it open so that he could see the six-point star. "I'm the guy who's supposed to find out why there was an accident."

He studied the badge, taking in the fact that the county was adjacent. "I told the investigators everything I know."

"I'm sure you did, but if you think of anything else I'd appreciate it if you would tell me."

He nodded. "How long will you be staying?"

I picked up the keys to both rooms. "As long as it takes."

I ignored the signs, backed in, and parked in front of room 5. Dog jumped out and immediately began sniffing the surroundings as I opened the tailgate and handed Lucian his overnight bag and the key. "How well did you know Holman?"

"Not that well; we worked a few cases together."

"Children?"

He nodded. "A daughter; she's on the school board here."

"Think she'd be worth talking to?"

"Hell, I don't know. I never met her."

"You're a liar; I heard you ask Phyllis about her—and what's the story on the room in the basement?"

He studied me. "Her name is Connie but Gerald used to call her Izzy for Isadora Duncan, the one that got killed in that Bugatti when her scarf got caught in the spokes of the wheels back in '27?"

"Actually, it was an Amilcar, but her chauffeur's name was Falchetto and she used to call him Bugatti."

He shook his head at me. "Anyway, Connie was one of those ballet dancers, they say a really good one, but she got caught up in drugs trying to keep her weight down and . . . Anyway, Phyllis and Gerald kept her in that basement bedroom and got her clean. Model citizen, these days."

I turned to watch my pet Kodiak snuffle the tires of a Jeep Cherokee. "Dog." He sniffed a few more times just to show his independence and then joined the two of us at the door. "Lucian, you take him and get settled in."

The old sheriff looked up at me. "Where the hell are you going?"

I stuffed the folder Sandy had given me under an arm. "Upstairs, to twelve."

"Plenty of time for that tomorrow."

"I still have the greatest of hope that I can salvage my trip to Philadelphia."

He stared at me for a moment, said nothing, and then slipped the key in the loose lock. Followed by Dog, who never met an open door he didn't consider an invitation, Lucian flipped on the light and shut the door behind them; I stood there listening to the eighteen-wheelers Jake-braking on the interstate.

As I turned to go, I saw the curtain in the window of number 6 slowly pull closed. I thought about knocking on the door but instead walked over and looked at the only other vehicle parked in the lot, the one that Dog had irrigated, with Idaho plates, 6B 22119. Ada County, city of Boise; there was also a Boise State snorting bronc sticker in the rear window along with the black-and-white sticker of the *lauburu*, otherwise known as the Basque cross.

Even with the Basque population of my county, an odd vehicle to be parked in this lot.

"If you're here to run me off, it's not going to work."

I turned and looked at the tall young woman with a thick mane of dark hair pulled up in a ponytail, backlit by the light from room 6. "Excuse me?"

She hugged herself, and I figured it was the cold but maybe just a habit. "I'm not intimidated by any of you."

I glanced around to indicate to her that I was alone. "Okay."

"I saw you . . . looking at my car."

"It's a nice car."

"Well, it's not going anywhere."

I repeated myself. "Okay." Feeling I should make some kind of effort at western hospitality, I stepped forward and raised a hand to shake hers. "Walt Longmire, I'm the sheriff of Absaroka County."

She stared at my hand, her arms still wrapped around her chest, one set of fingers clutching the doorknob in an attempt to not let too much of the cold enter the room. "This is Campbell County."

I pushed my hat back on my head with my now-free hand. "Yes, it is—and you are?"

She sighed and said her name mechanically. "Lorea Urrecha."

"Basque?"

Her chin came out a little farther and her head turned, the

high brows and cheekbones highlighted in the small amount of illumination—classically beautiful but with character. "Yes."

My attention was drawn to a Cadillac Escalade EXT that had entered the parking lot to travel down the rows of rooms, the vehicle slowing when it got in front of us. The windows were fogged, but from the dash lights I could see that it was a woman behind the wheel. She slowed almost to a stop but then looked more closely at my truck—the stars and the bars—and quickly pulled away.

I got a glance at the plates as she rounded the Aces & Eights bar and café at the corner of the motel at the 17—Campbell County. Turning back to the young woman, I stuffed my hand in my pocket. "Been at the motel long?"

She didn't say anything at first but then spit the words. "Is this an interview or an interrogation?"

"Actually, it was just a question."

She turned her head away from me, and I lost her profile.

I glanced back at the closed office and the now lit NO VACANCY neon light that Rankaj Patel must've turned on just before turning in. "I can always ask the motel manager, if you'd like."

"I'd like." She stepped back, her lips compressed, and shut the door in my face.

I stood there looking at the closed door and then raised my fist. "Go Broncs."

You crafty devil, you certainly played her like a Stradivarius.

I turned and started up the metal steps by the office, stopped at the landing, and looked at the numbers on the rooms until I got to the one with the yellow plastic tape that read POLICE LINE DO NOT CROSS. Thoughtfully, the Gillette PD and the Campbell County Sheriff's Office had simply put the barrier on the door so that you could open it without having to retape.

Convenient.

I slipped the key in and turned the knob, stepped inside, and closed the door behind me as I turned on the light. The heat in the room was off, and it was cold, cold enough to still see my breath.

Like a meat locker.

With more than thirty thousand suicides a year, the act is the tenth leading cause of death in the United States. The rates for those above sixty-five years of age are much higher than the average, and Holman was sixty-seven. Fifty-six percent of male suicides are a result of firearms, whereas with females the predominant choice of departure is an overdose.

Most suicides occur as a result of depression, but there are some where the motives are never fully ascertained. This line of thought is of little comfort to the survivors but sometimes helpful to the investigating officer, who can become so immersed in the case that he or she is tempted to slash his or her own wrists.

I flipped on the light in the bathroom and took in the chipped, stained porcelain, the worn tile, and the mold on the shower curtain. The thin towels were still hanging folded on the rod, and the little cakes of soap were still wrapped in paper and sitting beside the unused sample bottle of shampoo/conditioner. Even the toilet paper still had its folded and pointed edge—my compliments to housekeeping.

I turned off that light and moved into the main room, past Gerald Holman's suit jacket and three-quarter-length parka, both carefully draped on hangers below the chrome shelf where his bone-colored cattleman's hat still sat, brim up.

Nonetheless, his luck had run out—or he had run it off.

There were more tape lines set up that framed off the area

around the bed where Gerald actually shot himself, which was fine by me because I saw no reason to get any closer to the gore.

The majority of the blood was centered not on the bed but on the floor where he slid after he had shot himself. Evidently his upper body had been thrown back by the impact but then had bounced off the bed, which forced his lower body and legs forward where he slipped onto the floor and bled out.

Usually, when an individual shoots himself in the head, the weapon falls from his hand onto his lap, but from the photographs in this case I knew that Officer Holman had been well trained because the Colt Python had still been clutched in his constricted hand, a product of cadaveric spasm. This is a sure sign that the victim died with the weapon in hand; no one could place the revolver there and re-create the same effect.

In the movies, the individual usually slips the barrel of the gun in his mouth, pulls the trigger, and a brief spray of blood fans from the back of his head onto a wall, usually white for cinematic effect, then the victim's eyes roll back in his head and he falls sideways, leaving a relatively undamaged face with which the mortician can work.

I've seen the aftermath of more than my share of suicides, and I've never seen one that ended like that; instead, according to the armament, the effects are devastating. The photographs in the folder under my arm told the tale of the Remington 158-grain semi-wadcutter that had traveled through the roof of the investigator's mouth at over twelve hundred feet per second, taking off the top of his head and the majority of his face from the bridge of his nose up.

I didn't need to see the soot and powder trace results or the evidence of blowback material on the Colt to know who and what had done the deed—there was only one question that continued to puzzle me.

Why twice?

Because Gerald Holman was shot in the head two times.

The only scenario is that two weeks ago today, he had raised the big revolver up in his left hand and shot himself in the left cheek, then he had placed the barrel of the .357 in his mouth and finished the job.

He had started his career in law enforcement with the Wyoming Highway Patrol in the freewheeling fifties, then had accepted a job as a deputy in the Campbell County Sheriff's Office in the sixties, where he had been promoted to undersheriff in the seventies, ran for sheriff himself in the eighties, had lost, but then had accepted a position as an investigator; after retirement, he had returned to duty in the Cold Case Task Force that Sandy Sandburg had created for him.

A half century standing behind a badge, Gerald Holman knew where to point a weapon to kill a person.

So why would he shoot himself in the cheek?

There seemed to be only one answer, and it wasn't contained in the report from DCI. And that was that Gerald Holman did something that, to my knowledge of him, gleaned from his wife, Phyllis, and both Sandy Sandburg and Lucian, he had never done to another human being.

He had punished himself.

2

Aces and eights is a poker hand generally referred to as the dead man's hand. This particular combination of cards arrived at such notoriety by being the one held by Wild Bill Hickok in Saloon 10 at the time of his demise in Deadwood, South Dakota—a little bit east of where we now sat.

According to popular opinion, Hickok held only four cards—the ace of spades, the ace of clubs, and two black eights—the subsequent draw for the deprived fifth card having been interrupted by Broken Nose Jack McCall, who fired a bullet through Bill's head that exited his right cheek to rest in the wrist of a fellow card player, the fifth card being the least of Wild Bill's problems at that point.

Getting breakfast at the run-down café of the same name as the dreaded dead man's hand was as elusive as Wild Bill's hole card. The short counter was where the waitress supposedly served meals, but she was a little slow in responding, and getting a second cup of coffee was proving difficult. We'd gotten the first cup all right, but refills appeared to be in high demand, which was strange, since we were the only customers in the place.

Every once in a while the young Hispanic woman who had

poured us our initial cup rushed through the restaurant, and we'd ceremoniously hold up our mugs, but she would continue on and out the door.

Lucian watched as the girl breezed in again, once more ignoring our two-mug salute and disappearing through the swinging kitchen doors. "Damn, what'a ya got to do to get another cup of coffee outta that Mexican jumping bean."

"Lucian."

He flipped the side of his old hunting coat back, the one that had the 1951 Wyo. Rifle Association patch on the shoulder, and rubbed at the small of his back where the rented bed had not agreed. "What?"

I gazed into the kitchen, where I could vaguely see the smoky visage of the ghost of breakfast future. "I think she's cooking our Denver omelets."

"Think they'll be done before the fire alarm goes off?" The old sheriff studied the massive coffee urn at the bar-back, and I could see him eyeing the prospect of climbing over the counter to get at it.

The young woman passed us again, and we raised our mugs to no avail.

"So, what'd you see up there in room twelve?"

I sat my coffee down and looked at him. "Apparently . . . a man killed himself."

"I knew I trained you well." He continued to stare at the brushed stainless steel surface of the coffee urn longingly. "No question about it?"

I swirled the tiny bit of coffee at the bottom of my own cup in an attempt to make it last. "You read the report; look at the pictures?"

"Nope, I just called those assholes over here at the field office, and they made it clear that they were doin' me some kind of big damned favor by talkin' to me. They said that as far as they were concerned, he'd killed himself and that was that, case closed."

I reached over and tapped the thick manila folder that sat between us. "That the investigator who did the scene?"

"Two of 'em."

"I'll talk to them, but if I have to I can get in touch with T. J. Sherwin." I left my hand on the report. "Instantaneous rigor in the strong-side hand, trace elements."

He nodded. "I figured as much."

"There's one thing though." He turned his head at the tone of my voice. "He shot himself twice."

I watched the dark eyes sharpen. "With that big .357?"

"Yep." I sighed. "Wadcutters."

"Seems like once woulda been enough."

"If he had wanted it to be."

He raised his mug to his lips but then, remembering it was empty, sat it back down. "What's that supposed to mean?"

"Either somebody else shot him first, or your friend, Investigator Holman, raised that big revolver up and pointed it in his own face and pulled the trigger. Then he stuck it in his mouth and blew out the top of his head. Now, why does a man do that?"

Lucian scooted his cup toward me, and a sadness seemed to overtake him as he spoke quietly. "I don't know; I don't know what comes over a person to be driven to the point where they don't see any other way out than . . ." His words stuttered to a stop. "I just don't understand any of it. I guess I've fought so hard to keep my life that I can't conceive of a situation where I'd voluntarily give it up." The old sheriff sat there moving his jaw in anticipation of the words. "Why would he do that?"

"Possibly to punish himself?"

"For what?"

"I guess that's what I really have to find out." I glanced around. "And why here?"

"Hell, he was probably waitin' on a cup of coffee."

I repeated the question and then added, "Did you see his house? Spotless; he wouldn't stay in a place like this unless there was a reason."

He nudged the handle of his mug with a thick thumbnail. "Maybe he didn't want to make a mess for Phyllis to have to clean up."

I sat there quietly for a moment. "Hey, Lucian?"

"What?"

"That story you told me in the Holman driveway about the woman you used to come over here and see on Sundays? That was Phyllis, wasn't it?"

"By God, I warned her . . ." He turned and looked at me again. "I told her that you were a force to be reckoned with and that if she didn't want the answers, she better not have you ask the questions."

"You've got a lot of women in your past."

Absentmindedly, he lifted his mug and then slammed it down. "Yeah, and I'm pretty damned proud of it."

"Were you driving when she was hurt?"

He pivoted on his stool to look at me, and his glare was like a blast furnace. "No, I wasn't, and this doesn't have a damn thing to do with the case."

I didn't look at him but stared straight ahead and spoke in a low voice. "Maybe you better tell me the story, and I'll decide if it does or not."

"You go to hell."

"It'll be a matter of public record, but I'll be wasting more time looking it up."

"Wasting time is right . . ."

I didn't move, and if I'd had more coffee I wouldn't have drunk it. I did one of the things I do best; ask a question and then wait for the answer—something he'd taught me quite a few years ago.

Our waitress passed through again, once more leaving our mugs like ships in the night. After a while he turned back and thumbed his coffee cup some more. He took a deep breath, and I could feel the emotion leave him. "But I was in the car."

I continued to wait and then listened.

"We was headed down Route 59 for the rodeo in Cheyenne. Hell, I don't know, she wanted to see men fall off horses or some damn thing. We'd been drinking. This is back before she was married to Gerald. Hell, they didn't even know one another . . . You remember how it was, they used to hand you mixed drinks out of the drive-through in every bar in Wyoming—to-go cups."

"I remember."

He sighed. "She was in a hurry. Like a damn fool, I bet her a hundred-dollar bill that we wouldn't make it and let me tell you, she put her foot into that Eldorado and we damn well flew." His jaw moved up and down, chewing on the words he said next. "Wasn't even another car involved. We came around one of those big, sweeping turns and the thing just decided it wanted to go to Nebraska . . . She didn't have on her belt and flew out on the first roll."

He didn't say anything more and just sat there.

"You're not doing this for him; you're doing it for her."

He stared into the empty mug.

I let the dust settle and patted the report. "No signs of drugs, alcohol—"

"He didn't drink."

"At all?"

"Nope."

I dwelled on Phyllis Holman. "What did she say about him?" I leaned in closer. "Change in sleeping habits, lack of appetite, sex—disinterest in the job?"

He shrugged. "You'll have to ask her that."

"No, you will. You know her, and she's more likely to open up to you."

The waitress passed us again and both of our mugs levitated from the surface like some magic act and hovered there before slowly returning, in tandem, to the counter.

"I don't think I want that."

I was getting a little annoyed. "Then what do you want?"

He flipped his coat back again, and I thought he was going to rub his back some more, but instead, he quickly drew his service .38 from its holster, extended his arm, took careful aim at the coffee urn, and fired.

The sound in the enclosed space of the café/bar was like a falling tree, and the thing bucked against the bar-back like a wounded felon before spouting a single jet of coffee out onto the floor behind the counter. The old sheriff holstered the Smith & Wesson, hooked the handle of his mug with a forefinger like a talon, leaned forward, and held the cup under the stream to fill it.

The young waitress appeared at the door with both hands at her mouth. Lucian turned his head, grinned, and threw her a quick wave before she backed through the door and ran away.

After filling his mug, he took mine and held it just away from the gusher. "Cup of coffee?"

The sheriff's office in Gillette was a big one by Wyoming standards, and to me it looked like a fort set down in hostile territory. I didn't know anybody in the outer sanctum—Sandy Sandburg must have been in his office—but they all knew Lucian.

"There was this one time where we had this crazy guy from over our way that was after his wife and her boyfriend and drove over here. Killed both of 'em and was on his way out the door with a pump shotgun." I watched as the old man's eyes glinted in the storytelling. "There was a whole mess of us, but you know how those things can go when you're dealin' with the deranged— somebody's gonna get shot." He shook his head. "The crazy son of a bitch was on the porch wavin' around that twenty-gauge and screaming and yelling about how he was going to kill everybody, and we're takin' cover behind the vehicles when I reached in the trunk of my Nash Rambler for my own scattergun and noticed the vacuum cleaner I had in there."

I studied the plaques on the entryway wall and noted that Sandy was a member of the Wyoming Stock Growers Association, the Masonic Lodge, the Powder River Shrine, Kalif Horse Patrol, Elks Lodge, and the Wyoming Sheriffs' and the National Sheriffs' Associations.

"So I fetched the thing out and started walking toward this loony like I was there to sell the crazy bastard a vacuum cleaner." He turned and swept his eyes over the half-dozen deputies who listened in nostalgic rapture. "I had the thing in there to drop it off to get worked on, but I just walked up to that man and started telling him all about the benefits of having this vacuum cleaner."

I wasn't sure if it was the retelling of Lucian's story or the thought of all those associational responsibilities that was wearing me out, but I wasn't aware that Sandy was standing beside my chair until I heard him laughing at the old sheriff's story.

"Well, crazy as a waltzin' pissant, this guy starts screaming that he's gonna kill me, but I just kept tellin' him about the vacuum cleaner and how he was gonna need it to clean up the mess in there . . . Well, sure enough, he starts listening and after forty minutes I traded the crazy son of a bitch the broken vacuum for the shotgun."

Sandburg tapped on my shoulder and nodded toward the sanctuary of the Campbell County Sheriff's Office. Unnoticed by the assembly, I stood and followed him down the short hallway; he partially closed the door behind us so that we could still hear Lucian's voice. "He'll be tellin' that story for the next hour, and I'm betting you've heard it before."

"You'd be right."

He crossed around his large, wooden desk and sat in an oversized, oxblood leather chair. "So I hear you had a lively breakfast at the Aces and Eights this morning."

"Lucian has a somewhat unique perspective on self-service; I was just along for the ride."

He glanced at what I assumed was an incident report that had been taken by the nice young patrolman we'd met this morning and straightened the stack of papers on his leather-trimmed blotter. "Mr. Patel of the Wrangler Motel Corporation has agreed to not press charges if you replace the mortally wounded coffee urn today."

I glanced up at the mounted elk above his head. "Okay."

"They've got nice ones at the Kmart on South Douglas Highway; I had to buy a new one for the bullpen a month ago."

"Somebody shoot it?"

"Nope, natural causes." He leaned back in his chair and considered me. "It's where I get most of my supplies; kind of puts a whole different meaning to blue-light special."

"Yep."

He said nothing for a while but then spoke. "You seem kind of down, Walt."

I shrugged.

"Hey, I heard that little spitfire of an undersheriff of yours got sliced and diced in that cluster down near Powder Junction."

I studied him back but said nothing.

"Vic all right?"

"Yep."

He continued to look at me. "You want to talk to Richard Harvey?"

"I suppose so."

"Good, because he's standing behind you."

I got up and turned to meet Gerald Holman's replacement, a tall man, built like a fence post, with a weathered complexion, wiry hair, an impressive handlebar mustache, and caramel-colored eyes. I extended a hand, and he took it. "Walt Longmire."

He nodded, sizing me up. "Inspector Harvey."

I surmised from that that we were on a formal basis.

Sandy spoke from where he sat. "You wanna have a seat, Inspector?"

He placed his big hands in his trouser pockets, the action revealing a badge on his belt and in a holster a 586 S&W .357, the same type of weapon that Gerald Holman had killed himself with, but this one had ivory handles with some kind of medallion inset. "I'll stand."

So it wasn't just for me.

Sandy squeaked in his leather chair. "Sheriff Longmire is

continuing the investigation into Holman's death, and we're going to help him in any way we can."

The inspector jiggled his car keys and some loose change in his pocket.

"He's wanting to know about Holman's caseload."

"It's all in the file I gave you."

He sounded as if he was from the Southwest somewhere. "I'd like the individual files."

Harvey glanced at Sandy. "Those are ongoing investigations."

Sandburg smiled. "In any way we can, Inspector; now why don't you take the sheriff here down to your office and get him those files?"

Harvey tilted his head just a little, glanced at me, and then back to the Campbell County sheriff. Without any further word, he turned on a cowboy heel and started toward the door as Sandy called out.

"You're excused, Inspector."

The fence pole paused at the door and looked back at me. "You coming?"

I glanced at the sheriff, who was grinning, and followed the inspector down the hallway; taking a hard right, we passed Lucian, who continued to inspire the troops with tales of yore, stood at the elevator, and waited for the car to arrive.

"Phoenix."

He stared at me without a smile. "Albuquerque."

"Retired?"

"Once."

I nodded and watched the numbers rise. "How long have you been here?"

"Ten with Arizona Corrections, ten with the APD, seven

with Denver, and then transferred up here from the DCI Field Office about six months ago."

"Decide you wanted to shovel snow?"

"Something like that."

"Sandy trying to get rid of you?"

He glanced at me and nodded. "I don't think he likes me."

"As charming as you are—how can that be?" The small car arrived, and he gestured for me to step in. "Probably thinks you're going to take his job."

Harvey joined me in the elevator and punched the button, then studied me for a moment and stuck out his hand. "Richard."

I shook it as the doors closed, and the car silently descended. "Walt."

Appropriately enough, the Cold Case Files Division of the Campbell County Sheriff's Department was located adjacent to the Campbell County Sheriff's Department file room in the chilly basement of the building, and was devoid of the charms above.

I sat in what was certainly a cast-off green metal office chair beside what had surely been an abandoned green metal office desk out of which Harvey pulled a few file folders about an inch thick; resting them on the corner of the desk, he sat in the twin green chair. "Merry belated Christmas."

"Any order to them?"

He shook his head. "Not that I can tell, but he had them on the desk just like that."

I glanced around at the locked cages surrounding the file areas and could see only one window up near the ceiling, where people's feet, clothed in various winter footwear, walked by on the sidewalk above. "He worked down here alone?"

The inspector leaned back in his chair and placed his pointy-toed boots up on the surface between us on top of the files. "Now you know why he killed himself, right?"

I looked at the folders under his polished wing tips and even went so far as to flip the corners through my fingers. "Pretty skimpy."

He ignored my remark and glanced up through the abbreviated window. "I started trying to guess what people did for a living by looking at their shoes, but then I figured out they were mostly all cops and quit."

"There are a lot of them around here."

"Uh huh." His eyes returned to mine. "How 'bout you?"

"How about me what?"

"You a cop?"

I smiled, not making it easy on him. "In what sense?"

He didn't smile back. "Are you one of them, or are you one of us?"

"I'm just me." I closed my fingers around the files and yanked them from under his boots.

He slipped the lizard skin boots from the desk and stood, and I was standing right there with him, nose to nose.

"Gerald Holman was a friend of mine, and I don't want his name dragged through the mud."

I slipped the files under my arm. "Are you trying to tell me something, Richard?"

He didn't move. "I want to be sure about who you're working for."

"That would be my business."

He nodded toward the files securely compressed under my arm. "Those are now mine and that makes it my business, too."

"You want to wrestle for them?"

He looked me over. "You think I can't?"

"I think I've got you by about sixty pounds, and the first thing I'm going to do is grab that .357 on your hip."

"Well, I'll be grabbing that .45 at the small of your back."

I glanced around. "Boy howdy, I sure hope no one comes in down here while we're doing all that grabbing."

His face was stony, but after a few seconds fissures started to break through the façade, and finally the cracks formed a grin underneath the extravagant mustache and he chuckled. "Gets lonely down here." He laughed, outright, and then sat on the edge of the desk. "I hear you're pretty smart."

"For a Wyoming sheriff?"

He continued to smile. "You get a lot of press."

"Meaning?"

He drew a wide palm across the lower part of his face but somehow didn't disturb the mustache. "Look, Gerald was a good guy . . . ."

I sat and leaned back in the guest chair. "We all seem to be in agreement about that, but he's dead and his wife wants to know why. So, in answer to your question, I'm working for her." Confrontation largely avoided, I started shuffling through the files. "This is all he was working on?"

"The only things of any importance."

I nodded and left it at that. "His wife mentioned something about a missing persons?"

"Missing girl from out near Arrosa, a little crossroads east of here along the railroad tracks." He leaned forward and took the stack from my hands and flipped through until finding the one marked with a name—Jone Urrecha. "Classic case from the Itty-Bitty-Titty Club out there; got off work and disappeared, never to be heard from again."

He handed the folder to me, and I opened it. "Dancer?"

"Sure, if you say so."

"Missing five weeks . . ." I glanced up at him. "Not exactly a cold cold case."

"Nope, but Holman got all the leftovers." He glanced around the dungeon. "And shit flows downhill."

I rested my eyes on the photo of the young woman and found her features familiar. "Urrecha, that's Basque." I looked up at him. "I met a woman at the Wrangler Motel last night by that name."

"The sister—she's been talking to the press and harassing the department about our handling of the case—everybody around here just wants her to go home."

I glanced up at him. "How is our handling of the case?"

He pointed at the folder. "As near as I can tell the report got filed by another dancer about a week after the incident. A deputy took the statement, a detective followed it up, but there was nothing to indicate foul play. Her apartment was empty, and her car was gone, so it's a pretty good bet that she flew the coop—something she has been known to do."

"You contact Boise?" He looked confused. "Where she's from?"

"Hey, this wasn't my case until a week and a half ago."

I gestured with the file. "This one was on top?"

"Yeah."

"Any chance that she was involved with Holman?"

He made a face. "You're kidding, right?"

My turn to shrug.

He thought about it. "I know it's a reasonable avenue of suspicion, but he was three times her age and just not the type."

I looked at the next file—a waitress from the Flying J Travel

Plaza on South Douglas Highway by the name of Roberta Payne. "Another missing woman?"

He nodded. "Three months ago."

I flipped to the next file and another missing woman—a housewife from east Gillette from seven months previous, Linda Schaffer.

"These files are all missing women."

He studied me. "I know what you're thinking—Powder River serial killer, but there's nothing to connect them other than the fact that they were women and are missing, and the time span is not consistent."

"You think he just fixated and burned out?"

"It happens."

He was right, it did happen with an alarming frequency—police officers who grew so close to their cases that they simply couldn't accept the loss or the failure. I tucked the folders into my chest. "Do you mind if I take these and go through them?"

He stroked a hand across his mustache again and sighed. "Hey, I'm sorry about that, before . . ." He thumped my chest with the back of his hand. "The only thing I ask is that if you come up with anything you get in touch with me first." He stuck the same hand out. "Deal?" We shook, and I stood. "Where are you going to start?"

I glanced down at the file on top, just as Gerald Holman had left it. "Evidently, at the Itty-Bitty-Titty Club."

He smiled. "Never a bad place to start."

"But first I have to go to Kmart."

Whether from guilt or a sense of retail avoidance, Lucian decided to stick around at the sheriff's office, while Dog and I headed south on the Douglas Highway to the fabled Kmart; I parked and turned to look at him. "You want dog treats, or should I just go over to the meat section and get you a ham?"

His ears went up at the word *ham*; they say dogs have a vocabulary of about twenty words, and I was pretty sure seventeen of Dog's were ham.

Having taken his order, I got out and started in. It took me a while, but I found the ham and then the coffee urn. Vowing to get Lucian to reimburse me, I made my way out with the cumbersome box but stopped as I passed the bulletin board at the entryway where a shapely lass in a green Stormy Kromer hat and a vintage plaid hunting jacket was replacing a homemade missing persons poster using a heavy-duty staple gun.

After she secured the eight-and-a-half-by-eleven sheet on the cork with a slap, she turned and looked at me with the remaining posters hanging over her arm and the staple gun at the ready. "I've got permission to do this."

I looked down the barrel of the device and raised my one available hand. "Okay."

She studied me, probably noticing I wasn't wearing one of those nifty red Kmart vests. "Do I know you?"

"Walt Longmire, the sheriff of Absaroka County—we met last night. I'm staying at the Wrangler."

"The what?"

"The Wrangler Motel."

She nodded as the pneumatic doors opened and closed behind me, ushering in repeated arctic blasts from the outside. "Yeah, yeah . . ."

I pointed toward the poster behind her. "That your sister?"

Her chin came up. "Yes."

I lowered my finger, gesturing toward the remaining posters. "Can I have one of those?"

The chin remained steady, as did the gaze. "Why?"

The doors continued to open and close, so I stepped to one
side to avoid the sensors. "I thought maybe I could help."

She snorted, and it was an ugly expression on such a pretty
face. "Well, if you're as much help as the rest of the guys that are
supposed to be looking for her . . ."

I nodded and took a deep breath. "I think I might've discovered why there's been a little slowdown in the investigation."

"And why's that?"

I glanced around with as little drama as I could to make sure
that no discount shoppers were in earshot. "The detective that
was working on the case is dead."

"What'd he die of, old age?"

I stood there for a long time, giving her what my daughter
used to call the nickel-plated stare. "Evidently it was a suicide."

She looked back at the poster. "Good, maybe the next guy in
line will do a better job."

I glanced around again, a little embarrassed. "Maybe."

She stared at me. "You?"

I nodded. "Uh, kind of."

She didn't move at first but then clutched the posters a little
closer and dropped her arm that held the staple gun. "I'm sorry;
that was awful."

"It's okay."

She sniffed and then rubbed the red of her nose with the back
of a fingerless wool glove. "The old guy?"

"Gerald Holman."

"Yeah, him." She moved to the side with me. "That's why

there was a different cop when I went in there last week; Wyatt Earp, the guy with the mustache."

"Yep."

She stared down at her fur-lined, lace-up Sorels and then handed me one of the posters without looking up. "Really, I'm sorry."

I took the piece of paper and studied the copied photo of a beautiful young blond woman looking off to the right, laughing at something someone off-camera had said. "Pretty."

"Yeah."

"No other siblings?"

"No."

I glanced at the bulletin board. "How often do you change the posters?"

She looked back. "Every couple of days; I use a different photo each time. She was like that; no two photos ever looked the same."

I waited a moment before asking. "Can I buy you lunch?"

The Flying J Travel Plaza #762 off exit 126 on I-90 isn't all that different from the rest of the six Flying Js in Wyoming, other than its location next to the Kmart on the Douglas Highway, but it was convenient and had a nice view of the parking lot and my truck, where Dog sat in the driver's seat looking in at us longingly.

"Where did you get the plains grizzly?"

I sipped my coffee. "The Forest Service, he's Smokey's evil twin—at least when he's around ham." The truck stop groaned with the wind that had started up, and snow sandblasted the glass, pressing on the casings as I looked down at the poster on the corner table between us. "They said her apartment was empty, and her car was gone."

Lorea held her hot chocolate close to her mouth and blew in it. "Trailer."

"Excuse me?"

"She didn't have an apartment; she lived in a trailer behind Dirty Shirley's, the place where she worked."

"The strip club is called Dirty Shirley's?"

She looked at me over her mug. "Yeah."

"No one has heard anything from her at all, phone calls, letters?"

"No. We were close and used to text each other all the time and suddenly she just stopped."

"Credit card receipts—"

"Nothing."

I studied the poster some more. "Five weeks."

She took a sip and looked out the window at the monochromatic landscape of concrete and blowing snow. "Yes."

I was trying to figure a way of getting around to the subject and could come up with nothing better than just asking. "I hope you're not going to take offense to this, but—"

"What was a nice girl like Jone doing in a dump like Dirty Shirley's swinging from a pole with nothing on but body glitter?"

"Something like that."

Her eyes turned back to mine. "Upward of three hundred and fifty dollars a night, I'd suspect." She pushed herself into the booth with her back against the window. "She was an education major at State until the money ran out." As she curled her black legging-clad knees up under her chin, her dark hair draped around her face. "She said she'd gotten a job here in Wyoming with one of the methane outfits, which she said was only until she saved up enough money for next year. But my parents started hearing from her less and less—"

"What do they know?"

"That she's missing, and that's all." She glanced at me, the wool hunting cap casting shadows over her eyes. "They're older; there's nothing they can do, and I don't think they need to know that Jone was——"

"Was dancing all she was doing?"

She was about to answer, and possibly in a vehement way, when the waitress reappeared with a pot in hand. "You need a refill?"

I nodded and slid my mug toward her, glancing at Lorea, who was still giving me a hard look, as I slipped my hand down and opened one of the folders that I had at my side and held up a photograph for the middle-aged waitress to see. "Know this woman?"

She immediately looked sad. "Roberta Payne, she worked here over the summer."

I stuck out a hand. "Walt Longmire, I'm the sheriff over in Absaroka County."

She filled my mug, sat the pot at the edge of the table, and extended her hand in return. "Jane Towson. The cops come in here periodically to ask questions and retake statements." Her face brightened just a little. "You know Inspector Holman? He comes in here a lot."

"He's dead."

We both looked at the young woman seated across from me, and then I turned back to the waitress. "He passed away a couple of weeks ago——"

Lorea's voice stayed sharp. "He killed himself."

Jane slowly turned back to me, unsure of what to make of her tone. "I . . . I'm sorry to hear that. He seemed like a nice man."

Gesturing with the photograph, I brought the subject back to Roberta Payne. "Did you know her well?"

"Um, not really. I mean we worked here together and we were in a book club for a while, but I didn't know her really well . . . She was only here for a couple months before she disappeared." She picked up the coffeepot and glanced at Lorea before asking me, "Do you think it's possible that she's still alive somewhere?"

"Sure, it's possible."

The young woman on the other side of the booth shimmied out and stood there for a moment as she counted out some change, her voice rote. "Reports of missing persons have increased sixfold in the last twenty-five years, from roughly 150,000 in 1980 to 900,000 this year . . . More than 2,000 a day." Lorea tossed the change on the table but glanced at me. "Nobody gives a shit, lady." She walked away from the booth, her voice a shadow. "Nobody."

3

Linda Schaffer, the first of the women who had gone missing, had lived in East Gillette in a modest home, but the house was empty, the windows were boarded up, and there was a FOR SALE sign in the yard. There were shingles missing from the roof, and dead, dried weeds jutted out from the snow-filled, raised-bed boxes. A graffiti artist had spray-painted something colorful but illegible on the corner where a few bricks had fallen away—like a place that Vic once said had probably contained a lot of rage.

I thought about what happened when an integral part of a structure was removed, about how things can so easily fall apart. There was a period, after my wife died, when I don't think I left the house for two months. Dark days that got a little better, but almost drove my daughter away from me—the one thing my wife would not have wanted under any circumstance.

Delicate little families.

One of the members of my family whined, and I turned to look at him. "What?"

He smiled and wagged his tail.

"You and me, pal." I sliced off a piece of the half-unwrapped ham in my hands with my pocketknife and handed it to him. "You're not going to get married and run off, are you?"

He dire-wolfed the ham and continued wagging, his tail thumping the inside of the door like a leather quirt.

I peeled a piece off for myself, stuffed it in my mouth, and chewed as I looked at the empty house and thought about my daughter, and more important, the trip I'd put on hold for this investigation. Richard Harvey, for all his rough edges, seemed like a competent investigator; with all those years in correction, Albuquerque, Denver, and the Division of Criminal Investigation, he was more likely to break the cases that had led to Gerald Holman's suicide than I.

The radio under my dash sprang forth with the voice of Ruby, my dispatcher, moral compass, and practitioner of proper radio procedure. Static. "Come in unit one, this is base. Over."

I plucked the mic from my dash and keyed the button. "Ruby, can't you just say Walt?"

Static. "Unit one, is that you?"

I growled into the mic. "Yep."

Static. "I have Cady on line one from Philadelphia, do you want me to patch her through? Over."

"You mean unit one and a half?"

Static.

I keyed the mic again. "Or is it one and three-quarters?"

Static. "Do you want the call? Over."

"Yes, ma'am, please."

There was a brief squelch, and then my daughter's voice came on the line. "Where are you?"

I glanced around. "Gillette."

"Why?"

"Helping Lucian with a case."

"Uncle Lucian is retired, so he doesn't have cases."

"A friend of Lucian's, the wife of a man who committed suicide—a sheriff's investigator."

"That's Campbell County."

I glanced around some more. "My powers of deduction have ascertained that, yes, you are correct in that I am in Campbell County."

"Why isn't Sandy Sandburg taking care of this?"

"It's complex—"

"It always is." She sighed. "Anyway, it'll be convenient since you're flying to Philadelphia out of Gillette."

"I am?"

"You are; four days, which means Thursday at noon—got it?"

"Noon patrol. Roger that." I listened to the quiet and got a little worried. "What's up, punk?"

"It's nothing." I waited, and her voice became quieter and carried a different tone; one of those tones that when someone you love adopts, you feel like you're falling down a mine shaft. "Um, they say the baby's in a difficult position and that it might cause complications in the delivery."

I felt feather tips scouring the insides of my lungs. "What kind of complications?"

"I don't know, but I've got a conference with them later today. I'll call you after." She paused. "Did Mom have any problems along these lines when she had me?"

As always, I dropped back and punted with humor, even though the panes of my heart were cracking like ice in a warm glass. "No, she dropped you in the field and kept hoeing sugar beets."

"I'm serious."

"I know, honey . . . I don't remember anything like that, but that was back in the dark ages when they made the father sit on a bench in the hallway."

She laughed, and I could hear her wiping away the tears. "Well, you've got a front-row seat on this one, pal. They said I could have one more after Michael and his mother, and you're it."

I swallowed. "Okay."

"Noon, Thursday. Which means you have to be at the airport an hour early, okay?"

"Okay." I remembered the first time I held her; how amazed I was that anything that small could contain the amount of love I was pouring into her.

"I love you."

"I love you too, punk." The line went dead, and I hung my mic back on the dash and stared at the lifeless windows of the abandoned house.

Delicate little families.

I could just take Dog back over to Durant and drop him off with Ruby and run up to the larger airport in Billings and catch a flight to Philadelphia today, but the weight of my responsibilities held me grounded. I had responsibilities to Lucian, to Phyllis Holman, and in a way to Sandy Sandburg and Richard Harvey.

In a way, I also had a responsibility to Lorea Urrecha, but the real weight lay with Gerald Holman, Jone Urrecha, Roberta Payne, and Linda Schaffer.

Dead weight.

I sighed, placed the ham on the dash, and pulled out the aluminum clipboard from the side-door pocket along with the nifty flashlight pen I'd stolen from a highway patrolman a couple of years ago who was also now deceased. I scribbled down the phone number and address of the local realty firm that had the listing along with the address of the lonely house on East Boxelder Road.

I was about to pull out as a Gillette city cruiser slowed and parked beside me, the driver rolling down his passenger-side window and leaning across the seat to look up at me. I rolled my own down, and I judged his age to be late twenties. "Howdy."

"Sheriff Longmire?"

I smiled back, thinking he looked vaguely familiar. "Depends."

"On what?"

"You got warrants?"

He laughed. "Nope."

"You date my daughter?"

"I did." He blushed up to his blond crew cut. "The first time I came to pick her up you tossed me a shotgun shell."

"I did?"

"Yeah, you said they went a lot faster after eleven o'clock."

I nodded. "I used to think I was a tough guy."

He pulled off a black leather glove and stuck out a hand. "Corbin Dougherty."

"Your parents the ones that had the place near Spotted Horse?"

"Still do." He glanced around but mostly at the house. "Why are you in Gillette?"

"Gerald Holman."

He nodded. "I figured as much." I looked at him questioningly, and he continued. "As soon as a cop gets killed in this state, all the old-timers say we need to bring in Walt Longmire."

I ignored the flattery and threw a thumb toward the house. "Linda Schaffer was one of Holman's cases?"

He sighed. "And mine."

"Yours?"

"One of my first, and boy did I screw it up."

"Tell me how."

He got out of his car and shook his head. "Stupid rookie shit . . . I kept telling the husband and the little boy not to worry, that she'd be back any time." He looked at the abandoned house, and I could see a shudder run through him. "Turns out they had a perfect reason to worry."

"What happened?"

"She went to work one evening and just didn't come home." He glanced around the lonely strip of a road, not really country, not really suburbs, but the transition land between. "I would stop by periodically just to see if they'd heard anything, not only from us but from anybody."

"Anything?"

"Nothing." He shook his head and leaned away from my truck, still holding on to it in a modified push-up to drain some of the anxiety. "I kept coming by to check in, but one day they were gone. I guess it got to be too much for them, waiting for her to come home. I couldn't stand it and ran a check—they moved back to Spokane, where they were from originally."

I picked up the file from the center console, glancing through it but not finding the information I wanted. "Where did she work?"

"Kmart."

I glanced at the coffee urn on the passenger-side floor and then looked up at him. "You're kidding."

"Nope, why?"

"There's another woman who worked at the Flying J Truck Plaza, which is right across the parking lot, who has been missing for about three months, name of Roberta Payne." I shuffled through the folders. "And then another woman missing about five weeks now by the name of Jone Urrecha out near Arrosa, which is east of town?"

"Yeah, about eighteen miles—just go straight up Boxelder, left on Fox Place Avenue, and then a right on 51. You'll run right into the middle of the town or what there is of it, 'bout five hundred people."

I rested the files back on the console. "Thanks."

"You think there's a connection?"

I shrugged. "I'm sure they already thought of that what with the two missing women separated by only a parking lot, but the other woman ten minutes out of town—"

"Seems odd."

"Yep. You never heard about these other women in squad meetings, nothing?"

"No." I looked at him as he dropped his Oakley sunglasses and glanced in the direction of Arrosa. "Any of this have to do with that strip club?"

I nodded. "The Urrecha woman worked there."

He whistled under his breath. "Be careful out at that place."

"Meaning?"

He threw a shoulder in a half shrug. "We get warrants, do raids, they pay the fines, and nothing seems to happen."

"Somebody's connected?"

"All I'm saying is that nobody ever seems to go to jail, you know what I mean?"

He said nothing for a moment and then pulled a business card and a pen from his pocket, scribbled a number on the back, and handed it to me. "You need any help—day or night—you let me know?"

I glanced at the printed number on the front and then the written one on the back with a 509 area code. "What's this one?"

"Mike Schaffer's in Spokane, just in case you wanted to talk to him."

I held the card and noticed the pressure he'd used in writing it, almost as if he'd been engraving the paper. "You have it memorized?" He said nothing, and I watched as he climbed back in his unit, pulled out, did a U-turn, and headed back toward town without another word.

I made my own requisite turns, passing the Gillette Country Club, which I hadn't known existed, and then backtracked on 51 under the highway to make a quick stop at the Wrangler so that I could drop off the coffeemaker with the disgruntled owner.

As I headed east, the houses began thinning, but there were a few businesses along the way, including the Gillette Lightning Speedway, High Mountain Shooters—with a neon sign advertising GUNS & AMMO and an indoor shooting range—and then a Wyoming Department of Transportation Office, all of which were overshadowed by a rail yard and the monstrous tipple of the Black Diamond Mine that stretched across the wide valley and up into the sky far enough to be seen from Gillette proper.

I crossed some tracks and pulled up to the only stop sign in town, which was at the Arrosa Elementary School, HOME OF THE MUSTANGS, and the post office, and pulled through the intersection into the parking lot of a small bar with a large sign that read SIXTEEN TONS, BEST BAR IN ARROSA.

Glancing around for any other bar in Arrosa, I gave up, turned off the ignition, and pivoted in my seat to look at my faithful companion. "What do you think—post office or the bar?"

He stared at the dash and the red foil package.

"Ham is not an answer."

He continued to stare at the dash.

"I bet they'll let you in the post office." I opened the door, and he jumped out just as the railroad barrier arms dropped across the road that I'd just passed, the lights flashing and the bells ringing. "Hah, beat you."

I stood there watching the orange and black Burlington Northern Santa Fe thunder by, shaking the little hamlet of Arrosa like a righteous fist.

Beyond the freight, farther down the road, there was an illuminated sign at the top of a pole of a blond woman with impossibly blue eyes, her fingernail provocatively placed between her smiling teeth, and the words DIRTY SHIRLEY'S EXOTIC DANCING under her high heels. Down below was a lettered sign that could be changed daily which read TITTY TWISTER TUESDAY and below that, HUMP DAY AMATEUR STRIP-OFF.

I called Dog and walked across the parking lot to the modest post office, pushed open the door, and allowed the beast to go first.

"This is a federal government facility, and dogs aren't allowed." The voice came from an area beyond the P.O. boxes to my left behind one of those roll-up steel gates, where a handsome, lean man stood on a stool; he was taking down garland that must've decorated the federal government facility for the holidays just past.

"He could be a service dog."

He looked at Dog and then at me doubtfully. "And what kind of service does he provide?"

I walked to the counter, and Dog followed as I leaned a hip against the edge and pulled out my badge wallet and watched it flip out of my hand again and fall onto the floor. Dog nudged it with his nose and then looked at me.

Stooping down, I scooped the thing up and stood, badging the inspector general with the star of the Absaroka County sheriff. "Obviously, he's not a retriever."

He studied my star through wire-rimmed glasses, and I noticed he had a prodigious ponytail hanging down the middle of his back. "You're in the wrong county."

"I'm looking for a girl."

He stuffed the Christmas decorations in a box on the counter. "Aren't we all?"

"Her name is Jone Urrecha."

He sighed, walked away into the bowels of the office, and returned with one of those white plastic bins; scooting the decorations box aside, he replaced it with the basket. "I've called the number that detective gave me about a half-dozen times but nobody ever answered, so I was about to send them back."

I looked into the bin. "This is her mail?"

"The last couple weeks of it, yeah."

"Do you mind if I ask what number it was Detective Holman gave you to call, mister?"

He shook my hand. "Dave Rowan."

He disappeared again but in a moment was back with one of Holman's business cards that had a number scrawled across it that looked remarkably like the one the Gillette patrolman had given me. "You didn't call the office number on the front after you couldn't get an answer?"

The postman shook his head. "Nope, he was very specific that I only call that number written there. I left messages, but he never came in and never called me."

I leafed through the pile. "Hmm."

"Pretty shitty police work if you ask me."

"Yep, well . . . He's kind of gotten slowed down lately." I pulled the tub toward me. "You mind if I take this?"

"Nope, just bring back the bin."

"Okay." I read the address on the top envelope—it was from a student loan financier and was marked URGENT. "This her address?"

"4661-A, Highway 51."

I looked back at him. "You know the address of everybody in Arrosa?"

"For thirty-two years now." For the first time, he smiled. "They're my people."

"What was she like?"

He thought about it for a moment. "Carefree." He noticed the look, or lack thereof, on my face. "I know; most of them aren't like that—"

"The dancers?"

He pulled up the stool and sat. "Most of them are having substance difficulties, psychological problems, you name it . . . But she was different." He pulled at his ponytail. "You could tell she was smart, that she was going places, and this was just a stopover at the edge of the world where she could make some money and then move on—you know what I mean?"

"I do."

He adjusted his glasses and looked a little wistful. "Maybe that's what she did, you know? Just moved on."

"Maybe." I didn't sound convinced, even to myself. "Why here?"

He laughed. "Roses."

"Excuse me?"

"The town got its name from the Basque word for rose.

There are wild rose bushes all over the hills out here." He glanced out the window at the tail end of the train and the blowing snow that chased after it, almost as if the flakes were afraid to be left behind. "Not that you'd know it from recent temperatures." His eyes came back to mine. "She said she looked up exotic dancing clubs and saw this one and decided it was a sign."

"Any other name . . ."

The grin spread on his face. "Would smell as sweet."

"Anything else you can tell me?"

He shrugged. "Not really; I try not to pry into people's business—a lot of them are here for that same reason, trying to disappear." He glanced around. "Not that it's going to last much longer anyway."

"What's up?"

"This office is scheduled to be closed next year, so I'll be out of a job."

"Can't you just transfer to another office?"

He shook his head. "Too much of a free spirit; I don't think I can take orders anymore."

I smiled. "Me either."

I picked up the basket and started toward the door, booting it open and ushering Dog out. "I'll get the bin back to you before you close up for good."

I dumped Dog and the young woman's mail in the Bullet and trudged along in the hardened snow that was crusted on the side of the road toward the sign for the strip club.

I pulled my hat down a little harder and flipped the collar of my sheepskin coat up around my face in hopes of cutting off some of the wind.

As I got closer to the main building, I could see that it was one of those steel prefab ones with two windows and a small mudroom that gave a break to patrons before they entered the main structure.

There was a string of trailers behind it, an odd assortment mostly the size that hunters took to the mountains. Someone had sprayed letters on the doors, the first one marked *B*. I wondered where *A* was.

I cut off from the parking lot and waded my way toward the trailers and was about to reach the first one when a voice called out from the back of the brown steel building.

"You lookin' for something?"

There was an enormous individual in the doorway, almost as big as me, heavily muscled—the kind of muscles you get in a weight room, or a cell block. A black T-shirt spread across his chest as he held the door open with one hand and studied me.

"I'm looking for 4661-A?"

He did the white-guy hair flip, and his long, blond locks flew away from his face. "Gone."

I looked around as if he might've misplaced it. "Really?"

"Yeah."

I glanced back at the nearest trailer with the *B* on the door. "What happened to *A*?"

"Burned." Realizing I wasn't particularly intimidated, he stepped out, still holding on to the door. "You know the whole alphabet?"

"My numbers, too."

He nodded. "Good, that'll make it easy for you to find your way out of here."

I ignored him and continued toward the *B* trailer.

"Hey! Hey, I'm talking to you."

"Yep, and I'm ignoring you." I kept walking. "And unless I'm mistaken, that door in your hand is like the one at the back of my office, which is not a pass-through, which means if you let it close you're going to have to deal with me in that T-shirt and then walk all the way around the building to get back inside."

As I advanced on trailer *B*, I heard his voice just as the door closed. "Fuckin' hell."

I raised a hand to knock, but a frighteningly skinny young woman smoking a cigarette yanked the door of the rickety trailer open before my knuckles grazed it, leaving a shattered, etched glass storm door between us.

"What the hell do you want?"

"Hi, I'm looking for Jone Urrecha?" I threw a thumb toward the large building. "She was a dancer here?"

She pulled a polyester blanket from just inside, draped it over her shoulders, and inhaled. "Gone. You her dad or something?"

"Or something." I smiled. "Do you have any idea where she might've gone, or—"

"Look, Mac, she's gone, or something. Okay?"

I could hear footsteps crunching behind me and figured I'd better finish up before he got to me, so I gave her a wave. "Thanks for your help."

The door closed in my face, the second in two days, and I turned just in time to see a fist roundhousing its way into the side of my head. I leaned back in the nick and watched as the big guy, who had put on a blue and gold letterman's jacket, followed through and swung past, his momentum and a quick push from me sending him sprawling into the snow.

He recovered and moved faster than I thought he would and swung an elbow at me as he stood, but I palmed it over my head and gave him my best shot in the side, figuring that if that didn't knock the air out of him, I was dead.

He collapsed sideways and fell awkwardly, and it was about then that I felt something very hard hit me in the back of my head. I pushed my hat back up straight and turned to look at the skinny woman with the cigarette between her lips who had been in the doorway but now was holding a cast waffle iron. "Ouch."

She studied me. "You're the first one to still be standing after that."

I rubbed the knot at the back of my noggin. "I've got a hard head."

She held the waffle iron at the ready. "Leave Thor alone."

"Thor? Really?" I glanced at the big guy, who, having rolled over, was sitting up holding his ribs but showing no sign of wanting to stand, and then looked back at the woman. "He started it."

"Yeah, well I'm finishing it."

I held a hand out to the man on the ground. "Help you up?"

He brushed the blond hair away again and frowned. "Can't— my knee went out."

"I never understood why they called us offensive tackles; I mean, we weren't allowed to tackle anybody."

Sitting on a stool in Dirty Shirley's bar, I tried to explain the nuanced aspects of our shared football position. "It's from before, when eleven-man squads used to play offense and defense."

He massaged his kneecap and manipulated it in hopes of getting the thing to go back into alignment. "Before my time."

I sipped the can of iced tea the skinny woman from the

trailer had given me as she polished glasses behind the bar and carefully watched me. "Mine, too."

"And where'd you play?"

"USC."

"Leather helmets?"

I sighed. "Back in the sixties."

"Wow. What was your record?"

"Undefeated, my freshman year." I took my hat off and rested it on the bar brim up to make sure whatever luck was there stayed there. "Beat Wisconsin 42–37. Then we didn't win another big one till the year after I graduated."

"Oh."

Curtis "Thor" Hansen was from North Dakota and looked like he'd fallen off the road-show truck for *Li'l Abner*, aside from the Viking haircut and the acne on his neck. I'd thrown his arm over my shoulder and limped him around the building and back inside where he'd offered to buy me a beer. "What about you?"

"The Fighting Irish, Notre Dame—even had a tryout with the Seahawks." He gestured toward his knee. "Then this thing blew out on me."

"I'm sorry."

He waved a hand in dismissal. "I scored a thirty on the Wonderlic and they were looking at me for the third round—"

The skinny woman asked. "What the hell is the Wonder-whatever-it-is?"

The kid smiled broadly. "It's a short-form cognitive abilities test that the NFL Combine uses as a predraft assessment—limited to twelve minutes, only about two to five percent even complete the test."

I gestured toward the offending joint. "Why didn't you get it fixed?"

He smiled a sad smile. "No money, and the repair to the damage was iffy at best, so nobody would take the chance."

I kept my eyes on him, my expression neutral, the same one I used to give my daughter when her explanations for youthful transgressions were found wanting. His eyes darted away but then returned to mine. "What?"

I continued to say nothing, just staring at the acne on his neck leading down his back and into the T-shirt.

The skinny woman called out to him. "Curtis, you sure you don't want something to drink?"

"No, Kay—I'm good." He watched her for a moment and then came clean. "Steroids." He blew air from his lips in an unattractive noise. "Some speed . . . Nothing everybody else wasn't doing, but I got caught."

"Are you clean now?"

"Oh, yeah."

It really wasn't my business.

I pulled the piece of paper from my pocket and unfolded it, handing it to him. "Know her?"

He took the poster I'd gotten from Lorea and nodded. "The Basque Rose, Jone, yeah . . . She worked here for a while." He looked up. "She was kind of hard to miss." He looked at the poster. "We used to run together . . ."

Kay's voice sounded from behind me. "Just run, huh?"

He looked past me at the woman, who was finished playing at washing glasses and was now resting an elbow on the bar and pouring herself a stiff vodka without the rocks. His eyes went back to the poster. "Yeah, just running." The knee pained him again, and he winced as he shook his head. "The sister came by here a couple of times." He glanced up at me. "That where you got this?"

"Yep."

"I figured you were some kind of cop."

"Sheriff, actually."

He looked surprised. "Really?"

I nodded. "I'd show you, but it's in a new leather holder and I'd just drop it on the floor." I glanced down at the thick and highly suspect shag carpeting. "And to be honest, I don't know where this floor has been."

He glanced around. "I do, and I wouldn't get too close to it."

"What happened to her?"

"She just disappeared; got off work late, around two or three, and when I went to go knock on her door to get her to go for a run the next morning she didn't answer." He gestured toward the back. "Her car was gone, so I figured she was just out doing errands—but she never came back. A day or two later I busted open the door and all her stuff was gone."

I leaned on the bar and draped an arm on the surface. "Did a detective by the name of Gerald Holman ever come by here asking questions?"

"Couple of times, yeah."

I looked at him questioningly. "Only a couple?"

"Yeah, why?"

"Just curious. What about another detective by the name of Richard Harvey—tall, thin guy with a handlebar mustache?"

"Nope."

"You're sure?"

He shook his head. "Well, didn't talk to me, but that doesn't mean he wasn't here."

"What happened to the trailer?"

"What trailer?"

"4661-A, Jone Urrecha's trailer."

Kay interrupted. "Tommy sold it."

"I thought it burned." I turned to look at her. "Who's Tommy?"

She gestured to the building as a whole. "The owner."

"And where is he?"

She smiled. "Usually comes in around five."

Curtis gestured with a hand to get my attention. "It's not what you're thinking—"

"And what am I thinking?"

"That there's something going on. Tommy doesn't charge the girls anything but buys and sells the trailers all the time as a sideline."

The voice spoke from behind me again. "Tommy has a lot of sidelines."

I spun my hat. "And burns a few of them, too."

"Huh?"

"4661-A."

Curtis smiled. "Space heater; nobody got hurt."

"Glad to hear it." I glanced back at Kay, but she ignored me and sipped her drink. I stood and walked over to the kid. "Pick up your leg and put your ankle on your knee."

"What?" He looked at me for a moment and then did as I said.

"Now push down on your knee and twist your foot and stretch it out with your other hand."

I could see the immediate relief in his face as his knee popped back in place. "Oh, wow!"

I slugged down the rest of my iced tea like Philip Marlowe, rested the empty can on the bar, and picked up my hat. "You say Tommy shows up around five?"

The kid stood, looking more like his Thor Asgard self. "You want me to say you stopped by?"

"No, I'll introduce myself." We shook hands, and I went around a sticky brass railing and down the steps. "Little known fact: offensive tackles score higher on the Wonderlic than any other position."

"No shit; better than quarterbacks?"

"Better than quarterbacks—average of twenty-six."

He thought about it. "So, I'm above the average for the highest-rated position?"

"Looks like."

He waited a moment before asking. "You ever take the test?"

I slipped my hat on and started out the door. "Not in the NFL."

I sat in my truck outside the Sixteen Tons, the best and only bar in Arrosa. There wasn't anything to munch on since Dog had eaten the remainder of the ham, the red and gold foil remnants lying on the passenger-side floor mat.

He looked at me, completely unrepentant.

"You could've saved me a little."

I spent my time on stakeout leafing through the files, looking for something, anything, that would connect the three women. I rested them against my chest, also wondering why it was that Gerald Holman, if he was so upset by the disappearance of Jone Urrecha, had visited her residence and place of employ only twice. It was easier to understand why Richard Harvey hadn't made the trip to Arrosa, in that he was trapped in a basement with the cry and hue of Inspector Holman's career coming to rest upon him—like he said, shit rolls downhill.

After a few moments, I saw the inspector general come out of the post office, lock the door, and start toward my truck. I rolled the window down as he stood by the Bullet.

Dave Rowan glanced at the SIXTEEN TONS sign. "The bartender says to tell you that you're bad for business."

I rested the files on the center console. "I'm hoping not to be here for much longer."

"So is he."

"You know this Tommy who owns the strip club?"

"Some; I'm the one who sorts the mail and puts it in the box for Thor."

"The bouncer?"

"Yeah."

"Seems like a nice kid."

He stared at me for a moment. "You've obviously never seen him knock somebody down and kick their head for five minutes."

I glanced at Dirty Shirley's and the lurid blonde on the sign, thinking the kid might not be completely off steroids. "Bad news, is he?"

"Yeah. Sometimes in the afternoon, if his victims can't find anyone else to call them a cab or an ambulance, they crawl into the post office."

I sighed. "Does the owner of the strip club live around here?"

"No, or they wouldn't have their mail delivered to a P.O. box."

"Good point."

He glanced over his shoulder at the intersection, where a familiar Cadillac Escalade EXT rolled through the stop sign. "Speak of the devil; you can ask for yourself." He gestured with a hand and sounded like a sick Ed McMahon. "Heeeeeere's Tommy!"

I hit the ignition, flipped on the light bar, and pulled out as Rowan stepped away. "Thanks."

I was on the tail of the Cadillac and even blipped my siren before he could get to the parking lot of the strip club, but I guess he figured he was close enough that I wouldn't mind if he pulled in there.

He sat, waiting patiently, as I got out of my truck and straightened my hat the way the HPs always did, bringing my aluminum clipboard along just for appearances' sake.

The motor on the Caddy was still idling, and he had his license and registration hanging out the open window as I approached. I thought it was a little odd that he had on fingernail polish. "Hey, I . . ."

Snatching off the sunglasses, worn despite the cloudy day, the driver barked, "Do you know who the fuck I am?" As it turned out, Tommy was a Tommi with an *i* and a middle-aged woman with a massive pouf of reddish hair and a formidable chest.

I studied her for a moment, as if I were trying to remember where, exactly, we had met and then gestured toward her sign. "Dirty Shirley."

She lit a cigarillo and shook her head, unimpressed with my performance; her voice was like a foghorn through 60-grit sandpaper. "Very funny."

I gestured toward the only crossroad in Arrosa. "You didn't come to a complete stop at that sign back there."

She took a drag and blew the smoke toward my face, but the ever-present wind snatched it and forwarded it to the Black Hills. "You're kidding, right?"

"Nope, and with it being in the proximity of the elementary school over there, it could be a hefty penalty—"

Tommi interrupted me. "Do I know you?"

She probably wasn't as old as she seemed, but the alcohol, tobacco, and hard living had rolled up her odometer. "Probably not, and I don't know you—I thought we'd established that fact."

She studied my face, and then her eyes dropped to my chest in search of a badge. "You're really a cop?"

I began copying the information from her ID, just in case the conversation didn't improve. "I am."

She sucked on the small cigar again, as if it were life affirming. "Around here?"

"Pretty much."

"Not for long, bucko."

It was about then that I decided to give her the ticket. I'd just pulled her over so that I could start a conversation, but the chances of that seemed slim, so I held up a finger before she could continue. "I'll be back in just a moment."

"Are you fucking kidding me?"

I stopped and looked back at her. "Nope."

"Well then, fuck you, and the horse you rode in on." The whir of the electric window going up was the only other sound.

I shook my head and climbed back in the Bullet, unhitching the mic from the dash and changing the frequency to that of Campbell County. "Dispatch, this is Walt Longmire, I need a 10-14 on a black Cadillac Escalade, plate number 17—"

Static. "Who is this again?"

I keyed the mic. "Walt Longmire, I'm the sheriff of Absaroka County."

Static. "Where?"

"Absaroka County, just to the west of you."

Static. "And how can I help you, Sheriff?"

I read her the plate number along with the woman's name.

"Tommi, that's Tommi with an *i* Sandburg of Gillette; I've got her stopped for a traffic infraction, and I'm writing her up."

There was a longer pause this time.

Static. "I'm transferring you to the sheriff's office."

I keyed the mic again. "I thought this was the sheriff's office."

Static. "I mean *the* sheriff's office, the office of the sheriff, himself."

With a sinking feeling, I went ahead and asked. "Why is that?"

Static. "Because she's his sister."

4

"She's quite the charmer."

Static. "Isn't she though? She was worse when she had all her teeth."

I keyed the mic while looking at the smiling face on her ID. "She has teeth on her license."

Static. "Fake, some boyfriend or another knocked out the others."

"I'm giving her a ticket on general principles."

Static. "Okay."

"No argument?"

Static. "Well, she won't pay it, and I'm the one that's going to get the screaming hissy fit . . ." The airwaves over northern Wyoming went silent.

"You mind telling me why you didn't say that your sister owned the strip club on the edge of town?"

Static. "Didn't seem pertinent to the investigation; I thought you were working on Gerald Holman's suicide, not the case of the supposedly missing dancer—"

"Jone Urrecha."

There was a pause. Static. "You think there might be a connection?"

"It was the last case he was working on."

Static. "You want me to lean on my sister?"

"It might be helpful."

Static. "Take your time writing her up, and I'll call her on her cell phone and make up some bullshit about you being some kind of special investigator for the state."

"Roger that."

I took awhile writing the ticket by noting in great detail the conversation between us, practicing my cursive handwriting with special attention to the curlicues, dots, and assorted design factors, which were being eroded by the digital age. After a few minutes, Tommi Sandburg exited her vehicle, slammed the door, and crossed in front of mine, still puffing a cigarillo as she yanked open my passenger-side door.

"Not in here."

She stared at me, plucked the fresh one from her mouth, and made a show of dropping it from shoulder height onto the gravel; then she stamped it out with a full twist, the cigar being what I was pretty sure she wanted to be my head. Tommi with an i then climbed in my truck and closed the door behind her. "Well, you're a big fucking deal, aren't you?"

I paused writing her ticket. "It's on all my business cards."

"I find it hard to believe that you have business cards."

"I made that part up."

She glanced back at Dog, having edged away from the diminutive woman to go behind me; say what you will about canine intelligence, he knew when he was out of his weight class, teeth or no teeth. "This your girlfriend?"

I ignored her and got to the pointed end of the stick as I continued writing. "Jone Urrecha."

"Gone."

"Where?"

Absently, she pulled another cigarillo from the pocket of what looked to be a very expensive leather jacket, and tapped the end on my dash. "God, I wish I knew; that sister of hers is driving me up a wall." She pulled a Zippo from the same pocket and started to light up.

I stopped writing and looked at her.

With a long sigh, she repocketed the combustibles, turned in the seat to look at me, and nodded her head toward the winking sign down the road. "You know how many girls I go through on a yearly basis?"

I aimed the point of the flashlight pen above the ticket docket. "How many girls do you go through on a yearly basis?"

She stared at me with hazel death rays. "A shit ton."

"Define 'shit ton.'"

"Shit as in lousy, ton as in a bunch."

For absolutely no reason, I was beginning to like her.

She slumped in her seat and studied the 870 Wingmaster locked to the transmission hump of my truck and then turned her attention to the barren hills a couple of hundred yards up the road. "I mean, it ain't exactly the Folies Bergère around here—you know what I mean?"

I didn't say anything.

"We're on the circuit between Rapid City and Billings; I mean how are you gonna keep a naked girl down on the farm once she's seen those two cities of light?" She scratched her head. "The usual tenure is about six weeks or so, but she lasted longer than most—all of the summer and through the fall." She thought about it. "Smart kid, smart enough to not be doing this stuff, but I get 'em now and then—the ones that are having money problems, substance problems, personal problems . . ."

I watched as she extended a hand toward Dog as a peace offering. "Which one was she?"

Dog sniffed her hand and then turned and looked out the window. "Not very friendly, is she?"

"He."

She examined Dog a little closer. "Jone never said, and when they don't say and you can't see any evidence of the other two, it's usually personal problems."

"Who did she spend her time with?"

"Nobody. She was a loner."

I started writing again.

She watched me and then spoke up. "What the hell are you doing?"

"Every time you lie to me, I get the urge to finish writing this ticket."

"Who says I'm lying?"

"Just about everybody I've already talked to today."

She fumed for a while and then threaded her fingers into her hair, and I noticed her whole scalp moved, confirming my thought that it was a wig. "She used to pal around with Thor."

"The bouncer?"

"I think they used to run up and down the road and shit."

I stopped writing. "Any business on the side?"

She huffed again and then answered. "If there was, it wasn't through me—that shit leads to trouble, so I discourage it." She shrugged. "Which doesn't mean that it doesn't happen, but if it does it's not on my time or my books. Look, I'm no saint, but I try to keep the girls safe; it's in my interest, you know?" She tugged at the front of the hair, straightening it not unlike the way I straightened my hat. "Sometimes they've just had enough and they move on."

This was squaring with everything everybody was saying. "No contact then—no idea where she might've gone?"

"Nope. I still owe her a hundred and sixty-three dollars, so if you hear from her, let me know, will you?"

I thought about it as I studied the sign down the road and could see another coal train heading our way. "Don't you find it funny that a person with financial troubles would light out overnight without waiting for the money owed to them?"

"Honey, in case you haven't noticed, I'm in a funny business."

"I'm getting that. What about Gerald Holman?"

"Who?"

I started writing again.

She stretched a leg out and bumped my knee with a gold boot. "C'mon, I honestly don't know who the hell you're talking about."

"The sheriff's investigator who came around asking about Jone, the one who killed himself."

"Oh, him." She nodded. "Thor talked to him once, I guess. I wasn't there." She studied me. "Are you thinking . . . ?"

I ripped the blue warning ticket from the docket and handed it to her as the train sounded its air horns while passing through the crossing. "In case you haven't noticed, I'm in a funny business, too."

The bartender at the Sixteen Tons had never seen anybody eat one of the pickled eggs from the bar in the three years he'd owned the place, and neither the postmaster nor the BNSF highline driver said they'd ever seen anybody eat one in the thirty years before that.

"Slow movers, huh?"

The thickset railroad employee with the shaved head and tattoos nodded. "You could say that."

I glanced at the bartender. "What else have you got?"

"Frozen pizza."

I studied the off-color ivory orbs floating in the reddish liquid. "I'll go with the pizza."

He glanced over his shoulder at the illuminated Olympia clock on the wall. "Happy Hour, you wanna beer?"

"Rainier."

The cheery man glanced down at Dog—the monster was lying next to my feet. "Something for your dog?"

"No thank you, he just had a ham."

He extended a hand. "Neil Pilano."

"Walt Longmire. Nice to meet you, Neil." We shook. "So, you live around here?"

"I live over on South Douglas Highway." He glanced down at Dog. "What's his name?"

"Dog."

"Easy to remember."

The high-line driver stretched a hand out as he finished his beer. "Greg Fry."

"Good to meet you, Fry; you work the spur into Arrosa?"

He adjusted his American flag do-rag. "For a while now. You want a tour of the Black Diamond Mine sometime, just mention my name."

I watched as he walked out the door; the bartender searched through the coolers for my beverage of choice, and the postmaster moved down to the stool next to me. "You gave Tommi Sandburg a ticket?"

"A warning; her brother seemed to think she'd bite me if I gave her a real ticket."

"That or fall down out there on the road and start biting herself—she's had a rough life." He sipped his beer and nodded. "About a half-dozen marriages and counting."

The bartender sat a bottle of Rainier in front of me and lowered a plastic bowl of water down to Dog, who immediately stood and began lapping it up.

"The ham must've been salty." I turned back to the postmaster and took a sip of my beer. "Anyone next in the lineup?"

"Me, I hope."

I swallowed carefully, so as not to spray the beer all over the bar. "You're a very lucky man."

"I know. Crazy, huh?"

"Have you ever been married before?"

"A short period of time back, but I don't think either one of us took it very seriously—like my great grandfather used to say, nobody misses a slice off an already-cut cake."

I sat my beer back on a coaster that advertised Dirty Shirley's down the road and spread my fingers across the smooth wooden surface of the bar. "I think Tommi might be the kind that counts her slices."

He nodded as he sipped his Coors. "You could be right." He smiled to himself and, looking for a ring, studied my hand. "You married?"

"Widowed."

"Kids?"

"One, a daughter in Philadelphia getting ready to have one of her own—due at the end of the week. That's where I'm supposed to be, but instead I'm here."

He lifted his bottle. "That's the way most folks feel about Arrosa."

I lifted my own, and we toasted.

"Any word on Jone?"

"Nothing yet."

He eyed me through his funky glasses. "Any, you know, leads? From her mail maybe?"

"Leads?"

He lowered his beer and looked thoughtful. "Isn't that what you guys call 'em, leads?"

"Sometimes." I sat my Rainier back down. "No, just the usual junk forwarded from her previous address in Boise and some new stuff. But you must've noticed that."

The postman shook his head, the ponytail wagging back and forth. "Nope, I just sort 'em—I don't read 'em."

I thought about it. "No personal correspondence, nothing."

"Kids these days, they text, tweet, or use e-mail." He pointed to the USPS patch on his shoulder. "That's why we're going out of business."

"You'd think there would be something, though. Weeks of mail and not a single letter . . . Not even a postcard."

A youngish woman came through the door and looked around, pausing for a moment and then walking straight to me. Careful to avoid Dog, she stood a few steps away in her business suit, long wool coat, and sensible shoes. "Are you Walt Longmire?"

I glanced around the almost empty bar for comic effect, a move which was lost on everybody except Dog. "I am."

"Can I speak with you?"

"Sure."

She glanced around, perhaps for her own comic effect, and jiggled her car keys. "Somewhere else?"

I pointed toward the back. "I just ordered a pizza."

"This won't take long."

I stood and raised my voice so the bartender could hear me. "Mr. Pilano, have you already put that pizza in?"

A voice came back. "Just now."

"Can you take it out and put it back in when I return?"

His head appeared in the swinging doorway. "No problem."

Dog and I followed the woman out the door and were surprised when she kept walking toward the Arrosa Elementary School across the street—at least I was surprised. The parking lot was vast enough to allow the buses to make a full circle but right now held only a solitary blue Volvo. Beyond was a chainlink fence and a playground with equipment painted red and white, the school colors. We followed her through a gate in the fence, across the playground, and entered a door in the large, older stone portion of the building, which was, it turned out, the gymnasium.

She stood alongside the gleaming wooden surface of the basketball court, and turned to look at me, a large canvas satchel hanging from her shoulder. "I'm Connie Holman."

"The daughter."

She nodded. "I know who you are."

I studied her, clocking her age at late thirties. "Have we met?"

"No, but I've read about you in the newspapers, magazine articles, WyoFile . . . Sheriff Walt Longmire, they talk about you like you're some inevitable form of justice."

I smiled a tight smile and threw a thumb back toward the bar. "I stop for a beer and pizza every now and then."

She glanced through the metal grating of the multipane window and looked out onto the playground and past. "I'm sorry, but I'm a teacher here and on the school board, and it isn't good for me to be seen hanging around in bars."

I smiled. "That's okay. It's not so good for my reputation either, but I do it anyway."

She volleyed a smile back. "I'm not stalking you."

"I don't suppose that would be good for your reputation either."

"We had an in-service here, and I talked to my mother on the phone; she said something about having hired you."

"Uh huh."

"To look into my father's death?"

I walked to the window, and the clicking of Dog's claws on the gleaming wood as he followed me echoed as I leaned against the massive stones and looked up at the hand-forged girders. "This is one heck of a building for an elementary school gymnasium."

She glanced up, and I noticed she was thin and appeared to be stretched just a bit too far. "It was the old bus barn for the eastern part of the county."

The girders looked to be about twenty feet from the ground. "Not much headroom."

She shrugged. "Fortunately that's not a problem with elementary school basketball—not many granny-shot three-pointers." She swung the canvas satchel and hugged it to her chest, I guess to feel a little more secure, and then walked out onto the court. "I used to dance here when I was a kid." She did a half twirl and looked back at me. "I teach here now. It's actually the third evolution of the school; the first was an old one-room that got moved back up the valley."

I nodded and reached down to pet Dog's broad head. "Um, your mother didn't actually hire me."

"I figured that, seeing as how she doesn't have any money. I guess I should've said, played on your good nature and foisted this situation upon you?"

"Well, it isn't exactly that, either—she wasn't the one doing the playing or the foisting."

She shook her head and turned back toward the dying illumination of the day, albeit at four o'clock in the afternoon, which allowed me to enjoy the picture-perfect profile with the skin drawn tight across her face like some Degas painting. "Lucian Connally?"

"I don't mind . . ." I wasn't sure of what to say next, so I just let it trail off.

Her eyes stayed on the grime of the unwashed windows, and I have to admit that I wasn't prepared for her next question. "Do you think those two had a thing?"

I waited a moment more before responding. "I really couldn't say, and in all honesty it isn't any of my business."

"He was in the car when she broke her back."

I sighed and nodded, dropping my head to look at the shiny, lacquered surface of the court, polished to within an inch of its grain. "Well, that was before my time."

"Mine, too." She looked up at me. "And hopefully before my father's . . . Look, I'm really sorry my mother or Lucian dragged you into this, but there really isn't anything to investigate." She sighed. "My father was not a happy man, never was, and I think it was just a case of his unhappiness catching up with him."

"So you think it was a suicide?"

She studied me. "You don't?"

"Actually, I do."

"Well, at least we agree on something."

"If you don't mind me asking, why was he so unhappy?"

"Are you just being nice or do you really want to know?"

I tilted my head, as if in thought. "It might be both; I'm kind of playing the niceness and foisting the need to know."

She smiled but then cut it short as Dog misinterpreted and took a few steps toward her. "Is he friendly?"

"Overly." She reached a hand down, and I watched as she petted him, scratching behind his ears. I leaned in a little. "I'm thinking that's the reason your mother contacted Lucian, because she doesn't understand why your father did it."

"My father, Gerald Holman, never broke a law in his life; I mean it, never." She stood back up straight and folded her arms, dropping her head in thought. "Can you imagine what it's like, living with a man like that—let alone what he had to do to live with himself?"

"I understand he was a little inflexible."

She walked a few steps farther onto the court and stopped, her feet naturally falling into fourth position. "I wasn't allowed to speak to a boy on the phone until I was a senior in high school."

"I bet you got good grades."

She turned and looked at me, Dog beside her. "I'm just giving you formal notice that you don't have to do this—that it's not your problem anymore."

"Giving me my walking papers?"

She shook her head. "I'm relieving you of the responsibility of the sad ending of a very unhappy man's life."

"Are you planning on having this same conversation with Lucian Connally?"

She smiled. "I was kind of hoping you'd save me from that."

"I see."

"Not knowing him very well, I was hoping I could just talk to you."

"You've discussed this with your mother?"

The smile faltered. "Not at length; I thought I would speak with you first."

I folded my arms, listening to the creaking of my sheepskin jacket sounding like bark tightening. "I'll tell you what, you get her to tell either Lucian or me to drop it and we'll call it off."

She studied me and for the first time I noticed she had brown hair and chocolate eyes—not sweet chocolate, but the bitter kind that bakes. "Why can't you just take my word on this?"

"Because we agreed to do this investigation with her. I'm sorry, but that's just the way it works; she has to call it off."

Her eyes flared a bit, and the chocolate bubbled. "Some kind of code you sheriffs have?"

I smiled back. "Something like that."

"I'll speak with her tonight." She paused for a moment more and then walked past me to the door. "You might want to think about it . . . I've seen what those codes can lead to."

"You want a cup of coffee?"

I glanced over at the brand-new urn at the bar-back of the Aces & Eights. "No thanks, but I wouldn't mind a beer."

His fans at the Campbell County Sheriff's Office had dropped off the old sheriff, and I'd found him seated on a bar stool when I got back from Arrosa—I was going to have to find something to distract him as I investigated or every appliance on the high plains would be in peril.

"Hey, Haji." He raised his voice to the Indian bartender who had replaced the morning Hispanic girl in an attempt to be heard over the small crowd that had filtered into the tiny bar, mostly workers from the nearby oil refineries, their companies seeking lodging wherever they could, the tang of petroleum and dirt strangely comforting. There were four of these men seated by the door, who were laughing loudly at a story one of them was telling.

I leaned into him. "Lucian . . ."

He gave me the horse eye. "What?"

"You can't go around giving people names according to their nationality."

The small young man, dark-haired, with an enormous if crooked smile, approached from the back, and the old sheriff gave him the high sign for two more before leaning into me and whispering fiercely, "Damn it, his name really is Haji."

The bartender in question, who indeed had a name tag that said *Haji*, sat two more Rainiers on the bar along with a bowl of stale peanuts. "How are you?" He smiled an enigmatic grin and disappeared into the back as I took a sip of my beer in an attempt to wash down the nutty meal in my mouth.

"Where the hell did you go all day?"

I pointed toward the coffeemaker as the bartender reappeared and studied the oil workers with a worried grimace. "Kmart, for one . . ." I sipped my beer again. "Met with Richard Harvey, Gerald's replacement."

He nodded. "The pointy-head from New Mexico?"

"Yep."

"Never have figured out why they call that state by that name, it ain't new and it ain't Mexico—am I right, Haji?"

The bartender nodded and smiled again.

"What'd pointy-head have to say?"

"We just discussed the cases Holman was working on."

He pursed his lips and readjusted his prosthetic leg on the bar stool. "Like what?"

"A couple of missing persons; three women from this vicinity and all in the last year."

He grunted and gave the oil workers a dirty look as another outburst of braying erupted from their table. "Hey, you assholes wanna keep it down over there? We're tryin' to have a conversation."

They all looked at him, somewhat thunderstruck, and then waved him off and went back to yowling among themselves.

Lucian turned back around and grumbled. "Campbell County?"

"Gillette proper and within a ten-mile radius."

"Sandy know about all this?"

"I'm assuming, since it's his detective's reports I'm working from."

The door opened, and the oil workers hooted and howled even louder. I'd just about made up my mind to go over and badge them when I turned and saw that the biggest of the men was holding Lorea Urrecha's wrist.

Once again, the missing stripper's sister was holding a stack of posters and a staple gun, obviously intent on putting a fresh one up on the bar's bulletin board near the door.

The large man was trying to engage her in conversation even though she was attempting to pull away. He was kind of in shape but carrying a lot of beer fat and wore a jacket that read FOREMAN.

I slipped off the stool and turned, walking over to the table, catching only the tail end of the oil worker's statement: something about him, her, and a meaningful relationship of about three minutes. "Let her go."

He glanced up at me. "What?"

"I said let her go."

The nearest man turned in the booth, and I now had the attention of all four. The big guy pushed the bill of his greasy welding cap back and looked at me. "Hey pard, we're just havin' a little conversation. The lady and I know each other, so how 'bout you just run along?"

I glanced at the young woman, but she wouldn't make eye contact with me. "I don't think the lady appreciates the attention." I let my arms drop to my sides, my face growing cool and my hands still. "Let her go."

It probably would've ended there, maybe with a few parting barks, but it was at that moment that Lorea dropped the photocopies, raised the staple gun, and slapped a round in the guy's forehead.

I don't know how deep the thing went, but she'd put a lot of emphasis into the action and I had a sneaking suspicion it was going to take a pair of needle-nose pliers or a quick visit to the emergency room to get the thing out of the thin layer of skin that covered his thick skull.

The staple to the head had the expected response in that he let go of her wrist and grabbed his head with a roar, trying to get a fingernail underneath the staple to pry it from his face. He shouldered her as he lumbered around, and she fell backward into the wall where she bounced against a coatrack, taking it down with her.

I made a move to catch her, but the three other guys started climbing over the bench seat, possibly thinking that I was the one that had damaged the foreman, who was now trying to get his hands on me but was impaired by the blood flowing into his eyes.

He managed to slam an elbow down on my shoulder, and one of the others grabbed my right arm before I could get loose. Another grabbed the back of my coat and propelled all of us through the glass door onto the sidewalk, where we landed with a thump in the snow that had been piled in the handicapped spot.

I pushed off, but the three of them were still attached to me as the staple guy pulled my head back and swung, glancing a fist off the crown of my ducked head and busting a few knuckles in the process. I forced one of my assailants down and then got an arm loose just enough to push one of the others back into the one of the four who seemed undecided about the whole melee.

Getting my feet under me, I was half standing when the big guy brought a knee up, sending me flailing backward into the ice-capped snow. I started to get up, but he was on me pretty quick and was winding up with his left hand in a fist when, in the echoing chamber of the concrete alcove, there was the thunderous report of a gunshot.

The foreman froze, and as I forced my eyes to focus, I could see the four-inch barrel of a Smith & Wesson service revolver stuck in his left ear.

He slowly raised his hands as Lucian Connally spoke as though holding a pistol against someone's earlobe was an everyday occurrence. "You know, you look like one of those guys that lifts weights and I bet you are strong as a bull-ox." He leaned forward into the big man's line of vision, his grin in the half light looking like a death's head. "I been workin' out a lot lately myself—you know, gettin' in shape." He continued to smile. "But mostly I been exercisin' this finger enough so that I can pull the couple of pounds of pressure on this trigger that'll scatter your chickenshit brains all over this parking lot."

"Do I need to set up a sheriff's substation over here at the Wrangler Motel to keep you two out of trouble?" Sandy Sandburg looked at the two of us as though we were truants. "And remind me again about how the two of you are over here to make my life easier?"

"Lucian started it."

The old sheriff looked at me. "And how the hell'd I do that?"

"You called them assholes."

"Just introducin' myself, and I'm *not* the one who went over there and attempted to single-handedly take on Marathon Oil's second shift."

I adjusted my hat, held the bag of ice Haji had given me against the swelling on my head, and addressed Sandy. "How's Lorea?"

"We disarmed her and cut her loose." He looked over his shoulder at the big guy, now seated in the back of a Campbell County cruiser and being ministered to. "Damn, did you see the staple in that guy's head? I mean that was one of those big industrial jobs—"

"I think she wanted the thought to stick."

"One of my deputies is trying to pry it out with a Spyderco knife." He smiled. "The guy's got some priors, a battery and a few controlled-substance abuses; you want to press charges?"

"No."

"Well, he does."

"On me?"

"No. On her, but I think I can dissuade him if you want." He blew his breath out between his teeth. "I'm half a mind to let him have her and then send her butt back to Boise, she's been such a pain."

"She's just concerned about her sister."

He shook his head. "The stripper, the one that evidently packed up all her stuff into her car and drove off without telling anybody, the one that we haven't found any sign of foul play, the one that has a history of packing up her stuff and heading out for the road less traveled?"

"Just like Linda Schaffer and Roberta Payne."

He captured his lip with his teeth and then released it. "Who?"

I readjusted the ice pack on my head and stretched my jaw against the tightening there. "Linda Schaffer vanished from the Kmart parking lot seven months ago, and Roberta Payne disappeared from the Flying J truck stop three months ago." I studied him. "You didn't know about those women?"

"They were in Holman's reports?"

"Yes."

He looked over his shoulder at the cruiser again. "I need to see them."

"They're your reports." I waited a moment before continuing. "You really didn't know about them?"

His hand brushed the brim of his hat. "Vaguely, but I rely on my men to tell me the things I need to know."

"Why wouldn't Gerald Holman have told you about two missing persons cases?"

"I'm not saying he didn't, I just don't recall."

"What about Richard Harvey?"

The sheriff of Campbell County inclined his head. "We don't talk much."

I nodded but left it at that. "I'll run the reports by tomorrow. I want one last look at them."

"I'll make you some copies."

"There's an idea."

Things had quieted down, and I had even made the effort of going over and saying hey to the oil refinery workers, especially the one with the multiple holes in his head. They'd gotten the staple out, and an EMT had him bandaged up. We shook hands, and I wondered about the nature of things as I stooped to pick up the scattered posters on the floor of the bar/café.

I stared at another photocopied version of Jone Urrecha and wondered absently how many photographs her sister had of her. I crouched there by the booth and asked myself if my fixation on this particular young woman was irrational. The statistics said that all three women were most certainly dead, even though Jone was missing only five weeks. They say statistics by their nature don't lie, but in my opinion they sometimes do and damnably at that.

Scooping up the posters, I stood and was confronted with Haji, who was also holding a collection of the copied sheets. "Hey."

"These slid over near the bar, and I think you want them."

I shuffled the papers and placed them under my arm. "Where are you from, Haji?"

He smiled the crooked smile. "Mumbai, just to the south."

"You related to Rankaj Patel?"

"He is my father's brother."

"Mind if I ask how you ended up here?"

His face darkened as he stood the coatrack back upright, pushing it against the wall. "I worked the summertime in Yellowstone Park and then found job here with my uncle for the winter." He studied me. "All of my papers are in order—"

I raised a hand in supplication. "I'm sure they are; I was just curious."

He glanced around. "With the oil and gas industry, no one wishes to work at bar job. I am of hopes to buy motel self?"

"Buy a motel yourself?"

"Yes, in attempt of the American Dream." I started out the door, but he stopped me. "You are a sheriff?"

"Yep."

"And the old man with you, he is sheriff, too?"

"Yep."

He nodded. "Lots of sheriffs in Wyoming."

"I guess that's true, as of late." I reached a hand out, and we shook and I held on to his hand while percolating an idea. "Hey, you don't happen to play chess, do you, Haji?"

He stared at me for a moment. "Why you ask that?"

"Well, it's where the game originally came from . . ."

He smiled. "The Gupta Empire in the northwest in the sixth century; no one knows this . . ." He folded his arms in an attempt to look stately. "I am champion of the South-Western Administrative Province."

"Do you have a board around here?"

"No."

I nodded, figuring I was in for another trip to the Kmart. "I'll get you one."

"You wish to play?"

"No, not me . . . But if I get you a board, would you set it up and leave it there on the bar?" He looked at me strangely as I handed him my ice pack and exited the Aces & Eights.

It was really getting cold out, but I knocked on the door of room 6 and waited. There was some noise inside, and she shuffled toward the door before finally speaking through the cheap wood. "Who is it?"

"Walt Longmire, the sheriff who just got his ass kicked?" The door opened just a little, the chain still holding it secure, sort of. I held out the posters and slid them through the opening. "I thought you might want these."

She took them and then placed her face closer to the opening—I could see that she'd been crying. "They took my stapler."

"Yep, well . . . You have to have a concealed/carry permit for those things here in Wyoming."

She smiled. "I nailed him, didn't I?"

"Stapled him, to be exact. Don't feel so bad about it. I did something like that in Vietnam once." I waited a moment. "I've got to go back to Kmart tomorrow to pick up a chess set with which to distract my old boss, and I can pick you up another one. Smaller caliber, perhaps?"

She laughed again and tossed the posters behind her.

There was an awkward silence.

"Well, I just wanted to drop those off and make sure you were all right."

"Thanks." I started to turn but heard her unhook the chain, and she opened the door a bit more. She was wearing a pair of blue nylon shorts and a Boise State T-shirt with the snorting pony on the front. In deference to the cold, she hugged herself to cover the protruding aspects of her anatomy and placed one foot over the other. "I mean it, thanks. Look, I'm kind of vulnerable right now and I need a good word."

"Excuse me?"

Her head dropped, and the tears collected in her eyes. "I'm coming to the end of my rope, and I need something to hold on to, something to give me hope—tell me you're going to find my sister."

"I, well . . ."

She sobbed. "Tell me you're going to find her alive."

"I . . ."

Her face grew fierce and then slowly lost all emotion. "Please."

Usually capable of reading a dangerous situation, recent activity excluded, I stood there like a tower of crumbling stone, the only strong keystone in me, the two words I knew were the wrong ones to say. "I will."

She watched me to see if I was telling the truth and then wiped her eyes with the back of a hand. "You wanna come in?"

I stood there, making sure I was hearing what I was hearing. "Um, thanks but no . . . My head hurts, and I'm pretty tired."

"That's okay, it's an open invitation." She stepped back in, closing the door behind her.

As I stepped over to room 5, I noticed a handwritten note taped to the door that read *You have been changed to room 4.* The writing looked familiar, especially the emphasis on the period, which had stabbed a small hole in the paper, but I was too tired to analyze it, figuring Lucian and Dog had grown weary of my night-owl tendencies and had given me the boot.

It was just a few steps to number 4, and I found it conveniently cracked open.

I pushed the door the rest of the way in but then, fumbling for the light switch, I had my right hand caught in a reverse wristlock that turned me around and pulled me into the darkened room. A Browning tactical boot slammed the door closed behind us as my assailant dragged me back onto the bed, wrapped her legs around me, and bit my ear from behind, releasing it only long enough to whisper, "Good thing you fucking said no."

Boy howdy.

5

Lucian sipped his coffee and smiled, watching the two of us talk like it was Wimbledon.

"How was Belize?"

"I got a tan."

"So I noticed."

The old sheriff choked, swallowed, and then interrupted. "Got any lines?"

Victoria Moretti pushed a handful of blue-black hair back from her face and sipped her own coffee, sat the mug down, placed an elbow on the table and leaned in, looking back at him with a full load of tarnished gold. "You wanna try and find them, old man?"

He blushed, and I believe it was the first time I'd ever seen him do it. "I don't know if my heart is up to it."

"Maybe if you'd stop looking at my tits and look me in the face you could work up the nerve." She grinned at him, showing the elongated canine tooth. "Don't feel bad—many are called, but few are chosen."

"I didn't take you for a Sunday schooler."

She reached over and took a piece of my bacon, along with

a little bit of my heart. "That's where the phrase is from—damned if I knew; I'm schooled in other stuff." She bit into the bacon and narrowed the aperture of the cannons. "Why, you need a little teaching?"

He cocked his head as he slid out of the booth the oil workers had occupied last night and glanced at me for a moment. "I think I'm gonna go walk your dog."

Vic watched him slip on his coat. "Stay warm out there, thinking about me."

He pushed through the glass door and then stood still, frozen by her words for an instant. "I believe I'll do that."

I watched him head back for what had been our communal room and Dog. "I think that's the first time I've ever seen him scamper."

"I want to talk to you alone."

"I figured."

She slid out and switched over to the other side and took another piece of my bacon, being, after all, a carnivore. As she chewed I took the time to drink her in. She had gotten a tan and the blond streaks in her hair were incongruent in the depth of the Wyoming winter—a look I was more used to in the summer. Studying her was something you had to handle with care; volatile, like nitroglycerine.

"So, miss me?"

"Yep."

"A lot?"

"Yep."

She chewed and studied me. "Are you going to say something other than yep?"

"Yep." She waited, her eyes widening in comic expectation as I finally spoke.

"How are you feeling?"

"I've got a great scar."

"I know; I've seen it."

She nodded with a smile, staring at me in a way that made me think she hadn't had a really good look at me last night; not a feeling I was comfortable with. "Don't you think scars make better stories than tattoos?"

I fingered that little piece of my ear that was missing and draped an arm over the back of my seat. "If that's the case, then I've got a whole library on me."

"I've read it." She continued smiling and chewing. "And I really liked the ending."

She leaned back in the booth and looked out the fogged window of the Aces & Eights, a corpuscle-colored fingernail coming up and chipping at the frost cornering the edges. "The windows in Belize don't do this . . . Shit, who am I kidding, they don't have windows in Belize."

A quiet spread out over the table between us like a blank page covered with abandoned plates, glasses, and cutlery—but no words. "You stay at Jim Seale's place?"

She nodded. "Hotel del Rio, yeah. He's from around here, right?"

"Banner, over in Sheridan County."

"You ever been to Belize?"

"Nope. I think he's had that place for twenty years. He keeps asking me down . . . But I just never get away."

A smirk traced itself across her lips. "Look who I'm asking—you never go anywhere there isn't snow."

"I've spent some time in tropic climes."

She dismissed me with another flap of the hand. "The Vietnam War doesn't count."

"I spent six weeks on Johnston Atoll."

She stopped moving and then slowly turned her face toward mine. "After Vietnam?"

"Yep."

Her eyes sharpened to flints. "Okay . . . That's a month and a half of the two lost years unaccounted for after Vietnam in the saga that is the life of Walt Longmire. Where the hell is Johnston Atoll?"

I sipped my coffee, enjoying her full attention. "Seven hundred and fifty nautical miles west of Hawaii on a coral reef platform; it's one of the United States' minor outlying islands—about 1.3 square miles."

"A postage stamp in the middle of the Pacific Ocean with a single palm tree like you see in those cartoons in the *New Yorker*?"

"Something like that."

"What, were you shipwrecked or something?"

"No."

She glanced around, enjoying the illusion of covert activity. "What's there?"

I leaned back in my seat and studied her. "An air base, a naval refueling depot, and a weapons testing area, but not anymore."

"What kinds of weapons?"

"Nuclear, among others."

She leaned in. "No shit?"

"A dozen thermonuclear weapons were exploded there before the ban in '63, but they also had a twenty-five-acre landfill full of Agent Orange, PCBs, PAHs, dioxins, and sarin nerve gas from East Germany."

"Sounds horrible."

"Nope, it was beautiful . . . Well, not the landfill so much, but the rest of it was an island paradise."

"What'd you do there?"

"Swam, ate fish, fed the sharks, and sunbathed."

Her head kicked to one side. "For the government—you must've still been working for the military."

"Security." I shrugged. "I was on medical leave from the Marines and still attached to the Air Force through the provost marshal, so they shipped me off to a quiet place for the rest of my tour."

"Was it?"

I blinked. "What?"

"Quiet."

I thought about it. "For a while."

She wiggled on her seat. "Okay, let's hear about it—"

"Maybe some other time."

"C'mon."

I laced my hands behind my head. "So, how did Lena like Hotel del Rio?"

She whined. "C'mon."

"I want to hear about your trip, not mine; I know how mine was, and it didn't end well." I glanced out the window at the snow, the ice, and the cold, which was seeping through the windows in an attempt to freeze us solid. "I need a break from the winter; tell me about the sand, the surf, and how you got your tan . . ."

"Okay, but this isn't over." I sat there not looking at her and listened as she settled into her seat. "Mom stayed for a week but then got tired of watching me drink and went home." I turned back, and her eyes were now drawn to the frozen wasteland of the parking lot and the glaciers of snow piled against the building by the plows. "It was incredible; we had this cabana on the second floor where you could look at the ocean between the mangrove trees—the water was all shades of turquoise." She sighed and closed her eyes. "After the stitches healed up, I'd go lie in the salt water at the end of the pier and just soak in the warmth."

I thought back about a conversation I had had with her uncle Alphonse and his description of the teenage Vic who, walking down Christian Street in a one-piece bathing suit, had enticed most of the men back in her native Philadelphia onto the stoops when she'd sauntered by. "Sounds pretty great."

Her eyes remained closed. "These guys would come by with conch fritters and cashews, so you didn't even have to get up for lunch—just roll over and hand them some of that Belizean Monopoly money."

"And drink."

Her eyes opened with an ore wagon full of tarnished gold. "You weren't around and most people bore the shit out of me, so don't make it an issue."

"Right."

"I got enough of that crap from my mother."

"Right."

"I dove the Great Blue Hole."

I was surprised by the revelation. "You scuba dive?"

After a brief warning look, the eyes closed again. "They have this beer, Belikin, that comes in these really heavy, recyclable bottles—I did my part." Her head cocked to one side. "There was a little place about a quarter mile down the beach in San Pedro, The Sandbar—best pizza south of South Street . . . . I'd go down there in the evenings and eat and drink. Sometimes I'd have mai tais, but mostly I drank the beer." Her eyes opened, and she reached down, gathering our plates and stacking them at the end of the table where Haji could retrieve them. "I'd get toasted, and then Brittney and David, the owners, would drive me back up to the hotel in a golf cart and carry me up the steps."

"Sounds pretty nice."

"Yeah, I only had one rough spot."

I reached out and enclosed one of her hands, but her eyes remained closed. "What was that?"

"Well, like I said, they'd drive me home most nights, but they warned me that I needed to be careful walking home that late because there were a few bad characters around."

I squeezed the hand. "What happened?"

"Oh, they had a wedding at the restaurant, so I stumbled up the beach on my own; some guy got fresh and I told him to buzz off, but he got physical . . ." The eyes opened again, and she pulled her hand away as she slumped back into the bench seat. "I told you how thick those beer bottles were, didn't I?" She shrugged. "Turns out he was the police chief's nephew."

I nodded and then waited a permissible amount of time before bringing the subject up. "I'll ask again, how are you feeling?"

"I figure I'm just a hair's width away from having *syndrome* attached to the end of my name." Her eyes came back to me, and she cocked her head. "Now, huh?"

"Now what?"

"We're going to have this conversation *now*?"

I shrugged, thinking about the actions that had led us to the *now*—a very bad man, a knife, revenge, the loss of a child she may or may not know that I was aware of, her inability to ever have children, and a tsunami load of water under the bridge. "Why not?"

Her voice took on an authoritarian tone as it had with Lucian. "Question."

"Yes, ma'am."

"Tell me Tomás Bidarte is dead as Kelsey's nuts."

The very bad man.

I reached in the inside pocket of my sheepskin coat and tossed a long horn-handled switchblade knife that I'd been carrying for months with a clatter onto the table between the plates and us.

The knife.

She looked at it for a moment and then picked it up, sliding back the safety and pushing the button, the eight-inch blade slapping open with a deadly *snik*. "Tell me he's dead."

Revenge.

I said nothing.

She put a fingertip at the point, something she was wont to do in any circumstance. "If this is when we're going to have this conversation, you're going to have to do more in holding up your end."

"He's gone."

"Gone as in to the hereafter and buried by you and Henry in a shallow grave for a coyote buffet and then carried away in tiny, antlike bites, or simply gone?"

"Simply gone."

She stared at me, incredulous. "Henry Standing Bear couldn't find him?"

"No."

She smiled and shook her head. "There's no way I missed that son of a bitch with that many rounds."

"No."

She looked back out the window and set her jaw. "Maybe he is a ghost." She took a deep breath, and the eyes returned to mine. "So, where do you think he is?"

"Far, far from here." I waited a moment before adding, "Isn't that where you'd be?"

She laughed a laugh with no joy in it. "I'd like one more shot at him."

"Personally, I hope that never happens."

She sat forward and placed her hands between her knees, her voice suddenly low. "The doc says I can't have kids, not that I was looking to have any anyway." She stared at the leftovers on Lucian's plate. "I've got four brothers, so it's not like the Moretti name is at stake . . ." Her face came up, and her eyes were washed with salt water. "I just would have liked to have a say in the thing, you know?"

I slid out and moved around the table to sit beside her. "I know."

She wiped her eyes and laughed. "So much for hearth and home, huh?"

I gently placed an arm over her shoulders and pulled her into me where she pushed the lapel of my jacket away and stuffed her nose into my chest, and we stayed like that for a long time, her muffled voice finally rising up to my ears. "You smell good."

"That's because I smell like you."

She laughed.

"You could always adopt."

She laughed again, thank God, and then snorted and hic-cupped as she tried to stop, even going so far as to playfully pound my chest with a fist.

"Heck, seems like you adopted me years ago."

She pulled me in closer, and we stayed like that, but nothing more was said about the very bad man, the knife, revenge, her inability to ever have children, the tsunami load of water under the bridge—or the losing of a child I was now sure she thought I knew nothing about.

She nudged the blue plastic bag at her feet as I pulled from the parking lot. "Tell me again why we went to Kmart?"

I glanced down at the bundle I'd put on the floor in front of her seat as she held out a wrist for Dog to lick. "I needed a chess set to distract Lucian so that he stops driving me crazy, and I can't count on you because he might take you up on one of your offers."

"To coin one of your phrases, a dime's worth of me and a Fresca would kill him." She slid the files from the center console and began perusing them.

I cocked my head to one side. "He'd die happy."

She propped her boots up onto my dash, and I felt a surge in my heart at having her there. "So, what are we working on?"

I told her about Gerald Holman, the missing women, and about the sheriff of Campbell County not being particularly informed about the situation, resulting in a predictable summation.

"Fuck me." She thought about it. "What's the Clod Case replacement investigator's name?"

"Did you just call it *Clod Case*?"

She brushed my question away with a flap of the Dog wrist. "A Philadelphiaism."

"Inspector Richard Harvey."

"What's he like?"

I lowered my voice. "A dick."

She seemed preoccupied by the files. "A what?"

"A dick."

Her eyes widened in mock horror as she turned to look at me. "Oh my, Sheriff . . . Did you just call someone a *dick*?" She placed her chin in her palm. "A *dick*." She marveled, pretending to adjust a pair of make-believe glasses. "A *dick* by your reserved standards means he is some kind of colossal prick of proportions unlike we've ever encountered."

I shrugged and drove, trying to keep from smiling.

She glanced through the windshield and postulated in a pseudoscientific voice like some film you watched on a projector in high school. "Perhaps at one time he was a normal cock, but through contact with radioactive material in the deserts of New Mexico—"

"One of those blue-line guys."

Her hands flew up and out, measuring. "He grew to colossal magnitudes of dickdom!"

Dog barked, and I sighed. "I just think that he's more concerned with making sure that Holman's name goes unsullied than finding out why the man might've killed himself."

"Dickdom of a scale noticeable even to the demure sheriff of Absaroka County."

I mumbled, "Oh, good grief." But she ignored me.

"Dickzilla!" She shook her head, grinning as her attention, thankfully, returned to the files. "I gotta meet Dickzilla."

"Good, because we're on our way to the sheriff's office to give these files back to Sandy so he can read them—and did I mention that Tommi, female, by the way, and owner-operator of the strip club, is the sheriff's sister?"

"Wow."

"Yep."

"A *dick*."

I drove on, my diversion not having worked.

I laid the files on Sandburg's desk. "Richard's not here?"

"Probably out rogering the countryside."

I glanced at my undersheriff, then back to Sandy, and continued. "If you could make copies of these files for us, that'd be great."

The sheriff smiled at Vic and buzzed a secretary in, handing her the files. "One copy of all of these, Brenda."

"Two."

He nodded to the woman, swiveled in his leather chair, and looked at Vic. "So, is there anybody working over in Absaroka County?"

She propped her feet onto his handsome, vintage mahogany desk. "We've got people for that, kind of like you've got people to read your reports for you."

He stared at her boots but gave it up when it had no effect. "Well, we have a little more business over here—"

"Obviously more than you can handle."

He glanced up at me. "You wanna call her off?"

"I wish I knew how." I went ahead and sat in the other visitor's chair, not putting my boots on his desk, figuring there was only so much the poor guy could take. "Sandy, how involved do you think your sister is in all of this?"

"All of what?"

Vic interrupted. "Whatever."

He cleared his throat and thought about it as he pivoted back and forth in his chair. "She's a rough cob, believe me I know, but I don't think she'd be involved with anything that had to do with putting her girls in danger." He laughed. "I ever tell you about the time we raided the place and brought everyone down here and arraigned them—she posted their bail and paid their fines with singles; the girls in accounting put on plastic gloves to count all the one-dollar bills."

"Any other women ever disappear from there?"

He shook his head and kept his eyes on me. "You're sure there's a connection between Gerald Holman's suicide and this missing stripper?"

"No, but I'm sure there's a connection among the three missing women."

His voice was derisive. "A serial killer?"

"I didn't say that."

He sighed and dropped a hand onto his blotter. "Because you know what a shitstorm that's going to cause." He shook his head. "I can see the stories in the *News Record* now—"

"I could be wrong."

"You're not." Vic's voice was sharp. "It's possible that whoever he is, he hasn't worked himself up to serial level, but he's working on it; he's borderline, one more and it's official."

Sandy shook his head. "He, huh?"

"Only fifteen percent of serial killers are women." When I turned in my chair to look at her, she glanced back. "I assisted on a few cases in Philadelphia when I was going for my shield—before I gave it all up to herd cows with a cruiser." She studied Sandy's worried face. "Look, we could be wrong, but we'd be idiots not to approach this as a possibility in the investigative process."

The door opened and Brenda returned, placing the original files with the copies on the sheriff's desk and then quietly leaving in the silence.

Sandy shoved them toward me, picked up the originals, and dropped them in his lap to look through them. "Why didn't Gerald report this to me, and why the hell didn't Richard Harvey?"

Vic turned to me. "The dick?"

I nodded. "The dick."

Sandy's head came up. "Excuse me?"

"Nothing."

Vic stood, stuffing her hands in her jeans, and walked to her right where a large, matted, framed map of Campbell County hung on the wall. Her fingernail traced an area south and just a little east of Gillette. "All three are missing from this area; no more than twenty miles in radius." She turned to look at him, her fists now on her hips. "You're going to have to check and see if there are more."

"I'll put—"

"Don't put Richard Harvey on it."

He turned to look at me. "You really think Harvey is compromised?"

"Do I think he's involved? No—but he's not doing his best to come up with any answers, either. Is there anything you can do to get him out of our hair for a few days?"

He thought about it. "I've got an extradition of prisoner down to the psychiatric hospital in Evanston; that's at least a day down and a day back." He looked up at me. "Two days do it?"

I scooped the copies up from his desk. "Yep."

"Or I could fire him."

"Don't do that. I think he's a good man, just the wrong one for this job—maybe a little too close to Gerald or maybe somebody else?"

"But we'll be a man short." Sandy thought about it. "I could pull one of the guys from—"

"Actually . . ." They both looked at me as I thumbed the business card from my shirt pocket and held it out to him. "I've got someone in mind."

Patrolman Dougherty was surprised to be placed on loan from the Gillette City Police Department to the Campbell County Sheriff and had been doubly confused when we told him he could show up in jeans and a sweater.

He glanced between Vic and me, standing in the tomb of the cold case files and looking through the wire mesh into the room proper. "Have you checked with my shift sergeant on this?"

I leaned on the chain link that protected the file area and pushed my hat back to get a little light on my face in an attempt to let him know I was serious. "I didn't, but the sheriff spoke with your chief of police and he said we could have you."

His eyes stayed on the rows and rows of dented, green metal file cabinets. "To do what?"

I handed him the three folders and stuffed the other set of copies under my arm. "We need you to look for any cases that might pertain to the individual who we think abducted Linda Schaffer, Roberta Payne, and Jone Urrecha."

He looked at me. "You're serious."

Vic sat on the edge of Harvey's desk and punched Dougherty's cell number into her own. "As a heart attack."

He glanced at Vic as she handed him back his cell phone. "You really think it's the same guy?"

She shrugged. "Why not?"

Walking over to the grating that held the mountain of files captive, he threaded his fingers into the wire. "How long do I have?"

"About forty-eight hours."

His eyes widened. "Please tell me you're kidding."

I handed him the keys to the door. "You said you wanted to help . . . By the way, if a tall guy with a handlebar mustache should show up, tell him you were sent down from administration to straighten the files."

As Vic and I started for the steps, he called out after us. "What kind of connections am I looking for—what kind of suspect?"

Vic stopped and spoke over her shoulder. "Probably white, thirties to fifties, a loner with a reasonably high IQ involved with a menial job that he considers beneath him."

His voice echoed after us as we climbed the stairs. "That would be me!"

She shouted back, "Well, then, put yourself on the list."

At the top of the stairs, we buzzed ourselves out and turned the corner only to be confronted with Investigator Richard Harvey, standing in the hallway talking with another plainclothes officer.

As we approached, Harvey broke off the conversation and turned to face me, but Vic stepped between us and raised her hand. "Dick, so glad to meet you."

He glanced at me, but then took her hand, looking more than a little confused. "Richard Harvey, sheriff's investigator."

"Special Agent Vic Moretti, I'm supervising the sheriff here." She looked past him toward the outer office. "No offense, but you better scoot it up to Sandy Sandburg's office; I think he's got an assignment in connection with the Bureau that's of utmost importance."

He nodded, still looking a little off balance. "Okay, but I need to go down to my office and—"

She physically turned him around and escorted him back the

other way in a slow walk. "I think you better talk to the sheriff very first thing, he mentioned something about a high-priority situation that was going to need special handling and that you were the man for the job."

He paused for a moment. "Excuse me, but what did you say your name was?"

"Moretti, Victoria Moretti."

He nodded and then glanced back at me. "Sheriff."

"Investigator."

Without another word, he turned and continued down the hall.

Vic called out. "Nice meeting you, Dick."

He kept walking. "Richard."

"Right."

After he was gone, she turned and looked at me. "What?"

I shook my head as I walked past her.

"Don't you think I'm special?"

We stood at the door zipping, buttoning, fastening; it's what people in Wyoming do before they go outside in late December.

"What could these three women have in common?"

She snapped her fingers at me. "They're all missing."

We climbed into my truck and the atmosphere of Dog breath that had clouded all the windows. "I just keep going back to Gerald Holman."

"Maybe there's no connection at all; I mean, maybe he'd just had it."

"Why shoot yourself twice?"

"He was a lousy shot?" She tugged at her jacket. "Start this thing up and get the heat going. My blood must've thinned while I was in Central America—I'm freezing to death."

I fired the Bullet up and flipped on the heat. "A housewife, a waitress, and a stripper."

"Walk into a bar . . ."

I shook my head at her, and she rested her chin in the palm of her hand and smiled. Against my will, I smiled, too.

The Browning tactical boots lodged themselves onto my dash. "You did miss me."

6

"So nobody's died since Holman's suicide?"

I turned and looked at her as we sat in the parking lot of the Kmart, within eye-view of the Flying J Travel Plaza in the aftermath of an afternoon storm as a plow service pushed the never-ending snow over to the dividers. "As far as we know."

She skimmed through the reports. "I'm just sayin'."

I gripped the steering wheel of my truck with one hand. "He doesn't fit the profile at all."

She flipped a page. "Wouldn't be the first."

"Read to me about Linda Schaffer."

She shook her head and dropped the files in her lap. "If I know you, and I think I do, you've already read it to yourself about forty-seven times."

"Maybe forty-eight will be the charm—anyway, I like listening to you read."

She picked up and reshuffled the reports and held a hand out for the ubiquitous quarter I always paid her for the service.

I deposited the coin from my pocket into her palm as she began her dramatic interpretation. "Housewife with a full-time job at Kmart; worked there for three years . . ." She flipped a page. "I'm assuming after her son Michael was old enough to go to first grade. There are lots of notes . . ." Her face turned toward mine. "Was this Patrolman Corbin Dougherty's first investigation?"

"He kind of fixated on it, huh?"

Her eyes widened as she looked through the file. "Maybe we should take a look at him."

"He used to date Cady."

"So that means he's innocent?"

"I think he just got . . . too close."

"And now we're dragging him back into it?"

"Yep." I sighed. "If we need anybody to contact them, I guess we could have Corbin do it; I think he keeps in touch." I thought about it. "The husband . . . The one that moved to Spokane with his son?"

"Mike."

"Where did Mike work?"

"High Plains Energy, Inc. He's an engineer; designed coal mining equipment or modified it for use in HPE's three divisional operations here in Campbell County."

"How about the waitress, Roberta Payne?"

She flipped the pages again. "Divorced."

"Anything on the ex-husband—where he worked?"

"No."

"Phone it in to Dougherty."

She pulled out her cell and pressed the number. "He's going to love you." I listened as she relayed the request to the patrolman and then waited. "Corbin says her ex, Bret Bussell, works at a gun shop/shooting range on Boxelder Road, back toward Arrosa—High Mountain Shooters?"

"He still there?"

She conferred. "Corbin, the font of all knowledge, says yes." There was a brief pause, and Vic looked back at me. "And, stroke of luck, he says that Schaffer is here in Gillette signing papers to sell his house. He says he can talk to us at four."

I looked at the clock on my dash. "In the meantime we can go over to High Mountain Shooters."

Vic nodded and turned back to her phone. "Hey, Corbin, do you have a girlfriend?" There was a pause. "Well, you need to get one." She ended the call and looked at me as I started my truck.

"Kids?"

"No thanks, via nonelective surgery, I've chosen an alternative life plan." She grinned at me, but it was thin. "You can laugh—that was a joke." She studied me for a moment more and then went back to the pages. "No children at the time of her disappearance."

"Linda Schaffer had a son—how old?"

"At the time of his mother's disappearance, nine." She looked through the windshield at the skiff of snow swirling through the parking lot and dusting the cars with gray rime as I slipped into gear, circled around, and headed back toward Boxelder Road. "I don't know where you're going with the kid stuff, because the stripper didn't have any children."

"Far as we know."

Her tone became exasperated. "What, you think they've got day care over at Dirty Shirley's or they hitch 'em to the pole?" She sat the files on the console. "And she didn't have a husband, either."

I caught the end of a green light. "Far as we know."

"Will you stop saying that?"

I remained silent.

She stretched her arms out and laced her fingers, pivoting the arms and popping her knuckles. "Maybe they all shopped at Kmart, or maybe they all ate at the fucking Flying J . . . I don't know; it's like trying to find a needle-dick in a whorehouse. I hate cases like this."

"Gerald Holman."

Her arms dropped. "Gerald Holman."

"What did he know that made him kill himself?"

She chewed on a thumbnail. "Something bad." Then she completed the statement. "Far as we know."

"High Mountain Shooters, really? I mean, as near as I can tell we're hours away from any friggin' mountains."

We both leaned forward and looked up through the top of the windshield at the smiling mountain man holding a rifle. "I guess they're trying to capture the spirit of the thing."

We got out, and Vic gazed at the towering twenty-five-foot giant, complete with coonskin cap, beard, and a musket the length of a car. "I used to see these things over in Jersey when I was a kid, and they have always creeped me out."

"Why?"

She looked up at the slightly smirking face that all the statues displayed. "That is the classic expression of a child molester."

"They're called *muffler men*."

"Why is that?"

I looked at her for a while. "Because they started out holding mufflers." Walking over, I rapped the giant's leg with my knuckles. "Fiberglass; there was a boat maker who started putting these things out in the sixties, and they used to hold all kinds of things, mufflers, tires, axes, you name it . . ."

As she pushed open the glass door, she shrugged. "I've never seen one holding a muffler, but you should see what the one in front of the XXX Theatre in Camden is holding."

It was a well-lit, tile-floor sort of place done up in weenie-wood, which for the uninitiated is the bark-covered cast-off slabs from local, rough-cut sawmills. There were glass cases of pistols and revolving racks of modern rifles, but it was easy to see that High Mountain Shooters' heart lay in supporting the habit of reenactors; there were numerous assorted black-powder rifles on the walls, along with period clothing and accessories including a lot of coonskin and other assorted fur hats that mountain men might, or might not, have worn.

Vic plucked a fur hat from a mannequin head on the nearest counter and plopped it on her own, the fluffy tail and forearms draping onto her shoulders. "How do I look?"

"Cute."

She glanced around, finally locating a full-length mirror between the counters. "I look like a badger is humping my head."

"Umm, can I help you?"

We turned to find a middle-aged man in spectacles and a gray cowboy hat squeezing his way down behind the counters. "I'm looking for Bret Bussell?"

"Concerning?"

Vic took the hat off and placed it back on the mannequin backward. "We'd rather discuss that with Mr. Bussell."

The pleasant man adjusted his glasses and smiled. "Well, you are; I'm his father, Jim."

I went to badge him, but my new wallet flipped from my grasp and once again fell on my boots as he and Vic watched. I bent over, picked it up, and stood, stretching my star out for him to read. "Absaroka—"

He finished the introduction without looking at the wallet. "County Sheriff's Department." He gestured toward some monitors in the back corner. "Saw your truck when you pulled up in front of Jeremiah."

"Jeremiah?"

"The giant out front." He squinted his eyes at me. "Are you Walt Longmire?"

"I am."

"Saw you on the television last month, K2 out of Casper."

I shrugged. "You want to look at my badge, since I went to all the trouble of pulling it out?"

He nodded. "We've got a mirror over there if you want to try your quick draw; looks like you could use some practice."

"New wallet."

He gestured toward a leatherworking bench in the next room. "Want me to loosen it up for you?"

I removed the badge and handed it to him. "I'd appreciate that."

He flipped the piece of leather back and forth. "Cardboard."

I made a face. "It's supposed to be leather."

He held the edges up for me to see. "On the outside, but inside is cardboard; cheap Chinese shit. It'll fall apart before it breaks in." He dropped it on the counter. "I can make you a new one, but I'll need the badge."

"I'm afraid I'm working and need it."

He folded his arms and looked at me. "Working on what?"

"Roberta Payne."

He nodded to himself and then raised his face to look at the two of us. "You find her?"

I studied him back. "No."

He waited a moment and then responded, sort of. "Twenty minutes."

"Twenty minutes?"

He smiled. "I'll make you another badge wallet in twenty minutes, thirty if you want basketweave. I've got dark brown leather on the bench right now that'll match that holster you've got high on that right hip."

I smiled back at him and handed him my badge, something I rarely did with anybody. "Basketweave."

He nodded and looked at my star as if he were memorizing it. "Bret's in the back putting the finishing touches on a holster for a genuine Colt Walker—you can go back there if you want." As we followed him through the swinging saloon doors in the rear, he called after us, "I can make one to match that Glock that you've got, too, young lady."

Texas Ranger and then captain of the United States Mounted Rifles Samuel Hamilton Walker wanted a handgun for the war with Mexico, a weapon that would kill both man and horse at a hundred yards, and as the story goes supposedly sent the specs for just such a pistol to Sam Colt.

He made roughly 1,100 of the famed Colt Walker .44s, which in many ways turned out to be a touch too big, even for the great Captain Walker. End to end it is fifteen and a half inches long and weighs just less than five pounds, smokes a lot when fired, and was even known to blow out the chamber walls when loaded with sixty grains of black powder. The much-vaunted Sharps .45-70, with which I had a long and storied past, has a .45 round loaded with seventy grains of black powder; the Colt

Walker has a .44 caliber round holding sixty, and the Walker held six of them.

Full discharge of a round usually resulted in the loading lever dropping and effectively jamming the gun by sending the ram into a chamber's mouth. You had to check the lever every time you fired the thing, which proved more than cumbersome, but old-timers learned to loop a piece of rawhide around the rod and the barrel to hold it in place.

Later, the pistols were downsized and there were dozens of reproductions, but the one in Bret Bussell's hand when he turned to meet us was the genuine, unadulterated *Shooting Iron*.

"Howdy."

Bret was a small man, kind of a miniature Grizzly Adams, which did nothing but make the big Walker in the custom, four-point shoulder holster look even larger; the fact that he was dressed in buckskins from head to moccasined toe completed the incongruousness. "Can I help you?"

"Bret Bussell?"

He pulled some blond hair from his face and glanced at Vic. "Yes?"

"Undersheriff Victoria Moretti." She gestured toward me, and I was just glad she'd correctly and legally identified herself this time. "And this is—"

He slowly extended his hand. "Walt *Long-Arm-of-the-Law* Longmire."

I shook the hand as I looked through the wooden stands at the walls of stacked tires that protected the tin building's shooting area. "Have we met?"

"Nope, I saw you shoot once, though. I've got an uncle who's with the Highway Patrol and got to see you qualify for your certification down in Douglas when I was twelve."

I suddenly felt very old. "How did I do?"

He smiled a sad smile through the fur on his face. "Passable." With a quick spin, he twirled the big Colt like the protagonist of some Saturday gunslinger serial and slipped it into the patterned holster, complete with matching powder flask and a possibles box.

"Ahh." I pointed at the Colt Walker. "Is that thing real?"

He slipped it back out and held it toward me, handle first. "The genuine article; had a guy on the Internet offer me $11,400 for it about a month ago."

"I'm not touching it then."

He shifted toward Vic and held the big revolver out to her. "Go ahead, it doesn't bite."

"Loaded?"

He gestured toward the lubricants, percussion caps, box of lead balls, and bits of deer antler lying on the surface of the shooting bench, comprised mostly of the same weenie-wood as inside. "No, I was just getting ready to run a few rounds through it, but you can have a look first."

She took the magnificent weapon and held it up, marveling at the patina on the thing. *Hog Leg, Horse Pistol,* and *Smoke Wagon* are some of the names coined for the 1847 Colt Walker, the first commercially produced large-caliber revolver that then gave birth to the Colt Dragoon, named for the famed French dragon guns, and the 1873 Peacemaker—a couple of relatives of the semiautomatic I had high and tight on my right side.

Mexican soldiers, mistranslating the meaning of the word *revolver,* believed that the rounds fired from the weapon could actually turn corners and change directions, following the intended target as he ran.

"You actually fire this fucking thing?"

He nodded. "That's what it's for."

My undersheriff handed it to me. "Where in the world did you get it?"

"An old cowboy my dad knew out on the Powder River called him up one day and then brought it in. I told him I couldn't pay him what it was worth, but he insisted that he wanted to sell it to me, so my dad made me a loan for about half of what it was worth, and I bought it off him." I handed the Colt back; he twirled it again and placed it in the holster. "So, you needing some leather or hardware?"

"Actually, we're here to talk to you about Roberta Payne."

He looked like he could've been tipped over with ten grains of black powder. "You found her?"

The exact thing his father had said. "No, I'm afraid we haven't, but there are some other women who may have gone missing, so—"

"But nothing on Robby?"

"No."

He leaned against the shooting bench. "Would it be all right if I sat down?"

"Sure." I took his elbow and seated him. "You okay?"

"Yeah, yeah, I'm just . . ."

I glanced at Vic, who made a face and then covered it with a hand. "Sorry about that; we just need to ask a few more questions, knock on a few more doors, just to make sure that nothing was missed in that initial investigation."

"Yeah, I understand." He took a few deep breaths. "I just wasn't ready for that, you know?"

My undersheriff wandered off to a different shooting station, just to give the young man some space as I folded my arms and stood in front of him. "I do."

He took a moment to collect himself and then spoke into his lap. "Every time I think I've come to terms with it, something happens and I feel like . . ." He pulled the Walker back out and began disassembling it by rote in a mindless fashion. It seemed to settle his nerves, and the words started falling from his mouth as he clicked each empty cylinder. "When I was younger and just getting started in period shooting, this guy at a local gun shop told me I should top off every black-powder load with a couple of grains of Bullseye just to keep the fowling down; blew the nipple off and blasted the hammer back to full cock—still can't hardly hear anything out of my right ear." He looked up at me. "Three months, and it still feels like that whenever I hear about Robby."

I nodded and studied my boots. "My wife died a number of years back, and I still start conversations with her in our empty house till I remember that she's not there anymore."

He scraped his bottom lip through his teeth. "At least you know what happened to her."

"I do."

"That's the worst part, not knowing." He shook his head. "Wondering what happened . . . I like to think that she's okay; that she just decided to go somewhere else, you know? Like Florida or Hawaii. I like to think that she just got tired of her life, of me—and is laying on some beach somewhere."

Vic had wandered back, and I glanced at her, but she wouldn't make eye contact with either of us.

The kid kept talking, and I was really glad that the Walker wasn't loaded. "I mean, we were divorced for about six months, and she even went back to her maiden name, but I kept hoping that we'd get back together." He glanced around. "That's why I went in with my dad on the family business, you know, in hopes that she'd see that I was settling down and getting my shit together . . ." His eyes shot to Vic. "Sorry about my language, ma'am."

"Don't worry about it." She moved in closer. "When was the last time you saw her?"

"At the restaurant, the Flying J. I'd sometimes go in there just so I could look at her—nothing creepy, I just missed her, you know?"

Finally, Vic glanced at me. "Yeah, I know what you mean."

"It was lunchtime, so she didn't have any time to talk, but we made plans to maybe go see a movie later in the week—but then she never called." He reassembled the pistol and reholstered it. "She'd rented an apartment downtown, and I went by to check on her. Her car wasn't there, so I went over to the Flying J and her car was sitting in the parking lot, covered with dust, so I knew it hadn't been moved. I asked the manager to check the schedule, but he said she'd punched out two nights before and hadn't been back since."

"So, wherever she went, she went there from work and without her car."

"Yeah."

Vic leaned in. "Did she have any new friends, hobbies, or occupations?"

He shook his head. "No."

"No new people in her life?"

"No. I mean, not that I knew of." He sighed. "We were divorced, so it's possible she wasn't telling me everything."

Vic cleared her throat. "Was she seeing anybody else?"

"No."

"You sound pretty certain."

He stood and walked a little away from us. "I kept a pretty close eye on her after we split up." He turned and inclined his head. "Look, I know how that sounds, but I was just worried about her. Robby was good-looking, and you should've seen how those guys at the truck stop would hit on her, even when we were married."

I interrupted. "So you followed her?"

"I did. I know that sounds bad, but I'd just started lightening up on it when she disappeared. Can you imagine how that feels? I mean, if I'd been there the day she . . ."

I waited a moment before asking. "Did she have any friends or family out of town?"

"She had an aunt and uncle in Wisconsin, but she didn't like them."

"Nobody else?"

"No."

Vic interrupted. "What were her hobbies?"

The question surprised the young man, and he took his time answering. "She did plays with the local theater groups— she wasn't very good but she was pretty and always got cast." He thought about it. "She worked out and she ran, cooked; she was a really great cook."

My undersheriff leaned against the shooting stand beside me. "Are there any family members here in town that we could talk to?"

"Her mom—Sadie's got a place on East Eighth Street, next to the Mount Pisgah Cemetery, which is where the old she-devil belongs."

I smiled at the age-old war of son-in-law and mother-in-law; surprisingly, I'd gotten along famously with mine. "I take it you two don't get along?"

"Robby and her mother didn't get along."

Vic added. "Father?"

He looked at her and smiled. "Dead; that, or hiding out from Sadie. The old bat got hold of me about a month ago, trying to get a petition together for a . . . I don't know what they call it—one of those things where they declare you dead without finding your body?"

"Death in absentia?"

"Yeah, that's it."

"The state of Wyoming usually calls for the individual to be missing for five years before you're allowed to petition for a declaration of death."

"It didn't seem right to me, either. Anyway, she wanted me to sign a bunch of stuff and I wouldn't do it and I haven't heard from her since."

Vic pulled her duty notebook and a pen from inside her coat and mumbled to herself. "Sadie Payne? Sounds like a character from *Damn Yankees* . . ."

"What's that?"

Vic snorted as she wrote. "A musical where people sell their souls to the devil."

He nodded. "That's Sadie, all right."

"We'll go talk to her."

"Is there anything else you can think of that might help us, anything at all?"

"No." His voice broke. "I wish I could."

Vic handed him one of her cards. "If you do think of something, give me a call, okay? Unlike some other members of the Absaroka County law enforcement community, I have what they call a cell phone, a bastion of modern technology."

We stood there for a moment more, and it was as if he didn't want us to go, his hand dropping to the Colt Walker at his side. "You sure you don't want to try it?"

I stared at him for a second and then raised both hands. "I'm not going to be responsible if that thing blows up."

He turned toward Vic. "You?"

She shrugged and looked at me and then back to him. "Fuck it, why not?"

Shooting a black-powder pistol is a process that can't be rushed, which is why a lot of the old hands in the day carried five or six cap-and-ball revolvers so that as soon as they emptied one they could grab another or another in the face of a couple thousand Indians.

We watched as Bret dumped three nozzles' worth of powder into the cylinders and then stuffed each with a .457 round ball, before adjusting each cylinder to use the loading ram and pressing each round home. He thumbed off the tiny ring of lead from each chamber, indicating an airtight seal, and then applied some lubricant to each round to grease it up but also, he said, to guard against a chain fire.

"What's a chain fire?"

I continued to watch the young man work. "A loose spark that causes all six rounds to go off at once."

"I bet that's exciting." She watched as he picked up some of the smaller pieces of antler. "What the hell is that for?"

"Using it to press the percussion caps onto the nipples."

"I am all about nipples."

"If you don't get them seated tight, you get that chain fire."

"I am all about getting the nipples seated right." She pivoted toward me. "These chain fires, they happen a lot?"

I shrugged. "Not only will you have crippled your shooting hand, but you'll also have blown up an eleven-thousand-dollar piece of frontier history."

She spoke out of the corner of her mouth. "Bill me, chicken shit."

Bret held out the Walker to her again, handle first. "You ready?"

About fifty yards away was a standard 7-8-9-X silhouette target hanging from a guide wire and anchored at the bottom with clip-on fishing weights. Holding the revolver with the barrel in the air, she sidled into the stall, raised it, and held it up close to her face. "Born ready."

I mumbled to myself. "Boy howdy."

Bret and I, keeping a watchful distance, looked on as she reached down and moved the ear protection headset on the counter away. The mountain man called out to her. "You sure you don't want to use those?"

I had to smile, being familiar with my undersheriff's shooting tendencies.

She shook her head and called out over her shoulder. "I always like to hear the first one."

It was like thunder—very long, loud thunder. Black-powder guns don't tend to snap or jerk like modern weapons, but rather they give a strong and sustained push that resonates from your shoulders down through your spine and into your solid organs like a mortar.

I leaned forward enough to spot a rupture in the black silhouette of the paper target at the center of the forehead, and it didn't take much imagination for me to know that her target was Tomás Bidarte.

My undersheriff turned in the halo of white smoke with an undimmed and dazzling smile, almost as if she'd just arrived as a Faustian apparition—the kind you'd gladly trade your soul to. "Shoots about two inches high; I was going for the mouth."

———

I carried the Colt back into the gun shop proper, the cross-draw holster hanging from my shoulder. Jim was seated behind the main counter at the leatherworking bench and held out a beautifully crafted badge wallet when he saw me coming.

Vic stood at my side as I examined the workmanship, opening it up to see my star mounted in the basketweave setting. "It's beautiful."

He nodded. "Thank you."

I slipped the holster from my shoulder and handed it out to him. "Bret said to bring this in and give it to you."

"Where's he?"

"He's out there sitting on one of the benches. He said he wanted a little time to himself."

Bussell didn't take the holstered weapon, so I laid it on the counter. He removed his glasses and rubbed the spots where the pads rested on his nose with a thumb and forefinger. "I was afraid of that." He replaced the glasses and reached out to move the weapon. "You shoot it?"

I glanced down at Vic. "She did."

He smiled at her. "How'd you like it?"

"A lot." She looked behind us out the swinging doors that led to the range. "He gonna be okay?"

The leathersmith thumbed the loop off from the hammer and slipped the elegant-looking revolver from the holster. "You don't clean these things after you shoot 'em, they start corroding and pretty soon they're useless—I've told him that a thousand times." He disassembled the Walker and began cleaning the weapon very carefully, as befit the museum piece. "Loaned him the money for this thing, and you'd think it was his kid or something . . ."

"It's quite a weapon."

"Bret fell in love with it at first sight—kind of like he did with Robby."

I looked down at Vic as she leaned against the counter and reached out to put a hand on his shoulder.

"He's never been the same since she's been gone." He looked up at us, and it was one of those moments where you wished you did anything else but this for a living, like wash cars maybe. Bussell gestured toward the swinging doors as he cleaned out the barrel of the Colt. "I found him out there about a month ago with this gun in his hands; he'd been drinking . . . He said that he just couldn't put up with it anymore and that the pain was about to kill him and he'd rather do it himself." The gunsmith quietly reassembled the revolver, the barely audible clicks of the metal justifying the workmanship of its original manufacture. "He said that if he was going to do it, he might as well do it with the best gun he had . . ."

Neither Vic nor I said anything.

Bussell finished fitting the Walker together, loaded it, and then set after it with a polishing cloth so as to remove every fingerprint from the metal surfaces—almost as if he wanted to remove any traces of a human hand ever touching it. "Gave it back to him this week, and then you two walk in the door; I swear to God the thing is cursed." He slid it back into the holster, relooped the rawhide hammer retainer, and looked up at me. "Would you do me a favor, Sheriff?"

"Anything."

He glanced at the big pistol. "Take it."

I stood there staring at him but thinking about another vintage weapon, another suicide, and another lost and confused soul. Finally, with nothing to say, I laughed, but it was hollow and I desperately strung two words together. "I can't—"

"A loan; I just want to get it out of the shop and out of his life for a few weeks."

I glanced at Vic and then back to him. "Look, Mr. Bussell, I can understand your reasoning—"

His head jogged toward the shooting range. "He knows every hiding place, every combination to every safe, and has since he was eleven years old—do me a favor and just take it with you for a few weeks."

I sighed. "What if I lose it?"

"It's insured; anyway, you won't. I didn't say you had to use it—just lock it away for a while so that he can't."

Vic, her hand having slipped from his shoulder, slid the holstered weapon toward me. "That won't stop him." She glanced around. "There's always another way."

The gunsmith nodded. "Maybe, but it'll save him from using this one."

I raised my hand slowly and placed it over the weapon, careful not to touch the spotless metal. "What was the man's name?"

He looked up at me through the reflection in the tops of the lenses that covered his eyes. "What man is that?"

"The one who sold you this antique?"

He smiled for the first time in the conversation. "I figured you'd put two and two together faster than Noah—his name was Vanskike, Sheriff Longmire. Hershel Vanskike."

Outside High Mountain Shooters under the shadow of Jeremiah, Vic pulled at my arm. "So, Hershel Vanskike?"

I glanced up at the twenty-five-foot statue. "You remember Mary Barsad?"

"The woman from out in Absalom that ended up not killing

her husband; the one who had the horse that Cady rode at the wedding?"

"Wahoo Sue. Yep, that's her. Hershel was this old cowboy who worked for her, the one that Wade Barsad, her husband, killed."

"Oh yeah, the one who gave you the old rifle."

"The Henry in the office safe, yep."

"Next to the Cheyenne Rifle of the Dead." She reached up and fingered the holster on my shoulder. "You're putting together quite a collection of antique weapons."

"Yep."

As we climbed into my truck, Vic pulled the duty notebook out of her coat and looked at the address that we had gotten for Sadie Payne. "So, I'm assuming we're headed over to the she-devil's house?"

I carefully wrapped the leather straps around the four-point holster and opened my center console, gently placing the Colt Walker on the foam padding. "We are—after we meet with Schaffer at Jack's Tavern."

"Payne's daughter has been missing for only three months and she's trying to get her declared dead? I don't think we're going to be well received."

I tried to close the console, but the bulk of the Colt, powder flask, ammo box, and surrounding leather was more than modern truck designers possibly had had in mind. "Probably not." I suddenly felt very weary and slid my gloved hands onto my lap.

Vic attached her seat belt and then reached back and petted Dog before looking over at me. "You all right?"

"Hmm? Yep, I'm fine. Just thinking about that Bret Bussell."

She looked through the frost that had accumulated again on

the inside of my truck windshield from Dog's breathing. "A little young for that shit, isn't he?"

"Maybe—sixty-five and older have a 14.3 rate per 100,000, but young adults from twenty to twenty-four are pretty close behind at 12.7."

She stared at me. "Why do you memorize that shit?"

"My father had a photographic memory, and I got some of it." I started my truck and pushed down on the lid with my elbow and it somehow clicked shut. "It's just that it sometimes takes a while for it to fully develop."

7

As per Mr. Schaffer's request, we were to meet him at Jack's Tavern, a sprawling watering hole on the south side of town that housed a massive dance floor, pool tables, and dartboards. There was a spot for motorcycle parking that was under cover, which probably hadn't gotten much use since October, so I parked the Bullet and Dog there just to keep from having to push off the six inches of snow that were likely to be covering it when we got back.

"Don't you ever worry about him getting cold?"

"Who?"

"Dog."

I was confused by the question. "No . . . No. He's got a coat on him like a Kodiak; the only time I worry for his comfort is in the summer." I pulled open the door to Jack's Tavern and ushered her in. "He's tough, like me."

"You're not so tough."

I held a finger to my lips. "Ssh . . . Don't tell anybody."

Vic and I picked a corner booth on the unused dance-floor side of the place and quietly sat, unnoticed by the bartender. "I guess he didn't want the thin blue line showing up and queering the deal with the buyers."

"I guess."

She leaned in, even though we were the only ones in the bar, which was as big as a warehouse. "A biker bar?"

"Maybe he's a biker."

He was.

Ten minutes later, the man who slid in the booth with us was a young forty with a cleft chin, a little Dizzy Gillespie cookie-duster under his lower lip, and lots of ink. Mr. Schaffer wore a do-rag, sunglasses, a black leather jacket, and biker boots, and wasn't what I was expecting any more than the bar he had chosen.

"Hi." He immediately stuck a fingerless gloved hand out to Vic. "Mike Schaffer, how are you, Ma'am?"

She smiled, and I could see why he'd focused his attention on her first. "I'm good—you ride your bike over?"

The corner of his mouth kicked up, having taken no offense. "Too cold, even for me." He took off his sunglasses as his eyes shifted to me and he extended his hand. "Mike Schaffer. You the sheriff?"

I shook the hand as somewhere in the bowels of the massive building the Marshall Tucker Band began trying to get us to see what their women had done to them. "That's me."

"Corbin said you guys wanted to talk to me?"

"You've gotten to know Patrolman Dougherty pretty well?"

Schaffer nodded. "Oh yeah, he's a great guy. My son, Michael Junior, thinks he's like T. J. Hooker or something."

I glanced at my undersheriff, who waved me off. "Cop show on TV in the eighties where they specialized in sliding over the hoods of cars and shooting without the benefit of aiming."

Mike nodded. "He has a lot of contact with Michael on e-mail, but I didn't want to take him out of school to come over here, so I left him with my sister; that, and I just didn't want him reminded about what happened to his mother."

Vic tapped the file that rested on the table between us with a fingernail. "Linda?"

"Yeah." He looked a little unsure for a moment. "Corbin said there were some developments but that you hadn't really found anything more?"

"No, we haven't specifically, but there have been a couple of other women who've gone missing and we're wondering if there might be a connection."

He leaned back in the booth and caught the waitress's attention, her smile brightening as she approached.

"Mickey, how you doin'?"

"Tracy, are you playing the Marshall Tucker Band for me?"

"I am." She placed a hand on her hip. "It's slow enough that I'm waitin' tables myself, so I thought I'd cater to the clientele."

He gestured toward Vic and me. "Chief cook and bottle washer Tracy Jacobs, this is Sheriff Longmire and his fine partner Vic; they're looking into Linda's disappearance."

She looked at us. "You find her?"

"Um, no . . . We're just continuing with the investigation."

She pulled a pad from her apron. "Something to drink?"

Schaffer made a grand gesture. "Beer and a bump all around—I sold my house today."

I started to interrupt, but Tracy pursed her lips, looking a little downcast. "Damn, I thought you were maybe moving back."

"Nope, the check-cashing place bought it. I guess they're going to tear it down and add on to their parking lot."

I nodded toward Vic. "Just a couple of coffees for us, thanks."

She walked away, and I turned back to Schaffer. "No offense, but we're still on the clock."

"That's cool." He pulled a pack of cigarettes and a lighter with an Airborne insignia on it from the inside pocket of his leather jacket. "You guys mind? It's one of the only bars in Wyoming that still let you smoke, and I'm a little edgy from all this talk about Linda."

I changed the subject, just to give him a chance to settle himself. "Airborne?"

He lit a cigarette and blew the smoke skyward. "Fifth—Special Forces; you?"

"Marines, Military Police."

"Figures."

Vic asked. "Why is that?"

He smiled. "General enormity." He studied me. "Vietnam?"

"Yep."

"Iraq for me; you ever been?"

"Nope."

"Don't." He took another drag on the cigarette. "Got married, did two tours, then I quit, went back to school, and got a real job where I didn't have to get shot at."

I smiled back. "Sounds familiar."

He slid down his side of the booth and put his legs along the bench. "Maybe, but I bet you didn't lose your wife."

"In fact, I did."

"Sorry." He looked out at the empty dance floor, and I watched the sadness overtake him like a pack of hounds; I knew those hounds and had felt their gnawing. "Sometimes I get to where I feel like I'm the only one getting it in the shorts in this life, you know?"

Vic waited a few seconds and then asked, "You mind telling us about Linda?"

"What do you want to know?"

My undersheriff thumbed the files. "We've got reports, but we think that really knowing these women might give us more opportunities to catch whoever it is that's doing this."

He took another drag on the cigarette. "Met her here, right out on that floor; she was an incredible dancer." He grinned. "She had the shittiest laugh; really high and funny sounding . . ." He took a deep breath and then stuck the cigarette in his mouth again. "I'd give just about everything I've got to hear that laugh just one more time."

"Hobbies?"

"Jujitsu."

Vic snorted. "You're kidding."

"Kata and mixed-style, even Randori."

She made a face. "What the hell is that?"

"Random attack competitions; she was really good at it. She could kick some serious ass if you came at her; she whaled on me a couple of times."

My undersheriff and I looked at each other before I turned and asked Schaffer, "Did you tell Patrolman Dougherty that?"

"I don't know, maybe." Thinking, he stretched his jaw. "I don't know, man; it was months ago."

Vic opened the folder and searched the file. "Not in here."

"What's the big deal—is it important?"

Tracy brought the drinks over, sliding Mike his Coors and a shot of amber happiness and then setting the two coffees in front of us, along with a bowl of cream containers and sugar before addressing the biker. "You want a tab?"

"Please." He waited until she was gone and then asked again, "Why is jujitsu a big deal?"

"If it was an abduction . . ." I leaned forward and took a sip. "It tells us something about the abductor—that either he was incredibly powerful, capable, or . . ."

"Or what?"

Vic dumped her requisite three creams and five sugars into her coffee and stirred it with her pencil. "Or she knew him."

Schaffer nodded his head for a few moments, and I was pretty sure he wasn't even aware that he was doing it, and then downed the contents of the shot glass in a swallow, followed by a deep draught from the can of beer.

"Tell me about the night she went missing."

His eyes came back to mine. "She was supposed to meet me here for a drink, but she never showed." His eyes diverted to the table again, and he sounded like he was reading from a script. "It was a Thursday night, and I waited till an hour after she was supposed to be here and then drove over to Kmart where she was working, but by that time they were closed. I got one of the cleaning guys to let me in, but they said that all the regular employees had already left."

Vic leaned closer. "What about her car?"

He shook his head. "Wasn't driving one; walked everywhere, when she wasn't running." He drank some more of his beer. "I figured she'd just forgot we were supposed to meet and went home. I found the babysitter and Michael watching a movie, and I asked them if they'd seen her, but they hadn't so I drove back over here."

I turned my cup in the ring it had made on the table. "Then what?"

His voice rose, and he called out to the waitress/bartender/owner/operator. "Hey, Tracy, can I get another one over here?" His eyes came back to mine. "I ran into some buddies who were playing pool, and we had a few drinks . . . Later on, I just headed home and went to bed."

"What about the babysitter?"

"She had a car, drove herself."

"Remember her name?"

He thought as Vic worked her way through the files. "Shit, no."

Her face came up. "Would Michael?"

Schaffer laughed. "Yeah, he probably would." He reached in his pocket and pulled out a cell phone. "Just a sec." He punched in the numbers and waited, and when he spoke his voice changed instantly. "Hey buddy, how you doin'?" He waited. "Yeah? Hey, I've got a question for you; you remember the babysitter you had here in Gillette?" Another pause. "Yeah, her." He listened. "Yeah . . . you remember her last name?" He stubbed out the cigarette. "No, I'll be back when I said, I promise. Love you too, buddy." He punched a button on the cell. "Ashley Reich." He spelled the name for Vic, and she wrote it on the outside of the folder.

"Sounds like you have a pretty good relationship with that son of yours."

He looked back at me. "Why do you say that?"

"He said he loved you—in my experience you have to get that out of your kids with a crowbar."

He sat the phone down on the surface of the table, turned it, and slid it over to me. On the screen was a handsome boy with an enormous smile, holding up a pretty good-sized rainbow trout. "That, right there, is my life. He's all I've got left . . ." He swallowed and straightened up in time for the waitress to bring him another round. After she left, he spoke to the surface of the table, but it was meant for us. "Do me a favor?"

"What's that?"

"If you find him, whoever he is . . ." He glanced at Vic and then back to me. "Don't kill him right off; make sure that he suffers—a lot." He slammed back the second shot, and his head started bobbing again as he picked up the phone. "He looks like her." He sipped the beer and put the cell away, along with some of his thoughts. "And if you need any help with that, you just let me know and I'll be happy to get some guys to assist."

Some of the thoughts were put away but not all of them.

Mount Pisgah really isn't much of an ascent and ranks as the 1,336th highest mountain in Wyoming, but the real puzzle is that although the cemetery that has its name is in Gillette, the mountain itself is actually near Newcastle and is not even in Campbell County.

Mount Pisgah Cemetery is the crown jewel of the County Cemetery District and is located in the heart of the city. Atop one of the highest points in the town, the sprawling, fifty-seven-acre resting place is a beautiful spot in a not-so-lovely city with enough majestic old cottonwoods towering over the place that when they release their seeds in May and June, you would swear it was snowing. With rolls containing 5,600 burials, it has monuments dating back to 1879 and graves older than anyone can remember.

As I parked the truck in front of the large, Victorian-style house next to the cemetery, Vic turned and looked around the place. "Mount Pisgah in a pig's ass—this is a hill at best."

"It and the slope near Newcastle are named for a mountain in the Bible that's in a region directly east of the Jordan River and just northeast of the Dead Sea, usually referred to as Mount Nebo, the highest of the Pisgah range, a cluster of hills to the west of the Trans-Jordanian Plateau." I dredged up the chapter and verse. "'And Moses went up from the plains of Moab unto the mountain of Nebo, to the top of Pisgah, that is over against Jericho.' Deuteronomy, chapter thirty-four, verse one."

She pulled the door handle and slipped out, holding the suicide door open for Dog. "Jesus."

"No." I did my best Yul Brynner imitation. *"Mooooooses."*

"Was your mother some kind of religious fanatic?"

"No, but my grandfather spent most of his dotage reading and memorizing passages from the Bible, and since I spent most of my summers on his place it rubbed off." We looked up at the gate of the cemetery, and, as Dog did his business, at a strong snow beginning to curtain the landscape. "Pisgah is actually Hebrew for 'high place,' but lost its meaning over time and became the name of the range."

She thumbed through the files, holding them close to her chest and moving Roberta Payne to the top. "More developments from the photographic mind?"

"No, I had a Jewish girlfriend in college; you'd be amazed at what you can learn when motivated and with the right teacher."

"I bet." She glanced up; it was silting snow, which usually meant a foot or two before you knew it. "Have you checked the weather lately?"

I glanced around and noticed, indeed, that the landscape was sporting a contiguous white cloak. Never one to ignore the obvious, I nodded. "It's snowing."

She trudged toward the gate of the cemetery. "It's snowing a lot, and this looks like one of the ones that's going to last for a few days, bury everything, and shut down every airport on the high plains."

It looked as though the snow was smothering the land, almost as if the flakes were holding their breath in a snow globe. "It's a strange snow."

She glanced back at me from the gate, the tarnished gold embers dampening as if she were a centurion looking across Hadrian's Wall. "Yeah . . ."

A voice called out from behind us. "You people are supposed to have that dog on a leash, and he's not allowed on cemetery property!"

We turned in tandem and could see a tall woman wrapped in what looked to be an afghan who was standing on the extended porch of the Victorian.

"I'll get him, ma'am, but do you mind if we have a word with you?"

She stood there for a few seconds more, stooped to pick something up, and dusted the snow away by slapping whatever it was on her leg; then she eyed my truck with the stars and bars, about-faced, and went back in her house.

Vic looked at Dog, still irrigating the fence. "I'll give you a biscuit if you go shit on her lawn."

He came when I called him, and I popped open the door, allowing him ingress into his home away from home, and led the way toward the mansion with Vic trailing behind. "How 'bout I shit on her lawn?"

Stepping up onto the porch, I glanced back at her as I removed my hat and slapped the accumulated snow off. "I don't suppose you'd like to wait in the truck with Dog?"

"And not play with the radio? No thanks. I don't want to miss any of the fun, and anyway, I do get cold."

I reached up, knocked the heavy knocker, and noticed that the grand old lady of Eighth Avenue West was in need of a coat of paint, along with a puttying and sanding. After a moment, I could hear someone moving inside the house, then the sound of the chain being put on the door, then it opening about four inches. "Hello, Mrs. Payne, I'm Sheriff Walt Longmire and this is my undersheriff, Victoria Moretti . . . ."

She wedged her face into the opening to get a better look at me through the thick lenses of her bifocals, and I figured her vintage to be somewhere in her eighties, a little old to have a daughter Roberta's age. "I don't know where she is."

I waited a moment before responding. "That would be your daughter?"

There was a noise from back in the house, and she glanced in that direction. "She's dead."

I gestured toward the papers in Vic's hands, as if they had something to do with what we were talking about. "I understand you're petitioning the courts for a declaration of death in absentia, so we were wondering if you'd come across some information as of late that might've led you to believe that she was deceased?"

"No." She looked past me, trying to read the words on my truck as the noise from within grew louder. "What county did you say you were with?"

"I didn't, ma'am, but we're with the Absaroka County department."

"And what are you doing here?"

"There have been some other women who've gone missing, and we're thinking there might be a connection between them and your daughter."

The noise had reached a pitch to where I could now tell that it was a teakettle. "My daughter is dead."

"So you were saying, but if you'd allow us inside—"

"I don't have to allow you people in my home."

I listened to the screeching and figured I had an opening, so to speak. "No, you don't, but I was hoping we could ask you a few more questions, and it's kind of cold out here." I looked past her. "Is that a teakettle on?"

She paused for a moment and then, in a disgusted manner, disconnected the chain and pulled the door open, allowing us in. It was a large entryway with a sweeping staircase that led to the second floor. It had been a beautiful house in its day, but peeling paint, worn carpets, and distressed furniture indicated that the place had gone to financial seed.

Looking down just a little at Sadie Payne, still with the afghan wrapped around her shoulders, I got more of an idea of just how tall she was. "Beautiful home." I paused as I noticed the condensation from my breath was almost the same inside the house as it had been outside. "You can get that kettle, if you'd like."

She nodded her silver head and then started down a short hallway. "You people stay there, and I'll be right back." She exited through a heavy, swinging door with a window in it.

Vic took a step and pushed one of the partially open doors that led to the parlor a little further. "It's fucking freezing in here."

"Welcome to Miss Havisham's." I glanced up the steps but couldn't see anything. "I don't think she's got any heat on."

Vic glanced back at me and then rolled her head to indicate that I should have a look through the doorway where she stood.

With a quick take to the kitchen, I stepped back and peered over my undersheriff's head into an empty room. There were a few sheets lying on the floor, but other than that, there was nothing. We heard some noise and both stepped toward the chair and sideboard, the only pieces of furniture in the entryway. The noises continued, but she didn't reappear.

My attention was drawn to the mail that was lying on the table—it was a little wet and obviously what she had picked up from the porch. One piece was opened, and I noticed that it was from First Interstate Bank notifying Roberta Payne of her withdrawals from a trust account and dating back to the beginning of last month.

At that moment, Sadie reentered from the kitchen with a mug of tea, but I turned and leaned against the sideboard so that she wouldn't notice my snooping. "Mrs. Payne, you say you haven't had any contact with your daughter since her disappearance?"

She sipped her tea from a coffee mug, the tag from the bag fluttering in the drafty house. "No, none whatsoever."

Wishing that I'd had time to look at the statement a little more closely, I quickly made up a story. "Well, I was talking to Chip King over at First Interstate, and he said there had been some activity in Roberta's trust account as of late."

She dropped the mug, and we all watched it bounce off the floor with a loud *thunk*, the contents spilling on the hardwood floor, teabag and all.

I stooped and picked up the pottery, which somehow had not broken, and scooped the teabag as well. "Here you go."

Sadie Payne stared at me for a few seconds and then snatched the cup from my hand. "I want you people out of my house."

"Okay, but I'm going to be back pretty quick with a representative of the Campbell County Sheriff's Office and—"

Her voice became shrill. "Out! I want you people out of my house."

"And somebody from over at First Interstate Bank." She held the mug as if she might throw it at me, but I'd had things thrown at me before and wasn't that intimidated. "Maybe if you tell me what's going on with your daughter . . ."

Her head dropped, and she placed a hand on the table for support. "I've asked you people to leave my house, and if you don't leave I'm going to call the Sheriff's Department of *this* county and have you removed."

"All right."

She stared at me. "I mean it, mister."

"Sheriff, Sheriff Walt Longmire." I waited a moment before adding. "That's fine—I'd just as soon get some more people over here to get to the bottom of this."

She took a deep breath and sat the mug down, pulling the afghan around her a little closer. She gripped the blanket in a distracted manner, her fingers poking into the holes of the thing as she pulled it tighter.

Vic had given a name to the technique that we both used when questioning suspicious persons; I called it waiting, whereas she called it *running the Zamboni*, a term she'd brought from Broad Street, Philadelphia, where her beloved Flyers played—ask your question and then let the machine polish the ice.

"It's me."

Her voice had been so small I had to ask. "Excuse me?"

"I'm the one that's been making the withdrawals."

I glanced at Vic and then back to her. "You."

"Yes, me. I thought that if I kept the amounts under two hundred dollars that no one would notice."

I thought about the statement that showed that most of the withdrawals were well above two hundred dollars and let my eyes scan the decrepit house. "The money is Roberta's?"

She kept her head down. "A trust that her father left for her, but I've been using it to live on."

"For how long?"

"For a month now. There isn't any other money than what's in that trust."

"And that's why you've been trying to obtain a certificate of death in absentia for the last few weeks?"

She nodded and took off her glasses, wiping what I assumed were tears. "Yes."

I could feel Vic's eyes on me. "Mrs. Payne, it's clear that you've gone through a lot of difficulties lately, and we're not really here to add to your burdens but we need answers. We're just interested in your daughter, her disappearance, and the connection it might have with these other women." I pulled out one of my cards and placed it beside the stacked mail and then shoved my hands in my pockets. "We'll leave your home now, but if you do think of anything that might help us in the investigation, I'd appreciate it if you would give us a call."

Vic stepped in front of me and picked up the card, writing her cell number on the back and then handing it to the old woman. "Mrs. Payne, call this number and you'll get a faster response."

We walked out of the house and down the steps as my undersheriff punched my arm. "Okay, that's two visits that make me want to cut my wrists . . . Is Campbell County always this uplifting?"

"You should've seen what it was like before you got here."

"I improved your spirits?"

"Yep."

"I have that effect on people." She pulled out her phone and looked at it. "Uh oh . . ."

I pulled up, and we looked at each other from across the hood of my truck. "What?"

"Missed call."

"Patrolman Dougherty?"

"No, your daughter."

I froze, both figuratively and literally. "Cady?"

She thumbed the device. "Wait, there's a text." She read it and looked at me. "You're in trouble."

"How bad?"

"Bad."

"Bad bad, or just bad?"

She began reading from her phone.

"Dad, where the hell are you?! I've been calling the office! The doctors are talking about inducing and wanted to know if I had a magic number as a birth date for the baby, but I told them I was waiting till my father got here! The doctor I want for the delivery is only available one day this weekend and I want to make sure you're here! Would you please call me right now? Signed, your very pregnant daughter!"

Vic looked up at me.

I climbed in my side as she opened the door on the other. "That's not so bad."

Closing the passenger-side door behind her, she continued reading. "*PS: Now, or I'm going to kill you!*" She glanced at me. "The *now* and the *kill* are underlined."

I nodded.

"*PPS: I mean it!*" She lowered the phone and studied me. "*PPPS: I really mean it!*" She smiled. "Speaking from a personal standpoint, whenever a woman uses more than a half dozen exclamation points, four underlines, and three postscripts—you are in deep fucking shit."

"Gimme the phone."

She dialed the number and handed the device to me.

I put the thing to my ear and held it there as I fired up the truck and hit the wipers, barely able to move enough of the snow to clear the windshield. "Did I see an Office Depot back near the Douglas Highway in our travels?"

"Why, you want to go buy a chair to hit Sadie Payne with?" She thrust her chin toward the house we'd just left. "Little hard on the old broad, weren't you?"

I listened to the phone ring as I pulled a folded piece of paper from the pocket of my coat and studied it. "It was quite a performance."

"You're not buying it?"

The phone continued to ring. "Not particularly."

She studied me for a moment and then shrugged. "So why do we need an Office Depot?"

The phone rang some more. "So I can make a copy of this bank statement that says most of these ATM withdrawals in the last month were made at the Buffalo Gold Rush Casino in Deadwood, South Dakota. Some very large withdrawals . . ."

I turned to look at her just as somebody, a very angry some-body in Philadelphia, answered the phone in a tone of molten righteousness and wounded indignity.

"Hello?!!"

I could almost hear the exclamation points as I put on my best nonchalant voice. "Hi punk—you looking for me?"

"So, bad bad."

I nodded. "Pretty bad, yep."

"Have you called her since the one-legged bandit waylaid you?"

"Once, twice with just now."

Vic cradled her face in her hands. "Oh, Walt."

"I kept thinking I'd get out of here." I looked past Dog, now sitting between us. "Which is why I have to get this wrapped up by the end of the week when the two of us are going to have to get to Philadelphia."

She raised her head, brushing a wide swoop of black hair from her face, and looked at me. "Do you have a ticket?"

"An airline ticket?"

She glanced at the clock on my dash and tapped it. "If you take the bus, you're going to have to leave now."

I nodded and took a right on 85 onto the snowpack that was Main Street and then headed down the hill into Deadwood. "She says I have one for noon."

Vic shook her head and looked out the window at the snow that was continuously falling along with some freezing fog.

"We'll need to get me one." She looked up at the curtains of flakes falling gold in the illumination of the streetlights. "That is, if anybody's flying."

Deadwood, South Dakota, is a tourist town and, like most tourist towns, doesn't look its best off-season, but the architecture has been preserved here, and when snow covers the globed streetlights, I can almost see Bill Hickok, Calamity Jane, and Seth Bullock sauntering down the avenues of my imagination. "You've never been here?"

"No, but I saw the TV series."

"There was a TV series set in Deadwood?"

"Yeah. I liked it—they said 'fuck' a lot."

It had been a hard-fought battle getting here, and a South Dakota highway patrolman had pulled me over near Spearfish only long enough to tell me I was nuts. I crept up Deadwood's snow-covered brick streets and pulled my truck in front of the Franklin Hotel as a valet came out to meet us; he looked at the stars and bars. "You're in the wrong state."

Vic and Dog were already at the door of the hotel when I handed him the keys. "I think of myself as having a wide-reaching jurisdiction."

Inside, I caught up with the dynamic duo at the registration desk where Vic was arguing with the young woman on duty, wearing a name tag that read *Brittany*, as to whether Dog would be allowed to lodge with us.

"He's house-trained." Vic glanced back at me. "Which is more than I can say for this one."

I put my billfold and my new badge wallet on the wooden surface of the antique counter and had to admit that my badge looked a lot better in the hand-tooled leather holder that Bussell the Elder had made for me, and I liked the fact that it wasn't flopping around on the Turkish carpet like a dying trout. I thought about the big Colt Walker in the center console but then remembered that I'd locked it and flipped it back so as not to draw attention. "Brittany, I'm Walt Longmire, and I'm working a case and need a room—for the three of us."

Vic smiled and pulled out her own wallet, multi-badging the young woman. "With a tub, please, and don't make me get Dog's badge out, too."

Brittany blinked once and then took two keys from a drawer and handed them to us as I gave her a credit card. She stood on tiptoe, looking at the beast. "He doesn't bark, does he?"

"Not unless I sing, and I promise not to sing." I reached down to ruffle Dog's ears, letting him know I was abandoning him to Vic. "I'm going to head over to the Buffalo Gold Rush and spot the ATM—can I have one of the photos of Roberta Payne?"

She fished into the folder under her arm and brought out the most recent picture—the one from her employee-of-the-month plaque at the Flying J. "I'm going up and taking a bath. I'd be willing to take a shower if you'd join me, but I know you won't, so I'm going to sink into nice, warm bubbles and await your return."

"I won't be long."

She pulled at Dog's ear. "C'mon, Rin Tin Tin, let's see what we can find in the minibar."

I watched her lay a hand on the brass railing and flounce up the stairs with Dog in tow and wondered what the heck I was doing staking out ATMs at close to midnight in a blizzard.

Turning and tugging my hat down, I flipped up the collar of my sheepskin coat—the valet opened the door and watched me walk out into the fogged-over blizzard. Fortunately, the casino was only across the street about a block up, but I still had a quarter inch of snow on my shoulders and hat by the time I got there.

I shook off in the entryway and looked at the hello-officer red Corvette that somebody could win if he or she wrestled the one-armed bandits to the ground. Continuing into the din of electronic gambling, I made my way toward the cage that read HOUSE and asked the man sitting on a stool where the nearest cash machines might be.

"Whole bank of 'em behind this wall and around the corner. I can run a debit card from here though, if you need money."

I shook my head. "That's okay."

Walking as he'd directed me, I studied the half-dozen cash machines, then spotted a blackjack table within eyesight and decided to set up camp as long as the eighty-seven dollars and forty-three cents in my pockets held out.

Having returned Roberta's original bank statement onto the threshold between the storm and regular doors of the Payne home in hopes that Sadie would think she'd dropped it, I pulled the copy and noted the days of the week and the times of the withdrawals. There were a number of transactions in Gillette, but they were within the amounts that Sadie had mentioned, whereas the withdrawals that had been made here in Deadwood were much more substantial and growing more so. I pulled out my pocket watch. The days of the activity were random, but the times were not—all of them pretty much this time of night and within twenty minutes of each other.

Making a quick trip back to the cashier, I watched my real money transform itself into colorful plastic chips, and I strolled across the thick carpet back toward the vantage point I'd assigned myself at the blackjack table.

There was a chubby croupier with a beard, a bowtie, sleeve guards, a brocade vest, and a name tag that read *Willie* dealing cards to an east-of-the-Missouri-River farmer type, a brassy-looking blonde, and a broad-backed Indian. There were two guys sitting over at the bar, but other than that the place was deserted.

Covertly slipping my holstered sidearm off my belt, I stuffed it into the sleeve of my coat and draped the sheepskin over the back of a stool next to the Indian, took off my hat, tapping it against my leg just to make sure that I didn't drip onto the elaborate red felt, and took a seat. "Mind if I join you?"

Willie smiled a baby-face smile, probably wishing that we would all go home so that he could follow suit, and announced, "New player."

I piled my chips in separate stacks and nodded toward the farmer and the blonde, who, I assumed, was his wife, and turned to look at the big Indian, who had the most chips; he in turn looked at the dealer and nodded toward me. "I do not like his looks; he seems like the kind of man who cheats at cards."

I anted up. "Willie, has this Indian been drinking?"

The chubby man looked a little worried. "Um . . . No, sir."

"Well, let's get him started—give him a red wine, he looks like a red wine kind of guy."

Willie raised his hand, motioning toward a middle-aged woman—her name tag said *Star*. "What'll it be, gentlemen?" She was dressed in a kind of French maid outfit and uncomfortable spike heels and didn't look any happier than Willie at our reluctance to leave the table.

The big Indian spoke to her first. "Cabernet Sauvignon, *s'il vous plaît*."

She glanced at me, and I stared back at her. "Um, beer."

"What kind?"

I took a moment to respond, then straightened my chips and took a calculated guess. "You got Rainier, Star?"

"No."

I smiled. "Iced tea then."

The croupier announced the game and began dealing cards. "Blackjack, ladies and gentlemen—five-dollar minimum bet." He tossed the farmer's wife a king, the farmer a seven, me a three, a nine for the Indian, and finally a nine for himself, adding to his 25-to-2-percent advantage. "Lady has a king."

She grinned, her dentures shining. "Hit me."

He threw her a seven, and she sat pat. The next was an eight for the farmer. He brushed his fingers on the felt and was obliged with another eight, which carried him over the hill.

I stabbed the three, and the dealer laid a jack on it. I tapped again and was rewarded with a six. I looked at his ace, and decided what the hay. I tapped, and he sent me along with the farmer with a seven. "Ah, well . . ."

The dealer pitched an eight to the big Indian, who stared at his cards and then pointed at the dealer with his lips. The croupier paused for a moment and then flipped him another that skimmed along on a carpet of stale air—a deuce.

He looked up at the dealer with a smile as thin as a paper cut.

Willie gave himself a seven. The next card was a ten, and he followed the farmer and me down the road.

I watched as he deposited the chips in front of the Indian's pile; the farmer and his wife rose, and the older man laid a hand on my shoulder. "You high rollers are too much for us, we're headed for bed."

I smiled back at him. "Good night. Be careful out there."

"Oh, we're just down the street in a hotel—we're walking."

"Still, be careful. You could cut sheep out of the air with a pair of shears."

"We will."

I watched the older couple pull on their coats as the waitress arrived with our drinks, and I gave her a chip as a tip. "Keep us topped off, would you?"

"Sure."

The dealer was getting anxious as he looked at the Indian and then at me. "Another hand, gentlemen?"

I nodded and turned to Henry Standing Bear as we both anted up. "What the hell are you doing in Deadwood?"

The Cheyenne Nation nodded his head at Willie. "I am feeling lucky." As the croupier dealt cards to the three of us, the Bear smiled at me. "And besides, both Vic and Cady left me messages this afternoon. They worry about you."

We played a few more hands, and he explained. "Since I was already in Pine Ridge . . ." He gestured around him. "I decided to stop by."

Willie interrupted, ready to unload a few more cards. "Five for the cowboy, king for the Ind— Native American, and a three for the house."

Henry sipped his wine. "Why, if you do not mind my asking, are you here?"

I tapped the five and got another one. "Looking for a missing woman." I tapped again and landed an eight. "Hold." I pulled the photograph from my coat pocket and unfolded it on the table between us. "Roberta Payne—ring any bells?"

He studied it and then nodded his head toward the other room. "I would say she bears an uncanny resemblance to the woman with the man at the ATM machine over there." The Bear pursed his lips at the dealer again and got a three. He lip-pointed once more and got an eight, smiled the razor smile, and passed his hand over the cards as a blessing. I turned to see a tall, bald man, muscular in build, holding on to said woman's arm as she made a withdrawal.

I flipped my cards over. "That would be she."

Willie threw himself a jack and then a six. He looked at Henry, who paid him no attention, and then turned over a ten. He sighed and scooped up the cards, once again depositing the Bear's winnings in front of him. "You're lucky tonight."

The Cheyenne Nation stacked his chips. "Yes, I am."

Willie stepped back and dusted his hands together. "Would either of you gentlemen mind if I ran to the bathroom? It's right over there, and it's been a long shift."

We said nothing, just watched him go. Henry, speaking under his breath, turned back to me. "You do realize that he is going to warn this Roberta Payne and friend?"

I stood and reached for my coat, careful to reattach my holstered weapon, as he joined me in putting on his black leather duster. "I'm counting on it." We watched as Willie slipped behind the cashier booth through a door beside the cash machines. With one quick look back at us, he spoke through the cage to the couple at the ATM, opened another door, and allowed them inside.

We hustled across the floor, only to find that the heavy security door was fashioned with a large metal keyboard. I leaned back and motioned toward the man in the cashier booth. "Hey, would you mind—"

There was a thunderous crash, and I looked back and saw that the Cheyenne Nation had decided not to wait for approval and had let himself in with a size-twelve Caterpillar chukka boot; he extended his hand. "After you?"

We two-at-a-timed it down the steps and were immediately confronted with a hall. "You go that way, and I'll go this—first one to find something, sing out."

He nodded and disappeared to the left—I moved quickly to the right, finding another door, which read WOMEN'S DRESSING ROOM. I turned the knob, but it was locked. I was about to do a Bear when a young woman in one of the waitress outfits opened it and then stepped back, her hand to her chest. "Oh, my God."

"Excuse me."

I started to go around her, but she held up her arm. "This is the women's dressing room."

"I know, and I'm looking for a woman. Roberta Payne?"

"Never heard of her." The arm stayed on the door. "And you can't come in here."

I pulled out my badge wallet. "Yep, I can." I pushed past her, and across the room, I could see another door hanging open and moving. I threw what my father had called my field voice over my shoulder. "Henry!"

Hoisting myself up the steps, I threw the door open into the snow-covered alley behind the casino which, with the proximity of the surrounding buildings and the thickness of the fog, felt claustrophobic. I cranked my hat down tight and looked at the ground, where three sets of tracks went to the left toward the middle of town.

I felt the breath of someone next to me. "They are together."

"Yep." I stepped back and let the expert take over the tracking duties, watching as his left shoulder humped up and his right hand hovered over the ground like it always did when he was bird-dogging, and he loped off down the alley. I tried to keep up but was at a disadvantage running with the leather soles of my cowboy boots in comparison with the Vibram ones of his boots—at least that's what I told myself.

We tracked them two blocks, but then the Bear pulled up and stood at Lee Street, the snow already covering his raven-black hair like the mantle of silver on a grizzly. "They split up."

"Why in the heck would they do that?"

The streetlight flared off the surfaces of his face. "Two cars. There are two major parking areas in town, one over by Dead-wood Creek and the public parking garage on Wall Street. The croupier went toward the creek, and the couple went toward the garage."

"She's the one we want; we'll find out about the dealer later."

The Bear turned and was off again, trying to catch a glimpse of Roberta Payne in the freezing fog. "They are fast." He shook his head as we hurried across the empty street, the snow now approaching lower midcalf. "Try and keep pace."

Henry broke into a run, and I struggled to keep up as he took to the sidewalk—I just ran down the middle of the street. It was strange to see the usually busy little town like this, almost as if we were ghosts, haunting the place with our muffled, silent run. I saw Henry pause and then take a left on Wall toward the parking garage.

Sliding a good six feet on the smooth soles of my boots, I made the turn too, and lumbered after the Cheyenne Nation, almost running into him at the empty glass booth at the entrance. He stood, looking up, staring at the concrete ceiling and the floors above. "What?"

"Someone was trying to start a car."

I looked at the two passageways on either end of the massive building that stretched most of the length of the town. "You take *in* and I'll take *out*; working our way to the roof?"

He nodded and was off to the right as I moved left, looking at all the cars as I went, hoping to spot exhaust, movement, or the condensation that would tell me somebody was inside. There were more than a lot of vehicles—evidently guests from the surrounding hotels and employees who had given up the ghost had decided to just leave their vehicles in the safety of the garage for the night.

There was a Toyota pickup at the far end, sitting by itself with the motor running. Just to be on the safe side, I pulled my badge wallet from my rear pocket and held it open, placing my other hand on the .45 at my side as I approached the driver of the small truck and noticed that it was, ever so slightly, rocking.

I drew my coat back over my sidearm and walked a little forward where I could see a woman sitting on a man's lap. I had just started to move back when the guy saw me and screamed, honestly, screamed. Then the woman started screaming, and I held up my hands.

She slid to the side, and the middle-aged man rolled down the window and started yelling at me. "What the hell do you think you're doing?"

I put a finger to my lips. "Shhhhhhh . . ." I then held up my badge and whispered loudly, "Get a room." The window went back up, and I was able to get past before he threw it in reverse.

I turned up the ramp leading to the second floor. At the top, I looked down the length of the building and sighed through chattering teeth.

I was cold, it was late, and I was really tired.

I started working both sides of the street, so to speak, and was halfway done when I saw Henry, skimming along like a black panther, stooped and crisscrossing the lane just as I was. I shook my head and thought about the best buddy I had in the world, a man ready to drop everything in his life and rush out into a blizzard to help me try and catch a missing woman.

We met halfway, well, maybe a little more on my side. "Anything?"

"No, you?"

"A couple lap dancing in a Toyota."

"I heard somebody pull out and assumed you had it." He blew into his bare hands in an attempt to warm them. "Did you do your civil duty and tell them to get a room?"

"I did."

He glanced around in the darkness of the garage. "We could just wait at the exits, but she might freeze to death."

"I'm ready to just go back to the casino and see if they've got an address for Willie or either of them."

He looked at the ceiling. "In my experience, employees are usually relegated to the most inconvenient parking areas, so if they are friends of his . . ."

"Up?" I joined him in looking at the ceiling, and he nodded. "I'll double back."

On the third floor, there were fewer cars, and I was able to make better time but didn't see Henry as I got toward the middle. I kept going, finally approaching the ramp that he should've come up when I heard somebody running on the floor below. "Henry?"

His voice echoed up to me. "They're in the elevator!"

I ran for the steps at the southeast end of the building. Fortunately, there was no snow in the stairwell, but I could already hear Henry and the couple on the street below. Throwing myself against the walls, I bounced my way down, turned the corner at the ticket booth, and tripped off the curb just enough to send myself slinging onto the snow-covered street outside.

Picking myself up on one elbow, I could see the Bear climbing up the fire escape at the back of a three-story redbrick building to my left, and above him, barely visible in the cascading flakes, two people going onto the roof.

"Damn it." I grabbed my hat and pushed off, running the length of Wall back down to Main, keeping my eyes on the rooftops, and sliding another ten feet into the main thoroughfare.

Holding my hat in front of my eyes to give me a clearer view, I could see that there was a large turret on the corner building, and I could barely make out the shadow of somebody looking down from the front cornice. I shouted up at her, "Roberta Payne, sheriff's department—you need to stop!" She looked both ways and then behind her as the man yanked her away. "Whatever your name is, you need to let her go!"

He ignored me, and they both disappeared.

I moved sideways down the street, keeping an eye on the roof and trying to see, even though the falling snow was blinding.

After a moment, Henry appeared at the cornice. "Where did they go?"

"Not this way, they—" It was then that I saw something move on the roof of the next building, a full flight lower than the corner one that Henry was on. I pointed and yelled at the Bear, "They're down there; they must've jumped!"

The Cheyenne Nation flung himself from the taller building, but I couldn't see if he'd landed well or not.

Running sideways and hoping to spot a taller building that might impede their rooftop progress, I tried to keep up but watched as the couple made an easy traverse onto the next three buildings, with me, sliding along in my boots, desperately trying to keep pace on the ground.

Suddenly, I noticed that a half-ton pickup with its bright lights blasting up Main Street had stopped about fifty yards away. Bringing my hand up to shield my eyes, I peered through the fog freezing in the snow-filled air and finally figured it must be Willie.

I stood there for a few seconds, unsure of his intentions, when he revved the engine, lurched forward, and headed straight for me.

For all Willie knew, he was protecting the couple from a wild cowboy-and-Indian duo who might mean them harm. I would've liked to have shown my badge, but there wasn't time. Carefully, I pulled the Colt from my holster and leveled it at the rapidly approaching vehicle.

The truck stopped when I guess Willie figured out what he was up against.

I took a step forward and raised my sidearm, just to show him I wasn't intent on putting a bullet into him, and yelled, "Absaroka County Sheriff's Department." Unsure if he'd heard me, I yelled it again.

That's when he hit the gas and started straight toward me.

Unwilling to be run over, if by mistaken identity or not, but not wanting to hurt the driver, I fired low, figuring I would hit the front of the truck and something that would disable it.

The brakes locked up, and the truck slid at an angle to my right.

Tugging at my hat, I leaned my head to one side and tried to see in the cab to make sure the bullet had not deflected, but the snow and the reflection on the glass made it impossible.

Suddenly, the wheels started spinning and I raised my sidearm again, only then noticing that the truck was retreating, once more at a high rate of speed. He backed the vehicle into a parking lot at the end of the row, and as I ran after him, I saw Roberta and the unknown man leap onto a one-story building, swing around a billboard advertising the newest, biggest, and best of something, and lightly jump to the ground next to the vehicle in waiting.

I was getting closer but watched helplessly as they vaulted into the attacking pickup, which fishtailed out of the parking lot and headed off in the other direction, the billowing tunnel of snow in their wake closing off the air behind them.

Their taillights disappeared as the Bear dropped to the ground, both of us leaning over with our hands on our knees in an attempt to catch our collective breath.

He caught his before I caught mine, of course. "Who. Knew. We. Were. Chasing. Spider-Man . . . And. Spider-Woman."

I nodded and stooped to see a little antifreeze in the snow— I must've dinged the radiator—as another set of lights suddenly appeared from the other direction, along with a spotlight that blinded us. A voice rang through a loudspeaker mounted in the grille of a black-and-white Dodge Charger. Static. "Deadwood Police—don't move!"

Standing and holding my .45 high and wide so we wouldn't get shot, I shouted, "Sheriff Walt Longmire, Absaroka County, Wyoming!" I gestured toward Henry with a smile. "C'mon, we've got a ride."

"Follow *what* car?"

I'd gotten to say *follow that car* only one other time in my life, and the young patrolman was ruining the expectations I had with my second request. "It was a half-ton pickup, blue in color, headed east on Main . . ."

Tavis Bradley, who had turned out to be a part-time patrolman with the Deadwood Police, had cost us more than part time trying to figure out who we were and what we were doing, but had finally fallen in line and started the warm, if not hot, pursuit in his completely useless-in-the-snow Charger. "I called them in, even though you didn't have a plate number . . ." The car slid sideways as we joined routes 14/85 south, and I wished, once again, that I had been driving. "There can't be that many vehicles out here tonight."

"Turn your headlights on low, please?" The Bear, seated in the front seat with Tavis, peered over the hood at the surface of the road. "It is fast disappearing, but there is one, clearly defined set of tracks."

The young man did as he was told. "He's headed onto Sherman toward Cliff, but my jurisdiction ends where 385 branches off and goes south to Custer and the state park."

I leaned over the seat. "We're going to broaden your horizons tonight."

"Shouldn't we call the Highway Patrol? They've got a detachment in Custer and in Rapid City and can cut him off."

"Get 'em on the wire."

As the kid snatched the mic from his dash and talked to the HPs, Henry and I watched the road and tried to figure out what had happened in Deadwood. "I don't get it, why split up?"

The Bear pointed, urging the patrolman to go left.

I thought about it. "I can understand if you decided to change your life and hide out . . . Well, in all honesty I can't, but was she acting as if we were going to kill her or he was?"

He turned, giving me his usual horse eye. "I'm voting that she fears him much more than she does us."

The patrolman hung up the mic and glanced back at me through the rearview. "They're setting up cars on 44, 16, and

385, so he can't go south and he can't get over to Rapid, so can I slow down?"

"No. There are other roads he can take, right?"

"Small ones."

"Well, we're going to keep after him while we can still see his trail or else we might lose him to those small ones."

Tavis looked glum. "If I wreck this new cruiser, the chief is going to lose me."

"Who's your chief?"

"Emil Fredriksen."

I laughed. "Fightin' Freddie?"

"You know him?"

"Yep, I worked with him a couple of times back in the day, when I used to moonlight the Sturgis Bike Rally."

The Bear spoke out of the side of his mouth. "Dare I ask how he got the name?"

I shook my head, thinking back to a time when I was a struggling deputy with a wife, a child, a mortgage, and a car that needed a transmission. "Oh, every time some tough guy would say that Emil was just a tub of guts and that if he took off his badge and gun they'd kick his ass, he'd take off his badge and gun and kick their ass. I think his badge and gun got more wear from being thrown onto his dash."

In any other circumstance, it would have been a wonderful drive through one of the most beautiful and, according to the Indians, spiritual places in the world, but with the snow and fog, it was like driving underwater.

I had the kid shut off the lights on the light bar except for the warning ones at his rear, just so that if the SDHPs were out here moving around they wouldn't back-end us.

"Why no lights?"

"Henry can't see." I watched the road for a few seconds then tried to make out the signs, but they were enameled with snow. "Any idea where we are?"

I was talking to Henry, but Tavis answered. "Just south of Hill City, I think." He turned in the seat and looked at the Bear. "You Sioux?"

"Lakota. Some, but mostly Cheyenne."

"I never met a Cheyenne before."

The silence of the vehicle got to the kid, and before long he spoke again. "How 'bout telling us a story, I mean the sheriff and me have been talking the whole way . . ."

Henry nodded. "I know."

"Well, tell us a story, an Indian story to help pass the time."

The Cheyenne Nation glanced at him, then back at me, and then at the road. "You may not like my stories."

The kid wouldn't give it up. "What, do all the white people die in the end?"

"No, only white-people stories end with everybody dying . . ." He sighed and then smiled to himself. "There was an Indian and a *Ve'ho'e* traveling together—"

"What's a *Ve'ho'e*?"

I joined the conversation. "White person."

The Bear continued as if we hadn't spoken. "These two were on a hunting trip, but they were not doing very well, when suddenly a duck flew out of some rushes and the Indian shot it with an arrow at the exact same time as the *Ve'ho'e* shot it with a gun." Henry's hands came up, gesturing as he warmed to the story. "They plucked the bird and made a fire, burying the duck in the ashes so that they could eat it the next morning. As they were going to sleep the *Ve'ho'e* made a wager, telling the Indian that they should sleep well tonight and dream, and whoever had the best dream in the morning would be the one to eat the duck."

I had heard this story numerous times.

"The next morning the *Ve'ho'e* awoke very early, but when he looked at the Indian, he could see his eyes watching him and so the *Ve'ho'e* said, 'I have had a marvelous dream!'"

"The Indian, seeing his enthusiasm, allowed him to tell of his vision first.

"'In my dream, there were winged white women who came down from the sky who promised me everything forever if I would only join them in Heaven, but I explained to them that I did not have wings. So they lowered a ladder down for me and I began climbing up.'

"The Indian jumped to his feet and pointed at the *Ve'ho'e* and agreed—'I have had this same vision, a dream so powerful, so vivid that it must be shared by more than one person.'

"The *Ve'ho'e* nodded. 'It was as if it actually happened!'

"'Yes, I saw you climb up the ladder and disappear.'

"The *Ve'ho'e*, sensing he had won the bet, exclaimed, 'Yes!'

"The Indian continued to nod. 'So I ate the duck.'"

It was quiet in the cruiser as the Bear returned his hands to the dash and his attention back to the road.

The kid finally spoke up. "That's the end?"

The Cheyenne Nation's voice echoed off the windshield. "Yes."

"Well, that sucked."

"For the *Ve'ho'e*, yes." Henry smiled. "I told you you would not like the story."

For the sake of peace between the races, I tapped the kid's shoulder and asked, "You from around here, troop?"

"Sioux Falls, but they weren't hiring this time of year."

"How long have you been on the job?"

"Four weeks—got my criminal justice degree from Black Hills State."

"What made you want to be a police officer?"

"I just want to help people, right?"

The Bear looked at him again, and I slapped Henry's shoulder to get him to knock it off, the back of my fist making a loud smacking noise against the black leather. "Right."

Henry's voice rose with his finger. "Left."

The kid turned to look at him. "What?"

"Left, turn left."

"Right." He did as he was told, but after a moment, he spoke again. "What is it that this woman's done?"

I rested my chin on my arm. "Disappear, but the problem is that a couple of other women have had the same thing happen to them, and I'm hoping that she might be able to connect some of the dots for me. That, and I've got a dead sheriff's investigator to throw in the mix."

"How did he die?"

"Suicide."

The Bear raised a fist like a mace. "To serve and protect, right?"

I hit him in the shoulder again.

The kid looked at me. "How long have you been a sheriff?"

I shrugged. "About as long as you've been alive."

Some quiet time went by, and then there was a little edge to the young man's voice. "So, what about you?"

Henry shook his head. "What about me what?"

"Are you a cop?"

The Bear smiled. "No, I am freelance."

The tone was still there when he asked the next question. "So, what do *you* think we are?"

The Cheyenne Nation didn't look at either of us when he responded with a philosophy the young patrolman would develop sooner or later, if he lived that long. "Consequence." You could hear all of us breathing in the cruiser as we tracked along in the deep snow. "Consequence is what we all are."

9

"Stop."

Tavis hit the brakes, and we began a slow and agonizing slide on the cushion of snow, finally coming to rest at a diagonal, blocking both lanes. We'd been driving for what seemed like an hour, following the only set of tracks on the road, and all I could think was how embarrassing it was going to be if we were trailing a garbage truck. The young patrolman and I sat still as Henry leaned forward, looking past the kid through the driver's side window farther down the road.

"What?"

He gestured. "No more tracks."

I leaned back, wiping the fog from the inside of the window, and even though I was unable to do much about the outside, I could see that the Bear was right and that the road ahead was pristine and undriven. "The road less traveled?"

"They must have turned off."

I patted Tavis on the shoulder. "Can you get her turned around and go back?"

He nodded. "I think so."

As he tried, I scoped the outside to try and get my bearings.

"Shouldn't we have met up with one of the Highway Patrol road-blocks by now?"

"Seems like, but maybe they're just a little farther." He pulled the cruiser ahead in an arc, and we slowly started back up the invisible road.

"How could you see that there were no more tracks?"

The Cheyenne Nation shrugged. "Did not see it—I felt it. And heard it; the snow feels and sounds different when it has not been driven on." He raised a hand again. "Stop." We slid and then rocked back and forth like a moored boat as the Bear un-clicked his seat belt. "They went off the road here."

I looked out my window. "That's a road?"

Henry shook his head. "I cannot tell, but that is where they went."

I tapped Tavis's shoulder. "How 'bout it, troop?"

"What if it's not a road?"

"Then we're probably going to sink this Charger like a U-boat."

"I'd rather not do that."

I raised the collar on my coat and tugged down my hat. "Then we leave it where it's more likely to be damaged and walk."

He shook his head. "I'm not leaving this unit."

Henry gestured toward the supposed road. "That, too, is a choice."

Without warning, and I guess to show us that he was also ten feet tall and bulletproof, the kid spun the wheel and hit the gas. The big motor on the Dodge leapt at the opportunity and literally pounced into the tracks of the pickup, only to sink with a muffled thump like the plumping of four very large pillows.

I leaned forward between them and looked at the Bear. "What'd that sound like to you?"

He pursed his lips. "That we are, beyond even the slightest shadow of a doubt, stuck."

Tavis threw the cruiser in reverse and stomped on the accelerator before either of us could advise him against it. The Charger spun its wheels and, if possible, dug itself in deeper. "Shit." He turned to look at us.

"Looks like we walk after all."

"Shit."

Henry pushed open his door and climbed out. "My sentiments exactly."

"You want to open the door for me? There aren't any inside handles back here."

Tavis got out on the other side and trudged back up to the road. "Shit." He stood there and looked both ways. "I have no idea where we are."

Henry looked around with me and then pointed toward something hanging in the fog. "Is that a sign?"

The patrolman walked toward it and slapped the pole with his hand, whereupon the majority of the snow slid off on top of him. "Shit." He shook most of it off and then looked up and read the sign. "Oh, more than shit."

I stooped and shone my flashlight on the tracks, which illuminated a few drips of coolant in the snow. "What?"

"It's 16."

"Meaning?"

Zipping up his duty parka, he walked back toward us. "We're between the main roads leading to either Rapid City or Custer." He looked around at the twenty feet that were visible. "Probably somewhere in Custer State Park."

"I guess we're lucky he didn't go to Mount Rushmore." I joined the young man. "Are there any structures around? Lodges they may be trying to get to?"

"There are a few—Blue Bell and Legion Lake Lodges maybe, but I'm not sure where they are in this soup." He quickly added, "I've only been here once when I was a teenager, and we stayed at the State Game Lodge. I remember it because there was a photograph of Grace Coolidge holding a raccoon and she was a looker."

"A raccoon?"

"Yeah, it was the summer White House and she had this pet raccoon. I thought that was kind of weird, right?"

I glanced at Henry, who shook his head and then nodded toward the two depressions leading into the whiteout. "We better get moving before the tracks fill in." Henry and I took a few steps in that direction, but I noticed the kid wasn't following, so I stopped and turned to look at him. "You coming?"

He shook his head. "I told you, I'm not leaving this vehicle."

The Bear's voice sounded from out of the wall of white, muffled by the frozen condensation. "I do not think anyone is going to be able to take it without a tandem of tow trucks."

I stood there for a moment longer and then turned and followed the Bear. "Call the HPs and tell them where we are, would you?"

"Right." I could hear him crunch toward the cruiser but then stop. "Hold on; let me get them on the radio and then get the keys."

It was slow going; I was monkey in the middle with the Cheyenne Nation ahead and the puffing patrolman behind me.

"How far can they get?"

It was as if our voices were being struck by the tiny particles of snow and then steadfastly driven to the ground. Personally, I didn't feel like talking, but the kid was nervous so I tried to make an effort. "Hard to say, but he's got four-wheel drive. If there's a road around here he's got a better chance, but I'm betting that he's going to get stuck just like we did, or his radiator will drain out and he'll burn up the engine."

We huffed along for a while in silence, but then he spoke again. "Do you think the other guy is dangerous?"

"I don't know—either dangerous or stupid or both."

"Why's that?"

I pulled up, and he almost ran into me. "Would you be out here doing this without the right gear, if you had any choice?"

"No."

"Smart boy." I started off again but couldn't see the Bear, and I was getting worried that he was outpacing us to the point of leaving us behind, so I doubled up on my efforts. Out of the corner of my eye, I could almost make out something moving alongside, but it disappeared.

I squeezed my eyes together and then quickly opened them but couldn't see anything this time. I stared into the frozen fog, but the more I looked the more unsure I became. Off to my right, there was something dark outlined in the curtains of white gloom. Whatever it was, it must've moved fast to get ahead of us again. I didn't have any worries that it was Willie, the mystery man, or Roberta because human beings couldn't be that quick in snow that deep.

The kid's voice came up from immediately behind me. "Something wrong?"

"No, nothing."

I kept moving and scanned the area to my right but, responding to some kind of movement, I pivoted to the left and suddenly it materialized again. "What the hell . . ."

As soon as I spoke, the apparition disappeared.

Tavis was behind me and seemed spooked. "Hey, did you hear something?"

I stopped, and he caught up; now we were both looking outward in circles, like prey. "No, but I thought I saw something. Why, what did you hear?"

"Um . . . breathing."

"Breathing?"

"Right."

I stared at the path ahead. "We better catch up with Henry; I don't want him coming up on those three alone."

There was a thought that wavered in and out of my mind like the shadows in the snow, a déjà vu that reminded me of my time in the Bighorn Mountains a few years past and again when I'd been stalking some convicts in that same region only six months ago—it was not a welcome thought.

I was watching carefully as we moved on with more conviction, but there were no more shades in the claustrophobic storm. The kid had dropped directly behind me, and I listened to him breathe and sigh. "I bet you wish you'd never stumbled onto us back in Deadwood."

His voice sounded remarkably cheery. "Are you kidding? Other than the odd biker fight, this is the biggest adventure I've had since I've been on the force." Then he sighed again.

There was a little edge in my voice. "Why do you keep making that sound?"

"I'm not." He glanced around, but his eyes came back to mine. "I thought that was you."

There was a noise directly behind us.

Tavis stepped in closer to me. "Do you think it's your buddy?"

"No, not from that direction."

The patrolman edged in even closer, looking behind us. "Maybe he got lost."

"He doesn't get lost."

"Ever?"

"Ever."

It was quiet all of a sudden, and the only sound was our breathing and the snow crunching as Tavis adjusted his weight. "Maybe he—"

"Sssh." Something exhaled to my left. "Well, whatever or whoever it is, it's moving around out there in this storm at a pretty amazing speed."

"A horse, maybe? Or a mountain lion?"

"No, whatever this is, it knows what it's doing in deep snow and mountain lions don't make that kind of noise." I turned and started off. "C'mon, let's get going before we—" There was another sigh, this one directly in front of me that came with what looked like the exhaust from a steam train. I pulled up and stopped and took a step back, almost standing on Tavis's feet.

"Hey—"

"Be still—whatever it is it's in the trail right in front of us."

"Maybe it's a tree."

"That would mean the truck drove over it; besides, trees don't breathe." I leaned forward, but it looked like a rock, white with fissures and cracks running through it, darker than the snow, but not by much. It breathed out, twin billows that drove the flakes floating in the air like a double blast of a breathing shotgun. "It's a buffalo, and I think there are more than one."

As I whispered, a low plaintive noise emanated from my right that was answered by a snort from the animal in front of me. I slowly turned my head and could now see two more massive things to my left that swung their heads and regarded us— four, no counting the rest.

Having once roamed the grasslands of America in herds estimated at sixty to seventy-five million, the American bison became nearly extinct in the nineteenth century after being hunted and slaughtered relentlessly. Approaching twelve feet in length, six feet at the shoulder, and weighing well over two thousand pounds, the buffalo is the largest mammal on the North American continent. With the ability to fight grizzly bears, mountain lions, and entire packs of wolves to a standstill, they fear nothing. And because they're capable of reaching speeds of forty miles an hour, your percentages of being attacked by a buffalo in the national parks are three times greater than any other animal.

Tavis whispered, "There's a herd here in Custer State Park, a big one with more than a thousand of them, but they round them up and auction a bunch off in October."

"Including the bulls?"

"I don't know."

I sighed myself. "The bulls are bigger and meaner . . . I think we've stumbled into a herd of buffalo bulls, so don't put on your roller skates."

"What?"

"That was a joke."

"Oh. Right."

The one on the trail in front of us shook its head and came a step closer. I could see that it was the packed and melted snow on him that had made him appear to be made of rock, the snow and ice cracked revealing the dark coat underneath. He was close enough that I could see the horns and the broad, black nose that blew contrails into the snow around his barrel-sized hooves.

There was nothing we could do, and nowhere we could go. If we tried to back away or change direction it was likely that we'd just run into another of the shaggy behemoths—maybe a thousand of them.

The big bull took another step closer, bringing him within seven yards of us, but his eyesight, which wasn't so great in the best of conditions, was failing him in the still fast-falling snow and the fog.

"Should we draw our guns?"

I whispered out of the corner of my mouth. "No, the damn things have very thick skulls—all you'll do is piss them off or start a stampede and get us gored or trampled to death."

"So what do we do?"

"The hardest thing in the world—nothing." The bull took another step closer, stretching its neck out for that much more of a view and even going so far as to stamp a hoof. It was only a question of time, given the animal's natural curiosity, before he would eventually get close enough to realize that we were not part of the herd, and then all bets would be off.

I ignored my own advice and, humping my sheepskin coat onto my shoulders, I placed a boot forward and stamped it in the snow in order to convince him that we were buffalo, too.

The bull didn't move.

"What the heck are you doing?"

"It's what he did. Now, will you shut up, because I'm pretty sure he knows that buffalo don't talk."

I wondered where Henry was and then thought about Vic, safely ensconced at the Franklin Hotel in a bubble bath, but mostly I was just glad that neither of them were here to see me imitate a buffalo.

The real buffalo still didn't move and didn't seem to know what to make of my performance—hell, for all I knew I was asking him out to the buffalo prom, but as a rancher's son with a long history of dealing with large animals, I did know that when they get confused, they become dangerous.

I stopped moving, too.

Suddenly his head dropped, and I saw his tail lift and stick straight up.

There still wasn't anything to do; if I jumped out of the way the kid would get killed and I couldn't allow for that—the only other thing to do was to charge the buffalo myself.

All I wanted was to bluff him and not send all the others into a stampede that would leave us as bloody puddles in the snow, and I was just getting ready to make a bold and most likely foolish move when I heard a song lifted like the wind in a melody that was familiar.

"Oooh-Wahy-yo heeeey-yay-yoway, Wahy-ya-yo-ha, Wahy-yo-ho-way-ahway-ahway . . ."

The buffalo bull immediately pivoted to the right and then in a full circle to look at us again, shook its head, and turned its wide horns to the right and left—like us, unable to determine from where the song came.

It was silent for a beat, while the singer took a breath, but then he continued.

"Aho, hotoa'e! Netonesevehe? Netone'xovomohtahe? Eneseo'o . . . They are the foolish Ve'ho'e, the trickster people, and do not watch where they go."

The bull turned again, this time to the left, and waited.

"I am Nehoveoo Nahkohe, Hotametaneo'o of the Tsetsehestehese. Do you know me, big brother?"

The buffalo turned a bit more.

"We mean you no harm, and only wish to pass through this sacred place."

I watched as the buffalo bull's tail descended, and the muscles relaxed in the beast as he finally lowered his head and pawed at the ground again, this time in a disinterested manner, as if surprised to find snow on his buffet. Another moment passed, and he started off, up the slight grade to our right.

I sighed. "You still out there?"

"I am."

I still could not tell exactly where he was.

"Did I just see you attempting to imitate a buffalo?"

"You did."

"Do not quit your day job."

I buttoned my coat, flipped the collar back up, and started forward carefully with Tavis in tow. After a few steps I could see Henry in the pale gloom, a tall figure with a leather cloak moving in an imaginary breeze. "We lost you; where the heck did you go?"

He glanced at the buffalo—there were still a lot of them milling around—and whispered. "I was ahead of you when we walked into them; when I tried to double back they blocked my path. I was simply going to wait until they moved on, but then you started challenging the biggest one and I thought I should intercede."

I began whispering, too. "Challenging, is that what I was doing?"

"Yes."

I smiled. "I think I could've taken him."

The Cheyenne Nation did not look particularly impressed.

I kept my voice low. "Find the truck?"

"No, but the tracks continue toward the tree line."

Tavis broke in from behind me in a loud voice. "There's a tree line?"

The Bear looked at the patrolman and shushed him. "The buffalo are looking for shelter but must have gotten spooked when the truck drove through the herd." He glanced around at the hulking shapes. "They are just now settling down and getting their bearings, so be quiet."

I gestured with my chin. "Let's get going; I don't want to lose them."

Henry turned, and we started off, a little more carefully this time.

After a hundred yards or so, we started to climb, and I could make out a few small trees leading toward larger copses and eventually the tree line that Henry had found.

The Bear stopped, looked at the tracks, and then at what countryside was visible, all twenty feet of it. "This slope leads down into a canyon and I would suppose a creek, whereas the embankment to the right leads up to a ridge. If they are stupid, they went into the canyon, and if they are wise, they stayed with the ridge."

"If they took the canyon they aren't going far, so let's check the ridge."

He nodded and then frowned. "Unfortunate."

"Why is that?"

"It appears to be the same choice that the buffalo have made."

"Misery loves company." I could see at least a dozen of them in the immediate vicinity as I started after our Indian scout. "How many of these things do you suppose there are out here?"

"From the movement of the herd, I would say a couple hundred at least." He slowed as one of the bulls, tossing its head and huffing, tracked in front of us. "They are still very uneasy, and I am afraid that any movement or sound could set them off."

I nodded. "Just that much more of a reason to get to the tree line; if these monsters start charging around, I'd just as soon have a tree or two to put between us."

The Bear suddenly stopped and whispered, even quieter this time. "I can see the truck."

Bunching in close to Henry, I slipped my hand under my coat, pulled my .45 from the holster, and trailed it along my leg, watching as Tavis did the same with his Glock.

The Bear looked back at the two of us and shook his head. "Do not fire those weapons, unless it becomes absolutely necessary." He took a few more steps forward and then stopped again. "As near as I can tell, there is someone standing in the bed of the truck."

Of course, I couldn't see anything, but I was used to that in my dealings with the Cheyenne Nation's uncanny sensory abilities. "Do you think they've seen us?"

He watched the invisible landscape for a moment. "No."

"If I keep moving in this direction, I'll run into them?"

"Yes. This may take a while with the buffalo, so when you get to the truck, keep him talking." Without another word, Henry moved off to our left and gradually disappeared like a cipher.

"Where is he?"

I gestured for Tavis to follow. "Stick with me, troop, and don't fire that weapon until I tell you."

Another forty feet and even I could see the outline of the blue truck, and indeed, someone standing in the bed. "Look, we don't know that any of these individuals are dangerous, so let's just play it slow. Chances are, this guy just thinks a couple of crazies are after his friend and his friend's girl, and he's just try-ing to do the right thing."

He swallowed. "Is that what your twenty-five years of sher-iffing are telling you?"

"Not really, but there's gotta be a first time, right?" I looked at the kid and thought that I really didn't want to be shot in the back by the Glock .40 he was carrying. "Don't shoot anybody, okay? Especially me."

I turned, took another step, and lifted my voice just loud enough to be heard but hopefully not loud enough to spook the buffalo that surrounded us. "Hey Willie, how are you doing?"

A little distance away, one of the bulls turned to regard us.

The croupier moved toward the tailgate and yelled back at me, "I've got a gun!"

"Okay." I waited a few seconds, just to let the nearest buffalo know that we bore no ill intent. "Do you mind keeping your voice down a little? We're concerned that these buffalo might spook, and I'm sure that none of us want that." He didn't say anything, so I continued. "My name is Walt Longmire, and I'm

CRAIG JOHNSON

the sheriff of Absaroka County, Wyoming. I'm working on a missing persons case—"

"Whatta ya want?"

I watched as one of the bulls crossed between us, and I carefully took a few more steps to get a clearer view of the man. I could see that he was holding a rifle. "Well, this doesn't have much to do with you, but it has a lot to do with the other man and the woman who are with you."

There was a long pause before he spoke. "I don't got no woman with me."

I took a few more steps toward him. "Well then, the woman who *was* in your truck."

He gestured with the weapon. "That's close enough." He leaned a little forward. "Who's that with you?"

"Patrolman Tavis Bradley of the Deadwood Police Department." I held my free hand up. "The woman in the casino who was getting money from the ATM? We believe that she might be Roberta Payne, who went missing from Gillette, Wyoming, three months ago."

"I don't know no Roberta Payne." There was a long pause. "I don't know if I even believe you're a sheriff."

"If you let me get close enough I'll show you my badge, and Tavis here can show you a whole uniform, if you'd like."

His head turned as he glanced around. "Where's that big Indian guy?"

"He's not with us anymore—maybe he's with your friends?" An out-and-out lie, but it was all I could think of to say. I took another step and could see that there were two more people sitting in the truck. "Look, we just want to talk to you about the woman—"

"He says that somebody's after her."

I took a breath, just to let him know that he'd slipped up. "So, they are with you?"

He gestured with the rifle again. "I'm just telling you what he said before. Now, turn around and head back out of here before I make you sorry you followed me."

"What's your friend's name?"

"Go away."

I figured I'd put my cards on the table, so to speak. "Willie, you know I can't do that. I'm trying to find this woman for her mother, who doesn't know where she is or what happened to her. Now, if she doesn't want to go back there that's her business, but I need to speak with her and make sure she's all right and that there's nothing illegal going on."

He didn't move, not a muscle as near as I could see, and it was as if he were some kind of black cardboard cutout in a cheap community play, until the man in the cab raised the barrel of a pistol and aimed it at Willie and I heard a woman scream, "No!"

10

Willie fell forward, and another round passed through the collar of my sheepskin coat, grazed off my neck like a vengeful hornet, and yanked me sideways. I immediately raised my Colt.

I'm pretty sure that one of the buffalo rammed smack into the truck. Huge, wooly animals were shooting off in every direction as I turned to yell at Tavis to stay with me, but the young patrolman, clutching his side, with the Glock next to him and a lot of blood sprayed across the white hillside, was lying in the snow.

I grabbed him. "C'mon, we've got to get out of here."

"He shot me!" He tried to pull away. "I swear to God, he shot me!"

Pulling the kid up onto my left shoulder, keeping the .45 aimed on the truck, I staggered forward with buffalo galloping around us like cue balls looking for a good strike. One brushed extremely close, and I fell with the kid but scrambled up, dragging him by his arm as he screamed.

Another bull was hurtling at us, and I could see that we weren't going to make it, so I threw myself on top of Tavis in an attempt to shield him. He screamed again as my weight hit him, and I felt one of the hooves graze across the back of my head, the heavy, warm breath of the animal blowing down on us.

I lay there for a second more and then holstered my Colt, figuring it was about as useful as a peashooter in a shooting gallery, and pushed off again, this time grabbing Tavis by the front of his jacket. It was about then that I heard the truck start up and the billowing exhaust blew back at us from the twin tailpipes.

Lurching after it, my hand glanced off the tailgate, and I could see the card dealer lying in the bed, and the woman in the cab screamed, "Deke, don't!"

There were two people in the truck—the man whom I assumed was named Deke spinning the steering wheel, and the woman whom I believed to be Roberta Payne staring back at us with a look of horror on her face.

I slipped to the ground, the reverse lights flickered on for a second, but then the thing peeled out in the same direction it had been heading, spinning snow in my face and ice on all the rest of me.

Spotting a copse of evergreens to my left, I dragged the kid and pushed some of the branches away so that we could get close to the trunks and shelter ourselves from the charging herd that surrounded us.

I settled him on the ground but felt the branches cave in as one of the animals must've come a little too close to the tree. "Get the hell out of here, there's only room for two!" I fell backward onto Tavis, turned, and kicked at the thing to keep it away. The buffalo yanked its head around, stripping the branches in a cloud of needles that peppered the two of us, and I thought for some reason that maybe he might respond to a cattle call, so I started yelling, "Yaaaaaaah, yaaaaaaah—get out of here! Yaaaaaaah, yaaaaaaah!"

The bull, obviously having been herded in the State Park Roundup, recognized the call and immediately turned his big head and bounded away.

I sat there, stunned that my ploy had worked, and then rolled over, taking the flashlight from Tavis's duty belt to study him. He looked pale. "How are you doing, troop?"

He didn't say anything, but he wheezed and his chin trembled.

I rolled him to the right and could see the wound in his side, the blood saturating the bottom of his jacket. "This is going to hurt, but I'm only going to have to do it once." I unzipped his coat and then trussed him up using my bandana as a bandage to quell the blood loss. "You all right?"

He nodded.

"I've got to go out there and look for Henry, okay?" He nodded again. "I won't leave you, but I've got to make sure he's all right and bring him back here if he isn't." I glanced down at the kid with blood all over him. "We'll take you to the hospital over in Custer and get you squared away. You'll be okay."

He nodded again but still didn't say anything.

I stood and became aware of something warm and slick on the side of my head. I reached up and felt the spot where the buffalo must have kicked me and noticed blood on my glove that must have been dripping from the wound on my neck. I reset my hat, wiped my glove on my pants, and pushed through the evergreen canopy out into the open.

It was the middle of the night, and I was surrounded by buffalo in a blizzard with a stuck cruiser and as far as I knew no available cover for miles around—good going, Sheriff.

I trudged in the direction where the truck had been, pretty

sure that the Bear must've been close to the thing when everything had all gone to hell.

The buffalo appeared to have calmed down as I found the spot where the truck had been sitting. I bent and picked up the kid's Glock and then glanced around but could see no sign of my friend. A sense of dread began overtaking me—what if he was out here, unconscious or hurt and unable to call out, what if he'd been killed?

"Walt."

I turned with the flashlight and the .40 and could see the outline of what looked like a giant crow, the long black wings attempting to wrap close to his body, but ruffled and twisting ever so slightly in the wind. "You all right?"

He grew closer, and I could see that he was moving with a little trouble. "As well as can be expected—who was the idiot that fired first?"

"I assume it was the man named Deke—the woman in the truck yelled his name when they took off."

He nodded as he drew up next to me, and I noticed he held his side with one hand.

"You're hurt?"

"My back. I was attempting to negotiate my way around a particularly cantankerous bull when the shot went off. I got out of the way, but his horn caught my coat and we went for a ride."

"You should've done my imitation."

"There was not much time for interpretive dance." He grunted a laugh but then regretted it. He poked a finger at my neck, where a little blood had saturated the sheepskin. "You are hit?"

"Not bad, but it grazed me and got the kid."

He pursed his lips. "Where is he?"

"Under a tree over here—shot through a few ribs it looks like, but he's breathing okay, so it didn't get his lungs." We both stood there, looking at our boots. "His legs work, and you can get him back to the cruiser. I would imagine that the South Dakota Highway Patrol will already be there and they might have information on this Willie character, but also make sure they check out Roberta Payne and the mystery man, Deke."

"And what are you going to do?" I was still looking at my boots as he studied me. "You have no supplies, no gear, not even the proper footwear."

"I'll take the duty belt off Tavis, and you can take this." I handed him the Glock. "I'm just going to follow them. They'll probably come out on a road, and I'll be waiting for a ride, but if they get stuck or wreck that thing . . ." I reached out with my left and gently laid a hand on his shoulder. "That kid is hurt, and somebody's going to have to get him out of here."

He made a face. "I can track better than you with my eyes closed."

"I think I can follow a pickup truck; besides, you're hurt."

He cocked his head, studying first my neck and then the blood on the side of my face. "So are you."

My arm was aching, which must have been some sort of reaction to the bullet that had grazed my neck, and so was my head, but I decided to withhold those thoughts. "Not as bad as you, and anyway, it's my job."

He looked at the tracks leading toward the ridge and handed me his cell phone. "You need to be careful, this is an unpredictable situation—the worst kind."

I gestured weakly toward the tree where Tavis was hidden. "Get him some help, and I'll call you when I find anything."

He shook his head. "Where, exactly, is Vic?"

I converted my grimace into a clearing of my throat. "Room two thirteen at the Franklin Hotel, right across from the casino. I'm betting she's asleep," I added. "You can have my bed."

"What if she is in it?"

"Then you get the sofa and Dog." I started toward the trees and was already weary at the thought of traipsing through the snowbanks all night. "C'mon, I'll help you with him." I paused and looked at him. "When you get back to the cruiser, radio Emil Fredriksen—as soon as he finds out one of his own caught a bullet, he's going to want this Deke fellow's head, and other portions of his anatomy, I'm thinking."

My head was giving my neck a run for its money as I adjusted Tavis's duty belt to the first hole, took a deep breath, and studied the tire tracks, the only thing visible in the whiteout. As I'd suspected, they had followed the ridge and skirted the tree line before heading down a slight incline that flattened and opened up into an expanse of white.

Slipping in my boots, I continued down the grade until I could hear the muffled sound of rushing water, most likely under ice. Keeping the water to my left, I continued following the tracks and suddenly felt firmer ground underneath, almost as if it were paved. Pretty soon I could hear the heels of my boots clicking on the surface, and I was sure I was walking on a road, although I still couldn't see more than fifteen feet ahead.

I could feel a lump rising where I had been kicked by the buffalo. It didn't seem as though it was bleeding, but it ached like mad and wasn't feeling any better with me probing at it. I adjusted my hat a little forward so that the band didn't rest on the wound, and, since my neck was cold, I pulled up the collar of my coat and buttoned it tight, standing there for a moment feeling light-headed and weak.

The truck tracks were the only ones on the road, and I hoped they'd stay that way. I also figured that by now Deke would have become Black Hills Public Enemy Number One, and there were probably a dozen or so HPs out here prowling about like the buffalo, looking for somebody to hook. I just hoped it wasn't accidentally me.

The snow was getting deep again, and I couldn't feel the surface of the road any more, the drifts filling the area in with swales that started making the going a little rougher and forcing me into a few of the reflector poles.

It hadn't been high plains cold until now. I squinted my eyes to clear them, but it was as though my mind was trying to go on down the road without me. My teeth were beginning to chatter and my hands and feet were becoming numb as I clomped along, the mantle of snow I had acquired probably making me appear more and more like one of the buffalo.

I trudged across a bridge and as I yawned, trying to stretch my jaw in an attempt to get rid of the ache in my head and the one in my neck, I thought about what had happened back on the ridge. What had Willie been doing with Roberta Payne and why was she living in Deadwood, siphoning money from her own account? Where did the Deke character come in? Why did he shoot Willie? None of it made any sense, but until I got back to civilization and the backstory, my job was to find the woman.

I rounded a corner, looked up, and saw a large structure on a hillside near a giant cottonwood with bark like stripped bone, and I stopped to place a hand on it for a brief rest, but discovered my right arm was numb.

Using my left, I pulled my arm up and looked at the glove and the inside of the cuff where blood had coagulated and frozen. I would have thought the wound would have stopped bleeding by now, but as I half turned and looked back at the trail of red I'd left on the roadway slowly being erased by the snow, I suddenly felt a little woozy.

There was a sound to my left, and I could see another buffalo standing near the creek. He ambled up the rise into the falling snow, but when he got even with the tree, he stopped, turned his great head, and stared at me—he was completely white. At first I thought it was just the snow covering him, but from only a couple of yards away, I could see that under the frost his fur was indeed white.

We stood there looking at each other, but when I blinked he had completely disappeared. I blinked again and took a few more breaths, but he was gone. Thinking he had climbed the hill, I turned back toward the lodge and allowed my eyes to adjust— there was no white buffalo, but there was the back end of a dark-colored pickup truck.

Standing there huffing my breath through my mouth like the great beast, I tried to make sure I was seeing what I was seeing, but the image, though swimming, remained the same. Pulling off my left glove with a leather fingertip between my teeth, I unsnapped my Colt from the holster.

I moved forward and leveled the sights on the vehicle, which was parked in front of a rock retainer wall. There, lying in the truck with the majority of his blood having drained into its snowy bed, was Willie.

Reaching out, I placed a few fingers alongside his throat, but there was no pulse—and the rifle was gone.

I slipped up to the side of the vehicle and blinked to keep the ice from my eyes. Resting the Colt on the top of the truck, I got the Maglite from Tavis's duty belt and switched it on with my good hand to study the interior of the pickup. Most of the window was frosted over, but there was nobody inside—the keys were gone, but the hood was warm, so they must've not been here for that long.

Remembering Henry's cell phone, I holstered the flashlight and pulled the device from the inside pocket of my coat and looked at the bars, having become something of a master in searching for a signal in the Bighorn Mountains last spring. There weren't any bars, but I tried it anyway and dialed 911, holding the device to my ear but hearing nothing.

Tucking the phone back in my pocket and picking up my sidearm again, I glanced left and right while rubbing my arm to see if I could get some feeling back and finally saw a set of stairs composed of the same rock as the wall. Keeping my left-handed aim on the dark areas of overhang above, I negotiated the steps and noted a red sign to the left that read STATE GAME LODGE, ESTABLISHED 1920.

I took a breath and sighed; I suppose if you were going to hole up, you might as well do it in the swankiest place in the 71,000-acre park. If South Dakota was like Wyoming, however, the historic heritage lodges were closed in the depths of winter, while it was the newer, more insulated buildings that remained open.

The spacious porch was filled to the railings with snow, but there were footprints where two people had passed up the steps, and it looked as if someone had kicked open the door. Stepping to the left, I pressed the barrel of my Colt against the wooden surface and slowly pushed it wide, the hinges creaking like a crypt.

There were no lights on, but I could see wet prints on the dark, hardwood floors where the two people had crossed to the left, past the registration desk to the stairs that led to the second floor. I stared longingly at the phone deck with its multiple lines and buttons and wondered if it was working, figuring that was my next move; I just had to work up the energy to get there.

There was a fireplace to my right and a doorway to a hall that turned left and disappeared into the bowels of the massive lodge. Every surface gleamed, even in the dark, and the sheets over the furniture looked like ghosts taking a leisurely rest before a haunting.

I staggered a little entering the place, stumbled into a large wingback chair, and just stood there looking at my blood dripping onto the floor and remembering what Lucian had said about moving to New Mexico and how it was a bad idea because you could bleed to death. I felt cold, and it seemed like the entire right side of my body was numb—that, and there was a ringing in my ears that I couldn't seem to shake.

A voice called out to me from a distance, almost as if the person speaking might've been outside. "Oh my goodness; you scared me to death!"

Wheeling from the back of the chair, I crashed into the partially closed door, causing it to slam, and I raised my sidearm toward a brunette woman with deep-set eyes who was standing on the stair landing—she was holding a fully lit candelabra in one hand and a raccoon in the other.

I held the .45 on her and the raccoon until she raised her

eyebrows in an imperial fashion and spoke in an authoritarian voice. "Do you need help, young man?" I slumped there staring at her, and I assume she thought I was deaf because she sat the candelabra on the newel post and began signing to me with her free hand.

Entranced by those movements, I simply stood there looking at her but finally lowered my sidearm. "I'm sorry, I'm . . ." I tried to stand up straight, but my head ached and my neck hurt, so I just stayed there, leaning against the chair. "I'm chasing someone."

She dropped her hand to pet the raccoon and glanced past me to look through the Venetian shades that were partially open. "In this weather, and with a gun?"

"Evidently, I am."

"Then I can see why they are attempting to evade you."

I swallowed, fighting the swells of confusion that kept lapping against my consciousness. "I'm a sheriff."

She proceeded the rest of the way down the steps onto the Persian carpet. She was tall and wearing a cloche hat, with lips compressed in consternation. "You don't look very well—are you ill?"

"No, I—"

"Perhaps you should come in and have a seat by the fire?"

"There isn't any . . ." I looked around and noticed something orange flickering off the heavy beveled glass of the French doors to my right, and I turned to see a robust stack of logs burning merrily away in the hearth.

". . . Fire."

She walked past me. "It gets cold in the winters after all the help has gone, so I've become quite proficient at making and tending the hearth." She jostled the raccoon that had nuzzled her armpit and grasped her wrist with its tiny paws. "Rebecca here gets cold, but I can't imagine why, with the wonderful collegiate coat she's got."

I smiled, trying to be gregarious. "Spoiled."

She laughed a wonderful laugh, like music from a bygone era. "Not spoiled—pampered."

I wiped the cold sweat from my forehead with the back of my working hand. "You . . . you're in charge of the place?"

"For quite some time now." She gestured to me. "Come, sit."

I shook my head and immediately felt even worse. "I really should be finding these people." I took a deep breath. "Would you mind if I use your phone?"

"You're welcome to it, if you can figure it out. I've never had any luck with the contraption."

I nodded, smiled at her again, and turned toward the registration desk. "I'm not too good with . . ." The phone that had been there when I'd entered wasn't there any longer; instead there was a patch panel attached to the wall and an old Roman-pillar-style phone with an earpiece hanging from it.

". . . Phones."

She extended a fingernail and aimed it toward the wall. "It has to do with the apparatus of plugs, but I didn't ever have to do that type of thing myself, so I haven't learned." She grinned a vivacious smile. "Spoiled, I suppose you would say."

"I need to find these people."

"So you said." She picked up the candelabra. "Are you sure you wouldn't like something to eat first, especially since there's someone in the dining room who is waiting to see you."

"No, I . . . What?" Summoning my energies, I looked around and noticed that the sheets were no longer covering the furniture.

She breezed by me to the left, where wet boot prints led around the stairwell through a doorway. She turned, the light from the candles illuminating only one side of her lean and handsome face. "Shall we follow?"

I straightened, ignoring my arm, and raised the .45 up past my face. "Maybe you should let me go first?"

"As you wish." I stumbled forward, catching myself on the doorjamb as she watched me, and I was entranced by the reflection of her eyes. "Young man?"

"Yep?"

"Have you been drinking?"

"No, ma'am, but I sure wish I had."

She put the candelabra on the newel post again and crossed back to the desk, where she reached up and opened a recessed cabinet above her head.

"What are you doing?"

"Rebecca is very handy." She looked at the critter, who had climbed into the cabinet near the ceiling. "The bottle, Rebecca, if you will." A moment later the masked bandit reappeared with a small pint. "Thank you, dear." She extended a hand and the raccoon climbed out and jumped into the safety of her arms.

She turned and walked back over, holding the bottle out to me.

"What's this?"

"Medicine." She gestured for me to take it. "At least that's what the night watchman calls it."

I stuffed my Colt under my arm and took it, the label aged yellow with a discolored ribbon and stamped seal wrapped near the cork. I read the label aloud. "OLD TAYLOR, OVER 16 SUMMERS OLD." I tried to hand it back to her. "I don't think I should have this."

She fluttered a hand at me. "Nonsense, just a taste. I've been doing it for years."

Sighing, I opened the bottle and took a swig—it was like a little spark at the back of my throat, flavorful and delicate with no aftertaste of the alcohol. "It's good." I took another.

She reached up and spirited it away; corking it as she crossed, she handed it back to the raccoon. "All the way in the back, Rebecca. We mustn't let the night watchman know what we've been up to."

I had to admit that the whiskey had helped. I nodded my thanks and started through the doorway, but the raccoon reached up and touched the saturated sleeve of my coat, first looking at it and then up at me with her little bandit face, the only sound the drip of something on the gleaming floor.

The Pheasant Room, at least that's what the plaque above the door proudly proclaimed, was darkly paneled and appropriately full of pheasants, with a taxidermied bird forever captured in midflight adorning each panel above the mission-style windows that seemed to allow light in from the outside.

Maybe it was clearing up.

I stepped onto the wide-planked pine floor and glanced around the room at the dozen or so perfectly set tables—pristine, white tablecloths, sparkling silver, china adorned with those same pheasants, shining goblets, and fresh flowers in cut crystal vases finishing the arrangements.

Seemed a little over the top for a lodge that was closed up for the winter, but it surely was not my place to complain.

There was music playing from an old baby grand piano

tucked in the corner—I was a fan of boogie-woogie and knew it was Sophie Tucker, the last of the red-hot mamas—but there was no one seated on the bench. The keys depressed and the song was unmistakable; I just wondered who was really playing and singing. I wandered over to the instrument and touched the keys with the barrel of my Colt, but the second the metal touched the ivory, the music stopped.

I stood there for a few seconds but then felt as though someone was seated at one of the dining room tables, so I turned very slowly and raised my .45, but lowered it to my side as I became aware that there was nothing there.

Taking a deep breath, I noticed that the tracks I had been following led past the sideboard behind me.

I stepped to my left but stumbled into one of the chairs and was suddenly overcome with a sense of fatigue and cold again. Standing there for a few minutes more, I decided I'd better get a move on and started to the left out of the dining room where I found myself once again in the front lobby which was now empty. I started up the steps—the creaking of the treads was obnoxiously loud, even with the carpet covering them, but I finally reached a small landing one flight up that overlooked the dining room where I'd just been.

There were two stairwells that led to the second floor, but with my head really swimming now, I took the nearest one. The hallway was tastefully appointed with period wallpaper and antique fixtures that glowed and flickered. Gaslights. Odd.

I slowly checked each door, starting with the nearest one, but they were all locked except the one on the far end. There were two letters on that door that read KC, and I carefully pushed it open to reveal a very nice room with a highboy, a four-poster bed, and a small writing desk. I glanced down at the desk and could see a brass plaque that read CALVIN COOLIDGE'S WRITING DESK, 1927, WHEN THE GAME LODGE WAS USED AS THE SUMMER WHITE HOUSE.

I wiped the sweat from my forehead and backed out of the room, checking the knobs on all the doors in the hallway again, but none of them moved. I decided, as tired as I was, to go downstairs and wait until I heard something.

They went up, they would eventually have to come down.

Using the banister the entire way, I stopped at the mezzanine to look into the dining room and this time I could see that there was a hulking figure seated at one of the tables; he turned his huge double head and looked up at me.

I was glad to see him.

I seated myself opposite him—well, more like I had my legs collapse beneath me, making me park my butt on the chair and rest the Colt in my lap, which I covered with a napkin to honor the formality evident in the dining room. Leaning back in the chair, I rested my numb arm on my lap—the thing felt like it weighed a ton—and could hear the dripping noise that sounded like Chinese water torture but more delicate.

"Virgil White Buffalo."

He continued to smile, cocking his and the great bear's head sideways to look at me, the familiar smell of campfire, sage, and cedar wafting off him as it usually did. "How are you, lawman?"

"Tired."

His head and the one on the headdress straightened, and he leaned in, his face above mine with an expression of concern. "And hurt again, I see."

I looked at him. "Seems like I always am when I see you."

He placed an elbow on the table and tucked a fist under his

chin, the all-black eyes searing into me with a ferociously flashing intelligence. "Maybe that is when you need me."

I searched the opening leading toward the reception area but couldn't see the woman with the raccoon. "You bring friends with you from the Camp of the Dead?"

He grinned. "She is married to one of the great white fathers and talks a great deal, but her power is strong here." He folded his arms on the table, and I was entranced by the intricate beadwork on his shirtsleeves. "There are many who wish to see you, but I bring only those who are necessary."

"People say you don't exist."

He brushed my words away with a wave of one of his huge, scarred hands, the silver ring with the circling turquoise and coral wolves pacing around the wedding finger. "We are finite beings; how can we understand the infinite? It is enough for me that I have these opportunities to visit with you and perhaps assist you in the trials of this life."

I tried to bring my hand up to check to see if that same ring that I'd taken from his hand in the Bighorns was still on the chain around my neck, but it wouldn't work. "How did you get your ring back?"

He turned it on his finger in an absentminded manner, once again brushing away my words with a batting of his hand. "What are you going to do?"

"About what?"

"The ones you are hunting."

I took a deep breath and tried to keep my head level. "Wait. Sometimes it's the best thing you can do."

"Who taught you that?"

I laughed. "My father; he was a very good hunter."

His chin came forward in an attempt to catch my wandering attention. "He taught you lots of things?"

"Yes, he did."

"Remember those things." His eyes narrowed, and the blackness in them was boundless. "Above all else, you must remember the things your father taught you in the next few moments." He reached across and straightened me on my chair. "But right now, tell me, in this life, lawman—at what places have you stood and seen the good?"

I smiled a sickly grin. "Too many to count." I slouched toward the table again. "But you were right about the bad things, too . . ."

He studied me. "I am here to tell you they are not over."

I suddenly felt the scouring wing tips all along the insides of my lungs. "What do you mean?"

"Prepare yourself." He sighed deeply. "You will stand and see the bad. The dead will rise and the blind will see."

There was a noise from the landing.

I looked up slowly and saw that Roberta Payne and the man, Deke, who was holding a hunting rifle loosely aimed at me and a handgun on her, were standing at the top of the stairs.

I coughed. "Roberta? Nice to meet you, ma'am. And Deke—Deke, that's your name, right? Howdy."

"You know, I've made a study of you."

I did my best to adjust my eyes. "Is that so?"

"Yeah, I'm pretty careful about who I go up against—I like having an edge." He gestured toward my arm. "For example, I know that you're right-handed and that hand looks pretty useless."

"Something tells me you don't really make a living as a gambler."

"Oh, I do back in Vegas . . . But I also do a little work on the side."

"Why are you here?"

"To do what I do best." He smiled and leaned on the railing. "Killing two birds with one stone. I figured it'd be tougher than this—killing you." He let that one settle in before speaking again, and the only other sound was the delicate Chinese water torture. "I didn't suspect I could just waltz down those steps and find you in here all alone, talking to yourself like a loony."

I shifted my eyes across the table, but the legendary Crow Indian, as I'd suspected, was missing. I turned my head a little, just to make sure, but there was no one there—no woman, no raccoon, no pheasants, no table settings, and even the piano was gone.

"Did you know there was a contract out on you?"

"Me?"

"Yeah, somebody pretty important wants you dead." He smiled and gestured toward Roberta. "She was Willie's, but I took her when I found out about the trust and because I could. Besides, I figured if I kept pumping the money, it would be you that came after her." He paused and added, "Well, the guy that hired me did."

"Who was that?"

"Yeah, I heard you talking to someone and figured there must be more than one of you down here; I figured maybe the Indian."

I continued to stare around at the now unfamiliar room. "I . . . I guess I got distracted."

"I guess you did, and it's going to cost you, but first I've got some business to attend to." And with that, he raised the small-caliber pistol and fired it into the back of Roberta Payne's head.

The woman bounced off the paneled divider between the stairs and then her head and a shoulder went through the railing, and she hung there with an arm hanging straight out.

I lurched from behind the table, and it tipped and fell over as I brought my .45 from under the missing napkin and leveled it at him just as he fired the rifle at me.

The shot tore through the hem of my coat and grazed my leg as seven of my 230-grain rounds blew eleven inches into his chest at 835 feet per second, bouncing him off the back wall hard enough to push him through the railing to land on top of me.

We fell backward onto another table, collapsing it with a tremendous crash of splintering wood and dead weight.

He lay there on my chest, his face turned to mine. "You didn't study me well enough." His eyes flickered, and I knew he could still hear me. "My father was left-handed; all his guns were left-handed stocks and grips, so he taught me how to shoot with both hands." His eyes dimmed and clouded and I looked past him to where Roberta stared at me, a rivulet of blood trailing down her alabaster arm through her upturned hand where it pooled and dripped through her fingers onto the polished hardwood floor like Chinese water torture.

"It's my one saving . . ." My head lolled to the side, and I stared at a framed black-and-white photograph on the wall, a large portrait of the woman from the lobby, in the same clothes, hat, and pensive, handsome expression. She was holding a raccoon. Just below it, on the frame, was a small brass plaque that read FIRST LADY, MRS. COOLIDGE—1927.

". . . Grace."

11

They were sustained visions and with having dreamed them so recently, it was easy to summon them and try to make sense of the message they carried. I'd lain there on the dining room floor of the State Game Lodge, the images growing more and more real as the cold crept into me in tiny waves.

In the dream it was night and I was standing just below a frozen ridge surrounded by herds of white buffalo that had circled and watched me, their breath filling the air and warming it. The snow was deep, and from the tracks I'd left, I could see that I had come a long way; my legs were tired, and the cuffs of snow piled up against my thighs had stopped me in my tracks.

At the top of the ridge, at a place I couldn't seem to reach, a man was standing with his back to me, a tall man, broad, with silver hair to his waist. Independent of the conditions, he was in his shirtsleeves and stood there singing—a Cheyenne song.

I pushed off, but my boots slipped in the deep snow and I fell, finally satisfied, along with the buffalo, to just hear his song.

It was a clear night, the kind that freezes the air in your lungs with the advantage of nothing standing between your upturned face and the glittering cold of those pinpricks in the endless darkness, the wash of stars constructing the hanging road as it arced toward the Camp of the Dead.

The man had stopped singing and now half turned toward me, speaking from the side of his mouth. "You will stand and see the bad; the dead shall rise, and the blind will see."

It was a voice I'd heard before, even though I couldn't exactly place it. "Virgil?"

He half-turned toward me, his profile sharp, and I could see that it was not Virgil White Buffalo as he studied me from the corner of one eye. "You are bleeding?"

I looked down at the blood saturating the snow around me and the neck and chest of my sheepskin coat. "Um, yep . . . I think I am."

He turned toward me fully and walked easily over the deep snow, kneeling and taking my face in his hands, and I could see that he had no eyes. The empty sockets looked almost as if they shot through his head like twin telescopes magnifying the black, infinite space with only a few aberrant sparks of warmth from dying stars. "Good, we can use the humidity."

"I tracked the blood, and there you were, under the pile of bodies."

I started and looked at the both of them staring holes into me—as if I didn't already have enough extras. I watched my IVs drip and took a sip of my orange juice to gather myself until the quiet in the room became unbearable. "The two of you let me sleep away an entire day?"

My undersheriff's voice keened with an edge. "You were shot near the external jugular alongside the sternocleidomastoid muscle in your neck—the doctor said it was a slow-bleed, but without the pressure from your coat you might've bled to death."

Uncomfortably ensconced at the Custer Regional Hospital's ICU, I picked at my robe and lifted the neckline to try and examine my bandages. I'd had a look at the results of the wound when they'd cut the sheepskin coat off me as though it were a monstrous scab. My wife and daughter had bought the jacket almost twenty-five years ago; it was one of the most treasured items in my life, and now it was lying in the bottom of some hospital dumpster. "Why did my arm stop working?"

"Blast effect to the brachial plexus that's the nerve takeoff for your right arm, kind of like a karate chop." Vic slapped my hand near the IVs.

"Ouch . . ."

"I hope it hurts, I hope it hurts bad enough that you never do crazy shit like this again, but you and I both know that the only kind of hurt that will do that is a good dose of death." She stared at me, and I guess she felt a little sorry for the last statement because she added, "Speaking of which, how come you left a round in your gun?"

I glanced at Henry and shrugged, quickly developing the ability to do it with one shoulder. "We're in Indian Country—always save the last one for yourself."

The Cheyenne Nation nodded. "Prudent."

I thought about telling them about Virgil and Grace Coolidge, but they thought I was crazy enough, so I let it slide. "To be honest, I think I was just worn out from pulling the trigger." I looked back at Vic. "For the sake of the alliterative—Deke's dead?"

"Definitively."

"Too bad—I was really enjoying our conversation and was looking forward to talking with him some more."

She gestured toward my arm. "And letting him shoot at you again for the privilege?"

"When we spoke, he said he was from Las Vegas."

"Was this a long and wide-reaching conversation?"

"Long enough of one for him to shoot Roberta Payne and for me to shoot him seven times."

She shook her head. "Well, he was from Las Vegas most recently."

"You got a file on him?"

She glanced down at the folder in her lap. "A large one."

"And Roberta Payne?"

She looked up at me. "Dead, and it was textbook—the twenty-two enters the skull but doesn't have the power to escape and bounces around in there like a Mixmaster."

I looked back at the Bear. "How's Tavis?"

"He is fine, no damage to any internal organs." Henry straightened his coat and grimaced. "And Emil Fredriksen wants to drag Deke out from the morgue, prop him up on the nearest snowbank, and use him for target practice."

"And your back?"

He grunted and then squinted his eyes. "Spasms. They gave me muscle relaxers and a brace. They said to take the medication before it starts really hurting."

"Then you should have started taking it around 1967." I turned back to my undersheriff. "Did you talk to the casino people?"

"I did. The cocktail waitress, name tag *Star*, said that Willie was secretive about his personal life, but that there was a woman and maybe some other stuff; then the casino manager said that this Deke character showed up and the dynamic changed and the three of them were in there pretty much every night."

"Roberta was never alone?"

"Never as far as they knew."

I thought about it. "Deke said that he had taken Roberta from Willie—they all had to stay somewhere."

The Bear leaned back in his chair and glanced at Vic. "I am assuming you obtained an address for the now-deceased croupier, Willie?"

"Yeah, he's got, or should I say had, a crummy little house with an attic apartment."

"You have an address?"

"I do."

I started to pull the covers away. "Then what are we waiting for?"

The Cheyenne Nation placed a hand on my good arm. "There are four, very large, armed South Dakota highway patrolmen outside the door, who are charged with the responsibility of keeping you here until you have spoken with Special Agent Pivic of the Division of Criminal Investigation."

Bruce Pivic held a wide and long reputation in western law enforcement from his days as a fraud investigator with the South Dakota attorney general's office; meticulous and unrelenting, Bruce could boast of having taken down a lieutenant governor, a prosecuting attorney, and a mob boss who had attempted to launder money through an illegal cattle processing plant. I had sat in on one of Pivic's intense debriefings and swore that before I ever had to sit through another, I would gladly pound eight-penny nails into my head.

I glanced toward the door and scratched where the IV went into my arm. "How big are the troopers?"

"Not as big as you, but they outnumber us, and I think they can call for more, if need be."

Vic smiled. "Your hospital reputation precedes you."

"Hell." I sat back against my pillows and studied the two of them. "All right then, read me the Deke report."

Vic flipped open the folder and then held her hand out, palm up, in expectation of the two bits.

"I'll get you later." I looked around. "Where are my pants anyway?"

She raised an eyebrow, and the tarnished gold glistened. "That's three dollars and fifty cents you owe me." She looked down and began reading. "Deke 'Big Daddy' Delgatos is originally from San Diego, California, with a long list of run-ins, run-outs, and rundowns with the law. He did a seven spot in High Desert State Prison for kicking a guy's head in in a bar fight in Inglewood. While inside, it seems he got all giddy with the AWSFB." She glanced at Henry. "That would be Aryan White Supremacy Founding Brotherhood, or as my fed buddies over in Gangs and Bikers like to call them, Assholes With Shit For Brains."

He nodded. "Catchy."

"Delgatos continued perfecting his craft in Susanville, where he supposedly killed another inmate and had a hand in shanking a guard. Through overcrowding, they let him out, and Big Daddy got himself a brand-new bag in Vegas, where he falsified just about everything about himself down to his DNA and got a license with the Gaming Commission to push cards." She looked up. "Now, here's the funny part—Deke had a condo, a brand-new Corvette, a powerboat, a winter home in Puerto Vallarta . . ." She shook her head. "Either this scumbag's stackin' the deck, or he's got a little something on the side, right?"

I sat my empty juice cup on the tray. "He intimated to me he was a hit man—not exactly somebody you find on Craigslist."

Vic put a finger in to hold her place and closed the folder.

"She goes missing for three months and suddenly turns up two hours away?" She shook her head. "You think he was stupid enough to just keep siphoning money out of Roberta's account until you showed up?"

"He said he figured that I would be the one—I think he was counting on it."

Henry poured more juice into my plastic cup and drank it. "And why shoot her in front of you?"

"Just happened that way. I think she had become a liability; she certainly didn't know what was coming."

Henry nodded again. "She went to extraordinary lengths to stay with him."

"He was a hit man, and if I was making a guess, and this is a guess, mind you, I'm betting he told her he'd kill everybody she knew if she tried to escape."

The door to my room opened slowly and a smiling man with a gray mustache peered around it; seeing he wasn't disturbing anything, he entered, carrying a large stack of file folders. "Walter, I thought we had an agreement—you can kill as many people as you like in Wyoming but not here in South Dakota."

"Hi, Bruce." I watched as he pulled up a chair and sat by my bed. "Anyway, he tried to kill me first."

He tapped the stack of papers with a forefinger. "Is that how I should start the formal report?"

"You bet."

He glanced at Henry. "Mr. Bear."

"Mr. Pivic."

He smiled at Vic. "Have we met?"

My undersheriff turned on her most ingratiating Mediterranean smile. "Moretti, Victoria Moretti."

He carefully took her hand and actually kissed it. "Ah, you're Italian?"

"Udine, the Friuli–Venezia Giulia region."

He smiled and then smoothed his mustache and stared at the stack of papers in his lap. "Walter, this is going to take a while—"

"Bruce, I'd love to help you, but my neck hurts and my head hurts and I can feel a high-octane nap coming on."

He watched me, his mustache twitching under his nose. "I just spoke with the head nurse, and she said now would be an opportune time to speak with you."

I sighed and faked a yawn.

He stood. "I'll go speak with her again and arrange a more convenient time."

As he went out, I gave him a little wave and looked at a door to my right. "Where does that one go?"

Vic made a face and then covered it with her hand.

The Bear, figuring our odds, looked toward it. "An adjacent room, which connects to a short hallway leading to the fire escape."

I nodded. "Now the big question."

Vic spoke through her fingers. "Who hired him?"

I smiled at her. "Where are my pants?"

Lead, South Dakota, is pronounced as is the verb, not as the malleable heavy metal. Once home to one of the most productive gold mines in the Western Hemisphere, Lead now leads the area in twisting, straight-up-and-down, kiss-your-own-butt roads, currently covered with a foot or so of snow.

The address we had for Willie was half a duplex jammed into a hillside leading up to the city proper. There were side streets and a frontage road that ran parallel with Main, but even though it had stopped snowing for a bit, they were so choked with the stuff that there wasn't anywhere to park.

Vic slipped the Bullet in behind a covered Cadillac with Nevada plates and turned off the ignition, as I reached back with my good arm and ruffled Dog's ears. "Must be the place." I slipped off my seat belt shoulder harness, which was killing me anyway, pulled an emergency blanket from under the seat, and draped it over my shoulders.

Vic glanced at my outfit.

"What?"

"We're really going to do a forced entry into a place with you looking like that?"

"Like what?"

"A fluorescent homeless person."

I adjusted the optic-orange blanket. "It's all I've got until I can go shopping, all right?"

"You also don't have a weapon."

"Hop out, and I'll get my standby." I flipped down the center console with my good arm, opened it, and pulled out the holstered Colt Walker.

"You're kidding."

I palmed it in my hand. "Well, until the SDDCI gives me mine back, this one will have to do." I slung the vintage holster over my left shoulder, and we started slogging around the house, tramping a path toward the steps in the foot-deep snow.

Henry took the lead with me following and Vic bringing up the rear. "You know, we could go by the National Guard and get an antitank gun that we could tow around on the back of your truck; that way we could just set up out there in the street and lob shells in on people."

I ignored her and followed the Bear up the steps to the first landing, where we changed direction and found ourselves standing at a peeling, glass-panel door with tinfoil taped over the window.

The Cheyenne Nation drew the frightening knife that he always carried from the small of his back, the one with the stag handle and turquoise bear paw inset in the bone, and pointed at the foil with the blade. "In my experience, this is rarely a good sign."

"I agree." I reached out to check the door and was unsurprised that it was locked. "Kick it?"

Henry, always the thinking-man's felon, slid the blade of the knife between the door and the jamb, popping the bolt and gently swinging the door wide.

"I could have done that if I had had a knife."

He and Vic ignored me as they looked inside.

There was a large room with an efficiency kitchen which looked as if it had been assembled from appliances cannibalized from an RV, with a hallway where there were a couple of closed doors—I figured a bedroom and a bath. The Bear was about to enter when a tan and white pit bull appeared at the other side of the kitchen.

"You first."

He turned to look at me, and probably would have responded, except for being interrupted by the low, guttural growl emitting from the dog just before it launched itself toward us.

The Cheyenne Nation quickly slammed the door as we listened to the pit bull clawing and barking. He finally turned and looked at me. "Any other bright ideas?"

"You still have those muscle relaxers?"

We sat in my truck and waited about twenty minutes. I'd bought a container of hamburger at the convenience store at the bottom of the hill and had inserted one pill in each of two meatballs that I had made; Henry had climbed the stairs and had quickly tossed one of the balls onto the kitchen floor of the apartment. Not wanting to overdose the dog, I'd kept the other in reserve. The rest of the burger Dog consumed in a second or less.

"You think that did it?"

The Bear nodded. "Considering it is approximately a quarter of my weight, I would say yes."

Making sure I had the extra meatball safely ensconced in a paper cup in my shirt pocket, I pushed open the door of the truck, which was covered in a blanket of snow that was handy in keeping us out of sight of the myriad South Dakota law enforcement that was likely out prowling the Black Hills in search of us.

Quietly, we made our way up the stairwell again and paused at the door, where Vic pulled her Glock.

She ignored the look I gave her. "Fuck you, I'm not getting bit by Michael Vick in there."

Henry looked back at the two of us and then turned the knob, pushing the door open about four inches.

We listened, but there was no sound.

Carefully, he pushed it open a little farther and then stuck his head in, an act of bravery of which I was not so sure I was capable. He continued inside, and we followed.

The kitchen was as we'd left it, but the meatball was gone. "He ate it."

We all entered, and I shut the door behind us.

"C'mon." I could see a room in the front where an old table lamp without a shade, sitting on a cardboard box, had been left on. There was a plastic chair—one of those mass-produced ones that everyone bought from Kmart—beside the box, and a small flat-screen TV and DVD player, which were on the floor, along with a stack of homemade discs with dates written on them. Nothing else.

Vic opened a door to our right, Glock first, and closed it behind her. Henry and I looked at each other, but after a moment, there was a flush. Seconds later the door opened, and she shrugged. "Bathroom. Sorry, had to go."

Henry peeled off to the only other room in the place— what I assumed was the bedroom—as Vic kneeled, picked up one of the discs, and inserted it into the player. "Let's see what's on . . ."

"Walter?"

I turned and walked over to the doorway where the Bear lingered.

The pit bull, thankfully still breathing, was lying next to the bed. I stooped beside what was a she and ran my hand over her side and her eyes flickered, but nothing more. Other than the dog, there was a broken-down mattress and bedspring, yellowed sheets, a thin blanket, and lumpy pillows.

I straightened up and noticed that there were ankle manacles lying with their ends open, secured to eyelet bolts in the floor at all four corners of the bed, along with another plastic chair pulled up to a card table with a Canon video camera sitting on a short tripod. "Oh, boy."

The Bear took a few more steps in and kicked at a box on the floor.

"What's that?"

He pulled back a flap and peered in. "You do not want to know."

Vic appeared in the doorway with all of the DVDs in her hand, a strange cell phone, and a disgusted look on her face.

"Bad?"

"Worse than bad." She shuffled through them. "The ones dated within the last week especially—they are all Roberta Payne. Willie was an amateur in comparison to Delgatos." Her face came up. "Can we go kill them again, please?"

"We can petition Emil—I'm betting he'd be up for that. At the moment, however, they stay in the morgue."

"Maybe so, but Delgatos is still getting texts." The Bear and I joined her at the door. "Five minutes ago, somebody asked him if the job was done."

"Text them back." I watched as she pushed a button and waited. " 'Need to meet.' "

She typed in the message with her thumbs, and it buzzed in her hands immediately. She looked at it. "It's mystery guest number one and he's asking if she's dead."

"Tell him yes, need to talk."

She typed it in. "Looks like the area code is 702."

The Cheyenne Nation was the first to come up with it. "Las Vegas. Of course, that does not mean he is physically in Las Vegas."

The phone buzzed again, and Vic read the message. " 'Is the sheriff dead?' " She looked at me. "Who the fuck in Las Vegas wants you dead besides the dead guy?"

"I don't know." I felt the stubble on my face. "Tell him yes."

She typed it, we waited, and after a few seconds it buzzed. " 'You're sure?' "

"I'm sure."

She typed, and we waited. "He says you're lying." Almost immediately, it buzzed again, and Vic read, " 'Like your Indian friend, Deke never used contractions when messaging.' "

"Well, hell."

The phone buzzed, and she read, " 'Sheriff?' " The phone buzzed again. " 'You are a very durable individual.' "

"We need to meet."

Vic typed, and the response came back. " 'That would not be to my advantage.' "

"Are the other women safe?"

Vic read the response. " 'I'm not concerned with the women.' "

"This has to stop."

Vic typed and then read. " 'Not necessarily. Ever heard of Asociación Punto Muerto?' "

We all looked at each other. "Nope."

Vic looked up from the phone, a sickly smile on her face, and read the final text. "He says, 'You will.' "

12

"We got you a computer and a girlfriend."

Henry laid the pit bull next to Dougherty's desk on the dog bed we had purchased. "What's wrong with her?"

Vic put the computer, the cell phone, and the collection of discs on a stack of cardboard boxes. "She's got a substance abuse problem." She glanced around at the subterranean confines of the Campbell County Sheriff's Department. "Where's the Dick?"

Dougherty was still looking at the dog as he spoke. "He hasn't gotten back from Evanston yet. The sheriff came down and told me that he expected him around noon."

I nodded. "Good to know."

He studied the bandage on my neck. "What happened to you?"

"Got too close to a buffalo." I gestured toward Henry. "Him, too."

"Remind me to never go to South Dakota with you guys."

I moved a Gagliano's pizza box and put it with about twenty others on top of a nearby shelf and sat in the chair opposite him. "You guys must be single-handedly keeping the pizza joints in Gillette in business." I pointed at the computer and discs. "That stuff is from the dead guy . . ."

He adjusted a folder under his arm. "What dead guy?"

"The one who had Roberta Payne."

"The woman from the Flying J? You found her?"

"We did." I glanced at Henry and Vic, finally dropping my eyes to my lap. "She's dead."

His shoulders slumped, and he seemed to fall back into the chair even though he didn't physically move. "My God."

"I'm afraid so. Deke 'Big Daddy' Delgatos killed her."

"Who is Deke 'Big Daddy' Delgatos?"

Henry grunted. "One of the dead guys. It is complicated."

"Nothing on Linda Schaffer?"

"Not yet." I took a deep breath and explained, telling him about Deadwood, Custer State Park, and most of what had taken place at the State Game Lodge. "Evidently he was a hired killer, among other things." I leaned forward. "First, I need you to find out who with the Las Vegas number the last text on that cell phone came from, then crack the computer open and get as much information out of it as you can."

Dougherty nodded. "Will do."

I gestured toward the file under his arm. "Got anything for us, troop?"

He sat forward and petted the dog, even going so far as to put his face down near to hers. He straightened her ear, and she sighed—match made in heaven. "Almost nothing."

Vic leaned against the chain-link divider that kept the Campbell County files from making a break for it. "Almost?"

He sat back and handed the file to her. "I found the last reports that Gerald Holman didn't file."

I interrupted. "Where did you find those?"

He tapped a handle on one of the drawers in the desk. "Locked up in here."

My undersheriff opened the folder. "Holman did another series of interviews in Arrosa; so what's the big deal?"

The patrolman returned to petting the dog. "Look at the date."

She glanced at the report. "Yeah, so?"

"It's the day he killed himself."

Her eyes returned to the file. "Oh . . ."

Dougherty stopped petting the dog but left his hand on her head. "How do you do an entire afternoon of interviews and then check into the Wrangler Motel and blow your brains out?"

Vic handed me the folder. "More important, what do you find out in those interviews that leads you to do it?" Inconclusive, the file simply read that Holman had made stops at Dirty Shirley's, the Sixteen Tons Bar, and another location identified as *undisclosed* in or near Arrosa. I looked up at the group. "What other location is there, undisclosed or otherwise, in or near the town of Arrosa?"

Vic posited, "Private home?"

I thought about it. "There's an elementary school and a post office . . ."

Henry studied me. "Nothing else in the immediate vicinity?"

"No."

He smiled. "This should make things easier."

Vic's cell phone rang, and she pulled it out, looking at it and then to me.

"What?"

"It's your daughter." I didn't say anything. "The pregnant one." They all looked at me. "You answer it."

"Chickenshit." She held the phone up to her ear. "Hello?" She nodded her head. "Yeah, well he's around here somewhere . . ." She listened again. "Right." She listened some more, and I could hear the edges of my daughter's voice traveling through the airwaves from the City of Brotherly Love. "Yeah, yeah, he told me that . . ." She was silent for a moment. "It is a case."

I glanced at the Cheyenne Nation and then cleared my throat and held a hand out for the phone.

Vic shot eye-torpedoes at me and continued to speak, glancing at the Bear. "Yeah, he's around, too—helping your dad." There was another, longer pause. "I'll tell him." She pulled the phone from her ear and looked at it. "And a see you later alligator to you, too."

"What?" I slumped in my chair. "Please tell me she hasn't had the baby."

She deposited the phone into her other hand and pointed at me with it. "No, but they are inducing her tomorrow, and there are three tickets for the noon flight to Philadelphia at the Gillette Airport for you, yon Standing Bear, and me, and I was informed, and I quote, that if we were not on that flight then we could all kiss good-bye any thoughts of ever seeing the grandchild within our collective lifetimes."

"Gimme the phone." She did, but I handed it back to her. "Could you dial it for me, please?" She did, without comment, and gave it back to me.

It barely rang once, and my very angry daughter was on the line. "Chickenshit."

"Boy howdy."

"Daddy, I want you on that plane at noon."

"Cady—"

"I'm not kidding."

I took a deep breath, like I always did when facing total annihilation. "I know, it's just that there are some details that I'm going to have to take care of—"

"For who? A guy you never met who killed himself? Some women who've been missing for months now?"

"Well, there have been some developments—"

"I. Don't. Care. I, your only child, am about to have a baby, who is likely to be your only grandchild. My mother is dead, and it is your solemn and imperative duty to be here with me."

Feeling that a little privacy might be a nice addition to the conversation, I took the phone and started up the steps. "Cady, I promise I'm coming—"

"When? A week from now, a month?"

I turned the corner, walked down the hallway, pushed the outside door open, and stood on the elevated stoop behind the Campbell County Sheriff's Department. I leaned on the metal railing and watched the interminable snow continue to fall. "I just need a little more time to—"

"No, don't go on autopilot here."

"Honey—"

"Don't honey me." She took a moment to calm herself, and I could see her threading her long fingers through her auburn hair, and I was glad there were more than two thousand miles between us. "I knew this was what you were going to do to me . . . ."

I stopped myself from saying honey. "I'm not doing this to you; it's just that I have responsibilities."

"Your responsibilities are to me and the baby."

"I know that." I looked out into the parking lot and could see Dog looking at me through the windshield, fogging the glass with his breath. "Lucian is over here, along with Dog."

"Dog is also on the noon flight—I paid them more so he could go on the small plane—but you need to get a crate."

I pushed my hat back on my head and clutched my forehead. Of course, the Greatest Legal Mind of Our Time had gotten Dog a ticket. I smiled in spite of myself. "What about Lucian?"

"Uncle Lucian can drive the Bullet back to Durant so you don't have to pay for parking."

"We have free parking at all the airports in Wyoming, or did you forget?"

She shrieked, finally having had enough of me. "I don't care!" She was fighting valiantly, but I could hear the breaks in her voice as she spoke, and then there was a small sob. "Daddy, I'm afraid. Okay? They say there are complications and . . . I need you here for this."

I nodded into the phone, Virgil's words of disaster on the horizons of my life echoing in my head. "Right."

"Please."

"How much time do I have?"

It was silent on the line for a moment. "I knew you were going to do this—"

"When is the last moment I can leave?"

She literally growled into the phone. "You are not really booked on the noon flight."

That stalled me out, and I was unsure of what to say next, finally deciding on something original. "I'm not?"

"No, I just switched you to the eleven-forty-two P.M. one to Denver and then the red-eye to Philadelphia where you will get in a paid car and come to the maternity unit of Pennsylvania Hospital on Eighth Street by eight tomorrow morning—thus sayeth the Greatest Legal Mind of Our Time." There was a pause. "I know you."

I breathed a laugh and shook my head at my wet boots. "Yep, you do."

"Eleven forty-two tonight, got it?"

"Yep."

"That leaves you fourteen hours and forty-two minutes to break the big case."

"No pressure."

She pressed her advantage. "Now take Henry, Vic, and Dog to the airport so that they can catch their flight. Don't forget the crate."

"You said."

"Move."

"Yep." I quickly added. "Hey . . . ?"

"Yes?"

I tucked that tiny phone in tight, hoping she could feel me. "I love you, and everything's going to be all right."

She sniffed. "You promise?"

I took a deep breath and whispered the truest words I'd ever uttered. "That, I do."

Walking down the steps, I found Vic and Henry standing by the stairwell, and I was surprised to find the pit bull sitting next to Dougherty, with her head on his knee.

"Does she have a name?"

"Probably, but the guy that knew it is dead so make one up and let her get used to it." Vic shrugged. "She'll get fully awake here in a few hours but be careful because she might be a little wonky and she doesn't care for strangers."

I reached into my pocket and handed him a cellophane-wrapped orb. "If she gets really anxious, give her another magic meatball."

As we trooped out the door and up the stairs, Vic added, "Personally, I'd let her wake up and then post her at the door here for when the Dick gets back."

Dougherty called out after her. "Wait, she's aggressive?"

My undersheriff yelled back down the stairwell, "She's a bitch, after all; between her and the Dick—my money's on her."

As we trudged to the Bullet, I explained our newfound travel plans.

Vic buckled herself in the center seat as Henry closed the door and turned to look at me. "You should get on the plane with us; we can deal with this shit when we get back."

I started my truck and headed for the Kmart again. "I'll follow orders and grab the red-eye. I don't suspect I'll have much luck, but I'll follow up on what we've got so far."

The Bear leaned forward, making forceful eye contact with me. "You had better not miss that flight at eleven forty-two tonight."

I nodded. "Did Corbin get anything off of the computer or the phone?"

Vic shrugged. "Nothing on the computer yet, but he did get the information from the server on the phones; both of them are registered to Deke Delgatos, paid for by Deke Delgatos—"

"How about a listing of most recent calls?"

She slapped a Post-it onto my dash with the number engraved in the paper and a period that looked like it might've been made with an ice pick. "One number; the pay phone at the Sixteen Tons Bar."

After getting the crate for Dog, some toiletries and essentials along with a couple of carry-ons for Vic and Henry, and a cheap work jacket and pair of gloves for me, I pulled the Bullet to a stop as we found ourselves on the wrong side of another of those mile-long coal trains. "It's somebody in Arrosa."

"Yes."

Listening to the claxon warning and the thundering momentum of steel wheels, I glanced at him. "Any ideas?"

Both he and Vic shot me a look and then continued watching the passing train. "We have not met any of them to have any ideas."

"Oh, right." We watched the train together. Fingering the vents, I turned up the heat. "So Roberta Payne was sold to Willie and then taken by Deke."

Vic fingered the Post-it fluttering in the hot air. "I really called the folks over at First Interstate and guess what?"

Henry's voice rumbled. "The money from the trust ran out."

Vic nodded. "Yeah." She turned and looked straight at me. "You said he said he'd been studying you."

"Yep, but maybe that had to do with something else." I thought about it some more. "Maybe Roberta Payne was thrown in as a bonus, but after the money ran out—"

Henry asked, "Which would mean that the other women are alive?"

"Possibly."

"For what reason?"

"The answer to that might be on those DVDs."

Vic added, "You don't suppose you're pinning your hopes on that because it might mean that the victims are still alive?"

Both of them were looking at me now. "Maybe."

"Just remember that the cock crows at eleven forty-two post meridian, which does not mean that you arrive at the airport at eleven forty-one."

"Yep."

He glanced up at the sky. "Not to worry."

Henry had called the airport to check to make sure the airplanes were still flying, but although the snow had been steady, it hadn't been windy, so the plows were able to keep up, and flights were leaving relatively on time—but it was more than that. He breathed in through his mouth, and I watched him taste the frigid air. "It will stop snowing before midnight."

I watched as the Cheyenne Nation lifted the large crate onto his shoulder like it was a shoebox and led Dog into the airport on the leather leash, his back apparently feeling better.

My undersheriff stepped into my view as I sat there in the driver's seat. "Hey . . ." She glanced back and watched as Henry and Dog negotiated with the skycap at the outside desk, something I'd never seen at a Wyoming airport. "What are you going to do?"

I glanced at the Post-it, still stuck to my dash. "Just go over there again and poke around. That pay phone is outside the door of the bar, so I'm sure nobody's going to know who was using it or admit to it, but you never know."

She turned back to look at me and handed me her cell phone. "Take this. I gave the number to Dougherty so that if he found anything, he could get in touch with you."

I knew better than to fight. "Okay."

She studied me until I started to squirm. "Don't do anything stupid."

"Define stupid."

"Getting shot."

I popped the phone in my coat pocket and reached over and adjusted my arm sling. "Done that."

"Getting stabbed, getting punched, getting run over—or anything that might physically impair you any further."

"Right."

"Where the hell is Lucian?"

"Last I heard he was playing chess at the Wrangler Motel, but that was hours ago."

"You might want to find him and have him give you a ride back here to the airport."

"Right."

She reached over and pulled my face toward hers, the tarnished gold enveloping the world. "Walt, let's be clear about this. You are on somebody's hit list."

"We don't know—"

Her grip drew tighter. "A professional killer's list; just remember that."

"I will."

"And be on that plane at eleven forty-two or you won't have to worry about who's got a contract out on you."

"I promise."

"And make sure you don't stick your dick in a hornet's nest."

I nodded. "Something, I can assure you, I will endeavor to never do."

"Good, because I have plans for it." Her fingers dug into the back of my neck as she kissed me, her lips against mine as I gasped, breathing in her scent for the road. "By the way, happy New Year's."

I watched her walk into the airport with the two bags after Henry and Dog, and sat there, feeling like the loneliest man in the world. I thought about just parking my damn truck and running after them, but instead, I did what my daughter accused me of doing and put it on autopilot—I tugged the truck down into gear and pulled out.

The quickest way back to Arrosa was the interstate highway, but when I got to the on-ramp, the gate was down and an HP was sitting crossways, blocking the road. I peeled to the side and lowered my window, squinting into the stinging flakes. "What's up?"

The older trooper smiled at me. "Closed for business. How you doin', Walt?"

"Hey, Don. What's the weather report?"

"Shitty, with scattered shitty and more shittiness till sometime tonight."

"I've got to get a plane at midnight but first have to get over to Arrosa; any way you'd let me up on the big road?"

He shook his head. "Can't do it. They're plowing in tandem up there and they might push you into the guardrails."

I started rolling up my window. "Thanks anyway."

"Be careful with your radio, those old transponders down near there gave out; they're working on getting them going again, but I wouldn't count on my radio or cell phone if I was you."

"Thanks."

"Hey, I heard your daughter was having a baby?"

"That's it; rub it in." He gave me a quizzical look as I backed up and spun around one-handed, taking the surface roads to Boxelder and heading east, hoping that he and Henry were right that the weather would break before midnight—like eighteen minutes before midnight, to be exact.

There weren't very many cars on the road, and I made a little more time by cheating and jumping on the highway for the last few miles. As I slipped off the interstate, I thought about how I wouldn't make it to Philadelphia by tomorrow morning if I kept driving east and about all the players in this case and about how hard it was to keep a secret in a small town.

My shortcut turned out not to be such a great idea as I sat there watching another coal train pass by.

It can take three to four minutes for the average train, which weighs more than three thousand tons, to pass through a crossing. It takes a full mile or more for a train to stop; that's sixteen football fields; that's even after it's struck something. According to the Department of Transportation, the drivers of automobiles cause 94 percent of all grade-crossing accidents, and approximately every two hours in this country, a collision occurs between a train and either a pedestrian or a vehicle—that's twelve incidents a day. More people die in highway-rail crossings in the United States each year than in all commercial and general aviation crashes combined.

There was a honk from a horn behind me, and I glanced back to find a blue Volvo in my rearview—when I looked ahead, the train was long gone.

I pulled across the road into the parking lot of the Sixteen Tons with the Volvo staying close and was surprised to find a Campbell County Sheriff's undercover car sitting near the door.

Parking the Bullet, I watched as Connie Holman got out of the Volvo and jumped in the passenger side of my truck. "Sheriff."

"Ms. Holman."

"What are you doing?"

I glanced around. "I'm not sure I understand the question."

"I asked you to stop this investigation."

I cleared my throat and turned in the seat, the belt scraping my neck, the charge of pain making me wince. "Well, it's gotten a little more complicated."

She clutched her hands together, and I don't think it was the cold that caused her to do it. "You've got to stop this; you're destroying my family."

"In what way?"

She stared at me, her mouth opening to speak, but then she

shut it and climbed out of my truck, slamming the door behind her and climbing back in her car and driving away.

I cranked my hat down, started to zip up my faux Carhartt coat, but then stopped and draped it over my sling. I'm not quite sure why, maybe it was in light of the recent activities, but I thought about the big Colt Walker I had put back in the center console, hefted it from the holster, and slid it conveniently into the sling.

I sat there for a moment, looking at the brief shelter of the pay phone and the receiver hanging against the side of the steel building. There really wasn't anything tangible to tell me who it was that might've been involved, but I had some hunches—the kinds of things you couldn't really define but could most certainly feel.

I was about to get out of the truck when I felt something vibrating in my pocket along with some blaring rap tune that Vic had told me the name of along with the artist, but nothing I had committed to memory. I fished it out and answered it as quickly as I could, thankful I was alone. "Hello?"

"Sheriff, it's me, Corbin?"

"Hey, troop."

"I'm still working on the computer, but while I was doing it I did some research on that group you mentioned, Asociación Punto Muerto?"

"Yep?"

"Well, the information I got is sketchy, but it translates pretty much word for word and stands for the Dead Center Association; it's kind of an unofficial union for assassins and was started in South American prisons as a way for drug consortiums to get their contracts fulfilled, even if the hit man assigned to the job was killed or imprisoned. Once they assign a hitter for a job, there's a pecking order of associates that are responsible for ful-filling the hit if that individual should fail."

I sighed, thinking about the series of texts I'd received from the unknown person. "Oh, brother."

"It allows these hit men to charge more for their services, because the contracts are guaranteed." He was quiet for a few seconds. "Do you think this guy that you killed was one of them? Because if he was, that means there's probably somebody else coming for you, Sheriff."

I was tired, and this news didn't exactly pick me up. "Who knows? A lot of these types of associations from the prison systems tend to break down once the guys get back out into the real world. Anyway, it's not something that's going to keep me up nights."

"One of the signifying factors is a skull tattoo with roses in its eye sockets on a member's body, so you might want to get the authorities over in South Dakota to look for that on the decedent." I could hear him nodding on the other end of the phone. "I just thought it was something you should know." He paused. "And there's something else. When I was comparing the files between Holman and Harvey, there seem to be some discrepancies."

"Like what?"

"There's a Connie Holman—"

"The investigator's daughter?"

"Yeah, well, she's mentioned in one of the interviews, but Harvey appears to have omitted it."

I thought about that for a long time. "Thanks, troop." And then changed the subject. "How's your dog?"

His tone brightened. "She's better but tried to eat one of the corrections officers who came down here looking for payroll files."

"She's a little protective of her turf." I cracked open the door. "Call me if anything else pops up." I punched a button on the phone screen and looked at the image of my undersheriff in a bikini on a beach in what I assumed was Belize; I figured she'd left the selfie just for me.

I slid out of the truck and walked over to the phone, scooping up the handset and putting it to my ear where the operator advised me that if I'd like to make a call, I should hang up and try again. "The story of my life." I started to hang the thing up, but despite the cold or maybe because of it, there was a lingering scent in the plastic.

I headed for the door.

When I opened it I could sense a tension in the dim, smoky air and could see Lucian and Richard Harvey, of all people, seated at a table near the center of the room. I stood at the door, after having closed it behind me, and noticed the postman and the bartender having lunch—the gang being all here.

I cleared the cold from my voice and spoke. "Lucian?"

He turned his head a little but didn't take his eyes off the inspector. "Good thing you're here—I'm about to shoot this New Mexican."

My shoulders lost a little of the tension that had accumulated there. "Inspector?"

He stood. "I am truly pleased that you are here and that I don't have to babysit this cantankerous son of a bitch anymore."

"Who asked you to?" Lucian pointedly looked at me. "I got tired of playing chess with Haji and Sandy Sandburg sent this asshole over to give me a ride and we ended up here."

I pulled out a chair and sat, taking off my hat and motioning to the bartender for a cup of coffee, the wear and tear of the last couple of days finally settling on me.

Lucian stared at my sling, and I wondered if he noticed the

Colt Walker snuggled away in there. "What the hell happened to you?"

"Got shot by a fellow over in South Dakota."

"You shoot him back?"

"I did."

"You do a better job of it?"

The bartender, Pilano, arrived with my coffee, and I thought about sticking my face in it but settled for a sip. "Yep."

The old sheriff glanced at Harvey, just to let him know that some real Wyoming lawmen were on the case. "Have to do with Gerald Holman?"

"Maybe." I cut to the chase. "We discovered one of the missing women in Deadwood, but she was with this hit man, Deke Delgatos."

"Hit man?"

I nodded.

"Was?"

"He's dead, she's dead—he shot her and I, in turn, shot him."

"Lotta shootin' goin' on."

"Yep."

He studied my arm, my neck, and the lump at the side of my head. "You look like hell."

I sipped some more coffee. "I feel worse."

"What happened?"

"Buffalo and a few other assorted adventures."

Lucian raised an eyebrow, but Harvey interrupted the interrogation. "You think this Delgatos had something to do with why Gerald Holman killed himself?"

"Possibly. It appears he had control of the Payne woman."

Inspector Harvey's mouth hung open under his prodigious mustache. "How did you find that out?"

"Tracked the bank records in Roberta's name that had money being withdrawn from an ATM in Deadwood. Went over there and discovered a ménage à trois and a cell phone."

"What was the connection?"

I sipped my coffee. "You ever heard of the Dead Center Association?"

He stared at me, in a way I thought a little strange. "No."

I finished my coffee and noticed the bartender was quick to come over with the pot but that the postman stayed near the bar. "Me neither, but I'll tell you something I do know." I threw a thumb toward the door. "The only other recently dialed number on this killer's cell is the pay phone outside." I watched the bartender's hand shake as he refilled my mug, and then I raised my eyes to Lucian. "Hey old man, I was wondering if you could do me a favor and drop me off at the airport tonight around eleven?"

He nodded, studying me. "Are you planning on breaking this case before the New Year?"

I sipped my coffee and looked at the other three men in the room as I sat the mug on top of the ring it had made on the stained worn surface of the table, thereby freeing my hand. "Yep, I am."

13

Harvey's hand slowly dropped to his side as I skimmed my words across the surface of the table like the card that had floated on the cushion of air at the casino. "Hey, Richard . . . You don't have any tattoos, do you?"

He smiled a grin that was high and tight as he yanked the big .357 from his shoulder holster and pointed it at me precisely at the same time I leveled the long barrel of the Colt Walker across the table at him, both of us cocked and ready to shoot. We were both tall men with wide arm spreads, so the two revolvers stretched past each other. He looked down the barrel of the .44 and whistled. "Damn, did you find the grave of Wild Bill Hickok over there in Deadwood and dig up his gun?"

"South Dakota DCI's got my regular accompaniment."

He continued to smile. "Because of the dead guy?"

"Because of the dead guy."

Lucian leaned forward and looked back and forth between the two of us, finally resting his eyes on me. "What the hell are you two idiots doing?"

Harvey breathed a short laugh but kept his eyes on mine. "Seems to me you're kinda on a rampage, Sheriff."

I gestured, ever so slightly, with the Colt. "Gee, you think I'm done?"

His eyes stayed even with mine. "Not by a long shot."

"If you were actually a corrections officer in New Mexico, I find it hard to believe you never heard of Asociación Punto Muerto."

His eyebrows slowly crouched over the bridge of his substantial nose. "APM, the killers' union?"

"Yep."

"Well hell, I never heard of it in English."

Lucian swiveled his head, finally resting his attention on Harvey, and smoothly pulled his .38 out, shoving the barrel into the detective's ribs. "Buster, you better start coming forward with some of the correct answers, and that right soon."

I was mildly surprised and relieved at the New Mexican's response, mostly because it was what I would've said in like situation. "Why the hell is everyone in this room pointing a gun at me?"

"I think you know more about this subject than you've been letting on."

His eyes flicked to Lucian and then back to me. "You got any evidence along those lines?"

I nodded toward the big handgun he was still pointing at me. "Three hundred and fifty-seven thousandths of them."

He glanced at the pistol in his hand, slowly directed it away from me toward the ceiling, and then thumbed the hammer down, carefully resting it on the table. "Look, why don't we all calm down here?"

"Talk."

He aligned his mustache with a forefinger. "I might've got personally involved with the case."

I kept the Colt on him. "Do tell."

He made a pointed glance at my weapon and then Lucian's. "You fellows mind puttin' those damn things away?" He gestured toward the Walker in my hand. "Especially that one, since they have a tendency to go off kind of unexpected like."

I rolled the long barrel of the Walker up beside my face and lowered the hammer, setting it on the table in front of me. "There."

The detective glanced at Lucian's .38 still in his ribs, but the old sheriff's hand didn't waver. "The hell with you, mine goes off when I tell it to and you haven't said anything yet to convince me that it shouldn't." Lucian nudged him with the muzzle. "Gerald Holman was a friend of mine."

Harvey sighed in exasperation. "He was a friend of mine, too."

"Prove it."

Harvey laced his fingers and rested them in his lap. "The person I'm trying to protect is not involved with this."

"Okay."

"I did some things I maybe shouldn't have done—covered up some evidence and cleaned up a few files . . ."

Lucian nudged him again. "Hurry it up, you son of a bitch."

Harvey's head snapped around to the old sheriff. "Your buddy, your friend Gerald Holman, was dirty, you crotchety old bastard."

Lucian's face hardly moved when he replied. "The hell you say."

"He was cleaning up his messes, and things were starting to pile up against him so that he finally didn't have anywhere else to go but blow his brains out."

"Bullshit."

"It's the truth. He was suppressing evidence and rerouting the investigation so as to not draw attention to himself. I've got the files hidden away, but I'll be damned if I'm going to take the fall on this just because I'm trying to protect his name."

I interrupted. "Where are the files?"

"Back at the office."

I thumbed Vic's cell phone from my pocket. "Where in the office?"

Richard Harvey stared at me.

"Where in the office."

"In the bottom pizza box on the shelves as you come in from the stairwell."

Dougherty picked up on the first ring, and I told him where to look; he did and reported back. "It's the interviews all right— looks like much longer than the ones transcribed into the computer files."

"Read 'em and call me back." I tucked the phone in my pocket, gesturing for Lucian to lower his weapon. "It's all right, Dougherty's got the files."

The old sheriff didn't move. "Who's Dougherty?"

"The patrolman I borrowed from the Gillette PD." I glanced at the detective, his eyes widening just a touch. "You know him?"

"Yeah, isn't he the one that was fixated on Linda Schaffer?"

"Maybe." I took a deep breath and slowly let it out. "I've got just one question."

"There's a woman involved."

I sighed. "There usually is."

"But she doesn't have anything to do with this."

"If that's the case then why are you sitting here with my old boss's revolver in your side?"

He leaned back in his chair. "She—"

The sound of the weapon going off within the confines of the Sixteen Tons Bar was enough to turn your head and make you duck, which I did, and then immediately grabbed Lucian's gun hand and pulled it into the air along with him. "What the—"

"It wasn't me, damn it!"

We both looked at the detective as he clutched the lower part of his face, blood, tissue, and teeth scattering across the front of his shirt onto the table. He fell off his chair as another shot whizzed between us. I released my grip on Lucian, and he turned his .38 toward the bar.

I grabbed the Walker just as another round struck the table, sending splinters into the air, and I whirled in time to see the bartender attempting to take better aim. Lucian fired and hit the man in the upper right-hand quarter of his chest, spinning him around and throwing him into the bar-back with a crescendo of shattered glass before he slid to the floor.

Figuring I could count on the old sheriff to check his shot, I shoved the big Colt in my belt at my back and kneeled down by the wounded detective—the round had shattered his jaw but had exited through the other side. He was still clutching at the ghastly wound as I yanked a bandana from my back pocket and attempted to slide it beneath his fingers, the blood going everywhere.

He tried to speak as his eyes glazed over, and with the amount of blood in his mouth, I was afraid he might choke. "Don't try and talk; it didn't get your throat, so you're not going to bleed to death." I held the material against the side of his face.

"Hold on to this; he got your jaw. Keep your mouth shut and just lay there and try to not go into shock."

He blinked once, and then his eyes sharpened, followed by a curt nod.

I yanked my head up to look at Lucian, who had crossed to check on the man behind the bar. "Dead?"

The old sheriff nodded. "Or doin' a damned fine impersonation of it. How's the New Mexican?"

"Alive, but he's going to need some dental work. Take some of these bar towels and go over there and sit with him and keep him from going into shock. I'll get on the radio in his car and call in the troops."

I could've used the cell phone or the phone in the bar, but I figured by the time they got me patched through a 911 operator, I might as well have gone out and gotten on the detective's two-way. The snow which had covered the vehicles had just about stopped, but now there was a ground fog that obscured the landscape.

Whiteout. Like South Dakota. "Well, hell."

I stood there for a moment, feeling something out there in the blank, white parking lot—almost as if something was watching me. Ignoring the feeling, I walked over to the detective's cruiser and yanked the door open—it sounded like a glacier cleaving. I threw myself inside and turned the key, thanking the heavens that Harvey, like most Wyoming residents, had left it in the ignition.

I punched the mic and reported shots fired and an officer down at the Sixteen Tons Bar, whereupon the dispatcher asked me the location. "It's in Arrosa, about fifteen miles east of Gillette . . ." So much for speeding the process.

Static. "There are a number of communication towers down

in that area and with the weather conditions and the amount of responses we've got out it might be a while before they get there."

I keyed the mic again. "The officer is stabilized, but in pretty rough condition, so get us an EMT van and a couple of units as quickly as you can."

Static. "And who is this again?"

"Sheriff Walt Longmire of Absaroka County."

Static. "So you're not Campbell County personnel?"

"No, but Detective Richard Harvey is, and he's lying on the floor bleeding, hopefully not to death." I threw the mic against the dash and clumsily cut the ignition, figuring if I was hauling the detective into town I was going to do it in my truck, which had four-wheel drive.

Climbing out of the cruiser, I pushed at the bandage on my neck where I'd irritated it and stood there in the fog with the feeling of being watched overtaking me again. There was a breath of a breeze, and I looked across the parking lot where the fog had parted like a curtain and at the concrete-block building and the American flag that flapped feebly against its own pole, attempting to get my attention. I stood there for a moment longer and then charged into the bar.

Lucian was with the detective and was holding the side of his face with the towels. "Bartender's still dead, in case you were wondering."

"Lucian, wasn't the guy from the post office sitting on one of these stools before the shooting started?"

The old sheriff glanced around. "The horse's ass with the ponytail?"

"Yep."

He gave it a quick thought. "He was there earlier, but I don't remember him being in the place when the bartender shot Harvey here." He sighed. "You think he ran out before or when the shooting started?"

I stopped to pick up the detective's .357, undeterred by the bloody molar and chunk of jawbone lying beside it, and then moved toward the back door. "I'm not sure, but I intend to find out."

"What the hell do you want from me then?"

I gestured toward the wounded man. "How's he doing?"

Lucian looked down at the steady eyes peering up from the gory mess of a face. "He was trying to talk, but I told him to shut the hell up and wrapped those towels around his face along with a couple of sponges from the counter over there." He looked up at me. "You gotta hand it to these New Mexicans; they can bleed with the best of 'em."

I placed a hand on the door. "Help's on the way, but it may take a while with the ground fog out there. So collect as many teeth as you can and just try and keep him from bleeding to death."

"You goin' out there into the rain, sleet, and snow and gloom of night?"

"Late afternoon." I nodded. "The postman's the only one who can still talk, and he's not here and that speaks volumes."

"What do you want me to do when the troops arrive?"

I pushed the door open and stood there, waves of cold and bad feelings enveloping my exposed flesh. "Find me." I stepped out into the monochromatic landscape.

The postman's tracks traced to the left around his doomed office, the divots partially filled in but still visible. You couldn't even see the road for the frozen fog and the snow had started softly falling again—it was like walking into cotton batting, the flakes swallowing all sound.

I went around the building, almost tripping when I stubbed my boots on one of the covered parking curbs, and looked down at the area where the postman had evidently paused to watch me as I'd called in backup. That must've been the feeling I'd had.

It was possible that Rowan had just wanted to make himself scarce in a room full of flying bullets, but then why hadn't he returned? And why had he stood out here and studied me as I'd called in? I pulled the big Colt from the back of my pants and stuck it in my sling again, one gun possibly proving to not be enough.

The footprints led to the rear of the post office, where the back door hung open about eight inches.

I glanced at the only vehicle parked behind the building—a battered CJ 7 Jeep without a straight piece of sheet metal on it sat with a good eight inches of snow on the hood. I thought about checking for the keys or pulling the coil wire but figured the thing was derelict. I sidled up beside the back door of the building and gently swung it open with the barrel of the detective's .357—the storage room was empty.

Stepping inside, I made a quick sweep of the area, and then, dipping the Colt into the narrow aisleways and following the prints, worked my way down a couple of rows of eight-foot metal shelves.

There was a basket half overturned on the floor not unlike the one that the postman had given to me containing the collective mail of Jone Urrecha, so I nudged it over the rest of the way. It was empty, except for a sticker that had rolled up and was half stuck to its side. I stooped down and plucked it from the basket and read the typed address, a label redirecting mail for Linda Schaffer, the clerk from Kmart, to a box at this post office.

I stood and looked around at the mountains of paper ready to avalanche on me should I decide to start digging and wished I had Dougherty with me. It was just as I'd had that thought that the cell phone in my pocket started buzzing and I pulled the thing out and looked at it; Dougherty. I punched the button. "Hey, troop. I was just thinking about you . . ." There was no reply. "Dougherty?" There was still nothing. Evidently the reception was good enough to allow a call to go through, but not enough to retain it. I glanced around the post office, finally spotting a phone on a nearby desk. I picked up the receiver, satisfied with the dial tone, and punched in Corbin's cell number.

"Hello?"

"Dougherty, it's Walt Longmire."

"Yeah, I just called you."

"I know, the transponders down here are covered with ice and malfunctioning; nothing is working. Did you find something?"

"I've been going through those files and came across a transcription that wasn't in the computer, somebody else he talked to."

"Who?"

"A woman named Izzy—does that ring any bells?"

A faint alarm went off somewhere in the periphery of my head, but nothing I could place. "Izzy?"

"Yeah, Izzy. Evidently she was involved with the Dave Rowan guy in something that Holman seemed highly suspicious of."

I looked around, aware that I was still pursuing a felon. "Well, keep digging and get back to me."

As I hung up, I could still hear his voice. "How?"

Rowan had continued through a door into the commercial

area and around a counter where three P.O. boxes hung open, one with a key still hanging from the lock. There were wet boot prints there that trailed across the tile-covered floor and out the front.

As I pushed open the door into the silence of the outside, I saw that the tracks were much fresher and more defined, and that now there were two individuals walking. It looked as if they'd taken only one step out and then headed to the right, away from the bar toward the strip club and the scattered trailers belonging to the dancers.

There was a thundering noise growing louder to my left as I headed east on the frontage road, and all I hoped was that it wasn't a plow coming up from behind preparing to dump a few tons of snow on top of me. The sound became more familiar as it grew louder, and I turned my head in time to see the billowing vortex of snow being swept along behind another Burlington Northern Santa Fe. As it is with mountains making their own weather, the mile-long train drew its own along with it, clearing the road and the surrounding area as it carried millions of dollars' worth of not-so-hard fuel.

The pair of prints passed the trailers and angled into Dirty Shirley's parking lot, making a beeline for the back door where I'd first seen the bouncer. I tried it but it didn't budge, and then I thought about shooting the lock as they do on TV shows like *Steadfast Resolution*, but in reality, all that ever does is mess up the lock and not open the door.

Still thinking about that name, Izzy, I began the long trudge around the building and eventually got to the alcove that protected the front entrance. Where had I heard that before? I pulled on the door, it opened, and I eased it closed behind me.

It was dark in the interior of the building, and I couldn't see much beyond some half-drawn heavy curtains that led toward an elevated area. There were a few illuminated liquor advertisements behind the bar that were reflected in the numerous mirrors on the black velvet walls. I stood there for a few seconds, letting my eyes adjust, and thought I might've seen something move.

I watched the mirrors and finally saw the end of a baseball bat hovering in the blackness. Unsure from which direction it was reflecting, I figured I had to make a guess. Remembering that the bouncer had led with his right, I decided to move to the left and direct fire to the right, where he'd most likely be.

As mistakes go, it was a doozy.

He was on the left and caught me with the Louisville Slugger. Luckily, it was a glancing blow and I'd dropped my head, but unluckily, I tripped on the shag carpet and tumbled off onto the dance floor. When I hit the ground, the .357 clattered out of my hand and slid across the tile underneath the other platform.

"You know, you really should've left off on this one. Not only are you too old for this shit, but you're too dumb, too." He patted the wooden bat in the palm of his other hand with a continuous smack. "Now I've got to beat you to death, and I was just getting to kind of like you."

I rolled over and stared up at him. "Where's the postman?"

"Dave is taking care of business." He stopped at the step and took a few practice swings. "That's what we're all doing, taking care of business."

I pushed a little away and propped myself against a chair. "And what part of the business are you in?"

He palmed the bat again. "Right now, the tenderizing business." He stepped down. "USC, huh?"

"Yep."

He raised the bat. "Well, Trojan, say hello to the Fighting Irish."

I pulled the Colt Walker from my sling and carefully aimed it at his face. "Fight this."

He stared at the massive barrel of the vintage firearm.

"I've never seen a human being shot with one of these cap and ball jobs, but I've heard they about half explode on contact, so not only do you get the primary wound, but bits and pieces of the ball scatter all over you." I could see him weighing his chances. "But you won't have to worry about that because before I take another hit with that bat, as my old boss used to say, I'll spray your brains out of the back of your head like a manure spreader."

There was a tense moment, and then he lowered the bat onto his shoulder and sighed. "I don't want to go to prison; I just wanted to get my knee fixed."

"It might be a little late for that." I pushed off the floor, keeping the Walker on him. "What's going on around here, anyway?"

He reached a hand out, but I ignored it and stood on my own, watching his muscles tense in his shoulders as he thought about swinging the bat again.

I shoved the big Colt in his face. "I'm getting the feeling that you just aren't trustworthy." I pulled the cuffs from my pocket, tossed them to him, and motioned toward the pole at the center of the stage. "Hook yourself to that."

He stepped back. "No way, man."

I lowered my aim at his good leg. "Do it, or you're going to be rehabbing both of those knees."

He dragged a chair from one of the tables onto the stage and did as I said, slumping into a seated position with his wrist attached to the chrome pole. "Happy?"

"Give me the bat." He did, and I sat at another table with the lumber in front of me. "So I'll ask the question again—what's going on?"

"My question, exactly."

The voice that came from behind me was female, sort of, and was accompanied by the sound of a slide-action being pulled back on a 9 mm semiautomatic. I turned and was treated to the sight of the sister of the sheriff of Campbell County and proprietor of the establishment pointing a pistol at me. "Tommi."

She threw her purse and coat onto the bar and looked at the two of us. "What the hell is going on in here?"

Thor was the first to speak. "Thank God you're here, Tommi. I caught this guy snooping around and hit him with the bat, but he got the jump on me and cuffed me to the pole—"

I interrupted. "Call your brother; I'm working on a case involving the missing women. Your boyfriend, Dave, the recently deceased bartender of the Sixteen Tons, and the mullet with the mouth cuffed to the pole here are all involved."

She looked disgusted—then considered him and then me again. "Mister, I've done quite well in life knowing what aspects of my business I need to involve my brother in, and which ones I don't—another thing I've fine-tuned is my ability to sniff out bullshit when it's being shoveled my way." She came down, sat in the chair across the table from me, and then readdressed her aim to the bouncer. "Now, Thor, you tell him everything he wants to know or I'll shoot you myself."

The blond kid pleaded. "Tommi, you don't understand—"

The 9 mm went off, splintering a hole in the stage floor no more than a yard away from the kid's foot as he wrapped himself around the pole.

I sat the Walker on the table and cleared my nearest ear with the tip of a pinkie. "You mind telling me when you get ready to shoot that thing again?"

She casually lifted the semiautomatic and blasted another round in the stage a foot away from the kid's other sneaker, causing him to leap up, overturn his chair, and stand comically behind the chrome pole. She glanced at me. "I might be shooting some more."

"Thanks for the warning."

"Think nothing of it." She took out a cigarillo and a lighter and rested her elbow on the table in order to sight the pistol on Thor's private parts. "You were saying?"

The kid was on the verge of crying. "It wasn't my idea."

She puffed her cigarillo as if her life depended on it. "Comforting, seeing as how in the couple of years I've known you I've never known you to have one."

"It was the postman, honest."

I watched as Tommi's hand tightened around the pistol. "Dave."

"He always rings twice." Figuring the kid was scared enough, I reached over and lowered Tommi's weapon. "Tell me about Mr. Rowan, Curtis."

"It was his idea." Thor relaxed and leaned against the pole. "He gets these catalogs with women in them at the post office, and he figured he could go into the business himself what with it closing and him losing his job anyway."

"Mail-order brides?"

"Yeah . . . Well, kind of."

"Kind of?"

He nodded. "More like servants. We were all talking over at the bar one night, and he brought the subject up. We didn't know that he'd already done it twice with women from town, but we figured we had a supply of girls that we could use from the club—"

"You mean you abducted these women against their will and sold them?"

"Um, yeah."

I sat there, thinking that the report from Tommi's pistol had affected my hearing. "Slaves."

"Sort of, yeah."

She raised the pistol and aimed again. "Can I shoot him now?"

I pushed the 9 mm away. "Not till we find out where the women are." I turned and gave the bouncer my most immediate and severe attention. "At last count there are three—where are they?"

"Um . . ." He mumbled the next part. "All over."

"I'm shooting this little bastard on general principles."

I held the gun away. "Where are they?"

He shook his head as he spoke. "One might be somewhere in Florida, maybe."

"Rowan has the list?"

He nodded. "He knows everything."

"So, where is he?"

"I don't know." Tommi lifted the pistol again, and this time I didn't attempt to dissuade her, and Thor suddenly remembered the conversation. "He came in here and told me you were going to kill us all and that I was supposed to stop you no matter what it took."

"Then he left?"

"Yeah."

I thought about it. "There had to be a place where you kept the women before shipping them out or delivering them; where was that?"

"We kept them sedated in the trailer."

"The one that burned down?"

"Yeah."

I stood. "What about Jone Urrecha?"

"Who?"

I gestured toward Tommi. "Shoot him." She did, this time missing his foot by inches. "Your running partner, the Basque woman."

"The schoolhouse."

I stuffed the Colt Walker into my sling. "Over by the bar?"

"No, the old one back up the canyon road."

I walked to the stage and lifted the short curtain that trimmed the dancing area but couldn't see the .357. "There's a pistol that slid under there that belongs to the detective that's been working on this case. When the sheriff's department gets here to take golden boy into custody, tell them about it, would you?"

She nodded. "Will do. You headed for the schoolhouse?"

"I am."

"You can't see a damn thing out there." She stubbed her cigarillo out on the table. "You want me to send the troops and my half-wit brother after you, or do you just want to shoot that asshole Dave and leave him for the coyotes?"

"It's tempting, but send them after me."

"Will do."

I straightened my hat and zipped up my coat with my good arm, careful of the bandage on my neck. "Can I drive there?" She and the bouncer looked at each other. "I take that as a no."

"It's just a dirt road and all rutted out; in weather like this I think you better walk."

"How far?"

"'Bout a mile." She frowned. "And I was going to marry that son of a bitch."

When I came out the back door of the strip club and looked across the field, I could see that the Jeep was gone. I could also see the revolving lights of a Campbell County Sheriff's car. I hustled across the parking lot and down the road, getting to the Sixteen Tons Bar in time to see the present sheriff of Campbell County and the retired sheriff of Absaroka loading the wounded investigator into the backseat.

"Where's the EMT van?"

Sandy turned and looked at me as they made Harvey as comfortable as possible, his head wrapped with so many bar towels it was starting to look like the top of a snowman—all he needed was some coal and a carrot. "With this fog, you're lucky that radio call you put in with my dispatcher got through to me. I'll drive him over to the hospital and then come back." He glanced past me, toward the mail office next door. "I understand we've got somebody who's gone postal?"

"From what I got from Curtis, the kid I handcuffed to a pole over at your sister's strip club, he, the dead bartender, and the postman are running some kind of white-slavery ring."

He guffawed. "You've got to be kidding."

"I wish I were." I glanced at the hills behind the small town. "Supposedly they kept the women in the old one-room school-house up in the hills out here."

Sandy stopped laughing and nodded. "There's a road, but the fastest way to get there is to follow the railroad spur behind the school that deadheads about a mile down the canyon—and that way you can drive." He pointed to a line of empty coal cars. "They sometimes park the cars there before they roll 'em down to Black Diamond, where they fill them up. When you get to the end of the line, hop over the top of the hill, and the school will be right there."

I held a hand out. "Let me borrow your cuffs?" He handed them to me, and I reached for my keys. "There's a road beside the tracks?"

He nodded. "A lot better one than that goat path on the ridge."

I started to move off, but Lucian caught my arm. "What do you want me to do?"

I glanced at Sandy. "Is this the only road out of town?"

"In or out."

I turned back to the old sheriff, the man who had gotten me into this mess. "Stay here in case he decides to make a run for it. Take Harvey's car and set up out there on the entryway to the railroad crossing." I started off toward my truck. "You see him, you stop him."

Lucian called after me. "Like I did the bartender?"

I called back over my shoulder, "Or the coffeepot."

14

There was a BNSF high-rail truck sitting at the top of the dead-head, the kind that can run on railroad tracks when the gear is lowered, and I slowed down and stopped to yell out my window, "Any chance of you guys moving these cars in the near future?"

He smiled. "You chasing the mailman?"

"He go by here?"

"About twenty minutes ago."

I looked at the cars and at the narrow roadway on the side, clogged with snow. "Really, any chance of moving these damn things?"

He pushed the hood back on his Carhartt, and I recognized the man I'd met at the Sixteen Tons, *Fry* printed on a name patch. "In about forty-five minutes we're gonna move 'em out and fill 'em up." He jerked a thumb over his shoulder. "The mine is worried they're gonna get snowed in, so they're gonna take this spur train and attach it."

"No sooner, huh?"

He smiled. "Not unless you want to hook that big V-10 up and pull 'em yourself."

"Don't tempt me." I rolled the window back up and decided

that I didn't need the sling anymore. Pulling the cumbersome thing off and stuffing it in my pocket, I carefully slid my arm into the sleeve of my coat—my neck was sore, but I could deal with that. I spun the wheel, negotiated my way around the coal cars, and began the slow and arduous task of drifting my way down the sloped road in an attempt not to slip off into the ditch or run into the train cars.

There was a fresh set of tracks that rolled alongside in a straight line, a testament to the Jeep's more nimble design, but I kept turning into the slide and making progress. I glanced at the tops of the coal cars and could see that they were, indeed, empty.

The only way to keep any kind of forward momentum was by staying on the gas, even though I was traveling about thirty miles an hour sideways to do so.

Fortunately, when I got to the end of the line, there was a buttress of railroad ties and fill dirt, looking almost like a ramp, leading up to the last car, and, more important, an open area where I could goose the truck and climb up out of the ditch to straddle a flat spot.

I gunned the three-quarter-ton, dodged between two cottonwoods, both about as big around as a coffee table, climbed out of the Bullet, and looked at the Jeep tracks. I sighed and unlocked the Remington shotgun from my transmission hump, figuring if I was going hunting I might as well go prepared. Before closing the door, I reached in, snagged the mic from my dash, and thumbed the button. "Lucian?"

The old sheriff's voice rang back. Static. "What do ya need?"

"I'm at the end of the rail spur, but that damned Jeep of his was able to slip through and follow the goat path leading up toward the school."

Static. "There was a reason those drove into Berlin and To-kyo and not a bunch of pickup trucks, you know."

"Yep, but what I need is for you to keep an eye out in case he circles around on the old school road."

Static. "I'm backed up to the railroad crossing in the detective's car. These assholes from the BNSF say I'm going to have to move when they hook on to that spur of yours, but when that thing starts moving there isn't anybody going to be able to get through anyway."

"Make sure you and the interceptor are on this side, would you?"

Static. "Sure, I wouldn't want to miss any of the fun."

I tossed the mic back inside, plucked a handheld from the side pocket, and clipped it to my belt. I closed the door, stepping into the midcalf snow, threw the strap on the twelve-gauge on my good side, and marched off after the Jeep.

It was getting warmer, causing the whiteout fog to thicken like pudding, and the snow in the gulley was over my knees, but there was still not much wind. Luckily, I had the Jeep tracks to follow, so I switched off and began walking the tire-track tightrope, finally making it to a stand of naked trees and another slight depression that flattened out to the ridge where the old schoolhouse must've been.

As I got to the top of the hill, I paused to catch my breath and promised myself that if the postman made a run for it, I would just shoot him, pretty sure I was too tired to do anything else.

There was a discernible shadow to the left with a smaller shadow to the right, about the size of a vehicle. I jacked a round into the shotgun and continued to follow the Jeep tracks, hoping that I wasn't too late, but pretty sure that if Jone Urrecha was still alive, he would use her to negotiate.

It was about then that I heard the unmistakable whizz of a 9 mm round whipping past me into the distance. I immediately crouched, brought the Remington up, and pointed it in the direction of the report. "Rowan, you better throw down that weapon and call it quits."

There was silence for a few moments, and just in case he was a better shot than I thought, I moved to the left a little, keeping a low profile against the slope.

His voice was high and nasal. "How about we make a deal, Sheriff?"

I pinpointed his location to be in or near the Jeep, so I continued to the left, figuring I could work my way along the ridge and circle around, keeping the school between us. "I don't usually negotiate in these kinds of situations."

"I've got the woman."

"I know that."

"You better stop moving out there or all deals are off." There was more silence, obviously more than he could stand. "You want to hear my offer?"

I thought about letting him sweat, but I was concerned that as nervous as he was he might shoot Jone. "I'm listening."

"What if I leave her here in the schoolhouse, and you let me go back down the hill in the Jeep?"

"And I'm supposed to trust you?" Against my better nature, I thought about it. "You know I've got officers back in town, right?"

"I know you've got an old, one-legged sheriff down there, but I'd imagine that the rest of them are trying to get Richard Harvey to the emergency room or scraping the citizenry off I-90."

He had a point.

"I'll leave her in the school for you."

"Along with your gun."

"What?"

"You throw that pistol of yours out here toward me or it's no deal. I don't mind leaving you to the Campbell County Sheriff's Office, considering how you shot one of theirs—"

"I didn't shoot him!"

"Good luck explaining that in the heat of the moment." I let him think about it. "But I'm not letting you waltz out of here armed."

"What makes you think I don't have another gun?"

"Because if you had, you would've used it instead of that 9 mm. I'm hefting this twelve-gauge with a full-length barrel and loaded with buckshot." I let him think about that. "It might not get all of you at this distance, but it will get some of you— that much I can guarantee." It got real quiet. "I'm through negotiating, in case you're wondering."

There was no response, but something sailed through the air and landed with a soft *thunk* to my right. I moved in that direction and fished in the snow, finally pulling out a Ruger semiautomatic minus the magazine.

He found his voice. "I didn't figure there was any reason to give it to you loaded."

"Fair enough, but you better not be lying to me."

The ignition on the CJ-7 fired, and I listened as a door opened. "She's inside; a little drugged up, but I've found that makes 'em easier to handle."

"You're not going to get far."

"I'll take my chances; anyway, I've got friends."

"So I hear."

"Watch your back, Sheriff."

The sound of the door closing was accompanied by the revving of the engine as he spun the Jeep around and circled to the right to what I assumed was the regular road to the school.

I unclipped the handheld from my belt and keyed the mic. "Lucian, can you hear me?"

Static.

"Lucian, if you're reading me, the postman, Rowan, is headed down the hill; feel free to shoot the Jeep, but I'd like him alive so I can find out where the other woman is and about his partners in this little cabin industry of his."

Static.

I listened to the sound of the Jeep as I fastened the radio to my belt and started back up the hill. It sounded like the four-by-four was having a hard time negotiating the rutted road, and even as if it might've veered to the right and circled around toward the railroad spur, but sounds were strange and untrustworthy in this kind of storm.

Just in case, I pulled Vic's cell phone from my pocket and looked at the lack of bars; of course, NO SERVICE.

Depth-charging my way to the school, I could see the prints where he'd been standing but also where he had dragged the girl to the other side of the Jeep. "And that's what you get for having one shred of trust."

Just to make sure, I climbed the steps and yanked the door open—empty.

Leaping off the stoop, I tromped through the shallower snow on the ridge and pulled the radio from my belt. "Lucian, he's got the woman with him, so be careful taking him."

Static.

I headed off following in the tracks of the Jeep, which arced back toward the road we'd taken up from the railroad spur. "Now, why would he do that?" The road was worse but faster, so maybe he thought his odds were better doubling back and using the train for cover.

I had another hike ahead of me, but it was a path I knew and it was downhill. I sidled my way down the hill and back into the trees, where at least I could tell if I was upright.

There was a loud clanking noise, and I figured the empty coal train was pulling out. Great, just in time for Rowan to be able to drive on the tracks.

Increasing my speed, I finally got to the flat area at the bottom of the gulley where I could make better time. The sound of the clanking cars was thunderous, but I could still hear a high whining sound of tires spinning in the snow in an attempt to find purchase.

Moving into a hampered jog, I held the twelve-gauge with the butt under my arm in an attempt to keep it steady. There was a spot of darkness up ahead, but I was pretty sure that was either my truck or the buttress at the end of the line. I slowed when I got to the Bullet and looked around in all directions but still didn't see the Jeep. I moved around the ties and stood on the railroad tracks, peering into the distance where the train had disappeared.

I could still hear the noise but could see nothing.

It couldn't be more than a hundred yards ahead.

With a deep breath that imitated a steam locomotive, I pressed off and ran along the uncovered area where the coal cars had sat, finally seeing the Jeep turned sideways in a ditch where Dave Rowan must've pushed his luck just a little too far. The four-by-four was buried at the bottom of the trench, and the only thing it was doing at this point was throwing snow into the wheel wells.

I raised the shotgun and pulled the trigger, firing a round

into the air a little in front of me so as to avoid any double-ought precipitation.

Rowan let off the gas, and his hands shot up to the roof of the CJ-7.

I lowered the barrel on him and yelled as I walked closer, "Shut it off!"

He did as I said and then raised his hands again.

"Where is the woman?"

He didn't say anything, and I lowered the barrel of the twelve-gauge on him. "Where is Jone?"

He smiled a sickening smile and shouted back, "Jone who?"

I yanked the door open and grabbed him by the coat front, shoving the muzzle of the shotgun under his chin and forcing his head back. "Tell me where she is or I scatter the top of your head all over the insides of the Jeep."

His eyes widened, but his voice still had confidence. "You wouldn't do that."

I slipped the barrel away and blew out the passenger-side window.

He jumped, and I was betting he soiled himself just a bit. "Agha . . . !"

I jacked the slide mechanism, bouncing the empty shell off his chest, and shoved the muzzle back under his chin. "I've had a long day, and I wouldn't press my luck if I were you."

He was sobbing now. "Look, it wasn't my idea—"

"Actually, it was your idea; abducting and selling women out of Arrosa, Wyoming. I guess you figured you could get away with it because you were out here in the middle of nowhere, but the game's over. I don't know where Linda Schaffer is, but I'll find out. You sold Roberta Payne to the card dealer over in Deadwood, but now she's dead, he's dead, and the guy who tried to kill me is dead—and you're going to be dead if you don't tell me where Jone Urrecha is right now."

He glanced past me up the hill toward the tracks. "In the train."

I stared at him.

"She's in the last coal car."

I staggered back and looked up at the tracks, the train long gone. "Damn it!"

I pulled out the cuffs I'd borrowed, hooked Rowan to the roll bar on the Jeep, and snatched the keys as I dug back up the hill.

"What about me!"

"I'll try and remember that you're here." I snatched the radio from my belt and keyed the mic. "Lucian, are you there?"

Static.

"Lucian, the woman, she's in the last coal car of the train that pulled out from the spur. We've got to stop that train!"

Static.

"Lucian!"

Static.

I reached my truck and threw the radio into the back, climbed in, fired up the Bullet, and yanked the mic from my truck radio, which was more powerful than the handheld. "Lucian, can you read me?"

Static.

"Damn." I pulled the selector into gear and began the arduous task of backtracking along the roadway beside the tracks, almost sliding into the Jeep but then correcting and continuing down the slippery way. It was harder this time but probably because I was in even more of a hurry.

I finally saw the BNSF high-rail truck at the end of the spur with its emergency lights on and floored the Bullet, almost slipping down the bank in the process. I steered into the drift, blew by the high-rail, and locked up my brakes—all in all, an accidental show of remarkable driving acumen.

I threw myself from my vehicle and slapped my hand on the window of the rail truck; Fry dropped his coffee as I yelled into the glass between us, "Stop that train!"

Brushing the cup from his lap, he mouthed the word *What?*

I slammed the glass again. "There's a woman in the last car of that coal train you're loading!"

His eyes bugged like headlights as he looked past me down the road at the empty tracks. "Lord almighty."

"Get on your radio!"

He shook his head as he rolled down the window. "There's no radio reception; something must've happened to the transponders that relay out of Gillette."

I became aware of another vehicle sliding to a stop behind me and turned in time to see Lucian dropping his window. "What the hell is going on?"

"The woman, she's in the last coal car of that train. Rowan threw her in there in hopes of getting rid of her."

"Like the hobos?"

"Yep, like the ho— homeless." I started around. "We've got to catch that train and stop them from loading."

Lucian picked up the mic from the floor. "These damn things aren't working."

"I know."

The BNSF driver, Fry, yelled at me, "That booth is on the north side—there's nobody you can get on our side of that train."

I kicked a tire, in full realization that my options were running out. "Are there any other roads?"

He made a face as he looked off into the fog, the delineation of the horizon lost in all the whiteness. "One, but you have to go out past the highway, then down the frontage road, and then drive in on the gravel, and it probably hasn't been plowed."

I pulled the cell phone from my pocket. "Who can I call?"

"Nobody; it's a skeleton crew working tonight. We're supposed to load this train and then call it quits."

"Nobody has a phone?" The ludicrousness of this statement coming from my mouth was not lost on me. "Somebody?"

"No. There won't be anybody in the administrative offices, and without radios you won't be able to get hold of anybody in the chute section—it's all computer generated, and besides, as you might have noticed, there's no service out here." He shook his head. "There just isn't any way."

I stared at the tracks leading west, my mind racing like a runaway locomotive. I bit the inside of my lip and stared down at the steel wheels of the high-rail gear equipment on his massive truck. "Oh, yes there is."

As fast as the driver was working, it was still agonizingly slow. His voice was strained as he shouted down from the cab of the oversize truck. "This is a really bad idea."

"Give me a better one?" We watched as he lined the one-ton truck up with the rails, rapidly backing up and pulling forward. "And hurry."

Fry shouted down. "I don't get this thing right, we get derailed in the first twenty feet and then it's going to take a hell of a lot longer, I can tell you that much."

With a mechanical whine, the steel wheels lowered onto the

iron rails just enough to carry the weight of the vehicle but still allowing the traction to the tires that would provide us with power. The driver jumped from the other side and came to the front, touching a lever and lowering the front high-rail wheels onto the track with a loud, jarring noise.

He pushed back his hood again and smiled as he shook his head. "Just so you know, this goes against every safety regulation on the line."

"I'll take responsibility."

He nodded with the same smile as he turned and walked around, climbing in the driver's side. "You take responsibility for the three switches between here and the mine?"

Hoisting Lucian up into the cab, I followed, closing the door behind me. "What about the switches?"

He engaged the transmission, hit the gas, and we lurched forward. "No radio—no dispatch; we hit one of those switches and it's turned against us and we get hit head-on by another mile-long train going in the opposite direction."

I looked down the rails, feeling more and more like a maiden tied to the tracks. "That would be bad."

He nodded and studied me. "Very bad."

We gathered speed. "How fast can this thing go?"

"Pretty damn fast on the straight and flat—faster than you're gonna want to go."

"Bet me."

Lucian leaned forward. "And once we get there, what the hell are you going to wanna do?"

"I'll figure that out when it happens." We were picking up speed, and the high-rail began sounding more and more like a train, with the clickety-clack of the rail joints closing time like the second hand on a stopwatch. "How long does it take to load one of those cars?"

He glanced at the clock on his dash. "About a minute."

"How many cars per train?"

"A hundred and forty, give or take, but they've already filled those."

I looked at the clock, too. "So, where are we on the spur?"

He swallowed. "I'm betting near the end."

I braced a hand against the dash. "Speed up."

"You want me to go faster than this?"

"Yep." He did as I said, and the snow swirled and whipped around the windshield like galloping ghosts. "They have to slow the train to load it, right?"

He nodded. "They'll just run it at about three miles an hour." His head swiveled around, and then he turned back to look at both Lucian and me. "Did you see that switch indicator?"

"What does a switch indicator look like?"

He glanced out the window. "A very large, blinking green light."

"No."

Lucian interrupted. "There was a red one."

We both looked at him.

The old sheriff shrugged. "Large, blinking red light to the left."

The driver hit the gas even harder. "It's a train coming the other way."

Lucian and I looked down the rails joining in the distance at a vanishing point, fully expecting to see a BNSF locomotive heading straight toward us. "Where?"

The driver's mouth set in a straight line like a teeter-totter, weighing the odds. "I know this switchman, Bruce; he always throws early. I'll hit the horns, and he'll switch it back just long enough to get us through before that big son of a bitch comes over onto our rails." With that, he hit the air racks on the truck by pulling a cord near the headliner—three short, three long, three short.

I shouted, "SOS?"

He smiled. "He'll know it's me—we were in the Navy together."

We all peered through the snow and fog, and up ahead, in the far distance and barely a glimmer in the fog bank, was a light.

"Is that what I think it is?"

He nodded his head and hunched a shoulder over the steering wheel. "Another coal train, headed east."

"And through us?" Lucian joined me in bracing both hands against the dash, for all the good that was going to do. "How long before we know if he switched us through?"

The driver pushed the throttle some more, continuing with his Morse dots and dashes. "Any time now."

I peered through the windshield, trying to ignore the growing orb slightly to our left. "Will there be another indicator?"

"Nope."

"So we just have to get to the switch before the other train does?"

"You got it."

I glanced at the speedometer on the dash. "We go straight, right? I mean, we don't have to change directions, do we?"

He glanced down. "No, we'd roll at this speed."

"That's comforting."

"And then probably get run over by the train anyway." He glanced at me. "Say, who's the woman in the coal car?"

I stared at the man, amazed that he would ask a question like that at a time like this. "A woman by the name of Jone Urrecha."

"The Basque Rose?" He took the cigarette from his mouth and licked his lips. "The dancer from over at Dirty Shirley's?"

"You know her?"

He smiled and held the cigarette out, studying the glowing tip. "Oh, hell yeah. I used to go over there every week after shift until she left." His hands tightened on the wheel, and his head nodded up and down in determination. "We have to damn well make it."

I took a deep breath and glanced at the old sheriff. "Having fun?"

His jaw was tight, and his eyes widened as we both turned and looked at the oncoming train. "If I was next to the damn door, I'd make a jump for it."

With a sudden burst of clarity, the front end of the locomotive leapt into view like a building on wheels, a gigantic, stories-high building on wheels. The driver gave one last rhythmical blast of the horns as we shot through the switch, and I saw a man standing by the levers, looking up at us with an amazed and horrified look on his face.

The other train blew by us and continued east, rocking the cabin of the high-rail like a hundred fully loaded eighteen-wheelers, its own horns drowning out ours in an instant. All I could see in the side mirror were the flashing sides of the freight cars as they shifted onto the track where we'd just been only seconds ago.

The driver gave one last blast of the air horns. "Hell yeah, just like draggin' 'em down in Douglas." He turned to look at us. "We used to play chicken down there after they closed the drag strip."

Lucian turned and looked at me as I glanced at the driver. "How many more switches?"

"Two."

Lucian muttered, "Jesus H. Christ."

"Nah, the others will see Bruce pulled his switch late, and they'll figure something is up. They wouldn't send another train through on this line anyway, so we're good."

The rhythmical thumping of the rail joints continued to sound like a mechanical second hand, and all I could think of was a woman lying at the bottom of a coal car with the jarring off-and-on progression of two hundred tons of the stuff thundering into each container growing louder and louder.

"Can you climb out of one of those cars?" The driver lit another cigarette, clamped it between his teeth, and offered the pack to us. "No, thanks, even though the conditions have me thinking about taking it up."

He nodded and stuffed the cigarettes back in his shirt. "No way, the sides are smooth and close to twelve feet tall—I suppose if you were some kind of pro basketball player, maybe."

I remembered Rowan saying that he kept the women drugged—there was no way Jone Urrecha was getting out of that coal car without help. "How much farther?"

Fry checked his odometer. "About a mile and a half."

"When we get close, are you going to be able to stop this thing?"

"On a mercury dime, my friend."

I peered into the distance, the swirling clouds of snow worse with the passing freight that still roared and clanked only a few feet away. "I think you're enjoying this more than we are."

Fry nodded and pulled the cigarette from his mouth. "I rarely get to chase a train down with my truck and save a fair damsel in distress."

Lucian mumbled as he looked at me. "You would have to flag down the craziest bastard that works for the entire Burlington Northern Santa Fe Railroad."

I ignored him and watched the distance ahead, finally spotting a couple of lights, strangely enough, arranged almost as if in a cross. "Is that it?"

"Yeah, I think so."

"It looks big."

"Well, it's a train . . ."

My eyes widened as I realized, for the first time, that the back of this train was being pushed by a locomotive. My hands crept out to the dash, as did Lucian's. "Is that an engine?"

He squinted his eyes and took the cigarette from his mouth again, and I was pretty sure he was judging time by how fast he was smoking it. "Don't worry about it, it's a couple of pushers they've got in the back."

The lights of the coal train were impressive and enough to let the driver know to hit his brakes as the string lights of the coal mine's delivery system lit up the sky like Russian Christmas. "How are we going to gauge our gapping distance?"

"You said it runs about three miles an hour; doesn't the last car have a ladder on it?"

He tucked the cigarette into the corner of his mouth like the bolt action on a rifle. "Yeah, but do you know how fast three miles an hour is when you're out there slipping and sliding around on the ice and snow beside a moving train?"

I stared at the multiple lights. "How close can you get?"

He glanced at me and then at the train ahead, consistently applying pressure on the brakes. "I told you, I can put you nose to nose."

I began rolling down the window with the manual crank. "Do it."

Lucian looked at me. "What the hell do you think you're doing?"

I pulled the Colt Walker and rested it on the dash. "The hood of this truck gives me a six-foot height advantage; all I've got to do is make it from the front of this thing onto the observation platform of that locomotive."

He shook his head. "Have you lost your mind?"

I unbuckled my safety belt and nudged over to the door as Fry slowed, judging the distance between us and the back of the train. "I'm open to suggestions."

The train continued its crawl forward. The driver turned to look at me. "You see what we're up against?"

"I do." I took a deep breath. "From here to the loader, how many cars would you say we've got?"

He studied the distance. "Less than twenty, probably sixteen at best."

There still wasn't much wind, but the patterns of the few falling snowflakes were disorienting to say the least. I gripped the headache bar that protected the top of the cab and rested my rear near the windowsill. I started to reach out and pull myself up when I heard the crashing noise of the coal being loaded— one minute between loads.

That was a fast sixty seconds.

I waited until the driver roared forward and positioned himself right behind the train, almost to the point where I was sure we were going to run into it. Bracing my hand, I slipped a boot up onto the seat and could feel the strongest grip in Absaroka County latch on to my leg to make sure I didn't slip.

Lucian let go, and I pulled my other leg after and lodged my boot on the windowsill, pushed off and landed with my chest on the headache rack; then I grabbed hold of the spare tire that was mounted there with both hands, ignoring the numbness in my arm.

Lucian called out from the cab. "You all right?"

Standing on the sill, I edged forward, glancing down at the slick, white hood of the one-ton truck. "Yep." The clanking cacophony continued again, and the train surged forward with another tremendous crashing noise.

Another load. Another minute.

I held on as the driver crept forward, trying to buy me time. As soon as he stopped the truck, I took the leap of faith onto the hood and watched with satisfaction as it dented, providing me with a shallow divot in which to stand. I stooped and crept forward, extending my good hand toward the opening in the railing at the center ladder, figuring the more visibility I gave Fry, the better.

Looking past my fingers, I tried to gauge the distance beyond the high-rail gear, the tail mechanism that had taken the place of a caboose, and the front of the pushing locomotive—a good ten feet, at least.

The train continued forward with another thunderous load, and I looked down at my feet and laughed at the absolute absurdity of the situation.

I stepped back on the hood and placed a foot against the

windshield. Looking down at the driver, his face blurred by the reflection of the glass and the patterns of the snow, I shouted. "Nose to nose!"

I watched the determination tighten his face as he hit the accelerator, and I stepped forward just as the front of the high-rail struck the back of the train. I could feel my boots slipping on the sheet metal, and my arms involuntarily stretched out as I left the truck, the forward momentum lifting me up into the delicate flake-filled air.

15

There are few things in the world harder than a locomotive, let me tell you.

My hand locked around the top of the left-side railing in a death grip, while the rest of me swung to the right and tangled around the other railing and the headlamp mount. My face hit the chain between the railings, which damn near strangled me but hopefully didn't pull the bandages covering the wound on my neck, but it was the numbness in my right hand that caused me to slip. I kicked my boots into the hoses below me, hoping for any kind of purchase, finally wrapping a leg around the side long enough to get my other boot on a tread and ease the pressure.

Pulling my hat down tight, I scrambled up onto the platform and discovered that the ladder led to nowhere.

I turned and looked at Fry, and he stuck a hand against the windshield with a finger pointing up.

Great.

Hoisting myself, I landed onto the hood of the great orange and black beast, and even had time to glance in the cab, green-lit and eerily vacant. I climbed over the top and looked down the expanse of the thing, the cars disappearing in the ground fog. Loping along and feeling like a train robber in some sort of old black-and-white movie, I got to the end of the locomotive and was pleased to see another ladder leading down to another platform that provided easy access to the last coal car.

There was another loud noise as I started down the ladder, and once again, the only thing on my mind was . . .

That was a fast sixty seconds.

Jumping the gap between, I started up the ladder on the left and lunged over the edge to look inside. The ambient light from the mine illuminated half of the car, but the side closest to me was a contrast in complete darkness. I could see that there was a long board, possibly a two-by-twelve, sticking up from the middle of the coal car and extending to the corner and, on closer inspection, I could see another lying on top of it.

I concentrated on the darkness and yelled her name, in hopes that she might hear me over the tremendous roar of the coal being loaded. "Jone!"

My eyes began adjusting, but all I could see was the snow, sprinkled with a fine coating of coal dust, that had drifted in the bottom of the car. All I could think of was the remark that Lucian had made about the unfortunates who had met their demise at the bottom of two hundred tons of coal—pulverized pepper steak.

I stared into the darkness, willing my eyes to see her just as the mile-long train jerked forward, and I made the mental note that there had been four cars filled since we'd gotten there, which meant that if the driver's calculations were correct, we had only a dozen or so cars to go.

I looked down the rails, but with the fog I couldn't even see the cars in the distance, let alone count how many had been filled. Looking back, I shook my head and tried to figure out where she might be. "Jone!"

My eyes wandered to the boards half lying there, and I had the horrible thought that he must've walked her along on them and then dropped her in the next-to-last car.

There were five support rails spanning the last car's width, and I was going to have to fish the two-by-twelves out and get them up onto those supports before I could get to the next car up the line.

I was reaching for the boards when the thunderous noise came again, and I lurched forward, which almost threw me into the empty container. Scrambling, I counterbalanced, slapped my hands against the rungs of the ladder, and clung there, my right arm reminding me that it wasn't 100 percent.

I turned back to the job at hand and counted in my head— ten cars to go. It was an estimate, but the high-rail driver had impressed me as a man who knew whereof he spoke.

Grabbing the end of the top board, I leveraged it from the car and began the arduous task of trying to balance it on the edge, turning it toward the middle and getting the end up onto one of the nearest supports.

The edge of the board tipped, so I was going to need the other board to span the length of the car. Following the same maneuver, I leveraged the second board up and clattered it onto the supports parallel to the first one, but I was sweating like a bottle of beer in a biker bar.

Climbing onto the nearest board, I pushed the other one ahead, watching it slide on the ice and go about half the distance I wanted it to. Trying to gauge just how many of my sixty seconds were left and figuring not many, I loped a few steps ahead, grabbed the end of the second board, and pushed it, watching as it shot forward, bumping on the far edge and sliding past the end of the board where I now stood, creating a gap of about two feet.

"You have got to be kidding."

I crept forward onto the unsupported four feet that was left of the first board, feeling the length of the thing tip up behind me. There wasn't anywhere to stand, so I backed up and hunkered down in a three-point stance. I was getting an idea of the timing of the loaders and figured I could use the momentum of the moving cars to assist me in the traverse.

Clutching both sides of the board, I waited, and it didn't take long for the loading to recommence.

Nine cars to go.

Feeling the surge of the train as it continued pulling all its tonnage, I threw myself forward when I was sure we were moving together at peak speed, clomping down the two-by-twelve as if it were a wooden boardwalk.

Feeling the first board begin to give way beneath me, I leapt and watched as the train cars continued at their steady pace, leaving me to fly forward like a cue ball on a clean break.

I really hadn't had to worry about the gap as I sailed over that with no problem. What I should've worried about was landing halfway onto the frost-covered second board and sliding over the side between the two cars.

Gripping the two-by-twelve like a lemur, I put a hand out and was able to stop my forward momentum enough to slide sideways with my legs hanging down between the last and next-to-last cars.

Swallowing hard, I threw a leg back onto the board, reached

out, and grabbed the lip of the next car just enough to allow me to get mostly back on the board—wondering how Tom Mix did this shit on a regular basis.

I pushed the top of my body over the edge and looked down into the car and, in the contrast of dark and light, there, sticking out into the flat beam of the mine's arc lights, half buried in the drifts, was a woman's leg.

I forced the name from my mouth with all the air I could muster. "Jone!" Staring at the leg, hoping it would move. There was no response. "Jone!"

Nothing.

Edging to the side, I figured the only way to get down into the car, and, more important, back out, was on the board that had just tried to kill me. With a boot on the ladder, I brought it forward and tipped it down past her leg.

I looked at the angle, trying to judge if I'd be able to climb back out on the thing with a woman on my shoulder, and every voice in my head answered with an absolute negative. I thought that if I rigged the board from side to side as opposed to lengthwise, it'd certainly be a shorter distance and the side of the car would provide a better brace anyway.

Still listening to the noise of the loader, I braced myself on the ladder for the next short burst forward, throwing my arms over the side and hugging the lip as the thing clanked ahead for the anticipated distance and the noise began again. I wasn't sure, but it was almost as if it were becoming more violent.

Eight cars to go.

I grappled my way over the edge and turned toward the hateful board, hugging it so as not to take the entire slide at once, alternately gripping it and loosening to allow my descent into the darkness. It seemed to take forever, but I finally felt my boots kick against the steel of the car, notifying me that I'd reached bottom.

The snow had drifted on the trip from Arrosa, the bulk of it seeming to have flowed to the back of the car where Jone Urrecha lay.

Stepping around the board, I stooped to pull her up. She was lean and half-starved, and I lifted her easily, her long hair slipping against my chest; I could see the matted blood where her head must've struck the edge, but she was still breathing.

She was wearing a pair of jeans and a stained sweatshirt, and her body convulsed in shivers; even unconscious, she wanted to live, but she was not only drugged but concussed as well.

I pulled her face up and shook her gently. "Jone?"

Nothing.

"Jone?"

There was the slightest movement under her eyelids.

"Jone?" One of her eyes opened slowly, and then the other did the same, almost as if they'd been glued. Without the benefit of the flashlight all the doctors on television and in the movies seem to have handy, I was still pretty sure that her eyes were lacking any constriction. "Jone?"

A hand came up feebly but then dropped to her side, and she groaned, all good signs. "Jone, I'm going to need your help. We're in a pretty lousy situation, and I need you to do some climbing."

Her head jogged to one side and then lolled down with her chin resting on her chest.

"Great." I looked back at the board angling up to safety and wondered how far I could push her before she slid off the side.

When I removed my jacket, I noticed blood on the collar—my wound must have been seeping—but I gently wrapped the coat around her anyway. I moved onto the board, straddled the thing, and took a deep breath, looking at the angled climb as if it might as well be to the moon. I gripped the wood and started up, my boots slipping on the surface like a gerbil on a wheel.

I dug in a little harder and got enough momentum to slide my hand up and regrip. My boots continued to slip but provided just enough traction to allow another increment of advance—I figured at this rate we'd likely be out of the car by Valentine's Day.

I paused and took a deep breath, trying to calculate how many of my sixty seconds had gone by, figuring about thirty, which meant I had another thirty seconds to get Jone and myself out of harm's way.

I was almost to the point where I could grab one of the cross supports but was afraid that if I did, I'd lose traction on the board and we'd just go over. We needed to get a hell of a lot higher than this. So, repositioning my hand, I nudged us again. I pushed her even farther but was struck by the fact that she weighed less this time.

I raised my face and looked up to see Fry smiling down at me as he grabbed the young woman and pulled her up the board toward him. "Couldn't just sit there. Thought maybe I could help if you got her far enough."

I laughed. "How did you get up there?"

"The front of the high-rail is jammed onto the locomotive, so I just put it in neutral and climbed on the way you did."

"Did you get a hold of the men doing the loading?"

"No, so we need to get you out of there now."

As he pulled her from the car, I risked moving my left hand from the board and placed it on the support brace that ran from side to side. "Where's Lucian?"

He pulled Jone over the side and draped her over his shoulder. "Pretending to drive the truck, not that you have to—I think he enjoys being in charge."

With the force of a T-bone crash, the car suddenly vibrated in a clacking din, jarring the three of us like fleas on a shaking dog. I watched Fry grab the side of the car with one hand, still clutching Jone with the other so she wouldn't slip away. The two-by-twelve did its usual slide and clattered to the inside of the car, and I scrambled to hang on to the cross-member, finally giving up on the board and grabbing the support with both hands. Hanging there like a high plains piñata, my right arm reminded me that it was still half numb, leaving my left to support my two hundred and fifty pounds.

I flew through the air, landing on the floor in the middle of the car with a cracking sound.

That was a fast sixty seconds.

Seven cars to go.

Reaching for my hat, I shook my head and looked up to see Fry still there holding the young woman. "Get her out of here."

The sound of the car somewhere ahead filling with coal was so loud now I could hardly hear myself, but he had and replied, "What about you?!"

"Don't worry about me, I can climb out on the board." My eyes scanned the darkness of the car until I saw the end of the thing leaning against the corner and another buried in the snow and pointing toward me—broken in half.

I sighed deeply and probably loud enough for him to hear. "The board broke; maybe I can just climb out as it fills?"

"A hundred and twenty tons of coal?!" He shook his head violently. "It'll be like treading quicksand, and two inches of this stuff the size of a door weighs hundreds of pounds—it'll crush you like an egg!"

Rolling to my side, I pushed off and stepped over to see that the thing had broken in half at a knothole, probably where I'd been standing. I held the broken end up where Fry could see it, his eyes wide. "There's another board lying on the back car. Get Jone off of here, then get that board and throw it down to me, and I'll take care of the rest!"

He looked over his shoulder to where I hoped the board still lay, shifted Jone, and disappeared over the edge.

I dropped the piece of broken board and even thought about kicking it, but the way things were going I'd have only broken my foot. I massaged my arm, which actually helped make it feel better.

It wasn't that I didn't think Fry could get the board, but first he had to carry the woman to safety, then retrieve the two-by-twelve, and get back up here with it—a tall order at best.

Just as I was thinking of what to do, the cars shook, and the pieces of board clattered together.

Six cars to go.

I stretched my jaw and looked around, trying to figure some way of getting out of the damn car, but could see nothing that might assist—one thing I was sure of, this board and I were through.

I walked from one end to the other, looking for some sort of hand- or foothold, but it was useless; the loading and unloading of the coal had polished the insides like mirrors.

Looking up at the chutes, I could still see only the sporadic bulbs and machinery of my death; *like treading quicksand*—those words had stuck in my head. I stood in the feathery drifts of snow and, figuring I'd at least save myself the embarrassment of getting the crap beaten out of me when the cars loaded again, placed my back against the bulkhead.

I was leaning against the cold metal, closing my arms around me in an attempt to keep warm, and thinking about all the ways in my life that I thought I'd go, this not being one of them—squashed like a mouse at the bottom of a coal bin.

I looked up, hoping to see Fry but knowing there was no way that he could've accomplished his rounds that quickly.

The high-rail truck continued to blast its horn, but with the sound of the coal dumping into the empty cars, there was no way that they would ever be heard.

I'd always thought that I was a pretty capable guy with the ability to take care of myself in just about any situation, but it was possible that I'd finally met my match with a hundred tons of black rock.

That flight from Gillette would have one empty seat, and the red-eye flight from Denver would leave without me, and the car waiting for me in Philadelphia would never take me to the maternity room at Pennsylvania Hospital.

A promise, the most important in my life, would never be kept. I would never get to see my grandchild.

There was suddenly a vibration in the back pocket of my jeans, almost like a reoccurring thought attempting to get my attention. I reached down and pulled out Vic's cell phone.

The screen was cracked, but there were two bars, and I punched the button as fast as I could. "Hello?!"

"Are you on your way to the airport?"

I choked with a croaking laugh as I cupped my hands around the phone. "Cady?!"

"I can barely hear; where are you?"

I looked around and yelled, "You wouldn't believe me if I told you!"

"Daddy—"

The cars rattled, and I lost my footing but not the phone.

That was a fast sixty seconds.

Five cars to go.

"Cady, I need you to do something, and I need you to do it quick!"

She suddenly sounded exasperated. "How quick? I'm kind of busy having a baby here——"

"Like in the next four minutes, as if my life depended on it! Which it does!" I yelled into the phone, attempting to override the noise of the coal cars and the high-rail's horn. "I need you to call Black Diamond Mine in Gillette and tell them it's an absolute emergency that they stop loading the train in their yard—right now!"

"And what do you want me to tell them?"

"To stop loading coal!"

"Right now?"

"Now!"

"Do you have the number?"

"No, I don't have the damned number! Cady, look it up and call them right now or else I'm going to be killed!"

"Okay, you don't have to yell . . ." There was a pause. "What do you mean killed? Where are you?"

"At the bottom of a coal car that they're filling right now—call!"

"Oh, my God——"

The phone went dead, and I was at least pretty sure that I'd conveyed the immediacy of the situation. I quickly dialed 911 and was soon speaking with the dispatcher for the Campbell County Sheriff's Office, the same woman I'd spoken with before. "The Black Diamond Mine, out near Arrosa!"

The train shifted again, leaving me standing in the middle, where I'd just been.

Four cars to go.

"And you want us to tell them what?"

I stared at the phone and then cupped it back to my ear. "To stop filling the coal cars. There must be some kind of emergency number that you can use to get through to them!" I stood there looking up at my impending hundred-ton doom.

"There's an administration number, would you like me to call that?"

I held the phone to my forehead, attempting to send brain waves telepathically through the air. "No, they're not going to be in the offices this time of night, and it's New Year's Eve, for Pete's sake; how about an operations manager or the loading facility?"

"Sir, can you move to another spot? The place where you are is awfully noisy . . ."

I held the phone back out and looked at it again, suppressing the urge to bounce it off the metal walls.

"Lady, I'm standing at the bottom of a coal car, and if you don't get through to someone in the next three minutes they're going to drop a hundred tons of low-sulfur, subbituminous coal on my head like I'm at the bottom of a mine! Now, would you please try and get through to someone at the Black Diamond so that that doesn't happen? Please!"

I hung up, figuring that if this was the last three minutes of my life, I didn't want to spend them extraordinarily annoyed.

Walking to the front of the car like a caged prisoner on a three-minute death row, I scanned the walls again, hoping for any kind of irregularity that might provide me with a way out. Seeing nothing, I walked to the back of the car and looked up at the spot where Fry would hopefully appear.

The sound of the coal dropping only a few cars away was so deafening I doubted that anyone would hear me if I called them, but I felt like calling Cady again to tell her all the things she already knew.

I felt like calling Vic and telling her all the things I knew, things we hadn't discussed, things we should have.

I thought about calling Henry and thanking him for his help with all my harebrained schemes, and for being the best friend anyone could have had.

A granddaughter, at least that's what Virgil White Buffalo had prophesied on the mountain, when he had also told me that there were dark days ahead—*You will stand and see the bad, the dead shall rise and the blind will see* . . . Maybe I should've listened to him a little closer in the lodge, because I couldn't come up with a situation that ended more darkly than this one.

Taking a deep breath, I prepared myself for what I was likely going to have to do, maybe scramble up a corner as the thing filled, trying to imagine what the chute was like. As I recalled, it was large and square and started unloading at the front and then moved to the back at three miles an hour, the coal dropping straight down. That wasn't good, in that I was hoping that the stuff would fill the bottom so that I could keep stepping on it to get high enough to pull myself out.

More than likely, I wouldn't make it.

The phone rang again, and I looked at it, seeing it was Cady. I punched the button and shouted over the din of the roaring coal dropping into a car that sounded a heck of a lot closer than four away and braced my boots in the snow to keep myself from bouncing around like a Ping-Pong ball.

"Cady?"

I could hear her screaming on the other end of the line, but the noise was so loud that I couldn't make out the words. "Cady, did you get through?"

There was more, but I still couldn't hear what she said, not so much for the noise as the sight of the loader methodically moving through the next car in front of me, dropping its tonnage and shifting inexorably toward the car where I stood.

Fry had miscalculated by two cars, not a bad estimate really, and I was no longer in the last car but the next to last.

Less than one car to go.

"Oh, shit . . . " I looked down at the phone in my hand and then brought it up to my ear. "I know you did the best you could do, punk. I love you."

I hit the button and looked up, watching the curtain of black descending into the next car, the vibrations of impact causing my car to shudder as if in a death grip.

The dust wafted over the rim and floated back toward me like the transparent veil of some grim reaper. I backed into the bulkhead, forgetting that I was already at the rear and there was nowhere else to go.

Covering my nose and mouth with a glove, I watched the bottom of the chute as big as the doors on the trailer end of an eighteen-wheeler move the length of the car next to me, dropping a hundred tons straight down in a man-made avalanche.

Trying to keep my hands free, I tucked the phone in my pocket even though it continued to vibrate. No matter what happened, no matter the weight of whatever hit me, I was going to have to remember to keep digging up and out of the car.

Backing into the corner because I figured the majority of the coal would drop in the center, I braced my arms and prepared for the next-to-last load of the train. The rumbling noise subsided like a wave having crashed, and I raised my head—if I was going to die, it wasn't going to be on my knees.

No cars to go.

The gigantic chute was over me, and I could see the operator's booth, which for some reason had bullet holes in the Plexiglas, the shattered panes spidering cracks out in all directions.

The loader shut down suddenly, and a couple dozen chunks of coal tumbled into the car. I looked straight up, and Fry was hanging over me with the board lying on the rim. "Hey, you okay?"

Looking up at the loading chute and not completely sure I was absolutely out of harm's way, I caught my breath and coughed, maybe twice. "Um, yep."

As the noise dwindled, I heard the sound of a very large-caliber pistol going off and heard a *spak* as another round hit the control room window. The shocked operator lifted his glasses from his eyes and peered through the dust at me, and a familiar voice rose out into the night like the sound of a coyote. "And if you turn that son of a bitch back on I'll empty the rest of this hogleg into you!"

Fry, with his head turned, was obviously enjoying what I assumed was an epic romantic spectacle of the American West— Lucian Connally, waving the Colt Walker in the air, sitting astride the locomotive behind us. Fry turned and looked down at me with a bright smile. "That old, one-legged boss of yours . . . He's some kind of loco."

I croaked a response. "Boy howdy."

16

"No, I'm all right. Honest." I reached up and touched the thick bandage the doctors had wrapped all the way around my neck and tried to ignore Sandy Sandburg, two of his deputies, three highway patrolmen, Lucian, and Corbin Dougherty as they tried not to look interested in my call. Standing in the entryway of the Campbell County Memorial Hospital Emergency Room, I leaned against the wall and nodded into Vic's cell phone. "I know; it was a bad situation, but I'm okay now."

"So you're on your way to the airport, right, Dad?"

There was no use lying, she'd inherited her mother's unerring ability to spot dissembling at every level. "I've just got to make a stop on the way."

"What kind of stop?"

"I'll make the plane, I promise." I pulled out my watch and looked at it. "I've got an hour and a half, the weather has cleared, sort of, and it's on the way."

"I'm going to kill you myself."

"Honest, I just need to make one more stop to sew things up, then I'm off to the airport."

I listened to her sighing on the line. "If you don't, I'm giving the baby your middle name . . ."

I smiled, confident that I was no longer in really big trouble. "Oh, don't do that."

"I'm serious."

I laughed. "What if it's a girl?"

"Then it'll be even worse, and she'll have no one else to blame but you." Another sigh. "Excuse me for asking, but isn't there a sheriff's department in Campbell County and a Gillette police force, and isn't Uncle Lucian involved in getting you into this?"

"Well—"

"Is he there?"

"Well—"

"Put him on."

I glanced at the old sheriff and then tried handing him the phone, but he acted as if I were trying to hand him a stick of dynamite, lit. He brushed the device away with a hand and stepped back into the fluorescent light of the Campbell County Memorial Hospital Emergency Room.

I pulled the phone back to my ear. "I don't think he wants to talk to you."

"Hold it out where he can hear me then."

I did as I was told and listened as she raised her voice to be heard from afar. "Uncle Lucian?"

He looked at the phone, then at me as if I were a dirty rodent, and then snatched the thing out of my hand. He took a deep breath of his own and plastered a smile on his face for the performance. "Hey, Cady, darlin' . . . How you doin', honeybunch?"

For the next two solid minutes, the old sheriff looked at the floor and said nothing except for a few monosyllabic grunts and a few yeps. After the final response, he handed me back the phone and blew out air through his puckered lips.

I listened, but she had already hung up, so I pocketed the cell and looked at him, pale as I'd ever seen him. "We need to get me on that plane at midnight."

He barked a short laugh with no joy in it. "In no uncertain terms."

"Did she thank you for saving my life?"

"She did."

I turned to look at the unofficial eight-man task force. "We don't need this many people."

Sandburg laughed and shook his head. "The only one that doesn't need to be in on this is you."

"Yep, well . . . I started it, so I'm going to finish it."

He turned to the assembled manpower. "Run along and try not to be an embarrassment to your collective departments." They nodded and did as he said, the automatic doors opening and closing, allowing the arctic wind to creep in, always uninvited. "I don't know if that plane of yours is going to get off the ground tonight. Not with all this fog."

Walking past him, I paused to let the air in again. "It will clear before midnight."

I held the door open for Lucian, and I helped him climb into my truck but then he stuck a boot out to hold the door open. "How 'bout we just get a head start over to the airport; I got a funny feeling about this one."

I stood there, the cold trying to creep up the backside of my

Fauxhartt Kmart special coat that the hospital staff had returned to me. "You getting scary in your old age?"

"Maybe so." He didn't move but sat there with his boot still propped in the door—a spanner in the works, Lucian style. "In all my years on the job, I don't think there's ever been a situation I've looked forward to less."

"Maybe you're the one who should sit this one out."

He studied the sticker on my dash, the one that read WARN-ING, USE OVERDRIVE IN HIGH SPEED PURSUIT, and the addition Vic had made in marker below that read AND DO NOT SHOOT THROUGH WINDSHIELD. He started to say something but then stopped and then started again. "I warned her that you were like a gun; that we had to be careful where we pointed you . . ."

I thought about how it had all started, how it had been a fa-vor for a woman with a set of legs that didn't work because of a carefree accident with to-go cups so long ago. I thought about how it had been a search to find out why a man who had never broken a rule in his life had checked into the Wrangler Motel, locked the door, and taken his life. "I'm sorry."

He looked at me. "For what, doing your job?"

I nodded. "This job is hateful sometimes."

His jaw clamped shut, but the words still escaped. "If I never taught you anything, I taught you that a long time ago." He moved his foot and gestured toward the door. "Now close that damn thing before I catch my death."

I shut it and thought to myself that it would take a sight more than that to kill Lucian Connally, and then walked around the back of my truck as the Campbell County Sheriff's car pulled up and stopped, the Campbell County Sheriff rolling the window down and airing an elbow. "How 'bout you just head on out to the airport, Walt?"

I stopped and looked into the muted distance at the southern hills. "Why is every cop in Wyoming trying to get rid of me?"

"We like you; that's what we do with people we like." He shrugged and gestured toward Dougherty, sitting in his passenger seat. "Right?"

The patrolman smiled a thin grin.

"You're playing backup on this one, Sandy, I don't even want you in the house."

He studied me. "You're sure about this, huh?"

"Yep."

"It's going to be a big deal."

I pulled my keys from my pocket. "Look on the bright side."

"What's that?"

"Your family's not involved after all."

I climbed in the Bullet and began the slow drive to the west of town and the Iron Horse subdivision. The weather didn't seem to be getting that much better, and although the snow had stopped, the term "socked in" kept coming to mind, and I started thinking about promises. There was supposed to be more weather tomorrow, but I hoped to be gone long before then.

The whole case wasn't ending the way I'd hoped it would, but that was usually the scenario in my line of work. I drove carefully on the unplowed Echeta Road, guiding the tires in an almost out-of-body experience. I looked over at Lucian, but he was staring out the passenger-side window, lost in his own thoughts. In some ways, I'm sure he was sorry that we'd ever become involved in this investigation, but like me, he knew that you had to ride the trail till it ended. It was a lonely pursuit we had chosen and one that always finished with reading one more report, making one more phone call, or knocking on one more door—and reading one more person their rights, if you were lucky.

I took a right and then pulled up to the railroad crossing and stopped, making sure I looked both ways.

"I bet you're gonna be a lot more careful around these things, huh?"

I pulled out and made the right into the warren of streets.

The only addition to the Holman household was a blue Volvo, sitting in the driveway, but other than that, everything looked the same as it had—even the Santa was still lying in the yard like a New Year's Eve drunk, the coal dust spread across him like Lucian's pulverized pepper steak. "You're not going to reinflate that silly bastard again, are you?"

"Yep, if for no other reason than good luck." I pushed open the door and started across the yard, picked up good St. Nick, and plugged in the tiny air pump, just as I'd done before. I watched as the sheriff's car pulled up behind mine and also saw three more deputy cars down the street, along with three from the Highway Patrol.

Sandy, Dougherty, and Lucian met me at the sidewalk as I gestured toward the assorted manpower. "What the heck is that?"

"I told 'em to go away, but they won't." The sheriff glanced over his shoulder. "It's your escort to the airport."

I glanced at the door. "You're still not going in."

"The hell I'm not, it's my county."

I cast my eyes at Lucian. "We started this, and we'll finish it."

He glanced at us. "You two armed?"

"Nope; there isn't going to be any shooting."

He nudged his hat back. "Nice to be sure about those types of things."

"Yep, it is." I turned and walked toward the front door with Lucian in tow.

I knocked and then rang the doorbell.

Nothing.

Lucian tried the knob, and the door floated open into the museum-like interior of the Holman home in a déjà-vu-all-over-again experience. With a glance back at the old sheriff, I entered. Everything was exactly as it had been the first time we'd walked into the place, our boots making strange, crisp sounds on the plastic walkways that crisscrossed the house.

Heading into the kitchen, I stopped when I noticed something out of place, a coffee cup on the kitchen counter with peach lipstick on the rim.

Lucian touched the handle of the mug, turning it with a finger. "Not Phyllis's shade."

"Any reason to check the upstairs?"

He shook his head. "Not that I can think of."

I moved toward the basement door, noticing that the wheel-chair was still parked at the top.

There was no muted sound of a ballgame as there had been before, just an uneasy silence and three black screens looking back at the woman. Easing my way past the stair elevator, I stepped to the side and Lucian joined me.

Phyllis Holman wasn't working; her fingers were laced in her lap over a knitted afghan. At first, I thought it might've been a commercial break, but there was no graceful tapping at the letters that would form sentences, that would form paragraphs, that would form the kind of entertainment that would distract people from their lives, lives that sometimes led to the situation we now found ourselves confronting.

The elderly woman stared at the blank screens, dark as the world collapsing around her, and refused to acknowledge our presence.

I stepped forward, positioning myself between two of the monitors. "Mrs. Holman?"

She didn't respond.

"Mrs. Holman."

She looked up at me, at first annoyed, but then focused on my face and the bandage around my neck. "You're hurt."

I took off my hat. "Yes, ma'am. It's been a long day." She nodded and then returned her eyes to the television without saying anything more, and I waited, but not very long. "No game?"

She didn't look at me this time. "No."

I nodded and stepped in a little closer. "We're looking for your daughter—we're looking for Connie." She said nothing. "Mrs. Holman?"

"She's not here."

"Her car is parked out front."

Her hands shook as she spoke. "She's not here."

"There's also a half cup of coffee on your kitchen counter with lipstick traces."

"That's my cup."

"You and I both know you never left a cup on a counter in your life." I took a deep breath and slowly let it out with my words. "It would be nice if life weren't so messy, but that's just not the nature of things; we want things to be perfect, but most of the time we just spend our existence cleaning up the messes we make—and sometimes the messes of other people, people about whom we care most in the world."

Her eyes came up slow, and the words came from her mouth in a staccato of verbal bursts. "Can't. You. Just. Go. Away?"

"You know we can't." I waited a moment and then continued. "That's what happened with Gerald, wasn't it? When he found out what your daughter was guilty of and that it was something that he couldn't clean up—at least not without breaking the law, which was something he'd never do—he punished himself."

"Go away."

"That's the problem with guilt, it's a two-way street; our children have to live with the things we do, and sometimes we have to live with their actions." I moved in closer. "We tell them that we can protect them, but we can't even protect ourselves from the mistakes we make—that's why I'm here."

"I told you—go away."

"He didn't tell you what she was doing, did he? He thought he could protect you if he killed himself and took the knowledge with him, but these things often can't be hidden. We found the report that he didn't file, the one where he talked to a woman by the name of Izzy. It took me a long time to put it together, but then I remembered that Lucian had referred to your daughter as Izzy, the nickname Gerald had used for her. I don't think your daughter is a bad person, Mrs. Holman. I don't know how she got involved in all this, but she's made some terrible mistakes and she's going to have to answer for them."

She finally looked at me, the words striking out like a machete. "I hired you."

"No, ma'am, you didn't. You requested my help and I came,

but nobody's paying me." I stood there with her glaring at me. "We've got a warrant, and there are about a half-dozen police officers out in front of your house right now, but I don't really want it to happen like that."

Her chin dropped to her chest, and she began fussing with the blanket that hid her legs, and I wasn't surprised when she pulled a small Smith & Wesson revolver from the folds and held it there pointed at the floor.

I sighed deeply and then placed my hand in my pocket and waited.

The sobs that wracked her body were horrifying to listen to and watch, and all I could think was that this poor woman had paid enough in one life.

I glanced at the door to our right. "Where is Connie?"

"It wasn't supposed to be like this . . ."

"I know."

"We didn't do anything wrong; we were good parents." Her eyes came up to mine. "I didn't know."

"I'm sure you didn't, but people have been hurt and people are dead."

She raised the pistol a little higher and looked at it.

"Where is Connie?"

She pointed the .32 at me, and all I felt was tired.

"Go away."

I shook my head. "You know I can't do that."

She pulled the hammer back. "I said, go away."

"That's not how this is going to end, all these horrible things, with one more horrible act . . ." I held out my hand. "It's just going to end quietly and with dignity."

There we were, the two of us staring at each other, neither

of us wanting to be where we were, doing what we were doing, facing what we were facing. I tried to imagine how far I would go to protect my child, but I was just too tired to measure that kind of infinite distance.

Phyllis Holman held the .32 on me until her hand began to shake and then carefully lowered the hammer, turned the thing sideways, and held it out to me.

I took it and then turned to see Lucian holding his own side-arm hidden along his leg as I passed him and headed toward the door to the right. "I thought you were unarmed."

He countered to the left and approached Phyllis as I continued on. "I ain't ever unarmed."

I turned the knob and swung it open to reveal a lonely room with only a single bed, a nightstand, and an old dresser. The wallpaper was peeling, and the carpet was stained, an anomaly in the otherwise pristine Holman house—a room to be used and forgotten, shunned and shut away, a cell. There were narrow windows above, two of them, choked with snow, and an old door in the far corner.

There was no one in the room, but the covers of the bed were pulled to one side where someone had been sitting, hiding, waiting. I looked behind the door to make sure there was no one there, stuffed the Smith into my pocket, and tried the other door. I pried it open to find stairs leading to a set of cellar doors, one of them pushed back, the fog rolling down the steps.

I launched up them as fast as my exhausted legs could carry me and stood in the backyard; there were prints leading toward the side of the house, and it looked like she'd started for her car but had seen the constabulary out front and had doubled back toward a small gate in a chain-link fence. Did she really think she had a chance of getting away? I thought about calling in the troops but figured she was probably tired, cold, and afraid and that I would rather try and talk her in myself.

Lifting the clasp, I stepped through and closed the gate behind me, turning to follow the prints as they made their way through an abandoned lot and then down a slope to a flat area. There were a few cottonwoods, bare and stark in the frozen fog, and it was almost as if I were rushing across a white desert.

There was a shape in the distance that looked human, but as I got closer, it seemed to fade away. I thought I could hear something coming, but sound was muffled and seemed to resonate from all directions. I thought about the buffalo in Custer State Park, and what Virgil had said, and it seemed like the natural world was closing in around me. Unconsciously, my hand drifted down to the confiscated .32 in my pocket; evidently, I never went unarmed either.

When I got to the edge of the hill, I looked to the west and could see the sheriff's department's light bar rotating blue onto the front of the Holman house. When I turned east I saw the figure again, just barely within my field of vision. I stepped and half slid down the hillside and started jogging down a path. After a moment, in one of those patches of clarity that happen on a foggy night, I could see her striding along Echeta Road, parallel with the train tracks, and eventually the highway.

Being in the state she was in, I suppose she thought she could just walk away into the fog.

I continued after her as she headed back toward the center of town, walking alongside the twelve-foot chain-link fence that guarded the railroad tracks, the spiraled razor wire making it seem as if we were in a prison.

In the distance, I could hear the horn of an oncoming train, possibly the one that Jone Urrecha and I had escaped from.

Hurrying my pace, I got within fifty yards of her and called out. "Connie!"

She stopped and turned to look at me, the slight wind pulling at her hair and long wool coat as if we were in some Brontë novel. She stood there like an unfinished phrase.

We looked at each other. I guess it was the most hopeful moment I had had, but I ruined it by starting toward her again. When I did, she turned and began running.

About twenty more yards down the road she slowed and dodged to the right through an opening in the fence, her coat snagging on the wire and holding her up.

Running faster, I got within an arm's length, but she shrugged off the heavy garment and left it hanging as she leapt forward and then began climbing the short hill leading toward the tracks. I tried pushing myself through the area where the chain-link had been cut and pulled apart, but the opening was too small. "Connie!"

At the top of the incline, she stepped onto the ties and turned to look down the tracks where the whistle blew again, closer this time. Then she turned and looked back at me, the breeze blowing her hair across her face, hiding half of it.

We stood there as before, looking at each other, but this time I could move no closer.

Seeing my situation, she seemed to relax, and then spoke. "I used to come here when I was a kid; we'd put pennies on the rails and then come back and get them."

I pulled her coat from the wires and held it out to her through the opening. "Come take your coat; it's freezing out here."

She stood there, unmoving.

The train horns sounded again, and she turned toward them, the hair blowing back from her face. "I used to dance."

I looked down the rails but couldn't see anything yet.

"I was really good."

I turned back to look at her and watched as she stretched her neck.

She went up on tiptoes, placed her arms in position, and turned, slowly at first, but then gaining momentum until she spun like a dervish. Coming to a stop, she faltered a bit and leaned forward, catching herself and laughing. "I'm a little out of practice."

I pulled at the fence, but the opening was only wide enough for me to fit one leg and a shoulder through, my face pressed up against the chain-link.

Her voice was high and just a little bit manic. "I used to practice all the time, trying to keep my weight down I got stuck on amphetamines and a bunch of other stuff . . ." She moved her feet up onto the rail and balanced there. "It never goes away, you know."

The train horns sounded again.

"You'd be amazed at the things you'll do; things you can't even imagine." She began walking the rail as if it were a balance beam in a portrait of poise, flexibility, and strength. "Dave got me involved in all this, and I helped him. It got more involved, and he sold Linda to some guy in Florida."

She twirled again and then stopped.

"I had this plan for my life, but when that fell through I decided I'd teach and help other people with their dreams . . . But I guess that didn't work out, either."

I could hear the train now, the vibration of the thing pounding the rails like punishment.

She stopped and turned to look in its direction. "I don't think I can watch it—don't have the stomach for it." Then she turned to look at my face. "I guess that makes me a coward, huh? I might jump out of the way or something." She turned on the rail and continued her performance. "Can't have that."

The horns sounded again, and now I could see the four headlights of the locomotive pushing through the fog, bound and determined to get somebody this time. Pulling on the post at the other side, I felt my jeans tearing and the canvas of my coat shredding as I tried to get through the ragged edges.

Struggling against the opening, I felt the wire ends drag across the side of my face, pulling at the bandages on my neck, and the sudden warmth of my blood as it trickled down my cheek and saturated the collar of my coat.

Breaking my head free, I yanked at the rest of me, but the opening wasn't big enough, and I just hung there like a side of beef and watched the big train coming down the line like a juggernaut of justice, inevitable and unstoppable.

She took a few more steps on the rail but then stopped and folded her arms over her chest, still facing the other way. "I guess it's time to go."

I grunted and pulled hard, and with one sudden yank, I staggered forward and fell on the ice in the ditch on the other side.

Pushing myself up, I could see the coal train only a couple hundred yards down the tracks, rumbling toward us at speed. I scrambled off the ice up the incline toward the woman, but slipped and slid down on the snow, gritty with coal dust.

When I looked again, it was a lot closer.

I figured it would take a few seconds to get the rest of the way up the incline and another few to get a hold of her and snatch her from the tracks.

I looked back as I dug in with my boots and, taking an angular route, scrambled up and could now see the details of the giant orange and black conveyance, the front rails with the safety chain hanging between, the treads that led over the hood, and even noticed that the front had a modified cowcatcher—that would be the part that struck us.

No way I was going to make it.

Even with the approaching roar of the train, I could hear the siren of a car pulling onto the road behind me and could see the revolving illumination of the blue lights on the snow. Doors slammed, and I could hear Sandburg and Dougherty calling from behind me but couldn't understand the words.

Catching a few good footholds, I felt myself going up the hill before I was even aware that I was trying, the snow and coal dust passing under my eyes as I just kept digging and trying not to look to my left, focusing so hard that all I could hear was my breathing.

Reaching the top with a roaring rush of my own, I finally glanced back and could see the train was on top of us, the horn blaring in a din that was deafening. I threw myself into her and felt the toe of my boot hit the end of a tie, and all I could think was that I was going to trip and land the both of us on the rails.

The train bore down with a sudden rush of wind, carrying the fog and thunderous din with it. Making sure to use my left arm to wrap her up, I carried the two of us across the tracks onto the downslope with a tremendous thump, tumbling and sliding to the bottom.

Still holding her next to me, I watched silently as the thing passed by, car after car after car. She began crying and clutched me, finally converting the sobs into a low and steady moan that unintentionally mimicked the train's whistle in a sad and wrenching lament.

EPILOGUE

The taxicab driver said that the regular route to Pennsylvania Hospital would be a parking lot this time of morning, especially with the snow piled to the curbs and the fact that it was New Year's Day and therefore the Mummers Parade but that he knew a shortcut.

He patted the dash of the run-down Crown Vic. "Beena will get us there, she used to work for the police department." He turned to look at me. "Baggage?"

"More than I can carry."

"Where is it?"

I closed the door behind me. "Sorry, I was joking."

He nodded and turned back toward the meter. "Cash or credit?"

"Cash."

"We'll get there even faster." He punched the button on his dash and then the accelerator. We drove, and he continued to smile at me in the rearview mirror. "I have to tell you, that's one bad hat you're wearing."

"Thanks." We drove on, taking a banked loop underneath the highway, which was, as he'd predicted, jammed.

"Texas?"

I watched the floating snow flurries, somehow different from that of the high plains. "Wyoming."

"Where's that?"

"Above Colorado and below Montana."

He edged the Crown Vic forward and then hit his horn as an individual in another cab cut in front of him and attempted to crowd his way into the lane escaping the airport. "There's a state in between those two?"

"Since 1890."

I could see him still studying me in the rearview mirror, probably taking note of the bruises, stitches on my face, bandages around my neck, and that little piece of my ear that was missing. "Don't they have doctors there?"

I breathed a tired chuckle. "Yep, but my daughter lives here, and she's the one having the baby." On cue, I felt the phone vibrating in my pocket. One of the flight attendants had been kind enough to plug the thing in and recharge it after giving me a glass of champagne or it would've been long dead. I pulled it out and recognized the number. "Sweet-pea?"

The voice of the Cheyenne Nation came on the line. "I am supposed to ask where you are. Please do not answer with any other location than the City of Brotherly Love."

"Just got in a cab from the airport."

Another pause. "There was a car waiting for you, did you not see the man holding the sign with your name on it?"

"Are you kidding? I'm lucky I saw the airport." I looked around. "Well, I'm in this one. Anyway, I'm on my way to Pennsylvania Hospital, right?"

"Yes, everyone is here."

"Well . . . Almost everyone, I hope."

"The only other member of the party is due at 8:20 A.M."

I nodded into the phone. "Thanks for the reminder."

"You have two hours to get to the hospital. Do you think you will make it?"

I leaned forward to get the taxi driver's attention. "How long to Pennsylvania Hospital?"

He studied the road ahead. "Thirty minutes, tops."

I repeated the response to the Bear, but this time it was someone else on the line. "Hurry up and get here, these fucking people are driving me up a wall. You'd think that no one had ever had a baby in the history of vaginas."

"By *fucking people* I assume you mean your family?"

"All of 'em, including my uncle Al who in the spirit of the New Year was the only one thoughtful enough to bring wine and glasses." There was a pause. "How you doin'?"

I stared at my reflection in the window. "I'm good."

"I heard you're even more torn all to hell than when we left you."

"A little."

There was a pause. "Where are you anyway?"

I spoke out to the driver. "Where are we?"

He trailed the words over his shoulder as I held the phone out. "Lindbergh Boulevard, driving past Suffolk Park."

When I returned the device to my ear there was real annoyance in her voice. "What the fuck are you doing all the way over there?"

"Avoiding the Mummers."

"Let me talk to the taxi driver."

"No."

There was mumbling in the background and then the voice on the phone changed again. "Daddy?"

I smiled at her voice. "Hey, punk."

"You're going to be here, right?"

"Come hell or high water."

"Do not get involved in any investigations between wherever you are and the hospital."

"I won't."

"I love you."

"I love you, too." The phone went dead, and I repocketed it as we took a right. There was an area of leafless trees, the dark branches reaching up into the metallic sky like veins.

"You are having a grandbaby?"

His voice breaking my reverie, I looked at the one eye I could see in the rearview mirror. "Yep."

The traffic became more congested, and we slowed. "Congratulations." We moved a little farther but then stopped again, and he handed me a card with his name on it. "If you have any need for a driver while you are here in Philadelphia, I would be honored to assist you."

I read it and looked up at him. "You're a Patel?"

"You know my name?"

"I know the occupation. You're sure you don't have any family running a motel in Wyoming?"

"We're everywhere, a third of all motel owners in the U.S. are called Patel, and it is a surname that indicates that they're members of a Gujarati Hindu subcaste."

"I know." I smiled. "The Patel Motel phenomenon."

"You actually know this?"

"I do."

He smiled at me in the mirror. "With your hat, you are a real cowboy?"

"No." We slowly passed under another highway and into the patchwork of blocks that made up most cities, red brick and buildings a lot older than 1890.

He drummed the steering wheel, venting his frustration with the traffic. "But they let you wear the hat?"

"I'm a sheriff."

He shrugged. "So you get to do whatever you want."

I thought about it and watched the landscape change from strip malls to light industry as we passed over the Schuylkill River. "Not exactly."

He eyed me again. "Looks like somebody did whatever they wanted to you—no offense."

"None taken." I felt the stitches on my face, feeling as if I were growing spines through my cheek like a porcupine; the itching had finally gotten so bad that I'd just taken the bandages off. "I've had a rough couple of days."

"Chasing bad guys?"

I smiled even though it hurt, his phrase reminding me of the answering machine message my daughter had recorded for me: *This is the Longmire residence, we're not able to answer your call right now because we're out chasing bad guys or trying on white hats . . .* "Something like that."

"Train robbers?"

"Nope." I had slept and dreamed the entire flight from Gillette to Denver, awakened briefly to climb on the second plane, and then had dreamed and slept from Denver to Philadelphia, but the dreams were crowded with white buffaloes and dark prophecies. I was still tired. Maybe it was because I was punchy, but every once in a while you find yourself in a situation where you want to talk, and sometimes it's to a total stranger, maybe even a stranger who doesn't know that a faraway place like Wyoming exists. "There was a suicide of a sheriff's investigator in an adjacent county, and I was called in on the case."

"Sheriffs have investigators out there?"

I glanced up at the skyline of the fifth-largest city in the United States and the back of William Penn or, at least, the Alexander Milne Calder twenty-seven-ton bronze sculpture of the man, one of two hundred and fifty bronzes that adorn the outside of city hall, with seven hundred rooms, the largest municipal building in the country. "Oh, I bet you've got them here, too."

"This Wyoming sounds like a rough place."

"Not really, we have about twenty homicides a year in comparison to Philadelphia, which averages about three hundred and twenty."

"Yes, but we are a big city."

"And we're a big state."

Calder had wanted the statue to face south so that the detail he'd wrought in Penn's features would be highlighted by the sunshine to better reveal the complexity of the work. There would be no sunshine today, but it didn't matter; the statue faces northeast toward my daughter's building in Old City near Fishtown, commemorating the site where Penn signed the treaty with the Lenape tribe to create the city. "Anyway, this suicide put me on the case of three missing women."

"Did you find them?"

"Yep."

He shrugged. "That's good."

"One is dead."

"That is bad."

"Yep." I sighed. "And I guess there's somebody out there that's put a contract on my life."

"I am sorry for your troubles."

It was a heartfelt statement. "Me, too." I spotted a cheese steak joint and felt my stomach growl and tried to think of the last time I'd eaten anything. "One of the women was found in Miami, and we turned all the information over to the FBI—the authorities there located her."

The phone vibrated in my hand. "Excuse me." I cupped it to my ear. "I'm ten minutes away."

"I'm hoping that's not the case."

I recognized the voice of the Gillette patrolman. "Dougherty?"

"Yeah, did you make it to Philadelphia?"

"I did, what are you doing working on New Year's Day?"

"The sheriff offered me the Cold Case position and I took it. He said I had a unique skill set that would be perfect for the job."

"He fire Richard Harvey?"

"He's out on dental leave."

"I bet. What can I do for you?"

"I just thought you'd be interested that the Las Vegas PD did a search on Deke Delgatos's place and found a bunch of personal correspondence with a guy in Mexico City who they think is the one who put the hit out on you. You ever hear of a guy by the name of Tomás Bidarte?"

I could feel my jaw tightening.

"Sheriff?"

"Yep . . ." I thought about the man who had almost killed Vic, the man who had gotten away. "Yep, I have."

Dougherty seemed sorry to have brought up the subject. "I just thought it was something you ought to know, you know?"

"Yep. No, thanks, troop. Any word on Jone Urrecha?"

"She's fine; a little worse for wear due to the concussion and exposure, but they're only keeping her a few days for observation so I'm having dinner with her sister."

"Corbin, you dog you."

"It's just dinner."

"Make sure she doesn't bring her stapler."

I hit the button and rested the phone on my knee. So, he wasn't dead, not by a long shot. I thought about how Henry and I had covered all that ground down near Sulphur Creek and hadn't found a trace of the man.

The driver interrupted my thoughts. "This is your first grandchild?"

"Um, yep."

"Girl or boy?"

"A . . ." I thought of white buffaloes and Virgil as I listened to the slush of the melted snow rhythmically scour the underside of the Crown Vic; I attempted to collect my wayward thoughts. "A friend of mine says it's a girl."

"Good, girls are best."

"And why is that?"

"Sons, they have their own plans, but a daughter or granddaughter, they will love you forever and take care of you in your old age." The traffic had slowed to a stop, and I couldn't help but pull my pocket watch out and check the time as he watched me. "Don't worry, we'll get you there, my man. What time is this daughter of yours scheduled to deliver?"

"Eight-twenty."

He shook his head. "Nothing to worry about. Take it from a man with five children; they always go later than they say. I will bet you a ten-dollar bill."

The exhale of my breath clouded the window beside my face. "You haven't met my daughter."

The car began moving again, and we'd almost made it to midtown when we lurched to a stop to allow a SEPTA surface trolley to go by. "These damned trolleys, they are so slow, and they take forever."

"How many cars?"

Not fully understanding my question at first, it took him a few seconds to answer. "Um, two."

I slipped my hat over my face and smiled, looking forward to seeing all my old friends—and a new one. "You're on."

Cady and Michael Moretti
Proudly Announce the Birth of Their Daughter

Lola Longmire Moretti

At 8:20 AM EST
7 Pounds
20.5 Inches

Craig Johnson's eleventh novel featuring Sheriff Walt Longmire is available in May 2015 in Viking hardcover.

Read on for the first chapter of

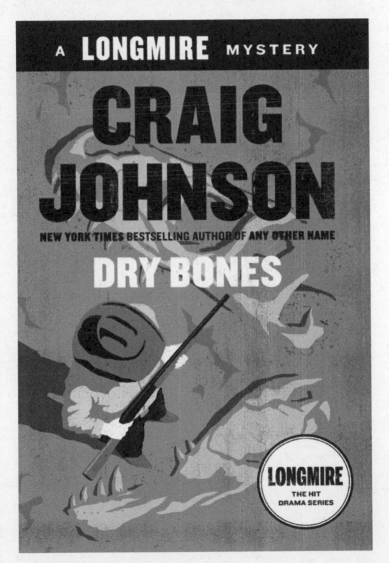

A **LONGMIRE** MYSTERY

CRAIG JOHNSON

NEW YORK TIMES BESTSELLING AUTHOR OF ANY OTHER NAME

DRY BONES

LONGMIRE
THE HIT
DRAMA SERIES

Craig Johnson's eleventh novel featuring Sheriff Walt Longmire is available in May 2015 in Viking hardcover.

Read on for the first chapter of

She was close to thirty years old when she was killed.

A big girl, she liked to carouse with the boys at the local watering holes, which of course led to a lot of illegitimate children, but by all counts, she was a pretty good single parent and could take care of herself. One night, though, a gang must have jumped her; they were all younger than she was, they had numbers, they might've even been family, and after they broke her leg and she was on the ground, it was pretty much over.

There was no funeral. They killed her and left what remained there by the water, where the sediment from the forgotten creek built up around her, layer after layer, compressing and compacting her to the point where the bones leeched away and were replaced by minerals.

It was as if she'd turned to stone just to keep from being forgotten.

It's interesting how her remains were found; her namesake, Jennifer Watt, was traveling with Dave Baumann, the director of the High Plains Dinosaur Museum, when they got a flat—not an unusual occurrence on the red roads the ranchers used for the more inaccessible areas of their ranches where the larger chunks of shale attacked sidewalls like tomahawks. The bigger rock is cheaper, but it's also the size of bricks and has lots of sharp edges, edges that like to make meals of anything less than ten-ply.

Dave had been trying to squeak another season out of the tires on the '67 Land Rover, but there they stood, staring at a right rear with a distinct lack of round, in the middle of the Lone Elk Ranch. While he fished the jack and spare from the hood and began the arduous task of replacing the tire, Jennifer unloaded Brody, her Tibetan mastiff, and went for a walk. Hoping to meet a friend on the place, she followed a ridge around a cornice, but the dog, who was 150 pounds with a heavy coat, began panting. Before long Jen decided that it might be a pretty good idea for the two of them to try and get to some shade, not an easy proposition out on the Powder River country; luckily, there was a rock overhang along the ridge with enough room for her and the dog to get out of the late afternoon sun.

She wore her blonde hair in a ponytail that stuck through the adjustment strap of her Hole-in-the-Wall Bar ball cap, and, pulling the collapsible dog bowl from her pack, she slipped out a Nalgene bottle, took a swig, and then poured the mastiff a drink.

Jennifer looked out onto the grass that undulated like a gigantic, rolling sea. It was easy to imagine the Western Interior (Cretaceous) Seaway or the Niobraran Sea that had once covered this land, splitting the continent of North America into two landmasses, Laramidia to the west and Appalachia to the east. The great sea had stretched from Mexico to the Arctic and had been over two thousand feet deep. She settled under the rock and petted the dog, her green eyes scanning the landscape.

Jennifer pulled her video camera from her pack and panned the distance, seeing things out there on the high plains, things that didn't exist, at least not anymore—predatory marine reptiles like long-necked plesiosaurs and more alligator-like mosasaurs almost eighty feet long. Sharks such as Squalicorax swam through her imagination along with giant, shellfish-eating Ptychodus mortoni.

When she'd been six, her father had brought her to this country from Tucson, Arizona, and had dragged her along on his private excavations that helped support his rock shop on the old highway out near Lake DeSmet between Durant and Sheridan. She still remembered what she'd said one day as they'd gotten out of his battered pickup, her fingers climbing up his pant leg until she found the reassuring hand with gloves worn like saddle leather, the adjustment straps with the transparent red beads. "There's nothing out here, Dad."

He surveyed the rolling hills that led from the Bighorn Mountains to the endless Powder River country, smiled as he pushed back his straw hat, and spoke gently to her. "There's everything here; you just have to know where to look."

Jennifer had learned to look and had never stopped; Dave Baumann's hands and hers were in the excavations that had led to the displays that crowded the High Plains Dinosaur Museum in Durant, and at twenty-six, she was still searching.

Truth be told, Jen liked dead things better than live ones—they were less trouble, the conversations being one-sided. A lot of investigators and paleontologists are more comfortable that way, able to accept the consensus of truth, disregarding the absolute as something that always carries the danger of being overturned by some new and extraordinary piece of evidence.

She lowered the camera, took another sip of water, and poured her dog more. Brody sighed and shook his massive head, and Jen leaned back under the rock overhang to try to decide what she was going to do with the old man's rock shop, a ramshackle affair near the lake that had started out as a trailer but through the years had evolved into a labyrinth of wooden fences lined with geodes, gems, quartz, and rock samples, most of them worthless.

He had died the year before, and she knew the land was more valuable than the structure itself, but she'd grown up there and loved the old place, as cluttered and tacky as it might be. She pulled the cap over her eyes and dozed until she became aware of a protracted growl in her dog's throat. She swatted at him, but he continued to rumble a warning until she finally lifted the bill of her cap to look at him. He was looking directly up. Jen's eyes followed to where a two-fingered talon stretched out of the rock ceiling down toward her, almost as if it were imploring. She grabbed the camera and began to film what would become one of the greatest paleontological discoveries in modern times.

Victoria Moretti sipped the coffee from the chrome lid of my thermos, leaned forward, and, peering through the windshield, watched the man with an intensity that only her tarnished gold eyes could command. "Is that some weird-ass Wyoming fishing technique I don't know about?"

I could see that Omar was tossing something into the water from the banks of the man-made reservoir.

"What the hell is he doing?"

Ruby, my dispatcher, had received a call from him early in the morning and had bushwhacked Dog and me with it when we came in the door. I had filled up my thermos and in turn bushwhacked Vic before heading out to the ten-thousand-acre Lone Elk place to find out what was up.

Outdoor adventurer, outfitter, and big-game bon vivant, Omar Rhoades had contracts with all the big ranchers and sometimes used their property for extended hunting and fishing junkets. Usually he kept his spots secret, but this time he'd told Ruby where he was and that I might want to come out and meet him.

Most everything was in bloom in late May, and I breathed in the scents from the open windows of my truck. As I stared at the aspens and cottonwood, they all began stretching to the sky like those cypresses in Italy that looked like thumb smudges.

My undersheriff turned and looked at me some more. "I thought he was in China."

"Mongolia."

The Custer look-alike was dressed in a state-of-the-art fishing vest, waders, and his ever-present black cowboy hat with more flies stuck in it than Orvis has in its catalog. All in all, I estimated the total worth of his outfit at somewhere close to two thousand dollars, and he wasn't even carrying the fly rod, which was sticking out the rear of his custom-made SUV that dwarfed my three-quarter-ton.

I leaned forward and stared through the windshield. We watched as he drew something from one hand, carefully took aim, and tossed whatever it was onto the smooth surface of the water, black like an oil slick.

Vic turned to look at me as she reached back and scratched the fur behind Dog's ear. "Do you think he's finally lost it?"

I pulled the handle and climbed out of the truck, careful to keep the Saint Bernard/German shepherd/plains grizzly inside. "Let's go find out."

The beauty of Italian descent followed with my thermos as we glided our way through the morning dew in the buffalo grass. "You know, the landed gentry get like this when they spend too much time alone."

I whispered over my shoulder, "Like what?"

"Fucking nuts." She increased her pace and caught up with me. "He's not armed, is he?"

"If he were, I don't think he'd be throwing rocks." I stopped at the worn path surrounding the reservoir, curious, but still attempting to abide by the protocol of the high plains angler so as to not upset the fishing—if, in fact, that was what he was doing.

"Hey, Omar."

He started, just visibly, and spoke to us over his shoulder as he continued throwing pebbles into the water. "Walt. Vic."

"What are you doing?"

He glanced at us but then tossed another stone. "Trying to keep those snapping turtles off that body out there."

We tiptoed to the edge of the bank in an attempt to keep the water from seeping into our boots, and Vic and I joined Omar in his target practice, Vic showing her acumen by bouncing a flat stone off the shell of a small turtle that skittered and swam into the depths. "Any idea who it is?"

Omar leaned forward and lifted his Oakley Radarlock yellow-tinted shooting glasses to peer into the reflective surface of the water at the half-submerged body. "I'm thinking it's Danny."

I stared at the corpse, which was a good forty feet from the bank, and tried to figure out how we were going to retrieve it, in that we had no boat. "Himself?"

My undersheriff squinted. "How can you tell?"

"Not everybody has hair like that." Omar nailed a big turtle that had risen beside the body like a surfacing submarine and had gotten caught in the mass of silver locks that had fanned out from the body. "Danny always had nice hair."

Omar reached behind him and, pulling out a fancy, stainless steel thermos of his own, poured the tomato-red contents into a cut-glass double-old-fashioned tumbler. "Libation?"

She stared at him, one hand on her hip. "It's eight o'clock in the morning."

He shrugged and sipped. "Sun's over the yardarm somewhere."

Omar and I watched as Vic expertly skipped a pebble across the glossy surface of the water, the pellet deflecting off another turtle. "How many turtles are there in this damn thing, anyway?"

Omar grunted. "Danny and his brother Enic protect them; nobody is allowed to hurt them—they're sacred to the Crow and the Northern Cheyenne."

Vic shook her head and nailed another. "Is there any living thing that isn't sacred to the Crow and the Northern Cheyenne?"

I tossed a stone but missed. "Nope."

Omar sipped from his Bloody Mary. "They're a totem for fertility, protection, and patience." He turned to look at me. "How are your daughter and granddaughter?"

There was a silence as I formulated an answer, but before I could speak, Vic chimed in. "Excuse me, but did I miss a transition in the conversation here?"

I tapped my shoulder. "Cady's got a tattoo of a turtle—reminiscent of her willful youth at Berkeley." I glanced back at him. "Should be here the day after tomorrow."

He nodded. "Lookin' forward to meeting Lola."

I smiled and picked up my thermos. "Any ideas on how we get him out of there?" I glanced at the big-game hunter. "You've got your waders on."

He shook his head. "Oh, no. The bank drops off ten feet out, and the reservoir is about sixty feet deep—used to be a shale pit."

I nodded and drank some coffee as Omar refilled his glass and Vic tossed a rock, this time missing her shelled target but causing him to duck his head and silently retreat into the depths. "Can I assume that nine-thousand-dollar Oyster fly rod of yours will do the trick?"

Vic crouched at an inlet on the other side of the pond. "I'm trying to resist saying something about the ironic aspect of a guy who protects the turtles but then falls in his own pond and becomes snapper chow."

"We don't know it's him."

"Sure we do." She held up a paper bag. "I found his lunch, and it's got his name on it." She read, "Daddy-O."

"Topflight detecting, that's what that is." I watched as Omar flipped the fly rod back and forth, trailing the line in cyclical patterns like gossamer wings, reflecting in the morning sunshine. "Think you can get him on the first try?"

He ignored my crass remark and flipped the fly forward, yanking it back to set the hook in what appeared to be the sleeve of a green canvas shirt. The outdoorsman carefully walked the banks and reeled in the body as we watched who we assumed was Danny Lone Elk spin slowly with his one arm extended like a superhero in flight, a trail of disappointed turtles in his wake.

As the body came alongside the bank, I reached in, grabbed it by the collar, and dragged the upper part of him onto the grass. "He weighs a ton."

"Lungs are probably full of water." Vic leaned over and

grabbed the other side of his collar and we both heaved the deadweight onto the bank, a forty-pound snapping turtle with a carapace the size of a washbasin attached to the dead man's left hand.

Vic dropped her side and backed away from the radially set iridescent eyes, the color not unlike her own. "What the fuck?"

The aquatic monster released the dead man's hand, hissed like a steam train, and extended its neck toward us, evidently not willing to give up its breakfast.

Vic drew her sidearm, but I pushed it away. "Don't. It doesn't mean any harm."

"The hell it doesn't; look at him." She considered. "I've shot people for less than that shit."

I kneeled down, and the beast stretched out his neck even further and struck at me with snakelike speed, the reach surprisingly far. "You know these things are seventy million years old?"

Vic reluctantly holstered her weapon. "This one in particular?"

"They appeared before the dinosaurs died out." I picked up a stick and extended the end toward the animal's open mouth. "See the little wiggly red thing at the end of its tongue?"

Vic raised her eyebrows. "What, that means he's popular with the ladies?"

"That's what he uses to ambush fish—they think it's a worm."

"That's disgusting."

I walked around him and raised his rear end, placing my hand underneath the plastron and lifting the creature, rather awkwardly, from the ground. His head swiveled back, and he snapped with the sound of a small firecracker.

Both Omar and my undersheriff stepped back. "He's going to bite the shit out of you."

"No, they can't reach if you're holding them from the bottom." A stream of something dribbled down the length of my jeans onto my boot.

They studied me, Vic, of course, the first to speak. "Did that thing just piss on you?"

"I believe it did." I swung the big beast around, lowered it back into the water, and watched as the creature settled in the mud and looked back at me, apparently now in no great hurry to get away.

"I guess he likes you."

I shook the water from my hands and studied the round eyes that watched me warily. "Might be a female."

"Well, anytime you're through turtle diddling, we've got work to do." She approached the cadaver again and rolled the body over, looked at what remained of Danny Lone Elk's face, and immediately turned away. "Oh shit, his eyes are gone."

Omar kneeled by the dead man and turned his chin. "Critters always go for them first." He sighed. "Those turtles sure did a number on him." They both turned to look at me as I stared at the body. "Walt?"

It was a man I'd seen before, in my dreams.

"Walt?"

In the dreams, he also had no eyes.

"Walt."

The man's words came back, and it was almost as if he were standing beside me, repeating the mantra of warning I'd stowed away: *You will stand and see the good, but you will also stand and see the bad—the dead shall rise and the blind will see.*

"Walt."

I took a deep breath. "You're sure it's Danny?"

Omar nodded and looked back at the body. "His belt says Danny." He paused for a moment. "And I recognize what's left of him."

"Does he have a wallet or anything else on him, like a fishing license?"

Checking the pockets of the dead man, Omar shook his head. "Nothing, but he's on his own property. I don't carry my wallet with me when I'm fishing—always afraid I'll dunk it."

I glanced at Vic. "Did you check his lunch?"

"Might as well; I'm about to lose mine." She reached down, picked up the brown paper bag, and, rummaging through the sack, called out the items. "Daddy-O had one can of orange soda, one cheese sandwich, one bag of Lay's potato chips, an assortment of celery and carrot sticks, and . . ." She fumbled in the bag, finally pulling out a withered, handmade billfold. "One wallet."

"Is it Danny's?"

She held it up for us to look at. "Well, seeing as how it has DANNY engraved on the outside, I'd say yes." She opened it and studied the Wyoming driver's license and the face of the elderly Cheyenne man. "He liked putting his name on stuff, didn't he?"

Omar reached out and straightened the collar of the dead man's shirt. "He was a good old guy—let me bring clients out here whenever I wanted and even let me fly my helicopter into this place."

I glanced around. "Where is the ranch house from here?"

He ignored my question. "There's going to be trouble." He pointed. "The eyes—the medicine men will have to do something about this or Danny will wander the earth forever." He looked up, and I could see tears for his old friend. "Lost and blind."

I nodded, fishing my keys from my jeans so that we could load the man into the truck bed and take him to Doc Bloomfield and room 32, the Durant Memorial Hospital's ad hoc morgue. "I'll get in touch with the family, Henry, and the Cheyenne tribal elders." Walking back to my truck, I thought about my vision and what Virgil White Buffalo and the stranger had said—that stranger, the stranger with no eyes, who ended up being Danny Lone Elk.

The last time I'd seen Danny was at the Moose Lodge at the end of town. It had been a few years back, and he had still been drinking. I'd gotten a radio call that there was a disturbance, but by the time I'd gotten there, cooler heads had prevailed and no one seemed to remember who had been involved in the altercation.

Asking why he was a Moose and not an Elk, I'd grabbed a Rainier for myself and joined him.

"They got a better bar down here."

He looked up at me and smiled. Lined with more wrinkles than a flophouse bed, the old man's face was cragged but still handsome and carried the wisdom of the ages. He reached over to squeeze my shoulder with a hand as large and spidery as a king crab.

Well into his cups, he spoke to me through clinched teeth; Danny Lone Elk always talked as if what he had to say to you was a very important secret, and maybe it was. "You off duty, Sheriff?"

"End of watch. I came here looking for trouble, but there isn't any."

"Can I buy you a beer?"

I gestured with the full can. "Got one."

He closed one eye and looked at me. "You too good to drink with an Indian?"

"No. I—"

"'Cause you gotta have a reservation." He kept his eye on me like a spotlight, guffawed uproariously at his own joke, and then leaned in close. "You wanna know why they called you?" He gestured down the bar where a small contingency of men did their level best to ignore us. "You see that sharp-faced man with the ball cap? That fella in the cowboy hat beside him asked him what he was gonna do on his vacation and he said he was gonna go to Montana and go fishing. Well, cowboy hat told sharp-face he couldn't understand why he was going fishing in Montana 'cause there was nothing but a bunch of damned Indians up there." Danny sipped his beer and looked past me toward the men. "Then sharp-face asked cowboy hat what he was gonna do on his vacation and cowboy hat said he's goin' hunting down in Arizona and sharp-face said he couldn't understand why he was going hunting down in Arizona 'cause there was nothing but a bunch of damned Indians down there."

I nodded. "Was that all there was to it?"

"No." He grinned the secret smile again. "That was when

I told them both to go to hell, 'cause there sure wasn't any Indians there."

His voice rose. "Bartender." He looked back at me, again smiling through the ill-fitting dentures. "I think that's when this guy called you."

The man approached somewhat warily. "Can I help you?"

He lip-pointed at sharp-face and cowboy hat. "Yeah; I think I better buy those guys down there a beer; I'm afraid I might've spooked 'em."

As the barkeep went about distributing the conciliatory beverages, Danny leaned in again. "I knew your daddy."

"Really?"

"Yeah, made the mistake of tryin' to get him to go to Indian church one time."

"Uh-oh."

"Yeah." He grinned again and nodded. "I was working down at Fort Keogh and lived out your way—had this wife that thought since your family lived so close we should go and invite them to go to church with us." He leaned in again. "Well, just my luck, your father answered the door, and boy did he give me an earful."

"I'm sorry; my mother was the religious one."

"He said he figured I was just tradin' one superstition for another."

I took a sip of my beer. "He wasn't a big one for churches."

"They still have that place out near Buffalo Creek?"

"I have it now—they've both passed."

He nodded. "I am sorry to hear that—they were good people." He was silent for a moment and looked down at his lap. "Do you ever see them?"

I turned and looked at him, thinking that I hadn't made myself clear. "They're dead."

He nodded again and then stared at the can in his hands. "Yes, but do you ever see them?"

"Umm, I don't . . ."

"When I am alone, hunting or fishing . . ." He breathed a laugh. ". . . And that is the only time I'm alone, by the way . . ." He looked at me. ". . . I see my ancestors, the ones who have walked the Hanging Road to the Camp of the Dead. When I see them, they are far away but watching me like the eyes of the stars."

Not quite sure what to say to that, I nodded. "That's nice . . . that they're looking out for you."

"I don't know if that's what it is." He took out some antacids, shook a few of the chunky tablets into his hand, and washed them down with some beer. "Mmm, peppermint, my favorite." He started humming the theme to *Dragnet*, which was also the jingle for the pills. "Tum, tum, tum, tum . . ." Then he opened a prescription bottle that he took from the pocket of his shirt, shook out a few pills, and swallowed them, too. He looked at me blankly. "What was I talking about?"

"Family."

"Oh, right . . . I am old, and I know I am standing on the brink of the life nobody knows about, and I am anxious to go to my Father, *Ma-h ay oh*. To live again as men were intended to live, even on this world, but I fear for the remains of my family."

I knew that his ranch was vast and there had been talk of fossil deposits, but I still couldn't understand Lone Elk's concerns. "You've got children, right? I'm sure your family will look after those things after you're gone, Danny."

It was a long time before he spoke again. "Maybe that's true, but I would take some things back if I could."

"I said . . ." My undersheriff raised an eyebrow and sighed, still holding her end of the now blanket-wrapped body. "Did you hear that?"

With Danny Lone Elk's voice still resonating in my head, I turned and looked around, fully expecting to see the man and his ancestors. "Hear what?"

She glanced at Omar, and then they both looked at me. "A gunshot."

I took a deep breath to clear my head and my ears. "Close?"

"What, you were having some kind of out-of-body experience?"

"No, I was just remembering when I had seen Danny last." I thought about adding more, but I hadn't shared my experiences in Custer Park with anyone. "Probably the hands who worked for Lone Elk, chasing off coyotes or plinking prairie dogs." I looked around. "Where was the shot?"

Vic looked toward the ridge. "Not far."

We hurried to get Danny loaded as quickly as we could, having decided to use Omar's massive SUV since it had better cover for the body than the open bed of the Bullet and, of all things, a slide-out game rack.

He gestured toward the passenger side. "Get in."

I glanced at my truck. "Maybe we'd better leave Danny in yours and take mine."

He shook his head. "This thing's faster—besides, it's bullet-proof."

Ushering Vic into the front, I climbed in the back and gaped at the leather and burl-wood interior. "Omar, what the heck is this thing?"

He fired up the engine, slapped the transmission in gear, and tore up the two-track toward the ridge, the three of us thrown back into the butter-soft bucket seats. "A Conquest, Knight XV—it's handcrafted out of Toronto."

As we flew across the prairie, I glanced up through the skylight. "What does something like this set you back?"

He shrugged. "Couple hundred thousand, I don't know—the accountant said I needed to spend some money fast, so I did."

When we made the top of the ridge, Omar wheeled the glossy black fortress to the left and stopped; we rolled down the windows to listen but didn't hear anything. Vic leaned forward in the passenger seat and pointed down the valley. "There are some vehicles parked at the fence down there through a few cattle guards; you want to go check it out?"

Spinning the wheel, Omar drove down the slope to a better-maintained road and started off toward the area Vic had indicated.

She turned to look at me. "So, you know the deceased?"

Thinking it best to keep the visions to myself, I told her about the Moose Lodge encounter. "I had a couple of beers with him one time a few years ago." I could feel her looking at the side of my face as I looked out the tinted windows. "There was a disturbance at the bar and when I got there it had settled down, so I had a beer with him. He was worried about some things, so we talked. It took a while for me to remember him."

She nodded, not buying a word of it. "What was he worried about?"

"Nothing, getting old, the land, family, the usual stuff."

"He should've worried about learning to swim."

I recognized Dave Baumann's weathered, light-blue Land Rover, emblazoned with the logo of the High Plains Dinosaur Museum, driving at high speed toward us. He slid to a stop alongside Omar's rolling fortress. A quarter of a mile away, I could see another gate where two flatbeds were parked nose to nose blocking the entrance, with some people milling about; beyond that was a working backhoe.

I rolled down the window and was about to speak when the paleontologist began yelling past the young blonde-haired woman in the passenger seat. "They're using a backhoe!"

I stared at Dave, an athletic-looking fellow with glasses, curly light-brown hair and beard, blue eyes, and an easy smile that made him popular with the young female scientists that sometimes came to intern at the private museum—they called him Dino-Dave.

"Excuse me?"

He took a deep breath to calm himself and continued. "They're digging up one of the most valuable sites in recent history with a backhoe."

"I'm no expert." I sighed and glanced at both Vic and Omar. "But that's probably not good."

"No."

"Who's in charge here?"

"I am." He studied me and revised his statement. "What do you mean?"

I had been involved in these kinds of conflicts where the university, the colleges, the museums, and the landowners quibbled about the exact location of digs, and I liked to get the full story before mobilizing the troops. "Is this official or something more loosely structured?"

"It's a straight-ahead deal; I paid thirty-seven thousand dollars last year for the fossil remains."

I opened the door. "I guess we'd better go over and take a look. Why don't the two of you jump in here with us, Dave?" They did as I requested, and I thrust a hand toward the blonde. "Walt Longmire."

A PENGUIN READERS GUIDE TO

ANY OTHER NAME

Craig Johnson

AN INTRODUCTION TO
ANY OTHER NAME

"Sheriff Walt Longmire, they talk about you like you're some inevitable form of justice" (*Any Other Name*, p. 76).

It's deep winter, and Walt Longmire's got no business being in Campbell County. The Sheriff of Absaroka County should be on his way to Philadelphia, where his daughter, Cady, is about to give birth to Walt's first grandchild. He would be, too, if his old boss, Lucian Connally, hadn't dragged him over county lines to investigate what looks like an open-and-shut suicide.

According to the autopsy report, Detective Gerald Holman shot himself twice at close range in a locked motel room. The first shot tore open his face and the next blew off the top of his head. His wife, Phyllis, is certain that Gerald would never kill himself and suspects there's something fishy about his death—something the Campbell County authorities aren't telling her. Lucian and Phyllis are old friends, but Lucian knows that there are limits to what an old man with one leg can do, so he asks Walt to help.

Sandy Sandburg, the Campbell County Sheriff, explains that Holman was the department's one-man cold case squad. When Walt looks through Holman's files, he finds that the detective was last working on a not-so-cold missing persons case. Jone Urrecha was a stripper at Dirty Shirley's in Arrosa, "a little crossroads east of here along the railroad tracks" (p. 35). Five weeks earlier, Jone went to work and hasn't been seen since.

Walt is all too aware that a stripper's disappearance isn't unusual. But then he learns that two other local women—waitress Roberta Payne and Kmart employee Linda Schaffer—vanished within six months of Jone.

Holman's replacement, Richard Harvey, insists "there's nothing to connect them other than the fact that they were women and are missing" (p. 37). Still, Walt can't shake the feeling that something more sinister than coincidence is at work.

Meanwhile, Cady's obstetrician is concerned about the baby's position in the womb and wants to schedule an induction. Cady was born "back in the dark ages when they made the father sit on a bench in the hallway" (p. 47), so Walt is both pleased and startled to learn that Cady wants him present in the delivery room. He's less pleased to hear that Cady's booked him on a flight to Philadelphia in just four days. Nothing can save Holman now, but Walt hopes the three missing women might still be alive.

With the clock ticking down to his scheduled departure, Walt heads out to Dirty Shirley's. Besides the strip club, Arrosa—Basque for "rose" —consists of little more than a post office and Sixteen Tons, a bar named during the town's heyday as a coal-mining hub. From there, the trail leads Walt out to a casino in Deadwood, South Dakota, just as a blizzard threatens to cover the culprits' tracks for good.

Fortunately, Lucian, Undersheriff Vic Moretti, and Henry Standing Bear have got Walt's back because an old nemesis has joined the mix of bad guys gunning for the Sheriff in this action-packed addition to Craig Johnson's bestselling Longmire series.

ABOUT CRAIG JOHNSON

Craig Johnson is the *New York Times* bestselling author of the Walt Longmire mystery series, now the hit drama series, *Longmire*, returning this fall on Netflix. He is the recipient of the Western Writers of America Spur Award for fiction, the Mountains and Plains Booksellers award for fiction, the Nouvel Observateur Prix du Roman Noir, and the Prix 813. He lives in Ucross, Wyoming, population twenty-five.

QUESTIONS FOR DISCUSSION

1. Lucian Connally convinces Walt to investigate Gerald Holman's death because he feels he is indebted to Phyllis. Was Lucian, in fact, responsible for Phyllis's accident?

2. Even though they've never met, Phyllis calls Jone Urrecha a whore because she worked as a stripper to finance her college education. What does this tell you about Phyllis's character?

3. As a widower, Walt has experienced his share of grief and loss. How does this inform his work as a law enforcement officer?

4. On their way to the Holman household, Lucian tells Walt, "they used to have bumper stickers over here that read CAMPBELL COUNTY— GIVE US ONE MORE BOOM AND WE WON'T SCREW IT UP" (p. 5). Discuss an instance in which a character's actions are driven by the country's current economic downturn.

5. Johnson always packs his novels with interesting facts and statistics. What is one of the most astonishing things you learned from *Any Other Name*?

(Spoiler Warning: Don't read on if you don't what to know whodunit!)

6. Walt is an enlightened spiritualist and a hard-boiled detective put together in one plain spoken, shearling-wrapped package. What aspect of Walt do you find most appealing? In what ways is he uniquely shaped by the traditions of the American West?

7. Both Connie and Thor have troubles stemming from drugs they used to further their aspirations as, respectively, a dancer and football player. Does society put too much pressure on young people involved in sports and other performance-oriented activities?

8. When her role in the crimes becomes clear, Connie tries to kill herself. Should Walt have intervened to save her?

9. The bond between parent and child is a recurring theme in the Longmire novels. Compare Gerald Holman and Connie's father-daughter relationship to Walt and Cady's. How are they similar? How far would Walt go to protect Cady?

10. Were you surprised to learn that Tomas Bidart—Walt's nemesis from *A Serpent's Tooth*—is still seeking revenge? Do you think Walt will tell Vic that Bidart is still in the picture?

To access Penguin Readers Guides online, visit the Penguin Group (USA) Web site at www.penguin.com.

Depth of Winter

A Longmire Mystery

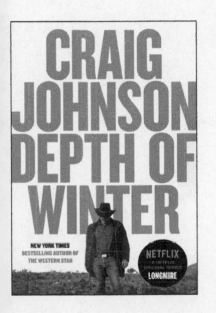

In Craig Johnson's latest mystery, *Depth of Winter*, an international hit man and the head of one of the most vicious drug cartels in Mexico has kidnapped Walt's beloved daughter, Cady. The American government is of limited help and the Mexican one even less. Walt heads into the heat of the Northern Mexican desert alone, one man against an army.

VIKING

 PENGUIN BOOKS

Ready to find your next great read? Let us help. Visit prh.com/nextread

09/22